MY SECOND TIME AROUND

J. C. Perkins

To my childhood safety net, my Grammy. You live on in me every day. Those who touch your life can never truly be gone. They've weaved themselves into your actions, thoughts, and spirit.

Restoration- noun

1. the act of restoring; renewal, revival, or reestablishment
2. the state or fact of being restored
3. a return of something to a former, original, normal, or unimpaired condition
4. restitution of something taken away or lost

CHAPTER ONE

It was never meant to be this way. When we pledged our eternal love on that mid-May afternoon, the botanical garden filled with the fragrant scent of peonies, surrounded by friends and family, we promised an eternity. I have never been good at breaking promises.

In an alternative universe, I was meant to be lingering at Starbucks over my second Americano, our Sunday morning ritual, my back sweaty from the first mile and a half of a three-mile run. Michael would be gently massaging his sore hamstring while I discussed the merits of a spring birth vs. a summer one, as we were finally ready to embark on the scary journey called parenthood. I was shaken from my reverie by the black SUV that was carelessly careening towards me, driver fiddling with her phone, nearly sideswiping my car and running me off the road.

"Watch out!" I yelled lamely into the open air. I could barely even hear my own cry. I didn't have the fight in me for anything more.

Glancing into the rearview mirror, my jade eyes reflected back the sorrows of the past months. It's no wonder they call eyes the window to your soul. My windows were wide open for anyone who bothered to look. Shaking my head at myself I thought, I was no victim. I alone was responsible for my happiness. It was my mantra. It was a tall order to fill.

I kept my eyes glued to the green exit signs, as I was nearing exit 17 off of 81 north. Throughout my marriage, I had grown accustomed to being the co-pilot, that was my role. Now I had to fulfill two roles, pilot and co-pilot. The wind whipped violently through my auburn hair turning it nearly into dreadlocks. I should have pulled it back when I put the top down on my sapphire blue 1970's Mustang, a present from Michael for my 30th birthday. He had it lovingly restored to mint condition, including the white soft top that matched the butter soft leather interior. If only he had put that much care into our relationship.

The autumn foliage managed to brighten my bleak mood. My peripheral vision was swirling with patches of orange, yellow, and red. The atmospheric farm country also had a calming effect. Surely something wonderful, my new improved life, would emerge from the tragic death of Aunt Virginia. I would make it my mission. It was hard. At the time when I received that call, I was left truly alone in the world. Aunt Ginny was the only family I had left.

Prior to my aunt's tragic passing, I was stuck. My sadness was like a foot of snow that had been iced over after one of those polar vortexes, shiny, hard, impenetrable. You couldn't walk through it. You could try to creep on top and your foot would sink in ever so slightly. If you held your breath and tread lightly, you could make it across without falling through. That phone call was the beginning of the spring thaw. I was heartbroken over Aunt Ginny, but it was a fresh beginning for me, a way out of my failed life.

I've driven the route to my favorite aunt's house many times in my life, but it felt different this time as I pulled down the winding driveway. I felt a desperate loss knowing she wouldn't be waiting at the screen door to scoop me in her arms, the smell of roses on her skin. It was the smell of home.

I needed to pause and catch my breath at the sight of the sprawling Victorian before me. I was shocked when, at the reading of her will, I was presented with a copy. It never occurred to me that I would financially benefit from Aunt Ginny's passing. I was so drained from all the emotional turmoil that when I read the words "To Ava, the daughter I never had, I leave my home and all its contents". It didn't really sink in that it was Aunt Virginia who would save me from my broken life for the second time.

CHAPTER TWO

I walked away from my marriage of ten years with lots of baggage but only four suitcases of things, mostly clothing. I managed to stuff them all into my car for the drive from Binghamton to Syracuse. I wasn't going for minimalism. I didn't want to be haunted by memories or ghosts of a life that never panned out, a reminder of my failures.

I parked as close as I could to the front door to haul the boxes out of the car. As I struggled with one of the bigger boxes, I felt a strong hand on my back.

I jumped, nearly losing my grip on the box and yelped as I turned to face an unexpected stranger.

"Sorry to startle you," the unnamed man drawled cooly. "You looked like you could use some help." He peered at the box that was about to topple as it was balanced awkwardly across my knee. "You must be Ginny's niece."

I focused on the man before me. He was classically handsome, in a spy novel hero sort of way. He was probably in his mid-fifties but took very good care of himself, tall, dark, and handsome. What, I thought curiously, is his connection to Aunt Ginny?

"Nice to meet you," I started, suddenly remembering my manners. "I'm Ava Zajaczkowski, Virginia's niece.

I could feel his gaze boring into me. "Sorry for staring you; it's just... the resemblance is uncanny." He continued to appraise me a moment longer before adding, "I live just next door," he motioned to the beautiful Tudor style house with a rounded red front door. "Peter White."

Peter took the box from my hands and escorted me to

the etched glass double doors of my pink Victorian house. I fumbled with the keys before pushing open the door into the giant entry way. It was almost the size of the living room of the old starter home that Michael and I spent ten years of our lives in.

"You can leave it right there," I said pointing to a spot right next to the expansive landing. "I wish I had something to offer you to drink. I'm only just setting foot inside for the first time since…" I let my words trail off, unable to bring myself to complete them.

"Don't be silly. I'll leave you to settle in, after I carry the rest of the boxes in from the car of course." Peter smiled, his eyes crinkling in the corners in a way that can only look attractive on a man. He turned to complete the task. I meandered into the kitchen to check things out. I was a little weary about letting this charming stranger in, however I was thankful for the assistance.

After Peter had placed the last box in a tidy pile, he came and found me in the kitchen. I was clutching a giant black garbage bag and removing the entire contents of the refrigerator and tossing them unceremoniously into the bag. I jumped when I heard his footsteps.

"Sorry to startle you," Peter said. His face revealed a slight smirk. "I'll leave you to finish...or rather start." He looked at me strangely, and it sent shivers down my spine.

I extended my hand for the second time. "Well Peter, it certainly was a pleasure meeting you. I will of course let you know when I'm having my housewarming party. You'll be number one on the list." I ushered him to the door anxious to be on my own in my new home, a house untainted by memories of my failed marriage.

After Peter left, I returned to the kitchen and the task at hand. I opened the vegetable draw and found a pool of rotted vegetables. Aunt Ginny was a real health nut, I remembered fondly. In a moment of weakness, I nearly collapsed into sobs, emotional over the whole mess.

I found a neatly wrapped plate of brownies stacked orderly in a circular design. They were displayed on a dainty silver plate with a filigree border. It was a shame they were moldy, as I could have really used a brownie about now. Looking at the stack, it was clear that only one was missing. Who could eat just one? Only Aunt Virginia.

I unwrapped them to dump the contents into my bag when I stumbled upon a note.

"Some sweets for a person who really deserves them."

The note was oddly typed on a typewriter and contained no signature, very curious indeed.

I was startled out of my thoughts by the sound of the landline ringing. As an afterthought, I rewrapped the spoiled brownies and stuck them back on the shelf where I found them. I hadn't changed the phone over to my name yet, so I was reluctant to answer. I just wanted the incessant ringing to stop.

"Hello," I stammered into the phone, trying my best to sound approachable.

"Ava," I was greeted by Fiona's cheerful voice. "I'm so happy you arrived safely, and on time!" she chuckled into the phone.

"Hi Fi. Yes, I got in about an hour ago. Thanks for checking on me."

"Are you excited about tomorrow?" she inquired teasingly. "I'll pick up some Starbucks on the way to work in the morning. Are you still drinking Americanos?"

"I should be picking up the coffee, as a thank you for getting me the job and all," I retorted.

"Nonsense, mom would kill me if I didn't give you a proper welcome," Fiona insisted. I had only met Fiona a handful of times, but her mother, Amber, was Aunt Ginny's best friend and mentor for at least two decades. I'm sure she's the one who supplied her with my coffee details.

"Well thank you so much," I said, softening my tone. "That would be great. By the way, do you know of any good places to workout around here?" Not only should I make an effort to bond, but keeping up on my health regime was an essential component of keeping me sane.

"As a matter of fact, I do! You have to join me tomorrow night for a *must* do class," Fiona sounded so excited that it was infectious. Maybe I made my first friend here. I hung up the phone feeling a little lighter. Tomorrow would bring my first day with my second graders, a hopeful new gym, and possibly even a new friendship.

I poured myself a glass of the malbec I brought along on my journey. Grabbing the elegant stem of the glass with one hand and one hand on one of the lighter boxes, I trepidatiously made my way. I knew it wasn't the smartest idea before I even began the trip up the dark stained, tiger oak paneled staircase. I stopped in awe on the first landing, unable to believe that this historic 1885 house, with all the elegance and opulence of the era, was mine. The late day sun was shining through the stained glass lighting up the staircase a peacock blue to match the peacocks in the glass. I raised my glass in a solo toast and took a sip of the rich plum, blackberry flavored wine. My story would begin now.

I didn't feel right taking Aunt Virginia's bedroom for my own, so I settled on a spacious spare bedroom that had a gorgeous view of the mountainside behind me. The windows were vast and gave way to a marvelous vista of houses and woods. I conveniently had an ensuite bathroom with white subway tiles and a clawfoot tub.

As I began to unpack the clothes in the box, I refolded them into neat piles. I put aside a pair of black cigarette pants and a black blouse with cream colored polka dots. I needed something suitable to wear for my first day. I previously worked in the same school in Binghamton for the last ten years. It was melancholy leaving my first and only place of employment since graduating college. I was desperate to make a good first impression.

After draining the rest of my wine, I dug deeper in the box. Not seeing any of my workout clothes, I frowned. I needed to pack a bag to bring with me to work tomorrow. I brought my wine glass with me as I went to retrieve another one of my boxes from the landing where Peter had so kindly left them.

As I deposited my glass on the kitchen table, I heard a bang in the yard. The sun had set leaving the world in twilight. The backyard was as magnificent as the rest of the house. Old growth hydrangea and rhododendron encased the sides of the yard and provided ample privacy. I peered into the semidarkness looking for a possible source of the noise. Not finding any apparent cause of the commotion, I shrugged and returned to the kitchen. It was probably just a neighbor closing their car door. I chided myself for my jumpiness. I wasn't used to being alone in such a big house.

I spent the remainder of the night unpacking the rest of my clothes. Finally managing to locate my gym gear in the third box, I retrieved a suitable outfit and put it to the side for tomorrow. Finally satisfied with my progress, I decided to settle into bed early with some Netflix. Tomorrow was going to be a busy day. I dozed off with a smile on my face, my first one in months, dreams of sunny days and rose gardens danced in my head.

CHAPTER THREE

"Boys and girls," Mrs. Avery, a fifty-something woman with an athletic build and a conservative, navy blue suit, my new school principal, was addressing my students. "I know how sad you were that Mrs. Mc Millan had to leave to have her baby, however we found you a wonderful teacher to take her place. This is your teacher for the rest of second grade, Miss. Z."

"Wow," one tiny little girl, with waist length blonde tresses, stage whispered, "wait until Amelia finds out I have Arielle for a teacher. She is going to be so jealous!" She finished matter-of-factly.

I chuckled to myself, happy that I had opted to wear my dark red locks loose and wavy. The ever so serious Mrs. Avery kept her face severe and excused herself, leaving me alone with my charges. A glance at my desk revealed that Fiona was true to her word and had left me a venti coffee complete with Post-it note. The words, *Good Luck!!,* scrawled in girly handwriting, complete with hearts and exclamation marks.

When the lunch bell rang at 11:15 am, I felt like I had barely blinked my eyes. The morning went swimmingly well. The students were adorable, and I began to feel like my old self. When Fiona had seen me at Aunt Ginny's funeral, she had mentioned to me that there was going to be a maternity leave opening at her school and encouraged me to apply. She personally handed my resume to Mrs. Avery, so it wouldn't get lost in the sea of overflowing applications. I was hesitant to leave Binghamton but was happy that I had taken the leap.

"Jenna can be our line leader; Jenna's table may line up," I announced. My little fan from this morning grinned widely as she grabbed her pink sparkle lunch box and darted to the front of the line. I put my finger up to my mouth, to signal silence in the hallway, and my class dutifully made their way into the corridor.

As I waited for the entire class to file out, I noticed the class across the hall from me doing the same. They were led by a male teacher with wavy brown hair and sharp cheekbones. I led the students down into the cafeteria, as I was shown by Mrs. Avery in my prior visit to the school. We followed behind the other class I saw in the hallway, waiting our turn to enter the room.

After depositing my students into the cafeteria, Fiona came running up to me clasping my hand. Her thin silver bracelets sang an excited song as they collided into each other, "Did you get the coffee?" she rhetorically asked, her raven-colored hair bobbing with her enthusiasm. Her corkscrew curls did a little dance with each movement.

"Fi!" I grinned wildly, so happy to see a familiar face. Her energy was contagious.

"Let me introduce you to some of the crew," Fiona said, dragging me up the stairs into the teacher's lounge.

As we entered the room, consumed mostly with a Last Supper like table, I felt 5 pairs of eyes trained on me. I always made friends easily. The only hard part about leaving Binghamton was the wonderful people that I had to leave behind. I was anxious to fill that hole.

Fiona went around the table, in order, and introduced me to the other second grade teacher who resembled Elsa from Frozen, the two third grade teachers, and the two fourth grade teachers. "We all have lunch at 11:15 am," Fi explained. "Everyone, this is Ava." With that, she sat gracefully down in an empty seat, tucking one of her legs underneath her. I took a seat beside her.

"Hey, I saw you in the hallway before," the wavy haired

guy I was seated beside announced. "If you ever need anything, just give me a holler, and I'll be there," he smiled.

"Prince Charming to the rescue," one of the third-grade teachers, a blonde twenty something, whose name escaped me teased, as she rolled her eyes.

"Hey we have to stick together," Coal Blake, the fourth-grade teacher, retorted.

I was grateful for the easy conversation and especially for Fiona's kindness.

The rest of the afternoon flew by just as quickly as the morning. I met Fiona in the parking lot at 5 pm, as we agreed during lunch. The sky was already darkening, the only part I didn't love about the fall. I came out to the car already in my purple capris and gray tank top.

"Oh good! You changed already," Fiona said revealing her own athletic wear. "I want to make sure we get there early enough to get good spots," she said seriously, looking down at her watch. "Class begins at 5:30 pm sharp!" Fiona said, jumping in her car. "Follow me!"

We pulled up in front of a building that stood alone from a nearby strip mall. The building was done with silver accents and shaded windows that made it impossible to see in from the outside. The only writing was a lone sign in a neon pink that read The Journey.

The reception desk was manned by two women dressed in all black athletic gear. It seemed like it belonged in an upscale spa. The women wore duplicate headbands in neon pink. They both had the appearance of just finishing up a photo shoot for the club.

"I'll go save us spots while you sign up," Fiona said, scanning her membership card from her iPhone. She ran to the left of the counter and disappeared.

"We are pleased that you decided to take the Journey," the woman with the sleek blond ponytail started. I almost laughed, but her deadpan face stopped me. She continued,

"We take your fitness seriously. I know Fit HIIT is about to begin. Marcia will be your instructor. Just sign here, and we'll give you your tour after class." She tapped her ballerina pink nail on the contract. I quickly scanned it and scribbled my signature.

"So, I come back here when the class is done?" I verified. The other woman with the long glossy black mane was staring intently at the paper. She furrowed her brow.

"Did I do something wrong?" I asked, glancing back at the contract.

"No, not at all," the blonde woman jumped in. "Yes, see you after class."

I retraced Fiona's route and went to the left of the reception desk. I had to give it to Fi, the club was stunning. The floor was done in silvery gray plank style flooring. There were several rooms surrounding the big room, each of them glassed in. The entire building shined from head to toe. To the extreme left I spotted Fiona through the glass, plopping down two sets of weights next to each other, beside a pillar in the middle of the room, and unrolling Yoga mats.

"Oh good, you're done!" Fiona exclaimed as I walked through the door and approached her. "I want to introduce you to some moms from the school. She led me to the right of the room. There was a gaggle of women in their mid-forties.

"Ladies, this is the newest teacher at West Syracuse Elementary, Ava Zajączkowski."

"Hi everyone," I said cheerily, giving my friendliest smile.

The women were quiet for a moment. I witnessed two of the moms, a thick dark haired brunette and a honey blond, exchange a look between themselves. Finally, a short red head woman spoke up, "Welcome Ava!"

We didn't get to continue the conversation because a woman with chestnut hair, arms, and everything else, toned, strutted in. Looking at her face she appeared to be about 50. Given her body, she appeared to be 30. I presumed she was the instructor. She went up to the front of the room and began fiddling with a mouth piece and the music. I guessed correctly. Fiona and I waved our goodbyes to the other woman and took our places that Fi previously procured. I looked around and the room had filled up. There were wall-to-wall women.

She pressed play and bass pumping music filled the air. "Let the journey begin," she screamed.

Fifty-five minutes later I was sweating and feeling better than I had felt in the entire last year. The instructor, Marcia, knew what she was doing. I looked at my smart watch and saw that I had burned 510 calories.

"Good, right?" Fiona said, rolling up her black mat.

"Definitely going to make it into my regular rotation," I said, pulling my sweaty hair into a ponytail to get it off my neck.

The instructor began walking towards us, about to leave the room, "Born running," she stated in a sarcastic tone.

"I'm sorry, were you talking to me?" I asked in dismay.

"Born running, your shirt," she said with a smirk as she flicked her ponytail and flounced out the door.

After taking the tour, I bought Fi and myself post-class green smoothies, and we settled in at one of the cafe style tables scattered around the juice bar. The seats were covered in butter soft white leather.

"I'm so happy you like to workout," Fiona said, her chocolate brown eyes looking earnestly at me. "Most of my friends, they just don't get it."

"Aunt Ginny is the one who taught me to find my calm in movement," I said grinning, happily thinking of how she rescued me from myself.

"Same for my mom," she answered smiling. "Only since I was a little girl, she taught me that life is an adventure, and it's ours to discover and make."

I was so happy to be having an a genuine connection with someone. It edged me on to share more than I intended, "You know that's how I met Michael, my ex-husband." Fiona was watching intently, waiting to hear my story, so I felt compelled to continue. "After mom and dad died on their way home from their grand Icelandic adventure, my world came crashing down around me. I was suffocating in my own feelings."

Fiona nodded, probably remembering the story from her own mother's perspective. Amber was Aunt Ginny's confidant. She surely shared my struggles with her.

"Aunt Virginia made it her mission to be my emotional guardian. While she was alive... I was never truly alone."

"So how does Michael fit into this," Fi asked curiously.

"At Ginny's insistence, I signed up for my first obstacle race. She even bought me a cute training tee. I wore it to school one day, and I literally ran into Michael as I was rushing to class. At first, he seemed annoyed by the collision, but then he looked up at me and his scowl turned into a grin. Next, he gazed at my shirt, and he was full-on beaming. He invited me for a drink that night. We were an item after that spending every moment together." For a minute, I felt nostalgic but then the reality of the years that followed came crashing back.

I took the last sip of my drink and stood up. Fiona followed my lead. I could tell that she wanted to hear the rest of my story, but I didn't want to ruin my great mood.

"To be continued," I felt compelled to say.

I rolled my windows down to enjoy the fresh fall air. I drove home feeling optimistic. It had been a great full first day. School had gone well. Fiona made me feel like we were old friends reunited, and The Journey turned out to be amazing.

As I pulled up to my house, I saw Peter in his driveway. "Hello neighbor," he said walking up to the car. "How is Syracuse treating you?"

"So far, so good. I started work today, and I'm just coming back from the gym."

"Oh, then I won't keep you," he said apologetically. "Don't worry, I'm keeping an eye on things for you." With this he turned with a wink and walked toward his house.

Monday October 10, 2021

My eyes must be deceiving me. I don't know how this could be. It took me several hours to calm down after seeing her. Only after two glasses of merlot was I able to relax a bit and begin to formulate... I can't decide if her being here is a blessing or a curse. Only time will tell. Until then, I must be patient and not act hastily. I don't want to ruin everything I've worked for.

CHAPTER FOUR

I have never been skilled in the art of sleep. I get upset if I sleep past 7 am, fearing I have missed half of my day, and all the excitement of the move and new job hasn't made it any easier to stay in bed. I woke up before my alarm, despite the extreme darkness at 5:30 am. I put on my iced blue velvety robe and plush white slippers and padded down the long stairway to the kitchen. I've always felt there is something so peaceful about the morning time. It's as if the world is encased safely inside a cocoon. Badness does not exist. The roads are quiet and all is safe. While everyone sleeps, I am living.

Yesterday the first thing I did while preparing for school was locate Aunt Ginny's percolator. She had it stored in the cabinet above the stove, right next to a stunning tea set that I've never seen before. When I laid eyes on it I carefully picked up the porcelain teapot with its delicate floral design in turquoise and coral to admire it. Flipping it over I read Digoin Sarreguemines France. Fancy, I wonder when she acquired this, I thought, replacing it precisely where I found it. I wasn't surprised though, Aunt Ginny was always traveling. She really knew how to embrace life.

I put the percolator on the stove to boil. Always the impatient one, instead of staying there to wait for it, I opened the back door and set out into the dark morning. I felt the chill of the October air and pulled my robe closer to me. My eyes adjusted quickly, I spotted Aunt Ginny's black wrought iron chairs and table. I would just finish making my coffee and bring it out here to drink, I thought to myself.

Choosing my favorite mug out of the cabinet, Miss New York 1994, in homage to Aunt Ginny, I emptied two natural sweetener packets into it. After adding a splash of oat milk, the bubbling sound alarmed me to the fact that the coffee was ready.

I tentatively grabbed the full mug and carefully opened the French doors, leading into the backyard, into my personal oasis. Sitting back onto the black iron chair, I breathed in the fresh autumn air. Taking a sip of my cafe Americano, I pondered why coffee always tastes better on a cold morning.

"Lila," I heard a soft call towards the back of my house, "Lila!" the voice became a little louder and distressed. I stood up and meandered toward the back part of the yard that is filled with ivy. Standing on an old cut tree stump, I peered over the back fence, to see where the voice originated from.

A petite woman of about seventy stood in a dark blue terry cloth robe. The second she saw me she started to fuss with her salt and pepper curls.

"Sorry, I didn't mean to disturb you," I offered at her surprised expression. "I just heard your calls and wanted to make sure you're ok. I'm Ava; I moved in here on Sunday," I stretched to offer my hand over the fence. She barely managed to reach it.

"Ah, Ava, it's nice to meet you. I'm Adelaide. You must be Ginny's girl," she declared, studying me closely. "So sorry to hear about her unfortunate passing, such a shame," she tsked.

"Yes, Aunt Virginia was wonderful. Is everything ok over here? You sounded upset," I said remembering why I was standing over my neighbor's fence with barely the beginning light of day breaking.

"Well, I hope so; you see Lila, my cat, didn't come home last night. She always comes scratching on the door around 9 pm wanting her dinner, without fail, but she didn't last night." Now my neighbor looked down sadly and called her name again.

"I'm going to have to go in, in a minute, to get ready for work, but when I get home, I'll come and check on you to see if Lila is home. If she's not, we'll start a search party," I told her. "It was nice meeting you. See you this afternoon."

My last words barely seemed to register as Adelaide continued to call feverishly Lila's name. I walked back to the patio, in the short time that I was talking to my neighbor, the day already seemed to have brightened a little.

Dressed in my soft brown cashmere sweater dress, tights, and booties, I surveyed myself in the long mirror. It was only my second day of work, and I wanted to get everything just right. I hoped that I would truly find my place in Syracuse, settle down and make it my home. Our school building was ancient, it was from the 1800's, and although the teachers had an awkward one -person bathroom off the teacher's room, it was equipped with a long mirror on the back of the door. I unlatched the hook that kept the door from opening and found Coal, the fourth-grade teacher, struggling with the copy machine. He didn't seem to hear me come out which left me with the opportunity to watch him. The copier door swung open, as he mumbled under his breath.

"What did that copier ever do to you?" I asked playfully, tucking a strand of my long auburn hair behind my ear.

"Oh, hi," he returned, standing up unconsciously smoothing himself out. His annoyance was suddenly forgotten. His scowl quickly turned into a boyish grin. "You laugh now," he teased, "but wait until the paper gets stuck and you only have two minutes to pick the kids up. Don't come crying to me," he finished.

I approached the copier, "If you don't mind," I said grinning to myself, "we had the same model in my old school. "I lifted the arm for number two, pulled the printer cartridge out and found an errant piece of paper. After removing the paper and replacing the cartridge, I flashed Coal my best smile. "You're welcome," I said satisfyingly as I did a little curtsy.

"I do believe I am forever in your debt," he said, moving a little closer to me. I felt my heart do an involuntary little flip. "Are you available for happy hour after work today? I can offer you a proper thank you," Coal asked, gazing at me with his brownish yellow eyes.

Before I could answer Fiona charged into the room at full speed. The moment, whatever it was, was over. "Did I hear someone say happy hour?" she asked. "Let's invite everyone; it will be a welcome to Syracuse for Ava."

"So, are you in then?" Coal asked, looking at me curiously.

"After I assist Adelaide in locating Lila; wild wolves couldn't stop me," I answered. "Now I must run before the kids think I've abandoned them on only my second day." I grabbed my cell phone off the table and noticed Coal giving Fi an indecipherable look. I'd have to ponder what it meant later.

"Who's Adelaide and Lila?" I heard Coal ask as I flew down the hallway to meet my class.

When the 3 p.m. bell rang, I was so preoccupied that I nearly ran into Samantha Asher, the other second grade teacher, as I spun around quickly, happy to be done with the task of delivering my students to their parents and bus stops. I wanted to leave right away today and get a run in before it got dark out. So far, we had only said hello in the lunchroom, and I was eager to cement a friendship.

"I'm SO sorry," I exclaimed, excusing myself for the near accident.

"No problem," Samantha laughed. She flipped her almost platinum blonde braid to the left side of her shoulder. "I'm anxious to get out of here as well. I guess we'll have a chance to talk tonight at happy hour," she finished offering me a smile.

"Ah, so I guess it is happening. Do you know where we are going or what time?" I asked clueless. Somehow Coal and Fi must have spread the word. Being new at school, I was so engrossed with my class that I didn't see a soul during the day, as I never even left my room.

"Yeah, Charlee's," she hesitated for a minute, "by the university. I'm not sure what time though."

"Ok, I'll check with Fiona. See you there," I said as I went to my room to collect my school bag. I stopped in the doorway of my room to text Fiona, but I found her standing by my desk.

"We're all set for tonight," she announced eagerly.

"I have to stop at my house to help my neighbor find her cat, and I was hoping to get in a quick run. There's a trail right by my house," I said while scooping up my brown leather tote bag.

"That's ok; we don't actually have to make it to happy hour. It's Charlee's, they have cheap beer all night," she chuckled.

"Great, how about 7 pm then? It will give me time to take care of a few things."

"Sounds good, are you leaving now? I'll walk with you, and I'll text everyone about the time." We walked to the parking lot together and parted ways at our respective cars.

After arriving home, I changed into running clothes. Although it was autumn, it was an unseasonably warm 70 degrees, so I opted for running shorts and my favorite turquoise tank top stating Make your Dreams Your Reality. When I finished dressing, I rounded the corner from my house and looked for the lemon yellow house that was located behind mine. Not seeing anyone outside, I rang the doorbell.

I could hear the shuffling of feet and make out a voice,

"I'm coming, I'm coming," through the four paneled plum colored door. Adelaide stuck her head out, her blue eyes looking perplexed as she registered my presence.

"Oh Ava, to what do I owe the pleasure of your company?"

"I've just come to see if Lila has made an appearance," I smiled. Adelaide relaxed her shoulders a bit as a look of understanding crossed her face, a very pregnant looking Siamese cat, as if on cue, came wrapping herself around Adelaide's legs.

"Noooooo," Lila called out as if trying to answer the question herself. We both giggled in response.

"My dear, thank you so much for remembering. You are a star. She showed up around 8 am crying at the back door. I was especially worried because, as you can see, she is fetching to be a mother any day now."

"Oh, my goodness," I cooed. "I just love kittens, well, all animals, I guess. We... I mean, I used to have a dog when I lived in Binghamton." Then I felt a little shot of sadness hit me. Spartan was Michael's dog first, so I lost him in the divorce.

"That is extraordinary!" Adelaide opened the door a little wider in excitement. "You will of course help me out by adopting one of her kittens," she asserted.

"Really?" I asked, a feeling of excitement built up in me.

"Oh, I insist. I want her to have a good home. You know family is everything dear."

I left Adelaide's house feeling as light as a feather. I was filled with excitement at the prospect of having a companion very soon occupying my space with me. The house would feel so much less lonely.

I crossed the street and went up the dirt slope to enter the running path that was so conveniently located in close proximity to my house. It was marked with a metal sign stating it was a Green Community. There were trees on either side of the path. It created a nice cool canopy of jewel toned colors as I began my jog. The path was littered with people trying to steal the final warm moments outside before the cold fall days finally took hold. I moved to the left to go around a boy with a mop of crazy curly red hair. He was simultaneously walking his black and white French bulldog and watching a YouTube video. I got around him just in time to avoid being hit by a woman on her red mountain bike. I went along like this for a mile and a half before turning around to finish the second half on the way back towards my house. It was such a nice running spot because you're not on the street but backed up to various people's backyards. Many of the people had gates that they could open to enter the trail right from their backyards. This was both cool and a little creepy, I thought, giving a shudder.

Once back at home, I jumped in the shower and took time out to blow dry my red locks pin straight. I carefully applied my purple and gold eye shadow. This would be my first night out on the town since I actually became a Syracusan. My thoughts were interrupted by the pinging of my smart watch.

Are you coming? xx Fi.

I didn't immediately answer her as I was doing one final look in the mirror for finishing touches.

Ping. *It's Coal. I stole your number from Fiona's phone. I thought we had a date. Are you standing me up?*" He finished his message with a frowning emoji.

I smiled to myself and shut off the bathroom light. I saw it as a sign it was time to leave. I located my actual phone on the kitchen table, secured the back doors, and quickly texted a message to Fi that I was on my way. Coal could wait until I got there I thought as I made my way to Charlee's.

CHAPTER FIVE

The city held an abandoned feel, crossing between the gorgeous Art Deco buildings and neglected Victorian masterpieces being left to fade from their former glory. Driving into the downtown area, I was swept right back into my college years. It's funny how a particular place, smell, or song can bring you emotionally back to a snapshot in time. You can feel precisely how you felt in that moment. I was caught in a moment in time when I thought that Michael and I would be together forever. Truth be told, he was never my ideal type. Other than being an athlete, he was not the type of man that drew me. He was an accounting major, lacking creativity in my book, sported a crew cut and had facial hair, all things that were not my style, however he was kind to me at a time when kindness was what I needed the most. Maybe I should have had the foresight to see that it wasn't meant to be forever.

Passing the SUNY Upstate Medical University, I punched my fist in the air as I pulled my sapphire Mustang into an empty spot right across the street from the Marshall Building. I counted my lucky stars that I wouldn't have to walk endless blocks in my purple three-inch heeled sandals.

I opened the door, the noise of people enjoying life enveloped the air and replaced my prior thoughts of Michael. Charlee's was famous for their high ceilings and industrial warehouse look. I involuntarily grimaced as my designer shoes stuck to the sticky beer drenched floor. Perhaps I had outgrown Charlee's after all.

"Over here," Fiona called, waving wildly. I looked to my

left and found Fiona sitting at a graffiti covered table with Samantha and two of the other teachers I had met the day before in the lunchroom. I went to sit in the chair next to Fiona.

"Oh, I have a seat for you right here next to me," Samantha said, moving her black quilted purse off of the chair. "Coal is sitting next to Fiona."

I wrestled with a feeling that I couldn't quite pin down as I went towards Samantha and gave her a kiss on either cheek. Her side braid was now replaced with Rapunzel like waves down her back. Then I made my way around the table to the third-grade teachers, the very sophisticated Tabitha who was dressed in leather pants, silky black tank top, and matching jet- black hair to finish her look, and the very young Marion the blonde 20 something who looked like she already was two drinks in, as she splashed her beer messily on the table. Finally, I went to kiss Fiona.

"Hmmm, Aren't you forgetting someone?" Coal was standing at the table holding a martini glass. "Oh, this is for you," he said, handing me the dirty martini with stuffed blue cheese olives. "I just took a guess. Now we're even." He winked at me.

"Perfect, my favorite! How did you know?" I placed my martini in front of my spot and Coal went in for an embrace.

"Glad you could make it," he whispered in my ear, so no one else could hear him. "I was getting nervous, for a minute, I thought you were standing me up." Then, he let go, and I went back to my seat bewildered.

We all took our place at the crammed table. I didn't mind, aside from the sticky floor and my expensive shoes. I was thrilled to be out, to be a part of something.

"So, what's your story?" Marion asked, finishing off her beer and placing it noisily on the table.

Everyone stared at me, and I could feel my pale skin warm. I did not enjoy being the center of attention, but I guessed this was how friendships were made. "Well, I moved here from Binghamton, where I worked as a second- grade teacher for 10 years," I started, pausing to take a sip of the martini sitting in front of me.

"So how do you like Syracuse so far?" Tabitha asked.

"Oh, I went to college here, so I am already familiar with the wonderful things, beautiful scenery and fun night-life, and the not so wonderful winters," I said laughing, remembering being snowed in the dorms with several feet of snow blockading our exit.

Marion, who originally started the conversation must have been bored already because she was back at the bar flirting with some frat guy dressed in all orange, she left midway through my explanation.

"It's not you," Tabitha inserted, noticing me watching Marion at the bar, "she's twenty-three is all."

I appreciated Tabitha's effort to make me feel better, especially since the time I met her previously she seemed so aloof.

"OMG," Fiona shrieked, "Did you guys hear about the fundraiser the town is hosting to raise money for the After School Arts Program?"

"Of course," Samantha inserted proudly, "Mrs. Avery asked me to be on the recruiting board." She looked as if she was offered a position in the Senate.

"Recruiting? Are they trying to get us to join the Army?" Coal asked with a laugh, as he caught my eye.

Fiona ignored his attempted joke and continued, "They want some of the teachers to dance with professional dancers, do our own version of Dancing with the Celebs."

"That sounds cool," I said remembering how Michael and I had taken dance lessons, a million years ago, to do our wedding dance. We did a rumba.

"I knew you would be up for it," Fi beamed at me. "How about the rest of you?" she asked, eyeing Coal, Samantha, and Tabitha.

"Up for what?" Marion asked as she plonked back in her seat, beer in hand.

"Are you trying to take my job?" Samantha whined, sticking out her bottom lip in a pout.

"Sorry, just excited is all," Fiona apologized looking at Samantha.

"I'm just kidding," she retorted, only it was obvious to everyone that she was not. "Did you guys hear who the MC of the event is going to be?" She suddenly grinned, happy to be revealing some new information.

"Who?" Tabitha asked.

"Mayor Whitherton, and it's going to be a black tie only event," Samantha continued. "Think of all those men in tuxedos! The event of the year! Tickets are two hundred dollars a piece with all of the money going to the arts program."

"Those dresses are expensive," Tabitha interjected. "All those expensive crystals and all."

"That's the best part! A famous dance dressmaker is donating the costumes, good publicity you know," Samantha finished beaming.

"Free dress, I'm in," Tabitha announced. "That seals the deal."

"Men in tuxedos! When I'm done dancing, they won't be able to look at anybody else," Marion bragged. We all rolled our eyes.

"So that leaves you Coal," Samantha eyed him mischievously.

"If Ava is in, I'm in," he announced. I noticed all the girls, except Tabitha, looked slightly put off. Although, it didn't stop me from feeling a little flutter of excitement in my chest.

Coal went up to the bar and ordered a round of cinnamon flavoured shots. I knew I would regret it tomorrow, but I went along with it in the spirit of celebration.

"To the arts program," Fiona declared as we raised our glasses.

"To hot men and free dresses," Marion announced downing her shot. "Now let's get out there and practice our dancing."

The group moved to the little area that was clear next to the bar. There was a DJ spinning, and a sea of college kids, dressed in orange, joined our group and started dancing too. For a little while, I forgot my troubles and lived in the moment, in the music. The mood shifted as a sad romantic ballad began to permeate in the air. I started to head away from the pack, to go regroup in the ladies' room

"Where are you going?" Coal asked, grabbing my hand and pulling me in close to him. He held me close, and I could smell the cinnamon on his breath. We swayed to the music.

A 90's R & B goddess crooned about love lost. I looked up and saw Marion hooking up with some random guy pressed up against the bar. My glance shifted to Fiona who had her gaze fixed steadfastly on us. When I made eye contact, she looked away.

"I'm really happy you came out tonight," he spoke into my ear.

"Me too," I answered.

The music stopped and the mood shifted as an early 2000's pop band, began screaming out of the speakers. Coal squeezed my hand before I broke our embrace.

The girls all came around us screaming out the words. After the song was over, we headed in mass back to our seats. I looked at my phone, and it was already 11 pm.

"It's only Tuesday," I said as, "I think I'm going to have to call it quits if I'm going to make it through the rest of the week."

"Totally," Fiona agreed. "The kids aren't going to care if we're tired tomorrow. They'll just overtake the class."

"We'll have a mutiny on our hands," Coal joined in.

We all laughed and gathered our belongings. We walked out of the bar still buzzing from the music and dancing.

"Thanks for a wonderful night, guys," I said, giving

everyone a hug goodbye feeling warm and content.

After arriving home safely, washing off my makeup, and changing into my bed clothes, I laid in bed enjoying the feel of the feather pillow beneath my head. My phone vibrated on the wooden floor planks indicating a text message. I reached down to the floor to retrieve my cell.

So happy to see you tonight. Maybe next time alone? Coal finished it off with a winky emoji.

I smiled to myself. I was feeling so at peace for the first time in a long while. I didn't want to do anything to jinx it.

We'll have to see about that, I teased as I typed my response. I added a winky emoji of my own.

I put the phone back down on the floor. I would leave it at that for the night. I had only just been officially divorced. There was no need to dive into the water blindly. I wasn't sure if it was deep enough yet, and I wasn't going to take a chance by jumping in and finding out the hard way.

When I arrived at school on Wednesday morning, the teachers' room was abuzz with the excitement of Dancing with the Teachers signup. Mrs. Avery had hung up the sign-up sheet right next to the coffee maker, where it was guaranteed to be seen by all. I noticed that Samantha's name was first on the list followed by Fiona's. I imagined the drama that ensued to be number one. Laughing to myself, Fiona materialized as though she could hear my thoughts.

"What are you waiting for?" Fi asked, as my eyes scanned the list.

"Nothing," I answered honestly. "I just need to find a pen."

Fiona's outstretched hand offered me a pen, as she watched me intently.

"You don't have to twist my arm," I said laughing as I wrote Ava Zajaczkowski on the list. "I love to dance. I'm actually excited."

Samantha came out of the bathroom just as I finished. "We get the names of our professional dance partners on Monday, as well as the dance we will be doing," she said. She obviously had been listening to our conversation from the bathroom.

"Are you up for class tonight?" Fiona asked, rolling up on the balls of her feet.

"Yes, I actually can't wait. I didn't bring my workout clothes though, so I'll have to meet you there."

"No problem, it's 5:30 pm again. If I get there first, I'll save you a spot!" she finished.

I glanced up at the clock. "It's show time!" I announced. "See you ladies later." Dashing out the door, I made my way to the side door, where I would greet my students.

Somehow, I didn't manage to see Coal all day. I was beginning to wonder if it was intentional on his part. He's right across the hall from me, yet we never crossed paths. After dismissing my students, I stayed only long enough to gather my grading and pocketbook, as I needed to get home to change.

As I was walking to my car, I noticed a blush-colored rose on my windshield. I felt my mouth involuntarily turn up into a smile. I carefully picked it up and admired its beauty. There was no note attached indicating its origin. I sighed and slipped into my car.

When I parked in my driveway and got out of the car, I remembered to grab my rose. I readjusted the strap on my leather school tote.

"Hello Peter," I called as I saw my helpful neighbor watering the grass on his front lawn.

"Hi Ava," he called as he strolled over to me. "Nice rose," he chuckled looking at the flower I was clutching in my right hand. He stood as though waiting for an explanation.

"Thanks," I answered, giving none.

"Oh, Adelaide, you know your neighbor that lives behind your house? She came around about 10 minutes ago wanting to talk to you."

"Really?" I asked, wondering what would bring her around. "Did she say what about?"

"Who knows, she's probably wondering when you're going to invite her to that famous housewarming party that you were talking about," he teased, pulling the black bar on the nozzle of his hose down to stop the water flow.

"Oh yes, I need to put it on my to do list. I would really love to meet all of the neighbors properly. Well, I've got to go, I've got papers to grade, and my class at the gym begins at 5:30," I finished heading away from Peter and into the house.

"Have a nice night," he waved, flipping the bar once more to release the water. "You've been here three days and have more plans than me," he mumbled under his breath, as I shut the front door.

I fumbled around in the cabinets in search of a vase for my rose. Was it from Coal? I wondered as I located several much too big containers, suitable for a whole bouquet of flowers. Remembering my empty malbec bottle from my first night, I fished the green bottle with the label Gato Gris out of the recycling bin. I rinsed it out, filled it with water, cut the bottom of the stem on a diagonal, and inserted the rose. Taking a minute to admire it, I placed it on the kitchen counter. It was still a mystery.

I was extremely happy to already have a full social life, however I just started this job and didn't want to fall behind in my work. After changing into a gym outfit consisting of cinnamon leggings and a matching tank top, I scooped my leather tote off of the kitchen seat and headed to the back yard. It was only 3:45 pm, and there was still at least 40 minutes of sunlight left.

Settling in at the table, I located a purple pen in my schoolbag. I began to grade our grammar assignment on articles from today. I got through half the class, enjoying the feel of the sunshine on my face. The weather had cooled down a lot from yesterday and felt like a true autumn day. I thought about going inside to fetch a sweater when I had an uneasy feeling of being watched. Looking up from my papers, I didn't see anyone, but I couldn't shake the feeling.

I stood up and walked to the gate. There was no one in sight. A lone robin walked across the lawn in search of worms. I walked to the back of the property. All I saw was the thick jeweled foliage still surrounding my yard. Probably just my imagination, I thought as I sat back down and completed grading the assignment.

Opening my school laptop, I figured out how to attach it to my wireless network. Thanks to the extender Aunt Ginny had installed, I was lucky enough to have internet that worked all the way to the back of my yard. After entering the students' grades onto our online portal, I moved on to their spelling sentences. I took great care in writing comments to help further their writing. I had a hard time concentrating as a niggling feeling kept me alert and looking up from my papers. The light was beginning to fade more, dusk was threatening to take over, so I decided to pack up my things and head inside.

When I arrived at the Journey and checked in, I went immediately to the glassed room to the left of the reception desk. I found Fiona already there chatting with the group of women from the other night.

"Oh, hey Ava, I set us up already," she shouted, pointing to two sets of weights and mats next to the pillar.

"Thanks, Fi, hey guys," I said brightly approaching the group.

I don't know if it was my imagination, but I could swear I saw one of the women grimace as I approached.

"Miss Z," a petite forty-something woman with dirty blonde hair said with a welcoming smile, "You're my daughter's new teacher. I didn't realize it last we met, but Jenna has wonderful things to say about you. She has absolutely loved school since you've arrived."

"I just love Jenna! Oh, I can definitely see the resemblance now that I know," I started examining her face closely. I was relieved that someone finally spoke to me and actually acted normal. I was beginning to get a complex.

"Are you here to socialize or workout?" the same instructor from last week questioned, as she strode by our group and took her place at the front of the room.

Embarrassed, I hurried over to my mat and weights. The teacher in me is a rule follower and doesn't like being reprimanded. I set up my smart watch to record my workout.

"Don't worry about her," Fiona said, twisting her curls into a topknot. She must have noticed my uncomfortableness.

The music began pumping, "Let the Journey begin!" she screamed as she started marching and leading us in our warmup. I followed along with exact precision. Until I thought she was going to go into heel digs, but she went down into a lunge instead.

"Don't anticipate! Follow," Marcia yelled over the music. She looked right at me in the mirror when she said it.

Maybe I was being too sensitive, I told myself as I did my best to follow along. When we went into squats, I was confident and finally felt that I could relax. This class was supposed to be a de-stressor, however today it was having the opposite effect.

"Head up and chest up, go down like you're sitting in a chair," she screamed, again looking at me in the mirror. Now I know that I know how to do a squat. I was doing them better than her. What was her problem?

The rest of the class went by without incident. Fiona and I walked out with the other moms. I was chatting to

Jenna's mom as we were leaving. We said our goodbyes and went our separate days. The parking lot had grown truly dark at this point.

Fiona and I lingered outside of my car. We stood in the dim light being given off from the street lamp.

"So, who's the rose from?" Fiona asked teasingly, giving me a sly smile. "The one on your car today," she added for clarification.

"You know, I'm not quite sure," I said, placing my gym bag on my trunk. I could almost hear Michael yelling at me for putting anything on the precious paint job.

"You can tell me," Fiona said, eyes wide.

"I really don't know; there was no note or anything." I don't know why, but something held me back from confessing that I hoped it was from Coal.

"Oh, a secret admirer!" Fiona announced.

Just then Marcia, our very own Miss Congeniality instructor, came out to her car, a black Jeep, which I was lucky enough to park next to. At least now I knew to avoid it.

"Goodnight," I called as she hopped into her front seat.

"Humph," she grunted and slammed the door.

As she sped off into the darkness, Fiona commented, "She woke up on the wrong side of the bed today." That was the understatement of the year.

Wednesday October 12, 2021

I've tried to calm myself down since originally seeing her, but when I get even a glance of her, I feel something take a hold of me. I'm afraid of what I am going to do. When I am in her presence, I cannot understand how she doesn't know how I feel, doesn't sense it.

CHAPTER SIX

When Friday finally arrived, I was feeling accomplished but exhausted. After an action-packed week, there was nothing I wanted to do more than collapse in front of the T.V. I hadn't worked since the end of June, and it always takes at least a month to get back into the swing of things. I felt like my battery was drained to 3%. As I was packing my things up to get ready to leave for the day, my phone buzzed with a text.

Long time, no talk stranger, followed by a wink, Coal.

Finally, I had only seen him in passing in the hallway, and I kind of just smiled and kept walking. I guess I was kind of annoyed that he hadn't texted me since Tuesday night, not that I had contacted him either.

Happy Friday. I texted back.
Do you have plans for tonight??

How should I answer? All of the sudden I felt a little less tired as adrenaline began to course through my veins.

Not really, I need to catch up on my grading, and there's always lesson plans, which is the highlight!
Coal responded immediately.

On a Friday night? No way. Did you decide yet if you wanted to go out, just the two of us?

My heart beat a little faster. Was I up for this? Was it wise to get involved with a coworker? All of these questions flooded my mind but my heart won this round.

I guess everyone has to eat dinner, right?

Despite how I felt, I didn't want to appear too eager. I saw the ... that indicated he was writing back and was a nervous wreck. I caught myself as I was about to start biting my nail. I hadn't felt this way since, well if I'm being honest, ever.

Address?? I'll pick you up at 7?

I typed in my address and added a thumbs up emoji. I pressed send and sat grinning at my phone. Lost in my thoughts, I didn't hear Fiona walk in.

"What's that smile about?" Fiona asked plopping down on the desk closest to mine and sitting with her legs criss crossed in her charcoal gray skinny jeans.

I debated with myself whether to tell Fi about my date. What to do? Was it a good idea to tell her? Was dating co-workers allowed, ethical, or smart? I panicked and decided to say nothing, for now. I didn't want to start the rumor mill churning.

"Just happy it's Friday," I said, smiling. I prayed my eyes wouldn't give me away and started to fiddle with papers on my desk. "Just trying to straighten up a little, so it is nice for Monday." I hoped that my attempt at looking busy would act as a cover for my nervousness about my lie.

Fi didn't seem to notice my jitteriness. She just kept right on talking, "So excited to find out about dancing on Monday."

"Oh, me too," I answered, finally looking at her, relieved for the change of subject.

"If you have a choice, what dance do you want to do?" she asked, recrossing her legs in the other direction.

I stared thoughtfully for a minute. My mind kept drifting to 7 pm tonight, however I didn't want to be a bad friend. "I've always loved the tango," I answered honestly.

"Yes, it really is beautiful," she agreed, "but not my style. I need something more cheerful."

"How about the jive?" I asked, pulling from the archives of my dance education that I acquired from watching movies. "You know that fast dance with all the kicks."

"Oh yes," Fiona smiled to herself. "I do believe you hit the nail on the head."

I was just relieved that the conversation was steered away from me.

"Are you leaving?" I asked, as I stood up and began to walk toward the door. She joined me in the hallway.

"Soon, just have a few things to take care of around here." Her eyes darted to Coal's room for a fraction of a second. It happened so quickly, that I wasn't sure if I imagined it.

When I arrived, full of hope, to my house, the first thing I noticed was that my mailbox was stuffed to the gills with mail. I'd neglected to collect it since I'd arrived on Sunday.

I deposited the hefty pile on the kitchen island and began sorting the contents. Sadly, I knew most of the mail would still be addressed to Aunt Virginia, probably the reason I had been letting it pile up in the letterbox. My heightened mood propelled me forward to finally complete the arduous task.

Among the debris, there was a creamy white envelope addressed to me. I curiously grabbed a butter knife out of the drawer and sliced open the envelope. I leaned against the granite top as I pulled out the card inside. The cover of the card was pink with gold lettering that said NEW CAT NEW FRIEND. It was written inside a heart that was formed by a big helium balloon. On the inside it read NEW FAMILY MEMBER! In beautiful loopy handwriting it said,

Dear Ava,

I am pleased to announce the birth of your new kitten. She

can't wait to meet you! Remember darling, family is everything. Please contact me when you are available to meet her.

Sincerely,
Adelaide

Well, that solved the mystery of what Adelaide was doing at my door yesterday. This was turning into the best day ever. First, I had my date to look forward to, and soon I would be bringing home a cat of my own. I tried to think about what I've read about kittens. What was the rule? I think they need to stay with their mom for about a month.

I scrambled to find my cell buried underneath Aunt Ginny's pile of mail. I googled "How long do kittens need to stay with their mothers?" and awaited my results.

"Ideally," I read, "kittens should go to their new home around 12 weeks of age. While some kittens can go home earlier, the closer you wait until 12 or 13 weeks, the better off the kitten will be."

I audibly sighed. I wouldn't be able to actually bring my baby home until the last week of December, but at least it would be around Christmas time and before New Year's. She would be my Christmas present to myself. We could ring in the new year together. I'm sure Adelaide would let me visit her in the meantime.

As I made my way up the stairs to my room, I made a mental note to talk to Adelaide later and thank her for the amazing news. I began rummaging through the drawer where I stored my athletic wear. It was contained in a heavy antique dresser with a mirror attached to the top of the dresser. I quickly pulled out a pair of bubble gum pink capris, matching sports bra and a white tank top that stated YOU'VE GOT TO BE KITTEN ME in neon pink letters, it seemed apropos with the news I had received.

After dressing, I pulled my locks into a side braid and headed out the side door. I made sure to lock it and place the key under the steps with some errant leaves covering the keys to obscure their view.

The running path the next street over worked out so good last time; I figured I would go again. As I rounded the corner onto Adelaide's street, I had to do a double take. Half-way down the street I saw a 1968 midnight green Firebird. The exact car that Michael has. I began to quicken my pace, passing the entrance to the running path. As I got closer, breathing heavy from the extra exertion, the car drove away. What was going on?

I was truly spooked. That had to be Michael's car. Right? Was he spying on me? I shuddered and backtracked half a block to the sloped entrance to the running trail.

Maybe I was mistaken, and it wasn't Michael's car after all. Surely there were others out there. He lived about forty-five minutes from my house, so I couldn't imagine him taking the time to drive all the way up there just to do a drive by.

The path was much less congested today; the weather had cooled, and it was starting to get darker earlier a little bit each day. I was happy I didn't have to spend my time dodging people and just ran at a nice steady pace. The sound of my feet crunching on leaves as I made contact with the ground soothed me and my worries about the Michael sighting. Well, if it was Michael, he was wasting his time. I glanced down at my running app and saw I was nearly at the mile and a half mark. I recognized from last time on the trail that I would turn around at the giant burgundy colored house with white shutters that butted up against the trail.

My thoughts turned to Coal and the evening to come. I decided on wearing my wine-colored satin belted cowl neck romper. This was a big deal to me. It was my first date since I got divorced. I was both nervous and excited at the prospect.

As I exited the trail the same way I entered, I took a good look around to see if I could catch a glimpse of the mysterious car. The sky had darkened quite a bit. Sliding up on the screen of my cell phone, I accessed my flashlight. I shined the light in all directions. There was no sign of the car, so I trepidatiously made my way around the corner and back home.

As I neared my house, Peter's motion light came on, and I could see there was a package waiting for me, on the rocking chair, on my wrap-around porch. As I cautiously went to pick it up and inspect it, Peter came out of his house.

"Hey neighbor, it's kind of late for a run by yourself. Isn't it?" he looked around, surveying the darkness.

I laughed, but it came out kind of nervous, "It wasn't dark when I started." I promised myself to get my own porch movement activated light. I didn't want anyone lurking around my house unseen.

"Did you see who put this package here?" I asked, trying to sound nonchalant.

He looked at the package in my hands. "No, can't say that I did, but I was just in the kitchen trying to see what to make for dinner."

I suddenly felt shivers up my spine. Examining the box in my hands, I saw that it was wrapped with brown craft paper and tied with brown twine. There was no writing on it to indicate that it was even for me, or who it was actually from.

"Ok, well hope you have a great weekend! I'll be sending out invites to my party shortly. I'm thinking of having a Halloween party," I explained. The idea had just materialized out of nowhere, but it seemed like a good plan.

"Sounds fun," Peter laughed. "I know just the costume to wear."

My heart was beating a mile a minute as I closed the front door, bolted it, and put on the chain for good measure. With shaking hands, I went into the sitting room and sat down on the purple velvet couch. The twine was loose enough that I could slip it off. I carefully undid the wrapping, afraid what I would find. There was an ordinary white box that you would use to wrap a present. It was the kind that you can find in any gift or craft store. It provided no clues. I unconsciously held my breath as I unfolded the tissue paper. Inside the paper was a little doll. It was about 6 inches tall. It had jade green eyes and her hair the exact shade of red as mine, crafted from yarn. It was dressed in a ballerina pink dress with tulle on the bottom.

There was nothing menacing about the doll. It was actually quite beautiful, I thought. trying to convince myself that there was nothing sinister at play, but why was it left anonymously?

I glanced at the clock, realizing that it was getting late. I wouldn't have time to wash my hair, so I would have to wear it up.

I moved the doll to the brown quilted leather sitting chair and propped it against the cream-colored throw pillow embossed with navy blue embroidering of roses. She sat there looking at me questioningly.

After taking a quick shower, without washing my hair, I reapplied my makeup, stepped into my romper, and twisted my hair into a chignon at the nape of my neck.

I headed cautiously out the front door. I felt myself doing a quick scan of my surroundings before heading to my car and reaching to lock the driver's side door. All the while, I was chiding myself for my paranoia, but it didn't stop me from keeping the door tightly secured.

Opening my text messages, I went to double check where I was meeting Coal. Just as I got his text open, without warning, I heard a tapping on my passenger side door window, and I literally jumped out of my seat, my heart racing.

Coal saw my reaction and rushed to the driver's side. I opened the door and stayed glued safely inside the soft leather seat.

"What's the matter?" he asked, his golden eyes filled with concern.

"What are you doing here?" I stammered.

"Did you forget our date?" He looked confused for a minute. "I said I was going to pick you up at 7," he added.

The details registering in my mind, I breathed a sigh of relief. I felt foolish realizing that I let the events of the evening send me into a tailspin. I had forgotten that Coal was coming to pick me up, and I wasn't meeting him there.

"Oh, my goodness," I said, smiling for the first time. "You wouldn't believe the night I've had already," I finally got out of my car and took care to lock and secure it.

"You can tell me all about it," Coal said, raising his eyebrows and reaching for my hand as he walked me to his car. He opened the door, and I slid in. Coal closed it for me and went around to get in himself. My heart rate was still slightly elevated, but it didn't stop me from noticing that he was a gentleman. He was so different from Michael, I noted.

Coal put the keys in the ignition but didn't immediately start the car. He turned to me, a smile playing on his lips, eyes focused on my face.

"Everything Ok?" I asked, switching gears from a ball of nerves to excitement.

"Perfect," he articulated, "you look absolutely stunning."

"Why thank you," I answered, all of the stress of the day leaving my body. "Where are we going?" The realization that I got into my car to leave and meet him, and I didn't know where we were going dawned on me. I couldn't believe that I allowed myself to get frazzled so completely.

"It's a surprise," he said with a wink, as he turned his car around and pulled out of my long driveway.

We arrived at Armory Square, the historic business district, located in close proximity to the college, so it was buzzing with activity. I felt nostalgic for my time at college. He found a spot right by the Starbucks, and Coal grabbed my hand as he helped me out.

I laughed and looked down at my silver strappy heeled

sandals, "Do we have far to walk? I brought along a pair of flats I can change into if necessary." I pointed to my pocket-book where they were currently located.

"No, not at all, but I like a girl that's prepared," Coal insisted as he stopped and put his arms around me. He nuzzled the top of my head, and I swear I felt my knees begin to buckle.

We walked along the street, arm in arm, taking in the old historic buildings. On Walton Street, Coal stopped us in front of The Blue Elephant. "Let's have a drink before dinner. Our reservation is at eight, so we have a little time."

He led me in the door into the pub. It was crowded with people, but Coal spotted two empty seats at the far end of the bar. We rushed over to them and happily claimed them. I rested my feet on the thick brass foot rail. We smiled knowingly as three new people entered and scanned the room for seats, with no luck.

"See I knew you were my lucky charm," he said gazing into my eyes.

A burly man with dark hair and an actual handlebar mustache, donning the plaid red shirt of a lumberjack and skinny jeans, appeared in front of us, "What can I get you?"

Coal turned to me. "Do you want your usual?"

I nodded my head in affirmation.

"We'll have a gin and tonic and a dirty martini," he said, placing our order.

"I love this bar. Look at the original carvings," Coal pointed to the scrolled wood work. "There's nothing like Old World Craftsmanship." He traced my lips as he spoke.

I heard the bartender place our drinks in front of us. Turning my attention to my cocktail, I took a slow sip. I removed my cell from my purse and opened up my camera app.

"Let's turn and get the bar in the picture behind us," Coal suggested.

I turned in my seat and handed the phone to Coal to take a selfie. "Not like that, silly," I told him while taking the phone. I pressed the button to turn the camera the other way. "When you take the picture facing you, the image quality isn't as good." I insisted as I set it up with the flash.

"This way you can't see yourself though, "Coal protested light heartedly.

"You don't trust me?" I asked, sticking my lip out a little in a pout.

"We'll do a little scientific experiment to test your hypothesis," he stated, the teacher in him coming out.

As this banter went on, unbeknownst to me, in the corner of the room, the band of women, the moms from my exercise class, were watching Coal and I at the bar. Lucky for me, I didn't see them as they whispered amongst themselves. If I had seen, it would have dampened my good mood, so I sat blissfully ignorant basking in the glow of possibility.

Coal listened at last and turned the phone to an angle he presumed would capture us. He hit the button and the flash hit us.

"Let me see," I said anxious to see if it worked.

"Wait, let me see if we do it *my* way," Coal said, withholding the camera from me. He turned it to selfie mode and our faces filled the screen. My cheeks were flushed with excitement. My eyes looked alive for the first time I could remember in a long while. It's a strange feeling to look at yourself and truly see yourself. Coal's smile was warm and mischievous. He hit the button, and our image was immortalized once again.

"Ok, let's compare the two," I grabbed the phone, all business now. I showed him the photo that he took my way. "This is my way, and here is your way."

Coal scrutinized the two pictures. "Ok, you do have a point," he admitted. "We are much cuter in your picture." He leaned over and kissed me on the cheek. At that moment, my face was turned towards the women from the gym, and I saw a flash go off.

I whirled around to Coal shocked. We both now

turned to face where the flash went off, but the women were turned talking to each other acting as if nothing had transpired.

"Did you see that?" I whispered in Coal's ear. "They took our picture," I practically hissed.

"I saw a flash," Coal admitted, "but I don't know if they were taking a picture of us."

"Well, I was facing them," I managed to get out without yelling, "and it was definitely us."

"Who cares anyway?" Coal said. "Maybe they just need a reminder of what happiness looks like." He tucked a stray hair that escaped my updo behind my ear, clearly not understanding why this was upsetting to me.

"Can we get in trouble? At work, I mean," I asked, my voice trembling slightly.

"No, there are no rules against dating coworkers," he said, grabbing both hands. "If you wanted to date me, I don't want to be presumptuous."

I took a big gulp of my martini, anxious to get away from watching eyes. Glancing down at my watch, I saw that it was quarter to 8. "We have fifteen minutes until our reservation," I said looking at Coal anxiously.

"We're just across the street," he said pointing towards the window, and that's when I saw it. The same green car from this afternoon was sitting outside of the big window of the bar. I felt a stab of dread in my stomach. Coal must have seen the change in me.

"You know, if you're not ready to commit to dating yet, it's cool," he said, assuming I was having second thoughts about him.

I shook my head from side to side, "It's not that," I said, almost a whisper. "I'll explain at dinner."

The magic of the night had disappeared as suddenly as it came. The spell was broken. I finished off my martini with one more gulp. I glanced back at the table. The women acted as if they didn't even know that Coal and I existed, sitting there chatting innocently. I looked back at the window; there was no green car in sight. Was I losing my mind?

Coal signaled to the bartender and placed some bills down on the table with the check. He helped me slip into my blush-colored wool blend longline coat that I wore in case the night turned chilly.

"Shall we?" Coal asked, taking my arm and leading me out into the dark night.

Coal was right; it took literally two minutes to walk up the street, cross it, and he led me down a brick alleyway that led to a beautiful courtyard. The building to the left was also brick with antique green trim around the windows. There was a tan canopy over a seating area. String lights dotted around the canopied area creating a fairyland feel. A beautiful tropical-like tree was planted in a boxed off area of the courtyard. Coal went up to the hostess stand marked with a wooden podium.

"Coal, party of two," he said to the twenty something hostess who was dressed all in black and donning a pixie haircut.

"Inside or out?" She asked with her best smile.

Coal turned to me to get my input. "It's so beautiful outside, and we have jackets."

"Out please," he smiled.

"Right this way." She grabbed two menus and a wine list and led us a few feet to an iron table with a glass top. It was directly next to a patio heater, which she promptly switched on.

After the waitress had left, I pretended to browse the menu, but my mind was a million miles away.

"Did I do something to upset you?" Coal bluntly asked.

"No, God no. It's been a beautiful night... with you," I stammered.

"Talk to me Ava, please," Coal pleaded, looking at me earnestly.

"Ok," I was nervous that the waitress would come back

any minute, and I hadn't really looked at the menu yet. "Let's just order, and then I will tell you everything."

Coal looked satisfied with my response and turned to the menu. I picked out eggplant parmesan and a glass of cabernet to compliment it.

After the waitress came to take our order, I looked Coal square in the eye. "I just want to start by saying, you have been wonderful."

"But...," he said, pausing. He looked crestfallen, waiting for the other shoe to drop.

"No but," I continued picking up steam. The waitress returned with a basket of warm bread and butter. I grabbed a piece and the butter melted immediately. As soon as the waitress left, I continued, "Things have been kind of weird for me."

"Weird how?" Coal questioned, genuinely interested in what I had to say.

I took a sip of the wine that the waitress had deposited in front of me, for courage. I told him all of the details of the day, from the strange coincidence of the '68 midnight green Firebird, twice, to the anonymous gift left on my rocking chair, and finally to the strange behavior of the moms from the gym. When I finished, I could tell that the color finally returned to my cheeks. They felt warm, and it felt good to finally let it all out.

His response was not what I expected, as he began to laugh a deep belly laugh.

"What's so funny?" I asked, narrowing my eyes.

He leaned over, this time kissing me softly on the lips. "I'm just relieved that it really isn't me. I thought you were just unsure about me. Listen Ava," he said leaning further in, so we were only inches apart, "I really like you. A lot. Whatever these problems are, I will help you get to the bottom of them. We will do it together."

Coal became serious for a moment. He frowned as if lost in thought, "Your ex, Michael, does he seem like the type of person who would stalk you? I mean," he took his time, as though really pondering his words before speaking them, "would he try to hurt you?"

"No," I answered a little too quickly. "He wouldn't try to physically hurt me." I finished, fairly confident that I had told the truth.

I finally felt able to smile. I felt relieved that I had told him everything. Well, almost everything. There were some things that were too disturbing to tell anyone. Maybe in time. At least I finally had an ally.

CHAPTER SEVEN

Saturday means not waking up with the alarm. I managed to sleep until 7:30 am and woke up with a start when I realized light was already filling the sky. I nearly jumped out of bed, afraid that I was late for work before realizing it was the weekend.

I leaned over the side of the bed and retrieved my cell phone. Hitting the app for photos, I stared at the picture of Coal and I at the bar from our date. What a night of mixed emotions, I thought as I gazed at the picture smiling. Coal smiled back at me, and I felt a tug at my heart. Oh boy was I in trouble.

I checked my texts, and there was a new one from Amber, Fiona's mom,

Hi Ava, are you available for dinner tonight? Please say yes; I'd love to catch up and find out what you're up to. xoxo Amber.

For a minute I felt a longing, so strong for Aunt Ginny, that I felt paralyzed to move. I must learn to be grateful for what I have and not dwell on what I don't, I thought to myself before writing back.

*I would love that! Time and place and I'll be there.*I finished and sent the message.

The ... appeared and I knew she saw it immediately.

6 PM. My house. Don't bring anything but yourself. xx Amber.

Amber was essentially the only "family" I had left. Hearing from her made me feel closer to Aunt Ginny. I couldn't think of a better way to spend a Saturday evening.

My phone pinged. There was an Insta notification. You've been tagged in one photo by @darkascoal. I clicked on the notification. It was a photo that I had never seen, only imagined being taken. An image of Coal and I from the bar. The one where he was kissing me on the cheek, as I was gazing at the camera. I looked so blissful, so carefree. I read the caption.

Night out with a special girl. #fridaynight #justthetwoofus #gettingtoknowyou #armorysquare #syracusenights". OMG. Where did he get that picture from?

Immediately, I switched to my text messages and frantically wrote,

Where did you get that picture from? I knew I wasn't imagining it! My hands trembled as I texted.

Samantha sent it to me. She got it sent to her by one of those moms. Guess she was trying to give me a heads up. Honestly, I was just happy for the amazing photo of us.

I thought for a minute. Why was I so upset? Coal was right. It was smarter to go public with us hanging out, so there was nothing to hold over us. I don't know why I felt like a criminal, but I did. Maybe because I lied to Fiona about what I was doing last night. Surely it wasn't because of Michael. I owed him nothing.

It is a good picture ;), I wrote. *Maybe I'll post mine too.*

I received back three smiley faces with hearts in the eyes.

Reopening my Insta account, I tapped the plus to add a picture. I started with the photo that I took my first night out, the one at Charlee's. I couldn't help but laugh, as the whole group was gathered together. Marion could be spotted looking not at the camera, but staring at some random guy in the background. I added the second picture of Coal and me. After adjusting the filters and cropping, I added hashtags of my own. #mynewjourney #myfirstweekinsyracuse #fresh-start #thankful #thankgodfornewfriends. I pressed share. I sent my photos out into the internet universe. I really do need to stop worrying about what other people think and take control of my own life, I thought as I got out of bed.

As I began walking out my bedroom door, a thought occurred to me. Who had seen the picture that Coal posted? I was in such a rush to find out who took it, that I didn't look closely enough. I leaned against the banister, in the hallway and clicked on Coal's account once more. It had 43 likes so far, and I didn't really recognize any of the people who liked it, but I did see FiFiFoFun had written- Aww cute!

I felt relieved. I continued my trip down the staircase. Fiona had seen it and written a nice comment, I assured myself. I just didn't want her upset with me for not telling her, especially since I was going to Amber's house tonight. Although she didn't say as much, I was sure that Fi would be joining us.

Passing the sitting room, my eyes were drawn towards the chair where I had placed my anonymous gift, the doll. She was propped up just like I had left her. Her eyes seemed to follow me as I walked across the room.

I made my coffee and took it outside into the yard. It was now after eight. The air was chilly, but the sun was shining brightly, making it an absolute joy to be outside.

The mystery of Michael's lookalike car being spotted twice yesterday was still irking me. I logged onto my Facebook account and typed Michael's name in the search bar. I was no longer friends with him, but his account was open, so I had just as much a right as anyone else to peruse his account. Although, I kept my account locked up tight.

As his account came up, I nervously began to pick at

my cuticles. I'm not sure what I was hoping to find, but I would just like some reassurance that he was not stalking me, or perhaps a post that let me know he had sold his car.

The first thing I noticed, as my eyes scanned his wall, was that he had changed his relationship status to: It's Complicated. I rolled my eyes and took a sip of my coffee, followed by a deep breath.

He had a new profile picture of him on a mountain bike with a navy-blue helmet covering his head. There were several likes, but no comments that might give me any insight into what was going on in his life.

Continuing to scroll down his feed, I noticed he had shared several Wrestlemania videos. How was I ever married to his man? I thought to myself.

Two weeks ago, he posted a picture of himself washing his prized possession, his 1968 forest green Firebird. The pristine paint job glistened in the sun, as he smiled proudly next to it. I zoomed in to examine the picture more closely. Well, as of two weeks ago, it was in his possession, and that was definitely the car that I saw not once but two times yesterday.

I scrolled a little further to no avail. No luck. I quickly exited his account worrying senselessly that he would be able to tell that I was on it.

"Ava," I heard my name being faintly called. "Ava are you back there?"

I moved to the back of the yard recognizing Adelaide's voice from the other day.

"Hey," I answered standing up on the tree stump again, "Hi Adelaide, I got your letter. I'm so excited. I can't believe Lila had her kittens already," I exclaimed, eyes shining.

"Oh, good dear," she tsked. "I was afraid since I didn't hear from you that you didn't receive it or perhaps had a change of heart." She sounded slightly wounded, eyes lowered to the ground.

"I'm so sorry Adelaide," I started, really not wanting

to offend her. "This was my first week in town and between school and getting to know people...." I trailed off.

"No need to fret dear," she jumped in, "I completely understand. I just wanted to make sure that you still were interested in the little guy. I want *each* of Lila's kittens to get a loving home."

I relaxed a little seeing she wasn't upset with me. "Actually, I can't wait. Will I be able to come by soon and meet her?" I asked, gazing past her and admiring her equally beautiful backyard. It was obvious that she tended to it with care.

"Oh yes," she said, "I was going to suggest it. Maybe you can come by tomorrow afternoon for a tea party, and you can meet the entire litter."

As we were talking, I felt the sensation of eyes on me. I searched the surrounding area to find the source of those eyes. After gazing around and not seeing anyone, I looked up and noticed a few doors down, to my right, stood a woman in a cream-colored silk robe, with glossy chestnut brown hair. It was hanging down the sides of her face, shiny in the sun. She was on her balcony, way up on her second floor, probably off her bedroom, staring down at Adelaide and me in conversation. She didn't even move to pretend that she wasn't watching us. I realized with a start that she had a full view of my backyard from her balcony, not as private as I initially suspected. I would recognize that face anywhere. It was Marcia, my instructor from the gym, and she did not look pleased to see me.

I lowered my voice to explain why I was distracted. "Sorry Adelaide, it's just, I know your neighbor a few doors down," I said, gesturing to where Marcia was standing on the balcony. Once she saw Adelaide looking up at her, she turned her back on us and laid down on her lounger, a glass of green juice held delicately in her hand.

Adelaide lowered her voice to an almost whisper, "Oh, Marcia," she said, contempt obviously present in her voice. "How do you know *her*?"

"She teaches classes at the gym I go to," I explained, glancing up once again to be sure she couldn't hear us.

"Be careful with that one," Adelaide whispered, "she's not to be trusted." Adelaide's face remained serious and stony.

"Thanks for the warning," I said, still keeping my voice low. I didn't want Marcia to eavesdrop on our conversation. I wondered at Adelaide's warning but didn't dare to discuss it any further with her right then. "So, I'll see you tomorrow, around two?" I asked.

"That's perfect," she answered with a wink.

"What can I bring?" I asked, anxious to wrap this up and get away from prying eyes and ears.

"We're just having tea," Adelaide said, "and maybe I'll make shortbread cookies as well."

"Sounds delightful," I responded. "I'm so looking forward to it. See you tomorrow."

Going back to my spot where my outside seating was, I tried to evaluate how far Marica could see into my backyard. I remembered her weird behavior in class and shuddered. I might have to move my table and chairs up a little, closer to the house, so her view would be obstructed.

After moving slightly, I settled back into my chair, marginally satisfied that her view was at least a little blocked. I grabbed my phone and noticed I had a text from Coal.

Love the pictures, but why is the group photo first? Coal questioned.

Sequence order, I wrote and added a wink.

Smart girl has an answer for EVERYTHING! he typed.

I smiled to myself. Michael and I never had this type of rapport, the entire time I knew him. I felt solidified in the choices I made to end the relationship.

I hit my Insta app to check the status of my recently updated photo. Some of my friends from Binghamton liked it. "Miss you" comments filled my screen.My heart felt full.

Fiona liked my photos and wrote: *So happy to have you in Syracuse!* See everything was fine, I reminded myself.

Coal liked the picture and wrote: *You bring the sunshine to Syracuse.* Several people liked his comment.

I opened my calendar on the phone and checked for the date of Halloween this year. It falls on a Sunday. Perfect. I would make my housewarming party for Saturday on October 30th. I didn't want to do it on the actual day because people might have plans already. I went into my notes on my phone and began to compose a list: Amber, Fiona, Peter, from next door, and Adelaide. I would send my neighbors on the other side of me an invitation, Coal, Tabitha, Samantha, Marion, I tapped my foot on the table leg trying to think. Should I invite Marcia and try to befriend her? It might just make my life easier. I would have to think about it.

The rest of the day was spent catching up on grading and lesson plans. There was a certain comfort in the routine of it all.

After finishing my work, I went into the old summer house in the back of the yard. It's painted an off-white color with antique green trim. I absolutely love it. I looked up towards Marcia's balcony, but she was nowhere in sight. Aunt Ginny kept her bike, which was now mine, in there.

I wheeled the blue bike out of the summer house and went for a bike ride around town. I brought my backpack and stopped to pick up a bottle of wine to bring to Amber's house and a can of condensed milk and cupcake mix, with pudding in the mix, to make cupcakes for Adelaide tomorrow.

Thank God when I arrived back home from my bike ride, there were no strange packages or cars lurking around town. Prepping for tomorrow, I put the condensed milk in the crock pot and put it on for 10 hours. Then I showered and wore my hair loose around my shoulders. I threw on a pair of high waisted black skinny jeans, a lightweight mauve sweater, and black ankle boots. Remembering to grab the bottle of wine before locking up the house, I turned on my dim front porch light, which would not suffice in the long run, and got in the car. I would need to invest in a security system as soon as possible and possibly flood lights for the front of the house. I breathed a sigh of relief as I got in the car without incident.

I texted Amber for her exact address. I had been to her house before, but I wanted to know exactly where I was going. Putting her address in my Maps app, I found she was actually only 10 minutes from my house.

Arriving in only eight minutes, I managed to catch all of the green lights. Sure enough, I saw Fiona's sky-blue Chevy Volt parked in front of the house. I sat in the car for a minute, touching up my lipstick, before grabbing the bottle of wine and exiting the car.

Amber must have been waiting for me because as I got out of the car, she emerged from the house. She looked stunning as usual, tall, lithe, dressed in snow white cashmere. Her blonde hair pulled into a classic bun.

"Ava," she embraced me. I didn't realize, until I felt the warmth of her arms, how much I was missing my family. I had been an orphan for quite some time now, but Aunt Virginia made sure I was never alone.

I could smell a homemade dinner wafting through the screen door.

"Thank you so much for the invite," I exclaimed, entering through the door that Amber held open.

"Oh Ava, you are *always* welcome. Don't be silly! Let's join Fiona in the kitchen. She is putting the finishing touches on dinner.

We walked down the white, wood panelled hallway into the kitchen.

"Ava," Fiona exclaimed, putting down the metal tongs she was holding to come hug me. I had interrupted her turning of the asparagus.

"It smells heavenly in here," I announced. "What are you guys cooking?" As I spoke, I handed Amber the bottle of sauvignon blanc that I had brought.

"I told you not to bring anything," she said shaking her head, "but it does compliment the dinner perfectly. I made my chicken cordon bleu."

I spotted a wine opener on the counter and set about opening it. "So, what have you been up to?" I asked Amber as she pulled a tray of chicken out of the oven. Fi did a dance to the side, so as not to get hit with the door.

Amber pulled three wine glasses out of the cabinet and rinsed them before handing them to me.

"Work has been really busy. Clients trying to stay the course with the holidays approaching." Amber is a very successful health coach. All of the society women in the area go to her for advice. She is a nutritionist, as well as having her personal training certification. That's how Aunt Ginny originally met her.

"Well, I'm glad to hear that business is good." I settled in on one of the leather stools at the kitchen island.

Amber turned to me. I noticed her immaculately made-up face softening, "Ginny would be so proud of you," she said out of nowhere. "You are so resilient, and you look particularly stunning today actually." She examined my face. I noticed the glistening of tears in her eyes.

I became suddenly shy, not wanting the attention on me.

"Does it have anything to do with your date last night?" Fiona teased, grabbing her wine glass and joining me at the counter. She sat down and crossed her legs in her black yoga pants.

"Not a date, really," I said.

"Oh, are you seeing someone?" Amber asked. Her eyes were now miraculously dry and sparkling. "How exciting! I wish Fiona would get back out there. She hasn't dated anyone in over a year. Being alone too long is good for no one."

Fiona rolled her eyes.

"Not really," I insisted, looking at the two of them. "Just a friend from work." I wasn't ready to admit to anyone, especially not myself, that I was having feelings for anyone. I didn't believe that I had the strength for any more disappointment.

"Just the same, I think it's wonderful." She came up behind Fiona and me, putting a hand on each of our shoulders. "My girls both deserve someone special."

"Thanks Amber," I answered, sincerely grateful for the support. Fiona looked more annoyed than anything else. "So, are you dating anyone?" I asked, turning my attention to her.

"That my dear is a story for dinner," she said mysteriously. "Can you girls set the table?"

I got up immediately, eager to contribute. Fiona went to pull dishes out of the cabinet by the stove.

"Not those dishes Fi, we are having a dinner party, use the china."

Fiona and I both went into the 1940's sideboard, in the huge dining room off of the kitchen. It was painted a soft dove gray. Fi carefully took out four plates rimmed in gold, with dainty purple violets, decorating the faces.

"Four?" I questioned. "Who else is coming?"

Fiona fussed with her hair. "Mom's boyfriend is joining us."

I grabbed the silverware and gold cloth napkins out of the drawer. "Oh, nice. I'm glad I will get an opportunity to meet him. Do you like him?" I asked, curious about the dynamic between them.

"He's ok," Fiona said, not committing to the idea.

We worked as a team and set the table. Then grabbing our wine glasses, we brought them to the dining room.

"Where should I sit?" I asked, surveying the table.

"Mom sits there," she said pointing to the head of the table. "You can choose any seat you want."

I placed my glass randomly down and went back into

the kitchen, "Do you need me to carry anything into the dining room?"

Just as Amber was about to answer, the doorbell rang, "Oh, just excuse me for a moment. Our other guest has arrived," she said, suddenly patting her hair and straightening herself, even though she already looked flawless.

While she went to answer the door, Fiona sidled up to me conspiratorially, "For real, how was last night? I want the details." She grabbed my hands, excited to share in my joy.

"It was actually really nice," I started, happy at last to share my little slice of joy with someone. "We just went by Armory Square for dinner and drinks, but it was weird because at the place that we went first, we ran into the moms from the gym."

"Oh yeah, what did they have to say?" she asked all wide eyed.

"That's the weird part," I paused, "they didn't talk to me. They took that random picture of Coal and me, the one on Coal's account, without our knowledge. I just saw the flash go off."

Fiona's eyes grew wide, "No way! Which mom was it that took the picture?" Now she really wanted the details, but we were interrupted by Amber's voice.

"Girls, can you bring the food into the dining room? I laid everything out on the counter."

"Ava, which mom?" Fi insisted, not wanting to end our conversation. She was obviously annoyed by the interruption.

"Later," I said, grabbing a pot holder to bring the chicken into the dining room. Fiona reluctantly grabbed the asparagus and salad.

As I entered the dining room, I saw that Amber had shifted my wine to the side.

"Oh, thank you my loves," she said as we placed the food down in the center of the table on the silver runner. "Ava, I believe this is your wine. You can sit here," she motioned for the seat across from Fiona.

"Thanks, "I said, feeling my cheeks redden because of course, I chose the wrong seat. I put the wine down and turned to my left to introduce myself to her guest.

"Nice to meet you, I'm...," I stopped mid-introduction because he finished the sentence for me.

"Ava, what a pleasant surprise," Peter White, my neighbor from next door, was sitting next to me. I was distracted and didn't get to look at his face until that moment. He was looking as debonair as usual. He wore brown wool pants and a caramel cashmere sweater. It looked as if Amber and Peter were ready to do a cashmere commercial.

I took his hand and smiled to myself. I guess the mystery of how Aunt Ginny knows him is solved.

"I didn't realize you two were acquainted. This is great. I'm planning a housewarming/ Halloween party on the thirtieth. You two can think of a famous duo, a couple's costume." I clasped my hands together excited about the idea. "What about President Kennedy and Jacqueline Kennedy?"

"I actually have an idea," Peter said, raising his eyebrow, "but you'll have to wait to find out."

Everyone was enthusiastically talking about the party and even went into their phones to save the date. It looked like my party was really coming to life.

The rest of the night was filled with easy conversation and laughter. I really felt like a part of a family again.

"Fiona, can you help me with the dessert and coffee? We can let Ava and Peter chat while we get it ready."

"Let me help clear the table," I insisted, getting out of my seat.

"Nonsense," she said, waving me away. "Relax, you deserve it."

I returned to my seat at her insistence and turned to face Peter.

"You've had quite a first week," Peter said, smiling charmingly.

"What do you mean?" I asked nonchalantly, taking a sip of the water in front of me.

"It's just you've been here only one week and you really have been on the go. I know I couldn't keep up with you."

I wondered how much he's told Amber about my comings and goings. The idea of being watched didn't sit well with me.

Feeling a little taken aback, I felt a need to justify myself, "Well I've really only been going to work."

Peter laughed and added, "And to the gym and running, I believe you had a nice gentleman pick you up last night. Adelaide paid a visit to you, and there has been a dark green car that keeps driving down our street, slowing down only in front of your house."

A nervous knot began to form in my stomach. I was not comfortable with Peter's familiarity with my schedule or the fact that he spotted the car going by my house multiple times. It seemed like the car thing was really a problem. I frowned lost in my own thoughts.

Thank God Fiona chose that moment to enter carrying a tray covered with strawberries, blueberries, and cut up mango. Amber was right behind her with a carafe of coffee.

"Everything ok here?" she asked, noticing the shift in my body language. Amber was very perspective, probably what made her a good wellness coach.

"Of course, dear," Peter replied, smiling his million-dollar smile.

I realized there were no coffee cups set on the table yet, so I jumped up and retrieved the matching violet ones from the hutch. I placed a saucer first, then a cup for each of us. Then I made a return trip to get dessert plates. While I was grabbing the plates, I saw a jeweled skeleton key, that hung from a nail on a crimson ribbon, in the cabinet.

"Wow, this is so pretty," I picked up the key, admiring the extensive jeweling on it. It looked to be antique and very valuable.

"I forgot that it was in there," Amber said, putting her hand to her chest with a wistful look in her eye. "That belonged to Ginny."

"Really?" I asked, with this new information, I was even more intrigued and closely examined it.

"She asked me to hold it for her, so I put it in the cabinet for safe keeping. You should have it. It belongs to you now," she dabbed her eyes.

"Are you sure?" I asked.

"Yes, of course. I'm not really sure if it opens something, or if it's just decorative, but either way it's beautiful and a family heirloom," she insisted, nodding her blonde head up and down.

I took my spot at the table and felt the key in the palm of my hand. The rough stones making tiny indentations, the smoothness of the actual skeleton key cool in my hand. It felt reassuring for it to be in my possession. I slipped the ribbon over my head and wore it as a necklace, close to my heart.

I turned my attention to Amber, "So how did you and Peter meet?" I asked, smiling innocently.

They both looked at each other at the same time, "Ginny!" they answered in chorus, smiling at each other.

"How long have you been dating?" I inquired.

"Well, we've known each other a while," Amber said with uncertainty, "but we didn't actually connect until Ginny's funeral." She looked down and appeared ashamed to mention it.

I involuntarily reached for the key around my neck. I noticed that Peter was staring at the key, but when he saw me watching him, he looked away quickly.

"Well, it's great that you found Peter to help you through your difficult time," I started to get a little choked up. "I realize it hasn't been easy for you either. You and Aunt Virginia have been best friends forever."

Amber got up and came around to my side of the

table. I sat there awkwardly, not sure what to do. "Thank you for saying that Ava, and for understanding." She bent down gracefully and hugged me right there in my seat, and I swear both Peter and Fiona gave me a strange look. I was really starting to lose it.

CHAPTER EIGHT

Waking up feeling invigorated after my night with Amber and Fiona, I decided that this Sunday morning, it was time to start new traditions. I gave up my Sunday running when things went south with Michael. It's as if I stopped going to punish myself for my failure. Today I will begin again. It was time to move on. I located my phone and texted Fiona.

Hey Fi, just wondering if you want to go for a run this morning and get coffee. If you're busy it's all good. Just figured I'd ask.

I was a little nervous to go alone after all the weird things that were going on, but I would if I had to. It was essential that I learned to be more independent.

While I was waiting to hear back from her, I spotted Aunt Ginny's key and put it in my jewelry box for safe keeping. Then I went downstairs to put my first coffee on. I never went for a run without it.

As I was puttering around in the kitchen, I felt the buzz of the phone in my robe pocket.

Great idea! What time? Where do you want to meet?

Do you know a good place for us to go? I wrote.

Yes! Onondaga Creekwalk! You'll love it. We'll need to drop one of our cars off at the end of it. It's about 5 miles, so we'll just do it one way.

Sounds great! Want to meet at my house? I can follow you to drop off your car? Can you be ready in half an hour? I have plans at 2 pm, and I need to bake cupcakes first.

Perfect! Address?

I gave her the details and rushed around to take the dulce out of the crockpot from last night. I was pleased with myself that I thought to put it on last night, or it would never be ready on time if I did it on the stove when I returned from my run date.

Opening the can and scooping the dulce out with a spoon, I transferred it into a mason jar. When the task was complete, I licked the spoon. Delicious. I would leave it out on the counter, so it would be easier to spread on the cupcakes when I got back.

I quickly changed into plum-colored leggings and a matching tank top. Pulling my hair into a quick bun at the top of my head, I wrapped it with two separate elastics to make sure it would stay.

Just as I finished putting my sneakers on, I heard the front bell. It was the old-fashioned kind that looks like a key. It's brass and has a carved decorated plate around it. You turn it to the right, like a crank, and the bell rings on the inside of the door. It rang three times.

"Fi," I greeted her as I opened the door. She looked adorable in a dark blue running ensemble. She was hopping from foot to foot.

"Hey Ava, so happy you texted. It's a perfect day for a run," she said, glancing up at the blue sky around us.

"It is, it is. Come in, I'll be ready to leave in like two minutes."

Fiona stepped into the entryway. I led her into the sitting room. "Have a seat. I just need to run upstairs for a second."

As I left her to bound up the stairs, she plopped down on the purple couch. I came down the stairs while putting on my Apple watch, to see Fiona staring at the doll on the chair.

"Cool doll," she said, walking over to pick it up. "I don't

remember Ginny having that before. Is it yours?"

"Yeah, it showed up on my porch anonymously a few days ago. Weird, right?" I shuttered thinking about it.

"Really?" she asked, turning it around, examining every inch of it. "That is kind of creepy. It looks like it's home-made. Doesn't it? Not to mention that the hair and eye color are dead on to yours and your Aunt Ginny's coloring too."

I winced at her use of the word dead.

"Well let's get going, so we have enough time. The creekwalk sounds awesome," I said, locking the front door and pulling at it to be sure that it was locked.

"Good morning, ladies," Peter appeared as if from thin air. He walked to the edge of my front lawn. "Where are you off to?" Although it was 8 am, he was fully dressed in dark blue jeans and a white button-down dress shirt. His casual look? I laughed to myself.

"Hi Peter," Fiona spoke up first, "Taking Ava to the creekwalk for a run."

"Nice," he said, flashing his megawatt smile. "Well enjoy, be careful."

We both got into our own cars, and I let her pull out first, so I could follow her to the end of the creekwalk.

To my surprise, she drove the same way that Coal and I went two nights before. I followed closely behind because I had no idea where our destination actually was. She pulled up on Walton Street and found a spot. Since it was Sunday, she didn't have to bother with the metered parking. I pulled up alongside her and waited as she hopped out of her car and into mine.

"That's so weird," I said when she pulled the door closed.

"What is?" she asked, wondering what I was talking about.

"This is the exact street that I went to with Coal the other night. I mean exactly the same." I pointed out the bar that we had gone to.

"Really? That's funny," she said, wrinkling her nose. "This is where our run is going to end. That's a strange coincidence."

"Where to?" I asked, wanting to get moving before a car came down the road and honked at me because they couldn't get by.

She led me onto I 81 and gave me turn by turn directions until we ended up parking at Destiny USA, very close to Onondaga Lake. We parked and got out.

"We get on the trail right over here," she said motioning towards the entrance. "To be honest, I'm also so glad you called because we didn't get to finish our conversation from last night."

"Where was I?" I asked, teasing her because I was very aware which part I was telling her about.

"The gym moms!" she nearly screamed at me, as we started on the path. The Onondaga Creekwalk turned out to be an urban trail along the creek. You could walk, run, or bike from here to downtown Syracuse. There wasn't a soul in sight, so I was happy that Fi had come along for company. There was safety in numbers, right?

"I know, I was just kidding," I smiled at her. "The mysterious picture I believe."

We were running along the path and went over a cute little black bridge. "So, who took the picture?" she asked, obviously intrigued.

Fiona and I were clearly good running partners, as we kept a nice steady pace and neither of us fell behind as we ran. We could comfortably talk simultaneously while running.

"I'm not sure. Samantha sent it to Coal. I guess one of the moms sent it to her. I suppose I'll have to ask Samantha tomorrow. Coal's not going to know."

"Ugh, Samantha, of course she's in contact with the moms. I'm not surprised at all. Very interesting and weird. Why would they take a picture of you and Coal? It's not like either of you are married, and it's scandalous or anything." She seemed to be pondering the situation aloud.

There was a plaque with writing and photographs accompanying them, coming up on our left. "Can we stop for a sec, so I can check out the plaque?" I asked.

"No problem," Fiona said, stopping right in front of it. "So, are you and Coal an item now?" she asked bluntly, as I was reading about the history of the Erie Canal.

"No, he did kiss me though," I smiled despite myself.

We continued on the path, following the signs as it weaved around. We went through old and new industrial areas. I could definitely get used to living in Syracuse, I thought.

"Did I tell you about Michael's car?" I asked.

"You mean your ex-husband," she asked, turning towards me.

"Yeah, I think I saw his car like three different times the other day, and at dinner last night, Peter told me he saw it driving slowly by my house on several occasions."

Fiona looked at me seriously, "For real? Has he contacted you?"

"No, he doesn't even have my number. I changed it after the divorce," I clarified.

"Why would you do that?" she asked, a look of concern coming over her face.

"He became a little possessive over me. That's part of the reason that I ended things." I glanced at the water as we ran on the pavers that made up the path winding beside it, hoping to find some peace with the lapping waves. I stopped abruptly alongside the white amphitheater, feeling tired all of the sudden. Fi didn't miss a beat and stopped too.

Fiona wrapped her arms around me. I sank into her embrace. "What do you mean by possessive?" she asked seriously. She pulled away a little to look me dead in the eye.

"I couldn't go anywhere but to work. If I stopped at the store, he would mysteriously show up there. I wanted so badly to start a family, but he was afraid that if we did, I would love someone better than him."

I instantaneously became cold from being near the water. I shivered a little, my skin damp with the sweat of our run. "It was just too much for me. I was suddenly in my thirties and miserable. I wanted to make it work, but he just wasn't the guy for me. He didn't love me for me. He loved me because I was his." I know I looked defeated as I stood, shoulders slumped staring at the water. "I never wanted to get divorced. I wanted to believe in true love. He was very kind to me, once upon a time."

"He didn't... hurt you?" she asked very cautiously.

"Not physically, but he was both possessive and emotionally withholding at the same time, a very toxic combination. Our friends had no idea and were shocked to learn that we were splitting up."

"I'm so sorry," she hugged me once again. "Ginny didn't know what went wrong between the two of you. She told mom how sad she felt that you were hurting."

"Yeah, I was careful to never say anything. I guess I was ashamed that I wasn't a very good wife."

"Why weren't you a good wife?" she asked, confused.

"I couldn't make him love me enough to want to make me happy," I swiped away tears that were starting to fall. "I'm not doing this. Today, it is about new beginnings. Let's go and talk about something else." I tried my best to appear strong in front of Fiona.

Leading the way, I started jogging again down the path. I could tell that we were coming close to downtown. Although emotional, letting Fiona in on some of my secrets had been cathartic, and I felt closer to her. Just a few minutes later we were back at her car.

This time I jumped in her passenger seat. "Thanks for that," I said, shutting the car door.

"No thanks needed, that's what friends are for," she said, smiling at me as she pulled up the block.

As soon as I got home, I started making the cupcakes for Adelaide's house. Immediately after mixing the batter and putting it in tins for the oven, I went upstairs to change for my afternoon date.

I settled on a pair of dark blue jeans and a blush colored, off the shoulder shirt. I figured I probably needed to be able to get on the floor with the kittens and wanted to wear something appropriate

After dressing, I still had time before the cupcakes would be done, so I went into the backyard. I found a pair of clippers in the shed and began to walk around the yard clipping all the dead heads on the plants that were around. It was actually very relaxing. I would have to gain some gardening skills if I was going to keep up with the rest of the neighborhood. Maybe Adelaide could give me some tips. Although I've always loved flowers, I've never tended a garden of my own.

Turning the corner, I walked around the block at 1:55 pm with my tray of cupcakes. I had washed the pretty tray that the brownies were on in the refrigerator, putting the strange typed message attached to them on the counter next to the bread box with the stained glass cover. Arranging the cupcakes on the tray, I put toothpicks in them so I could cover them without wrecking the dulce de leche icing.

Adelaide must have been eagerly anticipating my arrival because the door opened as I approached the house, before I even entered onto her property. It dawned on me that she probably wasn't used to having visitors; I suddenly felt sad for her. I would hate to be an old lady and have no one come around to see me.

"Ava, go through the garden gate on the side and come around back. I set everything up in the backyard," Adelaide insisted pointing to the right of the house.

Walking in the direction that she motioned, I saw there was a rounded black metal garden arch with ivy climbing all around it. I felt like I was entering a fairyland. I precariously opened the gate while taking care not to wreck the cupcakes in the process. When I stepped into her backyard, I saw flowers everywhere. Rose bushes and hydrangea were present, just like at my house, and she had mums and asters adding tiny dots of purple, orange, and burgundy throughout the yard. Adelaide suddenly appeared through her sliding glass backdoor. She was dressed in a yellow dress with a thick cream sweater over it. It belted at the waist to keep it secured. She had taken care in doing her hair and fastened a barrette on the left side of her hair. She herself looked like one of the flowers.

"Here, these are for you," I said, offering her my tray of cupcakes.

She took them and seemed to frown as she looked at the tray.

"I hope you like caramel." Suddenly I felt uncertain if I had chosen the correct thing to make. I don't know why I felt a need to earn her praise, but I did.

"It's my favorite!" She answered, taking the tray. Her frown turning to a smile, she carefully took the plastic wrap off of them and the toothpicks out. "How very thoughtful of you! This is going to be such a lovely tea party!" she finished clasping her hands together.

On the right corner of the deck next to the wooden guard rail, in a cardboard box, I spotted Lila, the beautiful mommy Siamese cat and five little kittens latched onto her feeding. I nearly squealed with joy at the sight.

"Sit, sit," Adelaide demanded, pointing at the chairs with the light green flowered cushions. "Let's have some tea first and a chat, and then we'll get to the business of the cats."

Listening to her directions, I sat at the big round glass table. She had set out a pretty little blue and white teapot set. Both the pot, cups, and plates had a cobalt blue diamond shaped netting pattern decorating them. Adelaide had it set for the two of us, and true to her word had made giant shortbread cookies, that appeared to be fresh out of the oven and smelled heavenly. They were my favorite. She had clipped an antiqued hydrangea bloom, the once vibrant blue bloom that had been faded and speckled with pink, from her bush and put it in a small crystal bowl, with water, to finish off her presentation.

"Thanks so much for having me; everything looks beautiful," I said, smiling a genuine smile. My thoughts turned to feeling thankful. My grandparents had all passed away, so it was nice to have this. Amber was like my foster mom and now maybe Adelaide and I could help each other as well. We all have something different to offer the people around us. Sometimes your family isn't by blood. Sometimes it's the people who are there for you.

"Of course, dear, how are you getting along in that big house of yours?" she asked, studying my face.

"I love it, and of course it will be less lonely once I bring my kitten home," I said, eyeing the box of baby cats once more. "Oh, I meant to tell you," I continued," I'm having a Halloween housewarming party on October thirtieth. You must come!"

This invitation did not evoke the type of response which I expected. Adelaide had actual tears spring up in the corner of her eyes.

"What's wrong?" I questioned, concerned. I felt guilty that I said something to upset her.

"It's nothing dear," she answered, dabbing the corner of her eyes with the white cloth napkin. "I'm just a silly old woman. I was feeling sorry for myself because it's been so long since I've received an invitation to a party." She looked frail at that moment; she seemed to have aged five years.

I guessed my hunch about her being lonely was correct. "Do you have any family around? Siblings or children?" I asked.

Adelaide sighed, "My husband died five years ago and left me alone in this big rambling house on my own. I have one sister, Betty, but she lives in San Francisco, and I haven't seen her in ages. I only have one son, but..." She suddenly stopped speaking, as her voice cracked. Her body was wracked with silent sobs as she hunched over trying to hide them.

I wasn't sure what to do, so I waited a moment. She composed herself and straightened up. "I'm so sorry about this display of emotion. I don't know what's come over me." She dabbed her eyes once more. "My son and I are not speaking at the moment," Adelaide sighed and took a deep breath.

I didn't want to pry. I figured she would tell me as much as she wanted me to know.

Adelaide went on. "My family is the most important thing to me, and my own son, my one and only, not talking to me… it is breaking my heart." She actually clutched her chest as though her heart was literally breaking in two right inside her chest. It was a hard scene to witness.

"Surely all families fight, give it a little time. I'm sure he will come around. You are after all his mother," I offered, trying to soothe her. I patted her arm feeling unsure about what to do.

Wanting to lighten the mood, I changed the topic of conversation, "Your yard is absolutely beautiful!" I declared gazing out at the gorgeous foliage. I thought my yard was stunning until I got a look at yours. Maybe you can give me some tips?" I asked.

Adelaide physically beamed at my compliment, "Well thank you dear. It is after all 40 years in the making. I didn't know the first thing about gardening when I moved in here. In the springtime, I will help you get your yard set up."

She delicately lifted the teapot and poured first my cup and then her own. The dark brown amber liquid filled the cup. "I hope you like it strong," she said, watching me gaze at the tea in the cup.

"Oh yes, I only like it strong, no milk," I said, taking my teaspoon and doling out a half of a scoop of sugar to add to my tea.

Adelaide watched curiously as I did it, "You know, your Aunt Virginia took her tea the same exact way." She said it as though talking to herself, unaware that I could hear her.

"Were you and Aunt Ginny close?" I asked curiously. I sat back enjoying the feel of the afternoon. With the sun shining so strongly and the cool nip in the air, it was a perfect fall day.

"Not close exactly," Adelaide spoke, carefully choosing her words, "but I've known her since she was a little girl. She was always a clever girl, that aunt of yours." She took a small sip of her tea and sniffed.

She reached for one of the shortbread cookies and stuck it on my plate, while she helped herself to one of my dulce de leche cupcakes. We sat in companionable silence for a moment enjoying the tea, treats, and company.

"These are delicious!" Adelaide announced after polishing off her cupcake. "Not good for my waistline," she said, patting her middle, "but worth it."

I smiled, happy that my offering was well received. I was still mid-bite with my cookie. "Yum, heavenly," I managed to get out, taking a sip of my tea to wash it down.

"Meow," a huge sound came from the tiniest kitten you've ever seen.

"That's your kitten you know dear," Adelaide said gesturing towards the tiny baby.

I stopped what I was doing and walked closer. My heart began thumping in my chest, a feeling of warmth spreading through my body.

"Meowww," the tiny kitten persisted looking in my direction.

"I love her. She is tiny and fierce," I declared looking at a miniature look-a-like of Lila. Adelaide nodded in agreement.

I sat back across from Adelaide and met her gaze, "So I researched. It looks like I can't bring her home until around Christmas," I stated, so disappointed.

"You can come and visit her my dear," Adelaide smiled. "I'll take good care of her until she can come home with you. Better to wait and get what you really want rather than just rush for something that is available."

She was talking in riddles, however what she said particularly struck me. This was a metaphor for my marriage.

"Really, thank you so much for trusting me to adopt one of the kittens. I didn't know how much I wanted her until I saw her just now." I felt a stirring of emotion, thinking of the baby I was supposed to have with Michael that would never be.

CHAPTER NINE

After surviving the hecticness of Monday afternoon, when the students had been dismissed, there was an all-call over the loudspeaker. "Attention all teachers that have signed up for the Dancing with the Teachers charity event, there will be a brief meeting in the library in five minutes. Please be prompt."

I walked swiftly to the door and into the hallway, not wanting to be the one who held everyone up. I saw Tabitha exiting her classroom as well. She walked toward me, her shiny black hair in a high ponytail swinging as she walked. She was wearing silver corduroy knickers and a plum dress shirt with sheer sleeves. There were dangling silver and black earrings hanging at her ear lobes.

"Love your outfit," I said, sincerely appreciating her style.

Tabitha smiled cooly. "Thanks Ava, how was your weekend?"

I wondered if she had seen the Insta posts. I really didn't think she would care either way. Tabitha didn't seem to be all about the gossip that the rest of them got caught up in.

"Pretty good and busy, I'm still trying to get settled here. How about you?" We walked down the hallway while talking and approached the library.

"Same here. I'm busy too. My fiance and I, we're doing a taste test to pick out a cake for the wedding. Pretty boring if it's not your wedding, but cool if it is."

We walked into the library and found seats set up in

rows. Spotting Fiona, we took the seats in the same row as her.

There was a group of non-teachers congregating together facing the seats. I could only assume that they were professional dancers. As a woman of Polish descent, I could spot all of the Eastern European faces. Dancesport is a very big thing in Poland and Russia and this group represented big time.

As the seats began to fill in with teachers that were exhausted from a day of herding young children, Coal came waltzing in and sat in the seat directly behind me, "You guys couldn't save your old friend a seat?" he asked teasingly, leaning forward to address us. He was wearing a green sweater that made his golden-brown eyes pop even more than usual.

"You snooze, you lose," I said with a smile, repeating the old rhyme we used to say as kids.

While I was turning around talking to Coal, in walked a distinguished man, about fifty, well-muscled, dressed in an expensive cut dark gray suit. His hair, raven black, was mostly devoid of any gray. His cheekbones were like chiseled granite, his eyes a cool shade of blue. A buzz could be heard in the air of people speaking in hushed tones as soon as he made his appearance.

"What's going on?" I whispered, turning to face the front where the mysterious man convened. "Who is that?"

"That's Mayor Whitherton," Samantha said, materialising out of nowhere. "Isn't he handsome?" she asked rhetorically, gazing starry eyed in his direction. Her pale complexion turned pinkish. In my head I was thinking, daddy issues?

Mrs. Avery rushed to the front of the room looking as frazzled as I felt. After a very busy day, her usually pol ished pulled back hair was threatening to escape in several places. She attempted to tame it by patting it down. She shook hands with Mayor Whitherton, and then went up to the podium that was set up. She tapped the microphone to be sure it was working.

"Teachers, thank you so much for coming and taking time out of your busy schedule to participate in this worthy cause. I'd like to introduce the man who is responsible for making this all happen. A man who needs no introduction, Mayor Simon Whitherton."

Samantha clapped enthusiastically, while everyone else clapped politely.

The mayor began his speech, electricity charged the air as soon as he grabbed the microphone, "Good after noon, it is truly my honor to be here with you today."

He took the time to scan the crowd and make eye contact with each person. He was the quintessential politician as he worked the crowd. The women nearly melted when they were afforded the opportunity to make contact with him.

When he reached our section, Samantha was practically salivating. His eyes flickered to me, and he smiled. When he went to move on and look at Fiona, a look of confusion hit him and his eyes flickered back to me, an indecipherable expression on his face. He quickly recovered and continued his speech.

"Physical activity and the arts are valuable assets that we need to provide to our students. Physical activity leads to better concentration in school and improved mental health. The arts are an outlet for our students to grow emotionally and creatively."

There was a smattering of clapping from the crowd. "Our goal with this Dancing with the Teachers event is to raise enough money to fully fund this afterschool arts program. In my estimation, there is no better way to reach this goal than to have the heroes of our education system model the dedication and beauty of dance."

At this, the entire library was filled with thunderous applause.

Mrs. Avery then handed Mayor Whitherton a crisp white typed sheet of paper. "I have a list of our teachers, and we will match you up with your instructor. You will have six weeks to practice your assigned dance. Then each of you will be showcased at the Gala in November. It is a black tie event and the word around town is that the seats are already at full capacity and tickets haven't even been released yet. We are considering moving the event from the school to a location where we can accommodate more people." At that,I felt a little nervous thinking about dancing for such a big crowd. He winked at the audience. Fiona and Samantha were hanging on his every word.

"After I call your name, you will go with your new dance partner to the gym where you can discuss the dance you will be performing and a practice schedule. Let's start with our first teacher, the very brave," he chuckled, "Coal Blake, Coal come on up," he encouraged.

"Coal walked up to the mayor confidently and shook his hand. "Your new dance partner will be Nathasha Dobrow." A very beautiful blonde woman with blue eyes smiled and shook hands with Coal. They walked off together through the library door, presumably on the way to the gymnasium.

Mayor Whitherton continued, "Next I'd like to call Samantha Asher."

Samantha got out of her seat and sashayed to the front like she was walking the runway. While I was embarrassed by her display and had to look away from her, the mayor was kind and smiled.

Samantha pushed her way to the microphone. She was nearly pressed up against the mayor. "I'd just like to give Mayor Simon," she giggled and paused after saying his name, "a big personal thank you for serving our city and organizing this event for the children."

He pretended to act coyly, however I personally felt like he enjoyed the obvious gushing. He introduced her dance partner, and they went off to join Coal and Natasha in the gym.

As more people began to be announced, I knew it was getting closer to my turn. I started to get butterflies in my stomach, both excited and nervous about the adventure that lay before me.

Fiona was next, then some teacher named Caroline that I had never met before.

When they were done, the mayor stared at the paper for a long while. It was probably only 15 seconds, but they seemed to drag on endlessly, like the days in a very cold winter, interrupting the flow of the meeting.

"Ava Zajączkowski," he said my name precisely, most people messed up the pronunciation. His voice was unfaltering, however I saw that look flash over his face, the same one that he had right when entering the room.

I walked to the front, just as all the others had done before me. Something wasn't right; I could feel it, but I couldn't pinpoint what it was. The air was alive with frisson. I smiled at the mayor and shook his hand. We locked eyes, and I saw something that I didn't quite understand. I saw fear.

"Ava," his facade returned, a polite smile on his face, "your partner for this grand adventure is Demitrus Nowak."

A slim built man of about twenty-five strolled up to us. He had sandy brown hair and blue eyes. He was about five foot nine. He shook my hand, and we walked together following suit with the other dancers.

Making our way to the gym, I knew I should be making small talk with my new partner. We would after all be working together for the next month and a half, a dark feeling filled my body, but I forced myself onward.

"So, how long have you been dancing Demitrus?" I finally managed.

"All my life since I was a baby," he responded, his Polish accent evident. It reminded me of my babcia, my father's mother. She had immigrated to America when she was a teenager and never quite lost her accent. "Do you have any prior experience?" he questioned.

I began to relax a little, having something to concentrate on. "Well, nothing to speak of. I did ballet when I was a little girl, and my ex-husband and I took lessons for our wedding dance. We performed a rumba."

"So, no rumba for you then?" he chuckled at his own joke.

I appreciated his sense of humor and smiled, "No thank you," and I laughed to myself. "I would really love to do Argentine tango, if we could."

Demitrus smiled, "Yes, I think we could arrange that." He looked relieved that I knew what I wanted.

When entering the gym, containing a gigantic banner in orange and gold sporting the words Welcome Dancers, I spotted Coal immediately. He looked up from his conversation with Natasha and smiled broadly when he saw me.

"So, we need to meet two days a week to start," Demitrus stated, as we sat down on some metal chairs designated for us. "Then as we get closer to the show, we will evaluate what we need to do. I can definitely do Sunday. I don't teach lessons that day. Would that work for you?" He paused and looked at me awaiting my response.

I really didn't have anything definite going on besides school and my classes on Mondays and Wednesdays at the gym, so I answered enthusiastically, "Perfect."

"Great, now you need to pick one day during the week that would work for you."

I glanced around the gym. Tabitha had entered the room with her partner and sat down near us. "How about Thursdays?" I asked.

"What time?" he questioned.

"Anytime after five is good for me. Wait, where do I have to go for our practices?" I asked.

He looked around. "Right here, the school offered us access to have all our lessons in the gym. This way, we do not have to pay for floor space at the dance studio."

"Oh wow, that's great. Ok, anytime after four is good then," I stated, adjusting my original time.

Coal stood up and began walking to the door, but he paused at the entrance, he smiled this sideways smile. He mouthed, "I'll wait for you."

I nodded in affirmation.

"Ok, let's make it twelve o'clock on Sundays and four on Thursdays. Do you have dancing shoes?"

"What kind of dancing shoes?" I asked.

He chuckled, "Your costume will be provided to you by a special designer- Brava Dancesport Creations, but you need to get a pair of shoes. You can look up Argentine dancing shoes. They have special wood bottoms that help you when you do your swivels. Look it up online. If you have trouble, you can contact me." He handed me a business card. I pocketed it in my gray trousers.

"Awesome, I'm so excited," I said standing up.

He followed suit, and we shook hands, "It was a pleasure meeting you, Ava."

"Same here, thank you," I said. He walked me to the door, then stood lingering to the side as he was obviously waiting for the other professional dancers before he would leave.

"How did it go?" I asked Coal as we made our way to our classrooms to collect our belongings.

"Good, Natasha said I should do a cha-cha," he announced, his golden eyes sparkling.

"I can't wait to see this," I answered with a mischievous grin of my own.

We parted ways at our own classrooms.

Upon entering, I erased the dry erase marker board that contained the day's work. Choosing an orange marker, I wrote Tuesday October 19, 2021, making the O in October into a jack-o'-lantern. I colored the eyes, mouth, and nose yellow, as though they were glowing. Thinking of my party in two weeks, I was getting into the Halloween spirit.

Getting sidetracked, I retrieved my phone off of my desk and pulled up my Insta account, searching for the other girls' accounts, so I could send them an invite to the party. I started with Samantha, since I knew her last name. I found it right away. Her account was private, so I requested to follow her.

I heard a knock at the door, and Coal entered. This was the first time he had come to my room, which I noted was somewhat surprising as he was only across the hall.

"Hey, it must be my lucky day," I said teasingly and Coal came and sat on the face of a child's desk at table number two, the group nearest my desk. He swung his legs lazily as he gazed at me.

"I realized I wasn't being much of a gentleman. I never asked how your meeting went." He raised an eyebrow at me seriously.

"Awesome," I said, tucking my red hair behind my ear, "I'm doing an Argentine tango." I did a mock swivel while holding my arms in dance hold.

Now his eyebrow went up about an inch. "With the Don Juan dancing guy?"

I laughed at his response.

He looked back at me seriously. "I'm going to be cha-chaing around like a clown while you are pressed up against a Polish dancing prince?" He attempted a laugh, but I could tell he wasn't happy.

Although I knew that he was only half-serious, I began to have flashbacks to my marriage, and I'd be lying if I didn't say that I was getting a little uncomfortable. I decided to change the subject.

"Oh, I meant to tell you; I'm having a Halloween/ housewarming party on October 30th. I hope you can come, "I added.

"Awesome," he immediately responded. "I love Halloween! Do you want to do a costume together?" he asked eagerly.

I had to smile to myself. Coal was not afraid to show how he felt. He was enthusiastic and had a sense of wonder that I found so charming.

"Depends what you have in mind," I retorted grinning.

"I'll think about it and get back to you, but I was thinking, what about Romeo and Juliet?" he offered nonchalantly.

I internally gulped.

"Well, we can figure out the costumes, but I'm glad you can come," I said quickly. I noticed his posture droop a little, but he immediately straightened himself out, for which I was grateful.

I drove home feeling anxious. I was anticipating a lurking car, a mysterious package, or something just generally menacing. I was thrilled that my intuition had set me astray. I pulled into my driveway without incident and rushed into the house to change for the gym. I was really cutting it close today.

I threw on a pair of black capris that I left draped over a chair in my room. Finishing with a sports bra and a cream-colored short sleeve shirt, I rushed out to the car, barely remembering to lock the door to the house.

I arrived at the gym just as the teacher arrived. Scanning the crowd, I found that Fiona was nowhere to be seen. I did spot the mom crowd but simply ignored them and claimed my spot. Luckily no one had gone next to the column. Marcia walked by my area just as I put my weights down.

"Hello neighbor," she sneered as she walked to the front of the room. I noted that Marcia had made extra effort today with her appearance. Usually, she taught her class bare faced, her hair messily put up. Today her makeup was immaculate, and her dark hair was blown out extra straight and glossy. She pulled back only her sides into a little smooth ponytail. She looked at least five years younger.

Jenna's mom turned around and waved enthusiastically at me. She wasn't among the moms that were guilty of stalking Coal and me the other night. She was probably at home spending time with her family, like a normal person. I waved back, and Marcia began the music.

We began the warm up, and I noticed one of the moms sneak a glance at me in the mirror. I met her eye line, and she immediately looked away.

The class went on without a hitch. There were no more comments directed at me from Marcia, other than the hello neighbor thing in the beginning. Fiona never showed, but I got an awesome workout. So overall, it was a win.

When the class was complete, and everyone was putting away their weights and mats, Marcia walked by to leave.

"Oh Marcia," I called out to her.

She seemed stunned that I had called her name, but she stopped and looked at me wearily. It was apparent that she didn't know what to expect. "I didn't realize that you and I were neighbors."

Marcia said nothing but continued to look at me, waiting to see if I had anything else to add.

"I'm having a housewarming Halloween party on the 30th. I just wanted to extend an invitation to you." I smiled, trying to thaw the tiny layer of ice that was formed between us.

She continued to study me and finally smiled, "Ok, great. What time should I be there?" she asked with a smirk on her face. I could almost see the wheels turning in her head.

"6 p.m.," I answered.

She nodded her head and left the room, not even turning back to smile or to thank me for the invite. She left me wondering if I had done the right thing. One thing was for sure, October 30 was going to be quite a night.

CHAPTER TEN

Upon returning home, I made myself dinner, an arugula salad with avocado, mozzarella, tomatoes, and cucumbers. I settled down in the cozy glassed room located on the right side of the house. Aunt Virginia had adorned the room with white wicker furniture. It was made comfortable by super plush sky-blue cushions. I put my feet up on the wicker footrest and rested my salad on my lap. When the days got colder, I looked forward to lighting the potbelly stove which would make the room toasty on even the coldest of days. I made a vow to buy some indoor plants that could decorate the room throughout the seemingly endless, bleak Syracuse winter. It could get frigid, especially with the antique turquoise and white ceramic floor tiles which while beautiful, could be very cold beneath your feet.

I located my phone on the end table and video phoned Fiona. I felt terrible leaving the meeting abruptly without talking to her, and then she never showed up at our class at the gym. I didn't even find out which dance she ended up with.

I could tell that she ended the call without picking it up by the abruptness of the call being sent to voicemail. That's weird, I thought. Is she mad at me? Just then the phone rang, looking at the screen I saw it was a regular call, Fiona.

"Hey Fi," I answered, "sorry I left without talking to you. I was rushing to class, and I figured I'd see you there." I frowned as I spoke, wondering why she didn't accept my Facetime call.

"Hi! No problem, I, umm...I just had something to do

tonight. No big deal." She sounded distracted.

"Oh, ok, well I missed you. How did the meeting with your dance teacher go? Was he good looking?" I teased.

"It went well. Listen, can I talk to you tomorrow?" she asked apologetically.

"Of course, no problem," I assured her. "Talk to you then."

I hung up the phone and decided to browse for tango shoes on the internet, first taking a bite of my dinner which sat on my lap untouched. If I could get them on Amazon, maybe I could have them in time for Wednesday, I thought.

I clicked on my Amazon Shopping app and typed in Argentine tango shoes and wood bottoms. Lots of Latin dance shoes came up, but I couldn't find them with wood soles. I made an impulse buy and bought a pair of tan strappy Latin dance shoes, with suede bottoms, that promised delivery by tomorrow evening. At least I could have something to wear for my first lesson. Once I found out what my costume looked like, I could order an authentic pair from Argentina and make sure they would match my dress.

Tap. Tap. Tap. I heard a weird sound against the window and shivered. A bead of sweat made its way down my spine. I got off the couch and walked towards where I heard the sound. It was almost impossible to see outside with the lights blazing in here and the total darkness enveloping the yard. The sound probably came from branches hitting the windows, I assured myself.

I attempted to look outside but could only see the outline of shrubbery, like big mounds surrounding the walls along the windows. A thought occurred to me, while I was in here with the lights on, anyone could see in and go unnoticed watching me. The thought made my skin crawl. I made a note, in my mind, to look for curtains or shades for this room, at least for the nighttime.

I refused to let my fear ruin my dinner, so I turned the overhead light off and located the sandalwood scented candle on the end table, next to where I found my phone. Using the pack of matches that was waiting next to it, I lit the candle.

Now with the low amber glow of the candle, I didn't feel as exposed. I asked Alexa to play tango music and the dramatic notes filled the air. The violin and bandoneon playing in harmony. It was so powerful, I felt as if the music was physically grabbing me. The ambiance was beautiful, and I felt resentful for being fearful.

Trying to put my trepidation aside, I went over the events of the day in my head. The dance meeting had gone well enough, and I was truly excited about getting started with my lessons, but why was the mayor so odd when he met me? Was I just imagining the weirdness because of all the strange things that had happened that week? I gazed out into the darkness again, but this time I felt sure that if there was someone outside, they couldn't tell what I was doing in here.

I forced myself to finish my dinner. Then I blew out the candle and brought my salad bowl into the kitchen, feeling proud that I didn't let my unfounded fright ruin my dinner.

Sitting at one of the champagne-colored leather quilted back kitchen chairs, I figured I better get serious about my party planning. I had invited most of the people, but I had to give everyone plenty of notice if I wanted them to show. Figuring I could find all the people from school's contact information on Insta, I opened the app for the second time that day. I used my detective skills and brought up Fiona's account. Tapping on her followers, I scanned the list for familiar names.

She had about three hundred followers, so I scanned the list from the top looking for a familiar name. Ah, ha, Tabitha Barelli. This has to be Tabitha from school I thought as I tapped on her name.

The picture was small, but you couldn't miss her stunning face. Tabitha had the looks of an Italian movie film star. As I suspected, her account was private, so I started a direct message to her.

Hi Tabitha, It's Ava from school. I'm having a housewarming/Halloween party on the 30th, would love it if you could come. Bring your fiance! Just let me know if you can make it.

I was really surprised as I continued my search for the other teachers that I immediately got a notification for a new follower, followed by a direct message. Of everyone, I never expected Tabitha to answer so quickly.

Hey, thanks so much for the invite. We will be there!

Although generally aloof, besides Fiona, Tabitha was my favorite of the teachers. She wasn't immature like Marion, silly and always chasing boys around, or high strung like Samantha. If her rubber band got wound any tighter, it was sure to snap. Tabitha seemed different, confident, like the type of person that did not befriend everyone she met, however if she liked you and considered you a friend, she would be there for you. A true friend.

After looking for a few minutes I found Marion. Her account was open for anyone to look at, not a big shocker. I took a look through her pictures and as suspected, there were several which seemed perhaps inappropriate for a teacher of small children. I shook my head. Maybe doing a keg stand for anyone to see wasn't appropriate for an elementary school teacher.

I followed her and sent a direct message about the party as well.

I leaned back in the chair. I think that covered all the guests. I either spoke to them directly, or messaged everyone.

I had to think. I vaguely remembered Aunt Ginny having a spectacular Halloween party when I was a teenager. She had the most amazing decorations. There were statues of creepy black owls and cats. They were memorable because unlike most Halloween decorations that were cartoonish, hers were elegant but spooky. There was a black lacy web that went across the dining room table. I think she even had a shower curtain that had a giant black cat on it! I would have to search and see if I could locate them. It was such a big house that I hadn't had a chance to really go through all of the rooms yet. I had only been in my new home for a week at this point, and I felt like so much had already happened.

I obviously had covered the whole downstairs in my first week here. The massive exquisite house had three stories, plus an attic. The downstairs contained the kitchen, dining room, sitting room, living room and the glassed room to the side of the house. It felt so extravagant next to the house I had lived in for the last ten years. Three rooms just to hang out in?

After you made your way up the grand staircase, the second floor contained Aunt Ginny's master suite, which I still didn't have the heart to venture in yet. My actual bedroom suite was on this floor. There was also a massive library. An actual library! Complete with tall dark wood bookshelves that reached from floor to the ornate crown molding surrounding the ceiling. As a school girl, I remembered exploring there and getting lost in all the books. I used to love to climb the wooden ladder to reach the novels at the highest point. The room also held an antique wooden writing desk and a gorgeous green leather sitting chair. I hadn't even stepped foot in there yet since I had moved in. The door had remained closed.

If you continued up the spiral staircase in the library, you reached the third floor. It was occupied by two more bedrooms, one complete with turret, and an exercise room, with mirrors on every wall. This would be a good place for me to practice for the dance show.

Then of course in one of the smaller bedrooms on the third floor, there was a hatch in the ceiling where you could tug on it and pull down a wooden ladder to reach storage in the attic.

Where to begin to look? I wanted to save the attic as a

last resort, since it was difficult to access and attics generally tend to be creepy.

I ventured up the beautiful staircase, turning on lights as I went. The thing is, I've never lived alone in my entire life. I lived with my parents until I went to college at Syracuse University. There I had a roommate. Immediately after college I got married and moved in with Michael in Binghamton. When we separated, I moved in for a very short while with my best friend from childhood, Clarice. She took pity on me. When Aunt Ginny left the house to me, I was so excited but also very nervous. I had always admired the house as a kid. The chance to actually own it and live in it seemed like an unattainable dream, yet here I was.

I stopped at the door to the library. Putting my hand on the antique octagon shaped purple glass door knob, I pushed open the solid door. I reached for the switch to the right of the door and the room was ablaze with lights.

The air was stuffy from lack of use. I wrinkled my nose and opened one of the windows to let in some fresh autumn air. It was a little chilly, but the room needed to be aired out. It needed life to be breathed into it once more. A layer of dust could be spotted over the writing table and cobwebs forming in the corners of the room.

If I wasn't going to have time to upkeep this gigantic house, I was going to have to hire someone to come in and help me. Maybe a few times a month they could do all of the things I wouldn't have time for. It felt disrespectful to not take care of this house like it was meant to be taken care of.

I scanned the room, seeing it with new eyes. It was as magnificent as I remembered. From across the room, I spotted a latch near the bottom section of paneling on one wall. I opened the latch and glanced inside. Sure enough, there was storage located in it. Aunt Ginny had never shown me this, and as a kid the latch escaped me, however I knew that Victorian homes contained many intricate little hidden details. I was excited to discover them all.

The first thing I spotted was a box filled with photo albums. I knew before I pulled out the box that I was going to get sidetracked from my decoration mission.

I hefted up the box and brought it to the writing desk with the green leather and wood top. Sitting in the comfortable old leather chair, I opened the ancient photo album.

The first page contained a picture of my dad, Aunt Ginny's big brother, when he was a baby. My dad was eight years her elder. He had the same auburn hair as both Ginny and me. What a cute baby he was! I felt a tugging at my heart. My sweet dad died so young. It would have broken my grandma's heart, if she was still alive.

Next there were pictures of Aunt Virginia as a baby. She was a surprise baby, coming when my grandparents least expected it. Ever since she was born, she contained a presence that was magnetic. You couldn't help but notice that she was in the room. Whether you liked her or not was irrelevant, her presence was known, it filled the room. Although I resemble her a lot, I had my dad's reservedness and didn't sparkle in quite the same way as she did.

Further in the album I saw a picture of her at 21. She was crowned as Miss New York. She wore a stunning gold gown. In the picture she was clutching a bouquet of flowers, as a queen behind her pinned the crown on her head.

Aunt Virginia was a perfectionist since birth, my father always told me. While he enjoyed staying in the background, doing his own thing, not wanting to be in the spotlight, Virginia was the exact opposite. She wanted to be in the center of everything, yearning to make an impact on the world.

While she was Miss New York, she spent her reign promoting the role of a healthy lifestyle, in maintaining good mental health. Her best friend in high school suffered from depression for many years and was able to combat it. With the help of her mother, and Aunt Ginny, she adapted healthy eating habits and learned how to manage her stress through exercise. It really helped her turn things around. Aunt Virginia wanted to help other girls around the country that might be having the same problems that her best friend had. She had a heart of gold.

She grew up in a house, close to this one, with my dad and my grandparents. Naturally living in such close proximity, Syracuse University was where she attended college. She had a double major studying both fashion design and writing.

Aunt Virginia became a freelance fashion writer. She traveled the world. She had been to places that would make even the most seasoned traveler jealous: Paris, Milan, Morocco, Belize, Madrid, Oslo, London and Buenos Aires. This is why I had the idea to do the Argentine tango.

Over the years, Aunt Ginny regaled me with tales of visiting Buenos Aires. Walking through the city, choking on the diesel fumes as cars would go by, the very attractive natives catching her eye. Drinking cafe Americanos at the cafes during the day, going to milongas, or tango dance parties, at night. There was one story that she told me that always stuck with me.

She was at a milonga one night around 11 pm, sitting at a round marble table with her glass of malbec. She was chatting with a friend. In walked a very elderly man, probably in his late eighties. He walked hunched over, clutching onto his cane for dear life. She said that as she observed him, she wondered what he was doing out so late and why at a dance party? He finally sat down as he approached a table filled with people, presumably his friends.

Ginny forgot about the man as she sat there enjoying the band, the music, and the dancing. A few minutes later, the old man stood up and faltered over to the dance floor with a much younger woman, probably in her fifties. She watched in fascination as this handicapped man glided across the floor, eyes closed, pressed up against this woman. They moved as one person. He led her with confidence as she swiveled and kicked her legs. His body was new again. He moved as though he were born to dance. It was magic. When the song ended and they broke their embrace, he limped back to his seat. The spell was broken, his body was his own again.

Ever since she told me that story, I wanted to find that magic. That magic that could take something that is broken and make it whole again.

With all this reminiscing, I lost track of time. When I looked at my cell phone, I realized it was already 11:30 pm, and I had missed notifications. The rest of the memories and quest for decorations would have to wait until tomorrow. I left the box of photos on the writing table, shut off the light, and closed the door.

After getting prepped for bed, washing my face, brushing my teeth and applying my moisturizers, I laid down feeling good and tired. I quickly checked my Insta account. According to her message, Marion would be at the party.

There was a new follower request on Insta as well. I didn't recognize the name, Chloe Smith, but I accepted it. It was probably someone that I couldn't remember at the moment.

Time was marching on, 11:50 already. I saw the numbers glowing blue on my alarm clock, a reminder that I really needed to get to bed.

In addition, there was a text from Coal.

Sweet dreams, hope I didn't upset you today. See you tomorrow.

I thought for a minute. What did he think I might be upset about? Then I remembered, he had acted jealous about Demitrus, my dance partner. Then he suggested that we dress as Romeo and Juliet. I had to remind myself that he was not Michael, and he was really unaware of our history. I couldn't hold it against him.

I typed back,

Not at all! Can't wait to see you tomorrow.

Then I leaned over, pulling the beaded metal cord, and turned off the lamp, with the stained glass shade, on the side table. I was asleep within a minute of my head hitting the pillow.

The next morning, I arrived at school to find a Starbucks coffee waiting in the middle of my desk, on top of the desk calendar. There was a sticky note on it with a drawn heart and the word Fi. I was early for a change, so I figured I would go find her and thank her.

The art room is located on the second floor, so I went towards the stairs to begin my trek up. With the echoey stairwells, I could hear the part of a conversation in progress.

It was obviously Fiona's voice, "Well why would she do that? Was it to start problems for me?" I had never heard Fiona sound anything but enthusiastic, other than when dealing with her mom, so it really alarmed me. I didn't know this person.

Samantha answered, "I don't know Fiona, why don't you ask her yourself?" She practically hissed.

I came around the corner, and they both buttoned up.

"Morning Ava," Fiona smiled sweetly, as she stood there looking angelic, you would never have guessed there was malice in her voice only a moment ago. "Did you see the coffee?"

"Yes, I did," I responded. My thoughts were on what they were talking about before I got there and why they stopped when I approached. I didn't know either of them well enough to be intrusive. "That's why I was coming up to see you."

"No problem, I was stopping, so I'd figure you could use a treat too," Fiona was back to her normal self now. She stood there in her navy trousers and white cotton shirt smiling at me.

Samantha continued to wait there, standing perfectly still with her mouth agape. I think she was still recovering from being caught discussing something private. "So, did you get my invitation Samantha?" I asked, letting her off the hook. She visibly relaxed a little and smoothed out her platinum hair which she held off her face with a silver headband. Today she was wearing a blue dress and looked more like Alice, from Alice in Wonderland, than Elsa or Rupunzel.

"Oh yes, I was waiting to talk to you in person. That sounds like a lot of fun. I'll be there."

Now we all started heading down the stairs towards Samantha's and my classrooms. The conversation turned to lively party talk. Samantha excused herself when we reached her room.

"Oh, come to my room if you have time," I told Fiona. "We didn't even get to talk about yesterday."

Fiona had a strange look of panic on her face. "What about yesterday?" she asked, fidgeting and pulling at her own raven curls.

"You know, the meeting. Why? What did you think I meant?" I asked, confused.

Her face turned an interesting shade of crimson. She was obviously guilty about something; I however had no idea what it was.

"Oh yeah! Sorry," she said, perking up. "I had plans with my mom last night, and she had a friend over. You'll never believe what she did. In classic mom style, she totally ambushed me. She tried to set me up with her friend's son. It was totally embarrassing." She paused for a minute, "That's why I didn't answer your FaceTime call last night; I was so humiliated and angry."

Her simple explanation relieved some of the anxiety that I was having. I was really starting to think that everyone was messing with me. That they were in on some big secret that I was not privy to.

"So how is your dance instructor?" I asked, my green

eyes widening.

"He's cool," she said. "I told him how I wanted to do the jive, and he sounded so excited about it. He also said I would be good at it, seeing as I'm so athletic," Fiona was beaming from head to toe from the compliment.

"I'm so glad you got what you wanted. I did too. I'm really happy we decided to do this," I said. Despite my words, my face became serious. My mouth was set in a straight line, my brow furrowed.

"Why don't you look happy then?" she asked earnestly. "Was there something wrong with your partner?"

"No, nothing like that," I answered, shaking my head. I was weary about telling anyone about how I felt. I didn't want to get things wrong and sound paranoid. Then a thought occurred to me, Fiona was there when everything happened. Maybe she saw something weird too.

"Well, what is it?" asked Fiona, practically begging me now, her face looking at me intently.

I continued cautiously, "I've never met the mayor before, but he acted so ... strangely when he first saw me and then again later on, when he heard my name. Did you notice anything?" I watched her waiting for an answer, hoping to get some understanding.

Fiona thought for a moment. "Maybe it's because you look so much like Ginny. I think he knew her. Maybe it freaked him out since..."

She didn't continue, but she caught my eye and I finished for her, "Since she died."

Fiona nodded her head slowly.

"I'm starting to feel like a ghost," I said, crestfallen. I spoke it aloud, but in a voice so low, I'm not sure that Fiona even heard me.

I glanced at the clock. It was time to start getting ready for my students. "Well, you're probably right. I never thought of that, but I guess I wasn't aware that they knew each other."

I was just grateful it wasn't in my head at least, a moment of clarity.

CHAPTER ELEVEN

The glow emanating from the two hanging domed lights in the library filled the room later that evening, and I decided to delve deeper into the storage area in search of the Halloween decorations. I needed to know if I had to go shopping, or if I had adequate supplies.

I've never thrown a party by myself. Michael and I used to have gatherings occasionally, but we had our tiny house to work with. The rooms would be so crammed with people, that decorations only needed to be a minimum. This was on a completely different scale. This was like preparing a venue that people would have high expectations of, and I was going to have to give myself plenty of time to prepare for this event.

I sat in the soft worn green leather chair and the thought occurred to me, as I spotted the bookshelves lined with dust, I should check with Amber to see if Aunt Ginny had someone who she used to clean her home. She used to travel so much; there was no way she would have been able to do the upkeep on this house alone. They would know better than me what needed to be done, and to be honest, I was working on a limited time schedule.

I found Amber's name in my contacts and sent a message.

Hi Amber, do you know if Aunt Ginny had a person she used to help with housework? Trying to get ready for the party, The house has been closed up for so long, so I could use a hand.

She answered right back.

Yes, I use the same person! She's great.

She forwarded me her details, and I wrote to her right away.

Hello Lina, I wrote, *my name is Ava Zajaczkowski. I am Virginia's niece. I received your information from Amber. I am living in Virginia's house now, and I was wondering if you'd have time in your schedule this week or next? I am preparing for a party and could really use your assistance. Please let me know. Thanks.*

After I finished typing out my message, I went back over to the hidden storage again. I yanked out the three boxes that were contained inside.

Opening the first box, I pulled a shoebox out. There was a thick stack of envelopes inside the shoebox. They were addressed to my grandparents. I opened the letter on the top of the box, and gazed at the yellowed paper. It was Aunt Ginny's report card from sixth grade, marking period 2: Environmental Science A, Reading, A, Math A-, History A. I chuckled to myself. I guess dad was right. She really was a perfectionist. She probably lost sleep over that A- in Math.

Putting the report card delicately back into the envelope, exactly as I found it, I sifted through the rest of the shoebox. It appeared she had saved every report card she had ever gotten, in addition to her letters from the National Honors Society and Honor Roll.

My phone pinged with a message. It was a number not saved in my phone, but at second glance I immediately recognized it was the one that Amber had given me.

Hi Ava, it read, *I was so, so sorry to hear about Ginny. She was an amazing person. I would love to stay on with you to help in the house. I can make it this Saturday, if that is convenient for you, and we can talk about future availability and pricing. Looking forward to hearing back from you, Lina.*

I felt a rush of excitement. Help was on the way, and it made me feel happy to know that she knew and liked Aunt Virginia.

I quickly responded,

Sounds perfect! Is 12 pm ok for you? If not, just let me know what you have available, and I will make myself available. Thanks again, I really appreciate it.

Looking at the boxes I had yet to open, I had an idea. Maybe Lina would know where the decorations were. Perhaps I would leave it until Saturday, rather than make a bigger mess. Putting the three boxes back neatly, I closed the latch on the compartment.

I spotted the box with the photographs on the writing desk. That could stay right where it was. I wanted to see if I could find some nice pictures of my dad and Ginny that I could hang up. Maybe she even had some photos of my mom and dad from their early years dating. I began to become excited at the prospect.

It was practically dark out, but I needed to get my exercise in for the day. Was it safe for me to run outside in the dark alone? I lived in a beautiful neighborhood, but it only takes a few wrong turns before you find yourself in a precarious situation. I wonder, I thought, if Fiona was around and would be up for a run.

Hey Fi, I tapped out, *are you busy right now?*

She didn't answer right away, but I busied myself with finding a running outfit to wear. Long black Lycra running pants and a turquoise fluffy top. Although beautiful during the day, the nights have turned cold now. With the sunshine dissipating, so did the warmth of the day.

By the time I was dressed and down in the sitting room

tying on my black and white sneakers, I heard a rapping at the door.

As I got up, I could see through the glass Fiona's thin silhouette.

"Hey," I said cheerfully, opening the door. "How did you get here so fast?" Fiona stood grinning dressed in her black running gear, her head was adorned with a matching black hat, and her raven curls were spilling out the back part of the hat into a ponytail.

"Funny, I was just going out for a run myself, so I figured I would just head over, rather than call," she explained, leaning on the arm of the couch while we were speaking.

"I didn't see your car in the driveway," I responded, puzzled how she got to my house so quickly.

"Ava, I live just two blocks away," she laughed, as though I should have known.

"Oh my goodness, I didn't realize," I said, locking the front door. Fi followed me into the kitchen and I grabbed the side door keys that were hanging on the hook next to the kitchen cabinets. "We'll go out this door," I said, gesturing to the side door to the left of the kitchen.

Fiona went out first. I then followed, locking the door, and put the keys in their hiding space under the stairs.

"Hi ladies," Peter appeared out of nowhere again, and I jumped upon first hearing the voice. I silently wondered if he saw me put the keys under the stairs. "Are you girls heading to the gym?" he asked, surveying our outfits.

"No, just a run in the neighborhood," I said with a smile.

Fiona had only been to my house twice, and both times Peter had appeared, like a heat seeking missile, the second we were outside together. It left me feeling a little unsettled.

"Safety in numbers. I knew you girls were smart," he said with a wink. "You know Ava, you really need to get some lights around your house. I was always after Ginny to do that, but you know how independent she was," his voice started to get choked up. "She insisted she was fine."

"No, I know you're right," I stated honestly. "I will definitely have them installed, along with an alarm system." It really did seem he was just concerned for my safety. He probably looked after me in honor of Aunt Virginia. I don't know when I became so suspicious of everyone. "Thanks for caring," I added as an afterthought.

Fiona and I set down the road. The night was pitch black at this point. The street was littered with colorful leaves that lay along the edges of it, like beautiful blankets encasing the road. We ran down the center of the street; there were no cars in view as far as you could see. With the darkness of the night, any headlights would be very apparent. We could move out of the way as soon as they came into view.

"I'll take you to the running trail right behind my house," I added, being happy to bring her somewhere nice this time, since she showed me the other running trail.

"I run here at least once a week," Fiona announced, as we entered the dark opening. I was a little disappointed that I didn't help her discover a new place, however I didn't say anything. What should I expect with her living around the corner?

We no longer had any street lamps to light our way, however the lights in people's backyards made it a little easier to see.

There wasn't a soul in sight, but running with Fiona, I felt safe. We ran the first mile in peaceful silence, just listening to the sound of the night, the crunching of the leaves under our running shoes, and our steady, even breathing.

"I start my first dance lesson tomorrow," Fi said, breaking the silence of the night. "I can't wait. How about you?"

"That's awesome," I answered, "but I guess you won't be able to make Wednesday classes at the gym for a while." I was let down, hoping that we would make our twice weekly exercise class a regular thing. "My lesson is on Thursday."

We passed a house where there was a family around

a fire pit in the backyard. I saw a slight little girl bundled up sitting next to her father. "That's Maureen's house, you know that woman from our class, the blonde. She's Melanie's mom," she gestured to the little girl sitting with her father, her face lit up with a beautiful orange glow from the fire.

"You'll have to point her out to me next Monday," I said. The girl wasn't in my grade, so I wasn't familiar with her. I wondered silently if she was one of the stalker moms who took Coal's and my picture that night.

We went beyond the point where I usually turn around, but the night was so beautiful, chilly and fresh. Our bodies were heated up from the exertion of running, so it didn't feel cold, only refreshing.

"So, you can bring a date to the party on the 30th, if you want to," I said teasingly.

Fiona sniffed. Her face became serious, "Not you too," she spat.

I stopped running. "I'm sorry Fi." She wouldn't look at me. Fiona was glaring into the trees, so I gently grabbed her by the shoulders. "I didn't mean anything by it. I only meant if you had someone you wanted to bring, you were welcome to bring them."

She finally lifted her eyes and looked at me directly. "Sorry," she said, "I know I'm being sensitive; it's just that my mom is always on me. I didn't mean to take it out on you."

I thought to myself how I wished that my mom could be around to give me advice, but I knew that was not what she wanted to hear. It would not be a well received statement.

We began to jog again. I was happy to have the distraction of movement.

"I suppose we should turn around now," I spoke. I looked down at my wrist. "My watch says we've run two miles, and we still have to run back."

Fiona didn't say anything.

"If that's ok with you," I added.

"No, that sounds good," Fiona answered begrudgingly.

We turned around and made the trek back the way we came. This time when we passed the house with the fire pit, I noticed the mom. She was the one with the honey blond hair. She was sitting with a boy of about three on her lap. She seemed to notice us as well. I wasn't even sure if she would be able to see us on the darkened trail, however I sensed her staring straight at us as we went by their backyard. Her gaze and the smell of burning wood followed us, lingering until the end of the trail.

As we exited the trail and walked down the slope, Fiona gave me a hug.

"I guess this is where we part ways," she said. She gestured to our left. "My house is about two blocks that way."

I leaned over and hugged her, "Thanks for coming with me. Don't worry about your mom," she gave me a sort of half smile. "She just wants you to be happy," I finished.

We waved at each other. She went to the left, and I pivoted to the right. I turned the corner, and I saw a car that was parked on the street. I could hear the engine running but no lights were on. As soon as I was close enough to spot the dark green of the car, the driver took off without even turning the lights on.

I paused in the street and began involuntarily shaking. I believed I was in the mists of a full-blown panic attack. I forced myself to move and breathe in deeply. In through your nose, out through your mouth, I repeated in my head. I stopped when I got to my house and sat on the curb.

"Ava," a gentle voice called, "It's me Peter."

Under normal circumstances, I found it creepy when he was lurking around. Tonight, I was thankful for a familiar, kind presence. I turned to look up at him but still said nothing.

"What's wrong?" he asked, his usual charming smile, replaced with a worried frown.

Peter then did something unimaginable to me, he sat down, in his expensive trousers, right there on the curb beside me.

"You're going to ruin your pants," was all I could think of to say.

Peter chuckled at my retort. His amusement was immediately replaced with concern, "Are you hurt?"

I gazed up wild eyed, "Have you seen that old green car around here lately?" I asked. I didn't know exactly how much I could trust Peter, but I didn't have many other options at that moment.

"Yes, tonight actually. That's why I was outside. It went by earlier, and I wanted to see if it would return. I was worried because I knew you girls were out running. "

He must have seen the fear on my face because he put his arm on my shoulder. "Ava, do you know who was driving that car?"

I nodded sadly. I could feel the tears threatening to spill over. I tried my best to stop them, but they had ideas of their own.

"Who is it?" Now Peter was on his feet, and he reached for my hand to pull me up. I only let him because international spy types aren't supposed to sit on a curb outside a house with a crying teacher. I didn't want to ruin his image.

"He's my ex-husband." It came out as a croak and the flood gates opened. I let Peter embrace me as my body was wracked with sobs.

He held me for a minute, "There, there..., has he actually contacted you? Besides his drive-by?" he questioned.

I pulled back a little to talk to him. My sobs were beginning to sound more like hiccups. I shook my head no, rather than attempting to speak. I was afraid the crying would start again.

We stood in silence for a minute. Peter was contemplating what he should say.

"Our marriage ended badly," I finally managed to sigh.

"Do you think you should contact the police about him hanging around by your house?" He asked cautiously. "At least get it on record, just in case."

My breathing had returned to normal, but fear hit me in my center.

My expression was solemn, but I spoke normally, "In case of what?"

"In case he continues to come around and you need to file harassment charges. You need to be able to prove that it has been going on for a while."

I nodded my head once more, "I don't want to do that quite yet, but it is smart. I promise if it happens again, I will go talk to the police. I'm really hoping that he will go away."

Peter looked at me skeptically, but he nodded. "Let me walk you into the house," he said, guiding me up my windy driveway to the front door.

We stood at the glass front door when I realized I left my keys by the side door. "Oh, I left by the side door, remember?" I asked him, although I didn't remember until that moment.

We walked together to the side. I bent down and felt around with my fingers to retrieve my key from under the stairs.

"With your ex-husband following you, you might not want to leave your keys outside," he looked at me seriously with a fatherly expression on his face.

"You're probably right," I sighed. "Thanks for everything." I went into the house and bolted the door. Peter stood there still for a moment after the door closed.

CHAPTER TWELVE

Upon returning home, my cell phone rang. It's funny that we even call it a phone, as we rarely actually talk to anyone on it anymore. It's mostly for texting and social media. I was startled to hear it actually ring instead of a text notification. I glanced at the Caller ID before picking up. Seeing it was Coal, I answered straight away.

"Hey Ava," he said, his voice sounding all husky. My mood picked up instantaneously.

"Hey yourself," I answered back. "Hay is for horses." I chuckled at my own dad joke.

"Are you home and up for company?" he asked, his voice sounding hopeful.

"As a matter of fact, I am." I was secretly thrilled to hear from him. I really didn't feel like being alone in the house after the whole Michael thing. "Come whenever you want. I just got home from a run with Fiona."

"Sounds great. Did you eat dinner yet?"

"No, I was just about to look in the refrigerator to see what I could find," I said. I was laughing to myself because unless someone secretly stocked the refrigerator without my knowledge, there was not much to be found.

"Well stop looking," he demanded. "I'm going to pick us up something on the way over."

"Awesome, see you in a little bit."

We hung up the phone and I got to thinking. Coal had been at my house to pick me up for our date, but he had never been inside before. My heart skipped a beat. We'd only been alone in public, but we'd never been alone, alone.

I wasn't sure how much time I had before he arrived, so I took immediate action. I didn't want to change out of my running clothes because I wanted to play it cool, so my black leggings and aqua fleece top would have to suffice. My hair needed help though.

Jogging up the steps to my bedroom, I located my dry shampoo in the bathroom. Spraying the top of my hair, I then flipped it upside down and sprayed it along my scalp. Finally, I used my fingers to comb through my hair. I had worn it curly today, so there was no way I could use a brush without my hair frizzing up.

I was still sweaty from the run, so I applied a generous amount of deodorant. Also spraying my favorite perfume on my neck, and a little in my hair to assure that the fragrance would stay for the duration.

I glanced in the mirror, my eye makeup was both smeared and faded from the run, a long day at school, and my crying jag. Finding my eye shadow palette, I applied some more purple eyeshadow at the crease of my eye and added gold near the inside corner of my eye, trying to make my tired green eyes pop. I threw on a coat of mascara for good measure. I didn't want to look like I tried too hard, but I didn't want to be a smelly mess either. I finished off with some dusting powder.

When I was finished, my hair looked a little 80's big, but I looked much better. He still wasn't here. Breathing a sigh of relief, I ran back down the stairs and lit a candle in both the sitting room and on the side glass room.

As I was putting my coffee mug and an errant drinking glass into the dishwasher, the doorbell rang. The second I heard it, I felt butterflies in my stomach. What a rush of crazy emotions it's been since I've arrived in Syracuse. Before coming, it had been a constant sadness, a black cloud over me, so I welcomed feeling alive again, in all its various forms.

I walked casually to the door, seeing his silhouette through the smoked glass. I recognized it was him by his stance and opened the door to greet him.

Coal's arms were full with a tray of food and a bottle of wine.

"Never come empty handed," he smiled, "that's what my mom always taught me."

"She did well. I see you learned your lesson. Here let me take that from you," I said, grabbing the bottle of wine. "You didn't have to bring all of this." I ushered him into the house and shut the door.

"Wow, your house is so beautiful!" he exclaimed whole heartedly, ignoring my comment and taking in the giant landing and stained glass. "I mean really, really amazing." He whistled as his head swiveled from side to side taking in the house.

"Let's put this stuff down in the kitchen, and then I can take you on a tour, if you'd like." I smiled, so happy that he liked the house. I remembered how he remarked about the wood carvings on the old bar that night of our date. He must have a genuine appreciation for the classic styles.

In the kitchen Coal put the tray down on the island. I peeled back the tin foil that covered it to have a sneak peek.

"It's food from the Portuguese grill," he announced as the smell of chicken and ribs wafted into the air. "Hope you're not a vegetarian. I just remembered you ordered eggplant last time we went out," he added looking a little concerned.

"It's perfect," I exclaimed, my stomach rumbling this time from hunger. Going into the dark wood cabinets beside the stove, I retrieved two plates and handed them to Coal. I then found two antique stemware wine glasses from the china cabinet in the dining room. They were Depression Era etched with a floral motif. I'd be lying if I said I didn't pick them on purpose to try to impress Coal.

I guess they did the trick because he announced, "Wow, these are perfect." He was grinning, as he admired the glasses I put before him. "I thought you were flawless before, after seeing your beautiful house, I don't even know what category to put you into."

Coal put the glasses down carefully on the counter and wrapped his arms around me. "P.S. You look adorable in your running clothes."

I tried to control my breathing and quietly inhaled deeply. I could hear the thumping of my heart in my ears. I didn't want him to see the effect that he was having on me. Wanting to take it nice and slow, I gave him a final squeeze and let go.

"Hope your taste in wine is as good as your taste in women," I teased as I handed him the corkscrew.

He chuckled and opened the bottle in one fell swoop. I watched in awe. If I had to do it, there would have been some swearing involved and multiple attempts of removing the corkscrew and reinserting before I got the cork out, either whole or in pieces. It was nothing I wanted someone to witness.

"Let's eat in the glass room," I said with a burst of inspiration.

The room already had an amber glow, as I had previously lit the candle. I put out two marble coasters on the glass table and put our wine glasses down on them. Coal followed close behind with our plates and forks.

"Wow," was all he said as he placed our plates down.

"I can't wait to show you the rest of the house after dinner," I said, both of us sat down on the coach, our legs were touching, but you didn't see either of us complaining.

I lifted the glass and sipped the wine. "I see your taste *is* impeccable. Malbec?" I questioned.

"Yes," he answered very quietly. His face was inches from mine.

I took another sip and put my glass down. I swallowed as I leaned back on the coach.

"We better eat before it gets cold," I said, only food was the farthest thing from my mind at that moment.

"Yes, good idea," Coal agreed, swallowing hard and not

bothering to hide it. The room was filled with so much electricity that I was sure we would be able to power a small town.

Forcing myself to reach over and take a bite, I tasted the hand cut French fries, "These are delicious."

"I'm really glad you were around tonight," he said, smiling shyly all of the sudden. "I've been thinking about you a lot since our date."

"Me too," I admitted looking at him longingly.

"I was afraid I scared you off yesterday with my remarks about Halloween."

"Shh," I whispered, putting my finger to his lips. "You did nothing wrong. I just need to take things slow, really get to know each other."

He wiggled his eyebrows at me, "I'd like to get to know you too. Slow or fast. I'll take you either way." His face looked so earnest, like a little boy. It gave me hope that his intentions were genuine. I actually felt my heart swell.

"Maybe we should have eaten in the dining room or kitchen," I said laughing. The love seat and the ambiance of the room seemed to make it impossible to concentrate on food.

"No, this is perfect," he insisted, taking a bite of his chicken, as if to prove his point.

We ate in silence for a minute, a comfortable silence which seemed to speak a volume of words. I felt like I was intoxicated, however I'd only had two sips of wine.

"Have you ever been married?" I asked, wondering how such a great guy was available. I took another sip of the wine and leaned back comfortably in the seat.

"No," he spoke slowly as if choosing his words carefully, intentionally. "I've dated plenty and have met some great women, but I knew that I hadn't met the one."

"How did you know?" I asked, really wanting to see the world from his eyes.

His eyes were searching mine now. I could see his internal struggle. He wanted to say something, but I could tell he was afraid. This intrigued me even more.

"Well?" I nearly whispered. "I really want to know."

"It never felt like *this*," he sighed and closed his eyes. I leaned in and kissed him, soft and hard all at the same time. We melted into one with that kiss. I was almost afraid of the storm of emotion that it stirred up in me. I leaned against his shoulder and laid my legs across his legs. We just sat, two separate beings breathing as one.

At last Coal spoke, "Have you given any more thought into costumes for the party?" he asked, lightening the mood a little. "How about peanut butter and jelly?"

"Obviously I would get peanut butter, you're the sweet one," I said with a giggle.

"I'm more like the Beast, and you are Beauty," he exclaimed.

Now we were laughing together. This time the spell was not broken. Despite everything that had happened in the last year, I felt joy. I swung my legs down to the ground and took another sip of my wine.

"I know," I said mischievously, "how about Bonnie and Clyde?"

Coal pretended to think for a minute, "Are you asking me to commit a crime with you? I knew you were a bad influence." He feigned disgust.

Now I really chortled. "I don't want to commit a crime, but it would be nice to have a partner to go on adventures with." My face became more serious than I wanted it to, however it didn't scare Coal in the least.

"It's a deal," he extended his hand very seriously, as though we were entering a business partnership together. "I would love to have a partner in adventure. If you think you're up for it," he challenged me.

"I know," I said standing up and gathering my plate of half-eaten food and wine glass. "Let's clean this up, and I can take you on our first adventure, a tour of the house."

"That my friend," he exclaimed, leaning down to kiss

me softly on the lips, "sounds like an excellent plan."

Coal followed me into the kitchen and began scraping his plate into the garbage. He grabbed mine off the table and did the same. While he did that, I refilled our wine glasses and put the remaining food in the tray into the refrigerator.

He went to the sink and actually rinsed off the plates before putting them into the dishwasher. I was so surprised, I almost cried out in joy. Michael used to leave them on the counter for me to do, or he would put them into the dishwasher coated in food.

I looked at him suspiciously. "Were you sent here as an undercover agent?" I asked, narrowing my eyes.

He just shook his head and laughed. I did a silent prayer in my head that what I was feeling and seeing was genuine, not some part of an act.

When he closed the dishwasher, I took hold of his hand and brought him back into the sitting room.

"You saw this room when you walked in, but this is the parlor," I said.

Coal stood silently observing all the details of the room. He surveyed the gold leaf painted crown molding and paneled sections of the walls, scanning over the vintage Persian rug in purples and blues that held the 1920's leather top coffee table. His eyes landed on the doll, which sat in the leather armchair.

"Is that the doll you received in the mail," he asked, eyes growing wide as he moved towards it.

I nodded my head in confirmation.

"Is it ok if I pick it up?" he asked, eyeing it suspiciously.

"Of course," I replied.

"It really does bear a resemblance to you. Whoever sent it to you got your exact coloring. It would be beautiful if it wasn't so creepy. Do you have any idea who sent it?"

"I sat down on the purple velvet couch, "Not really. I don't know anyone in town except the people from school, and I definitely don't know anyone well enough for them to go to such lengths," I chewed on my bottom lip trying to think.

Coal sat down next to me with the doll. "How about your ex-husband?" he asked seriously. "Has he been bothering you still?"

I wasn't sure how to answer that. I haven't heard a word from him, but there was no denying that someone, with a matching classic car to his, has been driving around town. More specifically, hanging around in my neighborhood. "I think I saw the car again today, after I left Fiona," I finally said.

Now Coal's face turned from concern to anger. "Do you have his phone number?" he asked me calmly; the rage in his face was betraying his voice.

I shook my head. "I'm not sure if he's changed it. I changed mine after we split."

Coal took both of my hands. The doll lay in his lap as though it were our child.

"He definitely didn't send that though," I said, staring at the doll. "It is definitely not his style. It looks handcrafted. The only thing he would try to handcraft is maybe a beer." My attempt at a joke that fell flat.

"Do you have any other ideas?" he asked, the concern showing in his face.

"Well, my Aunt Ginny, my dad's sister, used to live here. She left this house to me when she died. We looked very much alike, so I'm thinking maybe the doll isn't supposed to represent me at all. Maybe it's supposed to represent her." Now that I verbalized it, it seemed like it could be a reasonable hypothesis.

"That's not any less creepy Ava," he said gently, "if someone meant it in a benign way, they would have left a nice card with it."

I nodded at his reasoning. "Listen, I don't want to ruin this night. Let's finish the tour, and I promise we can talk about this again later."

"I want you to know," Coal said standing up, "I'm not trying to scare you." He paused for a minute, "I just don't want anything to happen to you."

His words sent chills up my spine. They felt like a foreshadowing of something dark. I didn't let him see this though. Instead, I smiled, "Thank you. I appreciate your concern."

"So, you really had this house left to you?" he asked as we embarked on the journey upstairs.

"Yeah, I'm practically the only family Aunt Ginny had left. Her husband was twenty years older than her and died about ten years ago now. My parents died when I was in college, and she never had children."

"So much tragedy," he said, more to himself than to me. He stopped in his tracks to regard the stained glass window with the peacocks. "I was wondering how you were able to afford such an opulent home. You should see the tiny house I have," he added for emphasis.

"I'm sure it's beautiful. I'm looking forward to being invited over," I said, as I ushered him onto the second floor. "Let me show you my favorite room."

I led him to the door with the purple door knob and opened it. He nearly gasped as I flipped the switch, and it was flooded with light.

"This is the most beautiful room I've ever seen." His eyes landed on the iron spiral staircase. Where does that go?" he wondered aloud.

"The third floor, but you need to see the rest of the second first. Don't ruin the tour," I said, our eyes meeting each other. I smiled coyly. We both relaxed a little.

For the first time since Aunt Ginny died, I opened the door to her bedroom. I didn't realize I was holding my breath while I did it. I wasn't brave enough to do it alone. I was grateful that Coal was here, and I could finally do this with some emotional support. "This was Aunt Virginia's room," I announced.

We stepped inside. Aside from a layer of dust on the dresser and vanity, the room was spotless. The walls of her room were lined with photographs in both black and white and color. Coal and I both went over to examine them.

Prominently in the middle of all the other pictures, there was a photograph of Ginny with her Miss New York sash and crown as she rode in a red convertible for some parade. She was wearing a strapless cream-colored cocktail dress and waving while sitting in the back of the open car. Her smile lit up the scene. Coal gasped.

"Wow, you really do look alike, it's uncanny. She couldn't have been too old if she was Miss New York in 1994," he said, examining her sash in the photograph. "How did she die?"

I started to tear up a little.

"I'm so sorry," Coal said, putting his arms around me. "I didn't mean to make you cry. It's just, she had to have been so young. I just want to know more, so I can understand. I want to help you get through everything...to be there for you."

"She died at home," I sniffed. "She had a heart attack."

"Really?" Coal asked, sounding incredulous. "She looks so fit in all of these pictures. It doesn't make any sense. Oh, was she taking prescription medication or something?" Now he looked worried with the realization that he might have said the wrong thing. Something I perhaps didn't want to talk about, something I might be ashamed about.

"No, nothing like that," I explained. "She had a pre-existing congenital heart defect. It's one of the reasons she kept herself in such good health. She knew the cards were stacked against her and wanted to give herself a fighting chance."

I sighed and began walking out of the room. Coal followed my lead. Since I had broken the initial barrier of going in there, I would go back another day on my own.

"Were you two close?" Coal asks as I heard the click of the closed door, indicating that it was shut securely.

I wasn't used to sharing so much of myself, with Michael my opinion and feelings didn't matter so much, so I felt a little uncomfortable. I didn't answer immediately.

We walked down the hallway now, my eyes focused on the parquet flooring. Coal was patient and remained quiet until I was ready to speak. I led him to my bedroom suite. I had left the door open a crack, and it squeaked a little as I pushed it open.

"This is my room," I announced.

I flipped the lights and saw the room through the eyes of Coal. I saw the five thin, long windows with stained glass at the top of each, the hardwood floors with the red and goldish throw rugs, and the deep red fainting couch under the window. It really was a room for a princess. I decided to focus on my good fortune instead of my misery.

Coal led me over to the fainting couch. We sat, together, his eyes fixed on mine.

"Yes," I finally answered with a sigh. We were very close. Even before my parents died, she was always more like a best friend to me than an aunt, and after they died, she tried to be more like a parent."

Coal nodded in understanding. He lovingly pushed a loose piece of hair behind my ear. "All you've been through is why you are so special. Without your experiences, you wouldn't have the depth of character that you possess now. I understand that it's been hard for you, but I love who you are."

I wished with everything I had that Coal was real. I said a silent prayer to God that I would be forever grateful if he was what he appeared to be. There was nothing he could have said at that moment that would have meant more to me. That's what scared me. There was something to be said for having nothing to lose.

CHAPTER THIRTEEN

I was sitting in my worn black swivel chair at my desk, in the mists of switching off between grading the long a and i word sort for phonics and trying to steal bites of my turkey club wrap, when a message came in on my phone from Amber.

Hi Ava, I hope you are not going to be annoyed with us, but I spoke to Peter last night about your predicament. I know it's none of our business, but we would like to help you out. I would like to arrange to have a security system and lights put in around your house. If you give me the go ahead, I'll have someone come straight away, my treat. Peter will come over to deal with the people. Please get back to me as soon as possible, so I can possibly make it happen today. xx Amber.

I read her text and didn't know how to feel. I was conflicted. On one hand, I felt weird about the fact that they were discussing me. If Amber wrote this to Fiona, Fiona would say that she was meddling. On the other hand, the thought that they cared enough to keep me safe made me very happy. It's very trying being an island. That made up my mind. I wrote Amber back right away.

OMG, thanks so much for helping me out. You are so thoughtful. If you want to arrange it, I would be very grateful. I'm not quite sure about how to go about making this happen on my own, however you don't need to pay. Thanks again xx Ava.

Amber must have been waiting, finger paused on the

keyboard.

Don't be silly, it's my pleasure. I'll get back to you with the details. xx.

Feeling happy about my decision to let Amber arrange it, I felt a sense of relief. I had been thinking on and off for days about how it needed to be done. Worrying about the feeling of being watched, mysterious packages being delivered with no one to witness it, but I wasn't sure what to do, so I was putting it off. Now there were no more excuses.

When lunch was over and the students were back in the classroom, I called the students, two at a time, to retrieve their laptops out of the computer cart. Upon receiving their computers, they immediately signed onto the website for science and social studies and began doing their social studies test online. I walked around and helped a few students who couldn't manage to log in. My watch vibrated indicating that a message came in from Amber.

My eyes darted to the door to be sure that no one stood at the window watching me.

Will you be home at 4? It read.

I wasn't really supposed to be on my phone, but I didn't want to delay Amber when she was trying to do me a favor.

I thought for a moment and quickly darted to my desk. I answered,

Yes, I'll be there at 4, but I have class at 5:30 pm. I looked up and saw that all the students were now working diligently.

No problem, you can be there at 4 pm to talk to the men and let them in. Peter will take care of everything after that. And yes, I am paying. I will feel at ease knowing that you are safe. xx

I typed back an orange heart and put my phone in my

purse. Then I got up and went to circulate around the room to see how the students' progress was coming.

When the day was finally over and all students had been dismissed, I shoved all of my papers and computer into my leather bag haphazardly. I needed to be sure to be home for the workers that were installing my security system.

Upon exiting my room, I saw both Fiona and Coal in the hallway, they heard my door open and turned to look at me, smiles on their faces. I stopped for just a brief moment.

"What are you up to, young lady?" Coal asked, trying to sound fatherly.

"Hi," I said, blushing a little, remembering the night we had together. I have to admit I was flustered. I usually had a quick comeback, but my mind was a little hazy now remembering our time. I felt like a lovestruck teenager.

Fiona must have noticed my reaction because she smirked a little, as though she were in on a big secret. "Are you still going to class tonight?" Fiona asked. "I have my lesson in twenty minutes. I can't wait."

"Oh that's right, awesome," I answered. "Yes, I'm going to class, but I need to go home first. Your mom arranged for a security system to be installed at my house. She and Peter decided it was a good idea," I finished with a laugh.

Fiona got a strange look on her face that I couldn't quite decipher. "Are you ok with this?" she asked, obviously annoyed that her mom had inserted her will on my life. "I mean if you're not, you should tell her."

"I think it's a great idea," Coal inserted, seriously. "Especially after last night."

"Why, what happened last night?" Fiona looked at me, surprised by Coal's statement. "We went running; you didn't say anything." She was watching me intently waiting to hear the story.

"No," I clarified, it was right after I left you. I ran down my street, and I saw a car in the distance running with no lights on. When I got close enough, I saw it was the same car from the other night. The one that I think might be Michael's car. It took off down the street as soon as I approached."

"Really?" Fiona asked. "I can't believe it." She stood there looking shocked.

"Well, I'm leaving now too," Coal said with a grin, "so do you mind if I walk you to your car? I can be your personal bodyguard."

"Sounds good," I said eager to get on my way. Coal popped into his room and came back within seconds with his own packed bag.

"Have fun at your lesson Fi. Let me know how it goes."

"Will do," Fiona said and turned to walk in the other direction, back up to her classroom.

"You look beautiful today," Coal whispered, the second we were down the corridor and out of Fiona's earshot. He looked at my thin deep purple sweater with the puff sleeves and brown corduroys and let out a, "Ooh la, la."

I smiled despite myself. I knew my makeup was probably running down my face. I was aware that I looked like a disheveled mess, but somehow when he said it, I began to feel beautiful.

Coal opened the door to let us out into the late afternoon sunshine and held it open.

When I arrived at school this morning, the parking lot was nearly barren. I parked when there were only two other cars in the parking lot, as I arrived bright and early to put up a bulletin board with their Halloween stories outside my classroom. My car was by itself, parked toward the back of the lot. I noticed that Coal's car was now parked right next to mine, keeping it company. I smiled again.

"You know, I really am glad you're getting that alarm system taken care of," he looked at me tenderly. It's awfully dark around your house." His eyes looked extra golden with his burnt orange sweater on.

"Yeah, I know it needs to be done. I'm going to my exercise class right after. What are you up to tonight?" It was the first time that I had ever asked him about his plans. Coal was still very much a mystery to me, and I didn't want to press him for information.

"I'm actually refinishing this table that I acquired. It's a 1940's French Louis XV Style. It's beautiful, but one of the legs is scratched up and needs some work. I'm sanding it down and then restoring it. I have a workshop in my garage," he explained. "Since it gets dark early, I have lights set up in there." He smiled sheepishly.

"Sounds amazing, you must have amazing patience working so hard to get things exactly right. Send me a picture," I said with a smile. "I'm sorry, but I really have to get going; it's getting late." My responsible side really needed to take over because all I wanted to do was stay suspended in time with Coal.

He looked around to make sure we were alone in the parking lot. The air was crisp. I could still hear the sounds of birds around me. Then he leaned over and kissed me, standing right between our two cars in the school parking lot.

"Are you trying to make me late?" I asked, holding on to his hand. "I thought you *wanted* me to get that alarm system."

"What time will you be home from the gym?" he asked.

"I'll be home by around quarter to 7. Hopefully the workers will be done by then. Peter is going to take care of them," I explained.

"Who's Peter?" Coal questioned. I could see him trying to think back on our previous conversations. "I know you've mentioned him, but remind me again."

"He's my next-door neighbor, and Fiona's mom's gentleman friend," I said with a laugh.

"Oh yes, I believe Fiona has mentioned him as well. Do you want me to come by then, just in case they are still there? It's up to you," his tone was very non-committal.

"Would you?" I asked, happy he brought it up. One of

the reasons I hadn't called about the alarm system is that I didn't want to be in precisely the situation that Coal was talking about, stuck in the house with strange men.

He was grinning wildly, "Of course I will."

This time I looked around, extra carefully, before standing on my tiptoes to give him a second kiss. I heard him groan softly.

I jumped in my car and threw my bags on the passenger's seat. Rolling down my window I said, "Until later then." I drove off leaving him standing there.

I arrived home to see Peter standing on his front porch. He was obviously awaiting my arrival, and my eyes flickered to the clock in my car to be sure that I wasn't late. I made it with ten minutes to spare, so I relaxed a little.

He casually crossed his lawn and then mine to meet me in my driveway. "The guys will be here in about ten minutes."

"Thanks so much for doing this," I inserted before Peter had a chance to say anything else. "I really appreciate it."

Peter examined my face closely, "We wouldn't have it any other way. Amber doesn't like what's been going on either. This way, if anyone approaches your house, we will see them coming."

I know he meant it to be comforting, but even in the late afternoon sun of this beautiful autumn day, it felt sinister.

"Come in, come," I said, suddenly remembering my manners. I unlocked the door and led Peter into the foyer. "Let me just put my things upstairs, and I'll be right with you. Have a seat if you like."

While in my room, I quickly changed my clothes. I was careful to pick a cute gym outfit, brown leggings and a pumpkin-colored tank top, as I knew Coal would be meeting me at my house right after the gym. Thinking for a minute, I re-

trieved Aunt Virginia's jeweled skeleton
key from my jewelry box. I put it around my neck, and it fell beneath my shirt. I wanted to bring some of Aunt Ginny's strength to my night.

When I made it back to the sitting room, I found Peter examining the photos on the dark stained oak mantelpiece, with carved stylized flowers, above the fireplace. There was a picture of Aunt Ginny and I in an antique silver frame from my first obstacle race, all those years ago. She came as a spectator to cheer me on and take action photos of some of my events. In addition, there were several photos of Aunt Ginny in various exotic locales. My favorite of course was a photograph of her dancing the tango at La Confiteria Ideal in Argentina. She was mid-foot flick and her face was glowing. Her partner in the picture wasn't revealed, as his head was positioned down, tango hat slanted to the side. Peter was so engrossed in the picture; he didn't hear me re-enter the room.

"Would you like a drink Peter? Coffee, tea, wine, water...?" I asked.

He looked up, his eyes looking haunted. "Oh, sorry." The look had passed from his face and was replaced with a pleasant smile. "Don't trouble yourself," he added.

"No, I insist. I really appreciate you helping me out. It's no trouble at all."

Always the gentleman, he replied, "That would be lovely, thank you. Do you have any red wine?"

"Of course," I answered, happy that he gave me the opportunity to do something for him. I went to the kitchen and found a half full bottle of cabernet sauvignon. I took a wine glass out of the cabinet, rinsing it to be sure there was no dust. As I stood at the sink, I could have sworn I saw a figure walk across the yard, but I did a double take and no one was there.

Feeling brave, probably because Peter was in the house, I put the glass on the counter and went out the French doors into the garden. As there was no one in sight, I quickly returned to the kitchen to retrieve Peter's wine. I didn't want to keep him waiting.

As I handed him the glass, he must have noticed my face because he said, "Thank you, everything, ok?"

Not wanting to be a drama queen, or cause any more unnecessary worry, I replied, "Everything's good! I hope you like cabernet."

He took a polite sip, "Perfect, thanks so much."

Just then the bell rang, I rushed to the door to answer it. Three men stood at the door.

"Good afternoon," a balding man of about fifty-five spoke. He was rubbing his paunchy belly as his eyes ran over me. "We're here to install an alarm system and motion lights."

Peter observed the interaction and my nervousness. He extended his hand, "Yes, thank you for your prompt service."

I was relieved Peter took over, as I didn't like the creepy vibe that the man gave off. I stood to the side listening as Peter spoke to them.

"Can you make sure there are motion lights by all of the doors to the house, the front, side, and back," he added for clarification.

"Are there any other doors?" Peter asked, turning to me for verification.

"Umm, the glass room has a door to the outside as well," I added.

The stout man scribbled a note down on his notepad. "No problem," he said, flashing a smile in my direction. Thank God Peter was here.

The man turned back to me, "Umm sweetheart, I'll need you to pick a pin code for the alarm system. You need something you'll remember but no one else will guess. Think about it."

"How long will the entire process take?" I asked, glancing at my watch.

"It'll be a few hours. Want to make sure your house is nice and secure for you," he eyed my chest as he said this. "A beautiful lady like yourself shouldn't be left unprotected."

"Very good," Peter said, noticing his gaze and taking control. "I'll wait here while you and your men work." He glanced at his two workers that stood in the background.

Peter was my new hero. I looked at him and silently mouthed, "Thank you."

He nodded back, closing his eyes looking satisfied.

"Help yourself to more wine," I said to Peter. "Would you like me to order a pizza or something while you wait?"

Peter shook his head, "No that's ok. I ate a late lunch, and I have chicken marinating for later."

"OK I'll definitely be home by 7; if you need anything from me, just text me, and I'll get right back to you." I gave Peter a slip of paper with my cell phone number on it.

"Sounds good," he said, slipping the paper into his pants pocket.

"Oh, by the way, my friend Coal is coming by around quarter to seven. If he comes, can you invite him in? I will be around right away, as soon as my class lets out."

Peter nodded and followed me out the door to my car. "I'll keep an eye on the guys for you. I know it's uncomfortable having them here right now, but it will be worth it in the long run."

"I know, thanks again," I said, sliding into the driver's side seat. Peter closed the door for me, and I went off to class.

Arriving fifteen minutes early, I was only the second person to class, as there was only one set of weights set up. I claimed my spot with my yoga mat and weights as usual. Then I went to fill my water bottle up. Who was standing at the water fountain but Maureen, the honey blonde woman whose house we had passed on the trail the night before? She didn't see me until she turned, putting the top back on her water bottle.

"Hi," I said, wearing my sweetest smile.

Her mouth was in a straight line. No attempt was made at even a grin. "Where's your friend?" she finally asked, looking around wildly as though Fiona would suddenly appear.

"Who? Fiona?" I was puzzled by her reaction. We had never actually spoken. I only knew who she was because Fiona pointed her out on the running path.

Maureen appeared to be getting impatient with me. I just kept on smiling as though I didn't notice.

"Yes," she said, now attempting a tight-lipped smile, her cornflower blue eyes gazing at me with mistrust.

"Oh, she's busy today, just me here I'm afraid," and I turned and walked away from her and back into the room where our class was being held. I wasn't offering that woman any additional information.

I've spent my whole childhood and adulthood worried about everyone liking me. I hated the idea of someone out there not liking me, but with this situation I didn't even know this woman existed. She had a problem with me that obviously had nothing to do with me, so I felt no need to try to placate her.

When I got back to the room, luckily more people had started filing in, so I wasn't left alone with Maureen.

I saw Marcia arrive, and Maureen caught her as she was about to walk through the glass doors. They chatted for a minute outside the doors. Both women fixed their gaze on me and then continued to gossip in whispered tones, putting their hands up to their face to block their mouths. Finally, they broke apart and entered the room.

Marcia made her way past me, "Good evening, Ava, looking forward to your party." Her voice contained an iciness as she spoke. I started to second guess my invitation. Wondering for a minute if I could revoke it without causing too much of a problem.

"Feel free to bring a date if you want," I replied, truly holding back from telling her that it was canceled, or she was disinvited.

At this, Marcia stopped and turned to look at me. Her snide smile disappeared. She looked as if I had stricken her.

"Thanks," she said. I could see that she too was holding back. I made a note to myself not to extend an invite to bring a date to anyone else. I thought I was being polite, however my politeness was apparently misconstrued. So far both Fiona and Marcia seemed to take offense at the idea. I was left scratching my head wondering if everyone had lost their minds.

I pulled into the driveway at precisely 6:45 pm. I certainly didn't want to stick around and chat after the chilly reception that I had received. I did have a great workout though, and that is what I was there for. To my delight, I saw Coal's steel colored Camaro parked off to the side in the driveway. Unfortunately, the work van of the security men was also still present. I parked my car behind Coal's, so they would be able to leave. Hopefully their exit time would be sooner rather than later.

The night had turned completely dark. It was such a crazy feeling because it looked like midnight, but it hadn't yet turned 7 o'clock. There was an extra full moon glowing in the sky, I could spot it between the trees, casting eerie shadows on the night. It was so full it looked as though it might overflow.

I turned my engine off and began to approach the front door. My entire porch lit up as I walked toward it. I guessed they had managed to get the security lights working.

The door opened to reveal Coal, grinning from ear to ear. "This," he motioned to the front porch, "is much better."

As I walked up the steps, he met me on the third step and threw his arms around me. At that moment Peter appeared at the door looking amused.

"Hey guys," I said, addressing both Peter and Coal, "how's it going?" I broke away from Coal's embrace and grabbed his hand. We walked into the foyer together.

"They're basically all set," Peter said. They're waiting in the kitchen to set up your alarm code and show you how to use the system.

I nodded. Of course, the creepy guy had told me I needed to pick a code. I had forgotten all about it.

"Good news Ms. Ava," the bald chubby guy said as a greeting, "your new system and lights are ready to go."

"That's great," I answered, relieved that it was done. "I saw the front porch was lit up beautifully."

"Yes, and it is the same at all your other points of entry. If someone tries to approach your house, they will be visible to anyone who is around. Are you interested in cameras in the house?" he asked, trying to up-sell me.

"No," I shuddered at the thought. "Too easy to hack. I don't need anyone to have easy visual access to the inside of my home."

"They're perfectly safe," he insisted. I could picture him looking in on women's homes on the daily with a bowl of popcorn and a beer.

"No thank you." I remained firm on my position.

"All right," he shrugged. "Let's get you set up with your alarm code for arming and disarming your system.

For about ten minutes, the man went through the whole process of how to enter my code. He made me practice one or two times, which I was grateful for. He had me pick a safe word, in case my alarm went off in error, so I wouldn't have the police showing up for no reason. Finally, they were ready to make their exit. His two assistants, who remained mute throughout the entire interaction, finally stood. They had been silently occupying the seats at my kitchen table.

I extended my hand to them. "Thank you so much for coming so quickly. I really appreciate it." I ushered them to the front door.

As they walked off into the night, Peter took this opportunity to make his escape as well.

"I'll leave you two to your night," he said, smiling at Coal and me.

"Nice to meet you Peter," Coal said, going to shake Peter's hand. "Thank you for helping Ava."

"It was my pleasure," he said with a slight bow.

"Hope you got your costume ready for the party," I said smiling at Peter.

Peter had a twinkle in his eye. "I sure do, and I'm truly looking forward to it," he leaned over and gave me a peck on the check. "Oh, and Ava, don't forget to arm your alarm before you go to sleep tonight. It only works if you use it."

CHAPTER FOURTEEN

Immediately following Peter's departure, I grabbed Coal's hand, it felt strong and I noticed the calluses on them, probably a result of his woodworking project, capable hands.

"Let's check out the rest of the lights around the house." I said gleefully, almost dragging him out the front door onto the front porch.

"Why don't we go through the back," Coal suggested gently. "This way we can lock the front door."

"So smart," I said, pulling him in close to me. We stood right below the porch lights and snuggled close for a minute. The night had grown cold, and the warmth of his body felt so good on my bare arms.

I locked the front door, and we made our way back into the kitchen. Exiting the side door, the area promptly lit up when we stepped outside.

"Wow, what a difference," I said. I was used to barely being able to find my keys under the stairs, having to root around until I felt the metal beneath my fingers.

I frowned. "The only problem is now everyone can see me coming and going, but I guess you can't have everything." I shrugged, and we went back into t he kitchen.

Entering the glass room, I was shocked to find that it was already lit up outside the exit. Coal immediately went and opened the door, peering into the night. This task was much easier thanks to the flood lights. I was right behind him, eager to see what had set off the lights. There was no one in sight. I listened closely to the sounds of the night. I heard a scratching sound and immediately tensed up. The hairs on my arms standing on end. The faint scratching was followed by a soft mewing, and I spotted Lila curled underneath the rhododendron bush.

"Oh, it's just Lila," I laughed, feeling instantly at ease.

"Who's Lila?" Coal asked. Looking down, he spotted the Siamese cat and joined me in laughter.

"Only the mother of my future kitten baby," I said, pretending to sound disgusted by his lack of knowledge on the subject. "You don't know me at all."

Now Coal bent down to talk to Lila. "Nice to meet you, beautiful," he said gazing into her big blue eyes.

"Nooooo," she answered in response, her tail flicking back and forth.

"Okay, see you later Lila."

I shivered in my slightly damp tank top. "I'm freezing."

We reentered the glass room satisfied that the kitty had set off the motion detector. That's something else I would have to get used to however, as long as it deterred people from lurking around my house, it was ok with me.

"Do you want to go out to dinner?" Coal asked when we settled down around the kitchen table.

"Not really, I mean I'd love to, but I'm not actually dressed for it," I said looking down at my gym clothes, "and I don't have the energy to go get ready now. I hope you're not disappointed."

"No problem, I just didn't want you to think that I was being cheap and didn't want to take you out anymore. I'd rather stay here," his voice became deeper and lower.

"Chinese food?" I offered.

"Perfect," he agreed.

We busied ourselves pouring over the Chinese food menu, ordered, and then sat down in the glass room to wait for the delivery.

Again, settling on the loveseat, I laid against him, my legs curled up. "How was your day?" I asked, relaxed at last.

"Not bad, and getting better by the minute." He

squeezed me a little tighter.

"How about you?" he asked, stroking my hair.

"School was good. I felt amazing after my class at the gym, but there's a mom there who acted really weird. Also, the teacher is not my biggest fan." I sat up to look at Coal now.

"What do you mean?" he leaned in, eager to hear more.

"This one mom came up to me and was questioning me about Fiona. Then the teacher and mom were both whispering and looking at me. I mean, I've only been here for a week and a half now, not nearly enough time to make enemies. What could I possibly have done to them?" I pouted a little as I finished my tirade.

Coal looked at me seriously, switching into problem solving mode. "Which mom was it?"

Her name slipped from my mind. "I'm not sure. I think Fiona said she has a daughter in kindergarten. Fi and I passed her house on our running trail, and I think she has a little son as well. She has honey blonde hair and really blue eyes."

"Ahh," Coal spoke with understanding in his voice. "That explains it."

Now I was leaning forward, willing Coal to continue and explain. I would love to finally get some answers.

Coal eventually went on, "A year or so back Fiona was dating some guy that had separated from his wife for a while. He had two little kids, not quite school age yet. Apparently, the wife, much to the husband's dismay, had asked for the separation, probably going through some midlife crisis. When she saw that he was dating, she suddenly changed her mind and decided to reconcile their relationship. Fiona was destroyed. That woman who asked you about Fiona, I think it was probably the wife. She fits the description that Fiona gave."

"Oh, wow. That would explain it. Fiona didn't say a word about any of that to me though." I sat in silence thinking to myself. It explained her disdain for Fiona but did little to shed light on their hostility towards me.

"The part that was the hardest for Fiona was that the guy only dated her because he knew the wife needed a reality check to get their marriage back on track. She told me how used she felt."

No wonder Fiona got so upset when Amber suggested that she start dating again. She was still trying to cope with the deception of this man who she thought cared about her.

The noise of the bell rang from the front of the house interrupting my thoughts.

"I'll get it," Coal said, getting up. "It must be our Chinese food."

"Okay, I'll set us up with plates in the kitchen."

We both got up and set to work. I pulled out two plates decorated with a white and red border and forks from the cabinets and set them up at the kitchen table on the silver filigree placemats that matched the fabric on the kitchen chairs. I selected a bottle of sauvignon blanc and two simpler small wine glasses, just to have a taste with our food.

Coal came walking into the kitchen carrying a plastic bag that contained Chinese food, looped around his left arm and two medium sized boxes which he held to his chest. He placed the bag of food down on the kitchen table and the two boxes on the kitchen counter. The aroma of the food already began to permeate the air making my stomach rumble.

"Your house is like Grand Central Station," Coal laughed, showing off his straight white teeth.

"What are those boxes?" I asked. I walked over to the counter and picked up the top one. It was addressed to me.

"Here," Coal said, handing me a utility knife from his pocket.

I cut across the brown packing tape across the middle and on the sides of the box and opened. A shoe box was contained inside.

"Oh, these are my dancing shoes," I exclaimed excitedly. With all the hullabaloo over the alarm system, I forgot they were supposed to be arriving.

"Were we supposed to get dancing shoes?" he asked cluelessly. "My dance instructor didn't say anything about that, and we have a lesson tomorrow."

"Me too! What time?" I asked, hoping I'd get to witness part of his lesson.

"I don't know," he said, scratching his head, "right after school I guess."

"You'll have to ask her about shoes tomorrow," I offered.

"You already have yours though, teacher's pet," he retorted as I pulled the strappy sandals out of the box. They could literally bend in half and had suede leather bottoms.

"I like to be prepared. Aren't they beautiful!" I exclaimed examining them.

"Yes," he said, kissing me softly, "but not as beautiful as you."

"What about the other box?" Coal asked. "Don't tell me you bought dance practice clothes too."

I glanced at the remaining box on the counter, a sick feeling immediately washed over me, my beautiful new shoes now forgotten as I walked over to the box. It had no label on it and was wrapped with craft paper and brown twine, just like before.

"Not again," I whispered, my heart began palpitating.

"What's the matter?" Coal asked, not understanding why I had suddenly gone so pale, standing there with my hands trembling.

I pointed towards the box.

Coal, for the second time, got out his pocket knife and cut the twine.

"Do you want me to open the actual box too?" Coal asked, as I stood there shaking like a leaf.

I nodded my head, unable to speak. After unwrapping the craft paper, Coal unveiled a generic white box. I knew what was coming. I unconsciously held my breath feeling like I was going to pass out, but nothing could have prepared me.

Coal turned and exposed the doll. I could only see it from behind at this point. It had the same auburn hair, this time adorned in a red dress and high heeled shoes, as he turned the doll around to face me, I gasped. There was a mouth and nose, but no eyes. Around the neck there was a necklace fastened out of silver thread. A thin sliver of paper containing a typed note was attached to the necklace. It read: *Why can't you see me?*

"We need to call the police," Coal nearly shouted. He was panicking and anticipating me protesting his demand.

I stood there against the hard granite countertop crying, not knowing what to think or where to turn. This couldn't be Michael, could it? I asked myself. The first doll could be ignored. It could have been meant as a gift, a nice gesture. However, this was the work of someone who was unstable. I needed to get to the bottom of this if I was ever going to feel safe again.

"Okay," I begrudgingly agreed.

"Call?" he asked, confirming before he dialed.

Coal fished his cell out of his jean's pocket and searched for the number of the local police. We agreed 911 was not the answer as it clearly wasn't an emergency. I was in no immediate danger, however it definitely needed to be dealt with.

After a few minutes Coal was connected with a local officer. I could tell by Coal's reaction that they weren't taking the situation seriously. The officer let him know that I should come down to the station to file a report. They informed him that technically, no crime had been committed. Apparently sending creepy eyeless dolls is not a crime, just demented. Driving on a public street is not against the law. I was welcome to get it on record in case a serious problem occurred. In other words, if I reported it, it would make the prosecution's case easier when the person went to jail for my murder.

Feeling defeated, I slumped down at the kitchen table.

"Do you want to go now?" Coal asked his voice, taking on a serious tone, as he took the seat by the other place setting, at the table.

"What's the point?" I asked, my head in my hands. "We may as well eat."

I opened up the bag and started removing the little containers and covering the table. "You heard them. I'll retell the story you gave. They'll "yes me to death", write down what I reported, and it will be filed away with no investigation."

I got up and opened the utensil draw to get extra spoons to dole out the food.

Coal looked at me critically, sensing my level of anxiety, he chose not to argue with me, at least for the moment.

"Can you open this?" I asked, holding out the bottle of wine. "I don't know how I'll ever sleep tonight."

Coal found the corkscrew on the counter and skillfully opened the bottle, pouring just half a glass for each of us.

"I know you don't want cameras *in* the house, but what if you got a security camera for outside the house. This way you can see anyone who approaches the house, catching whoever this is red handed," He put a heaping pile of rice on his plate along with some of the sesame beef.

"That's an awesome idea," I exclaimed, getting up to kiss him. "You are a genius!" I finally felt hopeful that we could get to the bottom of this.

I reached for my cell and found the internet browser. Searching outside security cameras, I clicked the link for Amazon wanting to get it as soon as possible.

"Please eat first," Coal said, trying to smile. "I'm worried about you. I promise you can get the security camera thing squared away after dinner."

"Ok," I agreed, "but I promise I feel much better now. Why didn't the security guy suggest this? Idiot." I took a forkful of food and felt my nerves begin to calm.

"Was Michael ever unstable?" he asked, trying to hinge the subject once more.

"Self-obsessed, but going to the lengths of making replica dolls of me with various clothing choices? I don't think so. My gut tells me it wasn't him."

Coal looked at me doubtfully, like I was just trying to protect Michael. I wished Michael no harm. I cared about him. We were after all married for ten years; it was just a toxic relationship for me. If I knew that he was guilty of something, I would be sure that I got justice. I didn't want to believe that he would actually hurt me.

"If not him, then who?" he proposed. "Someone out there is trying to get your attention; that much is obvious." He helped himself to some of the boneless spare ribs. I'm thinking maybe he is a stress eater.

"Well once we get the cameras installed, we will get answers, or perhaps whoever it is will get discouraged and go away." I pushed my half-eaten plate away. Unlike Coal, I found it impossible to eat too much when distressed.

I stood up and scrapped the remains of my food in the garbage can.

Coal took my cue and finished up his food as well, standing to help put away the partially eaten containers of food.

"Let's have a look at those cameras now," Coal said brightly. "By the way, you never did finish giving me that tour of the entire house. I believe we stopped at the second floor. Are you hiding something on the third floor? Perhaps dead bodies, or a boyfriend?" he teased.

"Ah yes, why don't we do our research in the library, and then I'll show you the third floor. This way I can prove to you that I have nothing to hide."

Before taking the trek to the library, we went around checking that all of the doors were locked and secured. I even engaged the alarm system. I was happy to practice using it with someone else there. I didn't want to accidentally signal the police to come and look foolish. Wanting them to take it seriously in case I ever did need them, I thought grimly.

In the library, I sank into my favorite worn leather chair, and Coal pulled up an ornate wooden chair that appeared too elaborate to sit in. We found it sitting to the left of the desk. He informed me it was an antique French black forest Alsacian chair from the mid 1900's. I silently wondered why he chose teaching as his profession, as he was obviously passionate about antiques.

I looked longingly at the fireplace and thought how beautiful it would be to make a roaring fire in the wintertime with Coal by my side. We could complete our lesson plans here, working in tandem, with the fire to keep us warm.

As we settled in, I went back to my previous search. Finding two systems that were in my price range, I showed them to Coal to get his opinion on which to choose.

"I think this one, here, is just what you want," he remarked, pointing at the screen. "It comes with three cameras, and it's wireless, which means I can install it for you."

"Sounds perfect," I said, taking my phone back and adding it to my cart. The best part was that it said it would arrive by tomorrow evening.

"Now that that's squared away, can I have my tour?"

Instead of answering, I stood up and walked towards the black iron spiral staircase located in the middle of the room. "Are you coming or not?" I asked as I began to ascend up the staircase.

Coal quickly followed suit but stopped on the second stair.

"What are you doing?" I asked, confused.

"Just enjoying the view from down here," he said slyly, wiggling his eyebrows at me.

"Oh brother, keep walking," I commanded, laughing the rest of the way up.

Upon reaching the top of the spiral staircase, we found ourselves in the hallway for the third floor.

"I still can't believe this is all yours," Coal remarked in awe. "This place is like a museum."

I took him into the first door on the right. We walked into the darkness and I felt around for the light switch. I hadn't spent nearly as much time on the third floor as the rest of the house, and the layout was a little unfamiliar to me.

"Are you trying to get me alone in the dark?" Coal whispered. "All you had to do was ask?"

I finally managed to find it and switch on the lights. Along the back wall, there was a full set of hand weights ranging from 2 pounds to 25 pounds, a set of four kettlebells, and a small pile of exercise mats. There was a sound system setup with speakers in the corners of the rooms. The walls were lined from floor to ceiling on all sides with mirrors. The floor was hardwood oak planking. At the end of the room there was a little door.

"Where does that door go?" Coal asked curiously.

"Let's have a look," I said leading the way. I glanced to the side and saw Coal in the mirror taking in his surroundings, amazed by what he saw.

We opened the door and were led into a spa room. There was a jacuzzi for two, a walk-in shower for two, and a massage table. The whole room was done in white marble with chrome accents. It was like being at a day spa.

"Ever used that tub before?" he asked, grinning.

"Not yet," I said, leading him out of the room.

"So, there's only two more bedrooms to see," I said, as we ventured back into the hallway.

"Only two? What kind of Victorian mansion is this?" he asked, sounding outraged.

"I know, it's not much, but it's mine," I said going to the first door on the left.

The room was done in creams, golds, and a muted

green. The walls boasted chair molding around the entirety of the room. The bottom was painted a soft cream color. The top was covered in wallpaper with a very faint diamond pattern in a soft gold. Green and gold curtains hung and showcased the windows. On the bottom, they were clear. On the top, they contained green and gold-colored stained glass. The centerpiece of the room was a fireplace with a simpler mantle than the one found in the parlor.

Coal stopped in the middle of the room. As he hugged me, the jeweled part of the key around my neck cut into my skin.

"Ow," I said.

"I'm sorry, did I hurt you?" Coal asked, eyes full of concern.

"It's not you; it's this key," I said, pulling it out from beneath my tank top, where it lay concealed.

Coal lifted the key up to look at it. "So cool, what's it for?" he asked intrigued.

"I'm not sure," I got it when I went to Amber's house for dinner. "She said it belonged to Aunt Ginny, and that I should keep it."

"I bet it grants access to somewhere hidden in the house," Coal said, looking around the room with new eyes. "These old Victorians are made with secret compartments and rooms. I bet this key opens one of them." He looked around examining every corner of the room.

"Maybe," I said unsure. "I just thought it was pretty, and I liked that it was Aunt Ginny's. That's why I'm wearing it," I explained.

"Of course, we'll save that mystery for another day, but I'm telling you, keep your eyes open. There might be a treasure waiting for you."

We visited the last bedroom, which sadly did not contain a fireplace, but it did have the hatch in the ceiling that you pull down to go to the attic.

"You're not interested in the attic," I said, waving the

thought away.

"Are you kidding me? In a place like this you never know what might be stored in the attic, but we can wait for another day. It might be kind of creepy at night."

I agreed and we started down the hallway and made our descent down the staircase, ending up back in the library.

"The whole house is amazing, but this room is my favorite," he stated, taking in the book lined shelves.

"Same here," I agreed, so happy that we had the same perspective.

Coal started walking around the room looking for any spot in the wall that might need a skeleton key to gain entry.

"I was just hoping this room had a secret passageway. How cool would that be?" Coal seemed like a little boy, thrilled at the idea. I just sat back and let him enjoy himself.

Looking down at my watch, I noticed that it was 10:15 already. I started to get nervous again when I realized that Coal would be going home soon.

"Want to go check my room for the secret compartment?" I asked, stalling for time and hoping he would stay a little bit longer.

"Only always," he laughed happily.

We left the library and went down the hall to my room. Coal immediately started examining the walls for secret compartments. He was on his knees feeling along the boxed-in wall paneling. I sat down on the bed and removed my sneakers before putting my feet up on the bed.

"Oh," Coal said when he realized I was laying down, "was the lure of the secret room just a ruse to get me in here?" he laughed.

I sat up and pulled his arm until he gently fell onto the bed, careful to keep his feet off of it.

I swallowed hard. I felt my skin turn hot as we sat there together.

"Thanks for everything," I said, breaking some of the tension that had just settled in. "Thanks for being a great person. I hope I haven't scared you off at all with the non-stop drama."

Coal looked at me seriously, his eyes looking nearly dilated. "This last week has been the best week of my life," he nodded in earnest, as though he expected me to argue. "You have made me feel more alive than I have ever felt in my thirty-something years." He traced a circle on my forearm with his thumb as he spoke. "I'm so grateful that I never settled for something less than this."

It was my turn to nod now. I wasn't quite ready to speak the full immensity of my feelings, but I agreed. From the way he was looking at me, I knew that he was aware.

I pulled his arm to bring him further down, from his upright position and his chest was on mine now. I could feel the weight of him and his heart thudding in his chest beneath his shirt.

Now he spoke again, his mouth just inches from mine. His voice was just a whisper, but each sound sent electricity through my body. "I still want to take this slow, no matter how much it is killing me, and believe me when I tell you it's killing me."

"It's okay, really," I insisted, trying to convince him, heat filling my chest.

"No, because I'm in this for the long run, and I won't do anything that might ruin that for us. Having you in my life permanently is a goal I will do anything to reach."

I gasped, the power surging between us undefinable. I kissed him hard, eyes closed, tongue lingering wanting to taste him, knowing he was right. I was still a little emotionally unable to move on completely. We shouldn't do anything that might send me running. For me it was easy to run. Everyone I cared about in my life was taken away from me. I wanted with all my heart for this to be different.

"You strike a hard bargain Coal Blake," I moaned.

He kissed the tip of my left ear that is formed into a little point.

We lay in silence for a long time. I listened to the sound of our breathing, his arms holding me tight. We both dozed off dreaming of the future.

CHAPTER FIFTEEN

My natural body clock woke me up at 5:00 am. I opened my eyes and heard Coal breathing evenly beside me. His feet were still partially hanging off the bed, even in his sleep he was considerate and made an effort to keep the bed clean.

I gently got up, trying my best not to wake him, and crept to his side of the bed. Removing his shoes and putting them down quietly on the throw rug, I saw him smile in his sleep. Picking up his legs, I rested them fully on the bed.

I would let him sleep for a little longer; I don't know many people who like to get up before the sun.

I went into the bathroom and quietly closed the door before turning on the overhead light. I looked at myself in the bathroom mirror, yesterday's makeup smeared on my face, my red hair sticking up unruly, but I recognized something beautiful in my face. I recognized the glimmer of happiness, of hope. Despite everything, I had hope, and it scared the crap out of me.

I opened the container of face cream and smeared some on my face, especially on my eyes, to remove my makeup. While I let that sit for a minute, I brushed my teeth. Then I fiddled with the shower water, waiting for the hot water to start flowing through the pipes.

Pulling my tank top and running bra over my head, I shimm ied out of my running pants before stepping into the claw foot tub to take my shower. I pulled the silver curtain closed around me. Taking care to shampoo and condition my hair, stopping to even shave my legs. Finally, I turned off the water, grabbing a towel off of the rod on the wall. I wrapped the plush forest green towel around myself. I reached into the closet, on a hook on the back of the door, I kept my special towel for my hair that would absorb water but not make my curls look frizzy.

I found my bag of moisturizers and applied some serum to my face, massaging it in, in an upward motion. It needed extra special treatment today, since I carelessly fell asleep without washing it. I never do that. Just as I was about to apply my second layer of moisturizer, I heard a gentle rap from the other side of the door.

"Come in," I answered shyly.

The door opened revealing a grinning Coal, complete with tousled hair. He was looking both goofy and handsome as can be.

"Morning beautiful," he said standing there in his bare feet, clothes from yesterday looking slightly rumpled.

"Morning... I don't know how this happened," I said, unsure what else to say. This man had just slept in my bed and here I was standing in a towel.

"Who cares, I'm just happy that it did. I haven't slept that good in years," he said grinning from ear to ear. "I know we said we were going to take things slow, but you are killing me walking around like this." He gestured toward my towel.

"I'm not actually walking around," I pointed out to him. "Technically you are the one who invaded my territory coming into the bathroom." I smiled, happy that our easy conversation had not left us and mysteriously disappeared leaving awkwardness.

"Good point," he said walking into the room. "Do you happen to have a spare toothbrush?"

I searched in the bathroom closet and found a brand new one still in the box.

Handing the toothbrush to him, I announced, "I'll leave you to it." I walked out of the bathroom, closing the door behind me.

While Coal was in the bathroom freshening up, I

quickly picked a green jumpsuit out of my closet to wear. I left my towel on and stepped into silky cream-colored underwear. Next, I stepped into the bottom of the jumpsuit pulling it up to waist height. I put on a matching bra, as quickly as humanly possible when I heard the door opening. I pulled the top of my outfit up and slipped in my arms before his face was in view.

"Can you zip me?" I asked coyly as he walked over to where I was changing.

"It would be my pleasure," he said, taking his time pulling up the zipper.

"I guess you better head home to change for school," I said laughing. "People might start talking if you show up in the same clothes as yesterday."

"I will, soon," he retorted, "but only for my students' sake. I have to set a good example by coming in with clean clothes. Let everyone else talk all they want."

"Do you want to have coffee together before you leave?" I asked, picking up the wet towel from the floor.

"That would be divine," he answered.

I quickly went back into the bathroom, hanging up my hair towel back on the closet hook, and the towel for my body back on the towel rack.

As I was doing this, Coal sat back on the edge of the bed briefly to put his shoes back on.

"Ready?" I asked as he stood.

"Born ready," he answered, following me out of the room.

"I'll make the coffee," I said. "You sit and relax for a minute. He took his spot from last night at the kitchen table as if it were the most natural thing in the world.

I went about measuring two scoops of espresso, instead of my usual one. Then I added twice the water to be sure that we had enough for both of us.

"So, dance class starts tonight," I said grinning at Coal. "I can't wait to see you in action."

"Please don't watch," he begged, "at least until I've had a few classes and have gotten the hang of it. Then you can gawk all you want."

"We'll see, I'm not promising anything," I laughed.

"I guess we will be seeing each other again tonight," he exclaimed looking mighty pleased with himself.

"You mean at dancing?" I asked, confused.

"No silly, your cameras are coming, and I want to get them installed as soon as possible."

"Oh, right, how do you like your coffee?" I asked, picking a mug out of the cabinet for him.

"I'll make it," he said, starting to get up.

"Don't insult me. I'm letting you put up my cameras, now you have to let me take care of you too."

"Yes mam," he responded, "two teaspoons of sugar and milk."

I opened the refrigerator and realized I had no milk, "I only have oat milk," I announced holding up the carton.

"Good, because that's what I wanted," he said with a kind smile.

After finishing making our coffees, I joined him at the table. It was still pitch black out, but after taking a shower, I felt wide awake.

I spoke first, "I'm glad you stayed over, even if it wasn't on purpose. I actually slept soundly, despite the creepy eyeless doll." I glanced toward the counter where we had left her laying.

"Just performing a public service, "he announced.

"What a Good Samaritan you are," I responded.

After Coal finished his cup of coffee, I got up and walked him to the door.

"Don't forget to disarm the alarm before opening the door," he prompted me.

I'm glad he reminded me because I totally forgot. I entered the code and opened the door, "I'll see you at school," I said.

"Until later love," he said, brushing a kiss softly on my lips and walking off towards his car. As soon as he got down the stairs, the light went on brightening the way for his trip.

Before leaving the house that morning I grabbed a little tote bag to bring my dance shoes in. I also remembered to bring an elastic for my hair, in case I needed to put it up for dancing. I threw in a water bottle for good measure. You can never be too prepared, and I wasn't sure what to expect.

I arrived at school to a half-full parking lot. Spotting Fiona's blue Chevy Volt entering the parking lot right before me, I pulled my Mustang up next to hers.

"Ava," Fiona smiled, getting out of the car and hoisting a gray tote bag over her shoulder, "Guess you had a busy night." Her voice was brimming with innuendo.

"What do you mean?" I asked, feeling confused. I was sure she didn't know anything about the doll. Who would have told her about it? I wondered.

She smiled a sly smile, "I saw Coal leaving your house this morning. I was going for a run before work and passed your house."

Oh great, just what I needed. The sad part was nothing even happened, I thought to myself.

"It's not what it looks like," I said defensively, but honestly who would believe me? Whenever anyone says it's not what it looks like, it's always what it looks like.

"No judgement from me," Fiona said, throwing her hands up in the air as we walked across the parking lot.

"Seriously, it was a rough night. The alarm guys were there pretty late. After they left," I paused for a minute as we were now entering the building. I didn't want to be overheard by anyone, and Fiona seemed to have understood because she didn't press me to continue.

We walked down the corridor to my classroom, and Fiona joined me in my room without an invitation. As soon as we walked in, I flipped the lights on, and Fiona closed my door.

"Go on," she prompted insistently.

"How was your dance lesson?" I asked as I put my heavy school bag down on the floor beside my desk.

"Ava," Fiona said looking at me, her eyes wide, "aren't you going to finish your story?"

"Listen, I don't want you to get the wrong idea. Coal is the first guy I've even spoken to since things went.... wrong. He came over after my class last night, so I wouldn't be alone with all those guys. After they left, we ordered food and things got weird."

"Weird how?" Fiona brown eyes were now nearly bulging out of her head.

I could see her mind working overtime. She was thinking I meant weird with Coal. I really had to just get out with it and clarify things.

"We ordered Chinese food, and when they delivered it, there was another mysterious package on the porch."

"Oh," Fiona said, some of the urgency had left her face. She just waited for me to continue.

Taking a sip of my espresso that I had brought with me, I braced myself to finish the next part.

"It was another doll that was fastened to look like me, only this doll was ... different." I could feel my voice start to tremble. I made myself continue, we were running out of time before school officially began, and I needed to just get on with it.

Fiona now came beside me and put one of her black clad arms around me for support.

"This doll had a face but no eyes," I looked up at Fiona now, my eyes brimming with tears and fear. "There was a note around its neck which read, "Why don't you see me?"

I saw Fiona physically shudder and release her arm from around me. "What!? That's crazy?" Her eyes now looked wild as though she was trying to process what I had just told her. All suspicions about Coal and I were forgotten.

"I know," I said softly. I took a breath and composed myself. "After dinner Coal stayed with me for a while, and we must have fallen asleep. All the stress took everything out of me."

"Wow, that's some story. I guess you were right; it really wasn't what it seemed," Now she narrowed her eyes at me. "So, what now?"

"Now I'm having cameras installed, so I can try to catch whatever weirdo is doing this," I sighed and looked at the clock. We had three minutes to go, and I had to run to the ladies' room while I had a chance.

"Let's walk and talk," I said heading to the door, "how was your dance partner?"

"Hot," Fiona said with a grin.

"Oh really?" I asked, happy that th e conversation had moved on to something less serious. "Do tell."

The gymnasium was abuzz with energy when 3:30 pm hit. Classes weren't due to start until 4:00 pm, but all the teachers that had lessons stayed at school to wait.

Coal and I walked together. I carried my purse and school bag with me, so I wouldn't have to schlep back to my room when it was over. I could use these doors to exit and make a hasty retreat.

When he opened the big metal doors to enter, they made a clanging noise as usual. We found Tabitha and Marion already there, along with some women with a short bleach blonde pixie cut that I had yet to meet.

"Hey guys," I called out to them as we crossed the gym to where they were standing.

The girl with the pixie cut smiled a warm smile, "Hi, I'm Chloe. I teach first grade; it's so nice to meet you. I've heard so much about you; I feel as though I know you already."

I shook her hand and returned her smile, "Nice to meet you too Chloe." Chloe, that name sounded familiar, but

I couldn't figure out why. It was niggling in the back of my brain. I knew it would come to me eventually. Also, I wondered what she had heard about me. I'd only been here a week and a half and barely knew anyone.

"So, are you guys excited?" I asked the room. Sitting down on the floor, I began to reach into the tote bag I brought with me. I came out with my brand-new dance shoes. The only package I received last night which was actually expected and wanted.

I removed my pointy black heels that I had worn to school, and I began to replace them with my dance shoes.

"Do you have special dance shoes?" Tabitha asked as she saw me switching out of the shoes I had worn that day. "Where did you get them?"

"Thank you," said Coal, throwing his hands up in the air. "I think Ava is the only one who got the memo that special shoes were required."

"Amazon," I replied to Tabitha, completely ignoring Cole's tirade.

"Oh well, not my fault my hunky instructor didn't tell me," said Marion, flipping her hair. She had changed into black shiny spandex pants and a turquoise sequin top, in honor of her lesson that afternoon.

We all chuckled.

I sat on the floor trying to fasten my shoes, but I was having trouble buckling the straps. Without my asking, Coal bent down to do it for me.

"There you go," he said with a wink. He had just successfully buckled both shoes.

"Wow, a real-life Prince Charming," exclaimed Marion. "Good thing we don't have our shoes yet, or you would be helping all of us."

We heard the tell-tale clanking of the doors, and in walked Demitrus with another instructor. He was tall and thin with black 90's hair and resembled the Nightmare Before Christmas Guy.

"Let the games begin," Tabitha said under her breath. "That's my instructor Henri."

"Oh la, la," I whispered back.

Tabitha smirked in response.

Demitrus walked right over to me and gave me a kiss on the cheek. "Ava, let's get started," he proclaimed and began to walk towards the lower right corner of the gym. I dutifully followed.

As soon as we claimed our dance space, he began. "In most of the dances, the lady walks backwards first. The Argentine tango is one of the only dances where the woman steps forward first," he explained.

I loved the idea of my dance breaking the rules. I was hanging on his every word, excited to embrace the magic of the Argentine tango. I definitely wanted to step forward in my life at this point. I didn't want to start by stepping backwards.

"Let's start with the hold," he said, grabbing both of my hands and adjusting how my arms were in contact with his. "The tango is to be danced very close to your partner." He pulled me in so that our chests were nearly touching. Now here we go." He guided me so I stepped forward, side, back, back, cross, back and side.

He said it over and over as I followed his lead and danced. This was the basic step in Argentine tango. He used his cell phone and played an Argentine tango song, counting as we practiced the basic step, over and over. Before I knew it, an hour had passed. By the end of the time, I could do it with my eyes closed.

I was so caught up in the dance, that I forgot to even glance in Coal's direction. I hoped his lesson was just as successful.

"Great job today, Ava, you are a natural," he said, taking my arm and spinning me. I will see you on Sunday?"

My heart was happy. "Looking forward to it," I said. All the while I was repeating slow, slow, quick, quick, slow in my head. It was on loop. "Thanks again," I added as I went over to my bags to change my shoes.

At this point I glanced around to see what everyone else was doing. Prior to this, I was so engrossed in my lesson, I barely knew that anyone else was occupying the room. I was in the zone, where everything else ceases to exist because you're concentrating so hard. They were all wrapping-up their lessons as well. Marion was leaning forward trying to nonchalantly push together her cleavage while speaking with her instructor. Tabitha was looking on in amusement as her spindly cartoonish instructor was trying to demonstrate what she was doing wrong. Coal waved goodbye to Natasha as he made his way towards me.

"Let me help you with that," Coal said, bending down once again to help me unbuckle my shoes this time. "By the way, I need to get dancing shoes. Did you know that?" he asked, voice dripping with sarcasm. He chuckled to himself.

"Really, are there special shoes you have to wear to dance?" I asked innocently. "I've never heard of that before."

We both laughed. Putting my dance shoes into the tote, I took out my black pumps and slipped into them.

As I stood up and gathered my things, Coal turned to me, not bothering to keep his voice low this time, "Do you want me to come over now to see if the cameras are here yet?"

"Sounds good, but why don't we stop at the supermarket. I'll pick up some things to make us a nice dinner, my treat," I said as we walked towards the exit door. I wasn't worried about who heard us either. This was dangerous territory.

"Great plan, only I want to cook together," he insisted as he walked me to my car. He wasn't right next to me today, as I had parked next to Fiona.

My heart fluttered. "Follow me. I'll meet you at the one on Kengsington Rd., in case we get separated."

"I won't let that happen," he replied with a wink.

I jumped in the car and shut the door before he had the chance to kiss me. I felt like I was on a runaway train. He seemed too perfect. You know what they say if something seems too good to be true, it probably is. This was the exact reason why we needed to take it slow. I had to talk myself down on the way to the supermarket, tell myself not to do anything hasty to wreck things. My pep talk to myself did little to calm my nerves, as we both found spots outside the store, parked, and got out.

Deciding to find some neutral ground, I spoke as we approached the entrance, "You know that girl Chloe, from the gymnasium today?"

"Yeah, she teaches first grade."

"Have you ever mentioned her to me before?" I questioned as we wandered inside the small store.

I spotted the produce and immediately went in search of portobello mushrooms. It was a small store, but luckily, they carried everything I needed. I pulled off a plastic bag to put the mushrooms in. Why do they make these so impossible to open? Predictively, I had trouble opening the top. Coal was laughing when my third attempt to open it failed.

There was a misting machine nearby, Coal went over and got his hands wet. Then he said, "May I?" Took the bag and opened it in two seconds.

"Show off," I said, pretending to pout but really laughing.

"You know how to fix the copier. I know my way around a produce bag. We all have our talents," he said, handing me the bag and placing a kiss on my nose.

"Please use your talents again and get me a head of garlic. Pretty please," I added, fluttering my eyelashes at him.

Coal completed his mission in under a minute.

"Wow, you are good!"

Next, we went in search of light cream, butter, and parmesan cheese. I navigated my way to the refrigerated section containing dairy.

"Why do you ask?" Coal said.

"About what?" I replied not remembering what we were previously talking about.

"About Chloe?"

"Oh," I faced him now. He was too handsome for his own good; that's why I was having trouble focusing. "I never met her before, but I swear I've heard her name. I don't remember why though. I thought maybe you or Fiona had spoken about her."

"I know her but not well enough that I would have spoken about her. Maybe Fiona did though."

"I'm sure it will come to me… I think I have everything else we need at home," I announced once we procured the dairy products.

Coal stopped me very seriously right before the cash registers. "You can tell me the truth, are we making meat-loaf?" He furrowed his brow and broke into a grin.

"You're so funny," I said, as I placed the groceries on the counter to pay. "We happen to be making my mom's famous fettuccine alfredo recipe. Don't worry, you can just follow my lead." I finished off with a wink as we walked out the door.

Arriving at my house only ten minutes later, Coal pulled in the driveway directly after me. He took the spot right next to mine in the driveway. Just as promised, as we walked up the path, the lights illuminated our way. There were boxes piled up on my porch."

Looks like we're ready to get to work," Coal said as he saw the boxes waiting expectantly for us. Logically I knew they were the cameras, but it didn't stop the pit from forming in my stomach.

Coal picked them up in his arms as I used my key and opened the front door. Panicking because I have to enter the code quickly, I rushed to the box. My fingers stabbed at the pin pad awkwardly, however I managed to get the code entered before the alarm went off. I breathed a sigh of relief.

"It's like defusing a bomb," I said seriously, my stomach

was in knots. "I don't know if I can take this daily anxiety."

"You'll get used to it, and it won't be so stressful. It's definitely less worrisome than thinking of someone in your house," Coal added.

"I won't set the alarm since you'll be working on the cameras," I said, more thinking aloud than speaking to Coal.

"Good idea, are you hungry right now? Should we cook first or do the cameras first?" Coal asked moving in the kitchen to set the boxes down.

I examined the labels of each box to be sure that they all actually contained cameras and no more surprises.

"If I just cooked for you, then we could do them at the same time," I proposed being practical.

"Yes, but then we wouldn't be cooking together, and there's nothing I'd like to do more than cook with you," he explained, kissing me softly on the lips. My knees nearly buckled in front of the stove. We started our morning here together, and now we were here again after school in the same position.

Coal retrieved his knife once again and began slicing open the boxes one at a time. They all luckily contained the cameras. He carefully laid out all the equipment and grabbed the directions. "Want to go sit in the glass room together while I read this over?"

"Sounds good, I'll join you there momentarily. Let me just get us some water to drink."

Coal went into the glassed room, and I realized I didn't retrieve my mail in a few days. I went to the front door and unlocked it. When I pulled it open, I peered down the driveway, and I saw an unfamiliar car sitting in front of my house. With the winding driveway it was a little too far to accurately recognize who it was, however it was definitely a woman with blonde hair in the car. She was looking down, presumably at her cell phone, so she didn't notice me until I quietly approached the car to check for myself.

Upon realizing she was caught and there was no escape, the driver reluctantly rolled down their window looking sheepish.

"Hey Samantha," I said, taking in my second-grade counterpart at work. She was sitting in her navy-blue car, wearing sunglasses in the near dark, and her navy-blue dress from the day. Her hair was scraped away from her face in a bun. I was completely confused about what she was doing here.

I saw Samantha's face blushed furiously. I could see her scrambling to come up with what to say to me. "Hey," she stuttered finally, "I thought you lived here."

"Yeah, I do, were you coming to see me?" I asked, not giving her the opportunity to wriggle out of explaining herself.

At that moment, Coal came strolling down the driveway with his hands in his pockets. Even with the dim light, I noticed that he tried to look casual, but I could spot the urgency in his face. He probably got nervous because I never returned with the water like I said I would.

"Hey Ava, everything alright?" Then he turned and saw Samantha in the car. "Oh, hey Samantha, I didn't know you guys had plans tonight."

"That's because we didn't," I responded, turning back to Samantha. "I was just asking Sam what she was doing here."

Samantha was staring at Coal. Her pale face contained a half smirk, half look of disbelief.

"Oh, my house is around the block and down the street a little. Fiona mentioned you lived around here. I was trying to see which house was yours," she said, looking off to the side as she spoke.

"So, you found me. Can I help you with something?" I could hear the sound of irritation creep into my voice, and I was trying to stamp it away.

Now Samantha was really flustered. I could almost physically see her trying to formulate an answer that made sense. I shivered waiting for her response. With the sun down, it was starting to get really chilly.

Coal startled me by being the first one to break the silence. "Well Sam, we need to get back to the house. If you need something, text me. By the way, you might want to take off the sunglasses to drive. It's dark out, just safer that way."

With that Coal grabbed my hand and we walked back up my driveway, leaving Samantha staring at us in disbelief. As soon as we made it to the house, and the front was lit up, Coal grabbed me, kissing me tenderly. His lips warm and plump and wanting. Finally, I heard her car pull away.

"Figured she came for a show, so it was only right that we give her one," Coal said, chuckling to himself. He went in for a second kiss, "Just in case she's still watching."

CHAPTER SIXTEEN

"What was that about? Why would Samantha be skulking in front of my house?" Now I was pissed as we went back inside and sat in the kitchen. I could feel the adrenaline coursing through my veins. I was reeling from the fact that one of my coworkers was basically stalking my house.

"Who knows," Coal responded with disgust in his voice, "probably just looking for gossip. Just annoying."

"Did you ever date her?" I asked, trying to keep my voice neutral when I asked. I sat and watched his face closely for an answer. I was hoping for a glint of something in his eye that would give him away. If he did date her, that would explain her strange behavior. It wouldn't excuse it, but at least I would understand.

"Sam? No way. She is *not* my type," he answered pointedly. There wasn't even a hint of anything off-base in his answer or tone.

"She's really pretty though," I reasoned.

"She's ok, but she's not "movie star beautiful" like you." He gazed into my eyes while he said this, and I was once again skeptical of his smoothness. You could never completely trust someone who always knew the right thing to say.

We opted to make dinner before installing the cameras. It was getting late, and we were both starving. I started to feel myself get that low blood sugar feeling where you start to feel a bit shaky, and I didn't want to start getting cranky.

Coal noticed my Alexa unit standing on the kitchen

counter. "Alexa, play French cooking music." The air was filled with the sounds of a French cafe.

I unpacked the bag from the store on the granite countertop and went into the cabinet to retrieve the box of fettuccine noodles.

"What else do you need?" Coal asked eager to help.

"Can you peel and grate two cloves of garlic and this parmesan cheese?" I asked, pointing to the pile on the counter where they lay.

"At your service my lady," he said with a bow.

"You can grate the garlic right into this little saucepan," I said pointing to the pot that I had already put on the stove. I grabbed a clear plastic bowl out from another cabinet. "Just put the cheese in here please."

We worked in companionable silence as I slowly melted the butter in the pan and sauteed the garlic into the pan. Soon the entire kitchen was filled with the delicious aroma of melted butter and garlic. The scent was wafting through the air; my stomach was really starting to rumble.

"You can't make this recipe without at least one glass of white wine," I informed him. I turned the burner down as low as it would go as I pulled a half empty bottle out of the refrigerator. I also retrieved the fancy fluted wine glasses. Pouring us each a glass, I went back to the stove to stir the butter and garlic.

"Taste this." I put a clean teaspoon in the mixture and raised it to Coal's lips. "Make sure you blow on it first. It's really hot."

Blowing on it for a second, he put the spoon in his mouth. A dreamy look filled his face, "Heavenly," he announced as he immediately took a sip of the white wine. "Wow."

I smiled, pleased that he enjoyed it as much as I did. He was right, this cooking together thing was fun. I was skeptical at first as I hated cooking by myself, but this was different.

Coal handed me the bowl of grated cheese, and I turned up the heat and added a little bit of the shredded cheese at a time, continuing to continuously stir.

"You really are a good sous chef," I said, winking at him.

"What should I do next?" he asked, coming up behind me and putting his arms around my waist.

It felt so natural, like we had been doing this for ages. Just two people cooking dinner together enjoying each other's company. It gave me a glimpse of a future that I could have, if things went the right way.

Suddenly remembering he had asked me a question, I replied, "You can cut the portobello mushroom into slices. They need to be sauteed in butter. Do you want me to show you how to cut them?" I asked.

"I think I can manage," he answered with a boyish grin. "Remember, I've never been married. I've had no choice but to learn how to cook."

That was another thing. I was grateful that he had never been married, less baggage. There was no obsessive ex-wife to contend with. No children that would forever bond you with said ex. He was still essentially a clean slate. I prayed that I could, would, be his story, his history. Of course, being wise, I left all these thoughts in my head. I instead kissed his lips, tasting the garlic, butter, and wine. I kissed him deeper, trying to show him how I felt, hoping my kiss would accurately convey my feelings. That he would read my thoughts, so I wouldn't have to say them.

"Oh no," I said suddenly, remembering the cheese sauce cooking on the stove. I pulled away from him and began vigorously stirring to rid it of any unwelcome lumps that began to form in my absence.

"Wow," he pronounced a second time, "that was better than the delicious sauce, and that's saying a lot." I could feel his eyes on me as I continued to add more cheese, bit by bit.

"What are you looking at?" I asked, pretending to be

offended. I was secretly thrilled.

"Beauty in action," was all he said. He looked at me so intently; I was afraid that he could see straight through me.

I lit candles in the dining room, and we ate using Aunt Ginny's good china. It was white with a silver band. Dinner was romantic and delicious.

After dinner was complete, Coal went about setting up my camera outside by the front door. I found my oversized Syracuse sweatshirt, that I got freshman year, and made Coal put it on to stay warm. While he was setting the camera up, I snapped a picture of him with my phone.

"No paparazzi," Coal said, waving his hand away, only he had a cute smile on his face while he did it.

I laughed and clicked on my Insta app. It had been a few days since I'd even gone on. I scrolled through, liking a picture of Tabitha and her handsome fiance. This picture must have been from their cake testing, I thought, as I saw him delicately feeding her a forkful of cake with a pudding and fruit center. Her eyes were filled with happiness. Physically the two of them were so well suited to each other. He had dark hair like her and crystal blue eyes. He was tall and lean.

I posted the picture of Coal up on a ladder with my Syracuse University shirt with the caption, "He can climb to great heights!" I didn't want to advertise about cameras, in case my stalker was watching. The less they knew the better.

The thought struck me to look at Samantha's account; she was on my mind since that random spotting in front of my house. I typed in her name. She posted an advertisement for the Dancing with the Teachers event, including a hashtag with Mayor Simon Whitherton. What a piece of work, I thought to myself.

I clicked on the hashtag and his account came up. It mainly contained political advertisements for things he was doing around Syracuse, including an advert for the Dancing with the Teachers event. I scrolled a little further and spotted a photograph of him with a woman I presumed to be his wife. She was reed thin. Her blonde hair was coiffed into an immaculate updo. She was wearing a red Jackie Onassis type dress, her arm wrapped protectively around her husband's back. I wasn't sure what I was looking for, but I hoped there would be something on his page that would shed some light on his weird behavior. Alas, I found nothing.

Something was niggling at me, I clicked on his followers to see if that would provide any useful information. Of course, I saw Samantha. Some other women I knew followed him as well, but there was nothing that stood out to me. Wait... someone I followed with the name Chloe. A lightbulb went off, that's where I knew her name from, I thought to myself. It has bothered me since meeting her. She must have recognized me from someone's page and requested me. Well, it didn't answer any questions about the mayor, but at least I knew why Chloe's name sounded familiar to me.

I decided to take a break from my detective work to check and see how Coal was doing. I found him out on the front porch.

"Hey pretty girl," he said, as I stepped out onto the porch. "Can I see your phone for a minute? I need to install this app, so you can access the camera with it."

I opened up my app store and handed the phone to Coal. My arm brushed his and a bolt of electricity surged through me. The look he gave me told me that he had felt it too. He searched the name of the necessary app and tapped the side button twice to download it. Once it was downloaded, he handed it back to me.

"Just enter the information they are asking for, name, address, date of birth, etc., and then I will take care of the rest for you."

I sat on the comfortable white wicker rocker and rocked gently as I entered my information. When they asked for the product registration number, I handed it back to Coal. "Your turn," I said.

"Your birthday is in May?" he asked, studying my information on the screen.

"Yes. I love spring, despite the rain. I know April showers bring May flowers, but it always rains on my birthday," I said with a shrug.

"So is mine," he said with a grin. "Two days before yours." He turned back to my phone and fiddled with the app for a minute.

I sat appreciating the stillness of the night. I breathed in the fresh air and closed my eyes rocking in the chair.

Coal broke my reverie. I opened my eyes and he was leaning in to display the phone screen. A clear, live picture of the front of my house was displayed. I stood up and went to the front walk. I watched myself on screen and waved for the camera.

"That is so cool. You are a genius," I said walking back over to Coal and running my fingers through his thick hair.

He grinned, "Aww shucks," he pretended to be embarrassed. "I'll do the other two cameras, but those should go quickly now."

We left the coolness of the night and entered the warmth of the house. I walked with Coal into the glass room. I took a seat for a minute on the wicker couch, while he headed outside to do the camera. He figured it made sense to do one by the glass room, more than the side door because there was access to a view of the inside of the house from here. As I draped my feet over the edge of the couch, my phone pinged that I had a notification.

It was on Insta, so I tapped the app and it opened. I hit the notification button and there was a direct message from Chloe.

Hey Ava, so glad we got to meet in person. How did your dance lesson go? Mine went pretty well, but I felt spastic because I kept confusing my left foot from my right. Ha! Btw, are you and Coal a couple? You look so cute together.

Hmmm, I thought to myself. I didn't know what to make of that message. I'd have to show it to Coal when he was done with the camera installation. I glanced out the window and saw him up on the little step ladder. I wouldn't write her back until I spoke to him.

Deciding I should accomplish cleaning up the kitchen while Coal finished up with the cameras, I walked over to the stove and brought the pots to the sink to be cleaned. After spending fifteen minutes washing all of the dishes and cleaning up the stove and counters, Coal finally came back in.

"It's all finished," he declared, collapsing in his kitchen chair.

"Awesome," I answered, folding the damp blue dish towel and hanging it on the stove. "Do you want some coffee or tea before you go?"

"Oh, so that's how it is," he teased, "get me to work for free and then send me on my way."

"Hey I'm a single girl. You can't blame me for taking advantage of free labor when it comes my way." I laughed, coming up behind him in the chair, and wrapped my arms around him. "Seriously though, thank you for doing that."

"I will take you up on that coffee," he said, his shoulders quivering a little from the cold.

While setting about making us a couple of Americanos, Coal began scrolling on his phone.

"Oh, I found out why I recognized Chloe's name," I announced after turning the flame on for the coffee, making sure the fire didn't go over the edge and blacken the percolator. I had done that on my own at home, but I was determined to do better in my new life.

Coal looked up from his phone. "So Fiona had mentioned her before, I presume."

"No, she requested me on Insta the other day. I guess she probably saw my name on someone else's account and realized I worked at the school. The weird part is she sent me a private message."

"Why is that weird?" Coal asked not understanding.

"I mean I guess it's not weird. We did meet in person today, but she asked if you and I were dating. She said we look cute together."

"Well, we do look cute together," Coal confirmed. "Not weird. She's just observant. I think all the weirdness going on just has you on edge. That thing with Samantha though. That was not normal. Who sits outside someone's house in the dark with sunglasses on?"

"Thank you. I was beginning to think I was the nutty one. Does she always act that strangely?" I questioned, trying to understand her motives.

Coal seemed to think for a minute, scratching his chiseled chin before he responded. "She is an extreme type A personality, driven beyond. If she sets her sights on something, you better believe she will work to get it."

"Ok, but what does any of that have to do with me?" I asked, not sure where he was going with this line of thinking.

"I'm not sure," he said honestly. "This is just what I know about her. We've worked together for a few years. She's not a bad person, just a bit obsessive."

Now I started to feel a lump in the pit of my stomach begin to form. What could her possible interest in me be? I thought.

Holding the mug of coffee I gave him in both hands, one of Aunt Ginny's favorites boasting a photograph of the Eiffel Tower, he continued to talk, "She wants to be number one at everything. She's a hard worker; I'll give her that."

I took my steaming mug and joined him at the table.

"Well, I'd rather just stay off her radar. I am in competition with no one," I said, taking a careful sip.

"Let's look online for Bonnie and Clyde costumes," Coal said, probably changing the subject so I wouldn't get in a bad mood. Never in my life has drama followed me like it has since I moved to Syracuse. In my old life I was friends with everyone. I was not used to getting so much negative attention.

"Yes, we are cutting it kind of close. Let's see if we can still order and definitely get it in time for the party. Let me get my laptop out so we can look together," I said, pulling my school computer out of my leather bag that was perched on one of the kitchen chairs.

I moved from the chair across from Coal to the one next to him, so we could look at the costumes together. We put our heads close together as I typed in Bonnie and Clyde costumes. As I scrolled, I was excited to see that we had most of the costume in our own wardrobes. Coal would wear dress pants and a white shirt. We only needed to buy him accessories. I located a set which included suspenders, tie, and fedora, and a money sack with fake money. I could wear a high waisted black pencil skirt and white blouse. I just needed to buy a wool beret and patterned silk scarf to tie around my neck.

"These are going to be awesome," Coal said happily as he went on his own phone to order his accessories. They were promised to him as two-day delivery. Thank God he mentioned looking into the costumes today.

"I know, I'm really pleased with them. I don't love that Bonnie and Clyde had a gruesome demise, but I do love the time period costumes," I looked up after ordering and put my phone down.

"So does this mean we are officially partners now?" Coal's usual teasing smile was replaced with something much more serious. It took me off guard.

I fiddled with my hair and looked into his amber eyes. "What do you mean exactly?" I had to stop myself from making a joke to lighten the mood, but I wanted him to be clear about what he meant. I wasn't jumping to any conclusions.

He took my hands and gripped them tenderly, "Are you officially my girlfriend now?" His face was so sincere, I had to believe that he meant what he was saying. I've never had a crazier two weeks in my life, and it didn't scare him off.

Coal was there every step of the way, helping me, cheering me one, and very willing to take it slow.

It was my turn to be serious. I nodded my head very slowly, lips together. I dabbed at the corner of my eyes, as I felt the beginning of happy tears forming in my jade green eyes. This time my stomach wasn't nervous. I just felt the expanding of my heart in my chest. I was so grateful for a second chance at love. This time I was wiser, at least I hoped.

"Who knew Bonnie and Clyde were so romantic?" he asked, breaking back into his usual goofy grin.

October 21, 2021

Her presence is causing a bubbling in my brain. I don't like this off kilter feeling. It's as if I'm on a seesaw going up and down at regular intervals. I can't keep up with my feelings. I both want to be close to her, and I want her to vanish at the same time. So much conflicted emotion. Maybe when we can be together as we were meant to be, the feeling will dissipate.

CHAPTER SEVENTEEN

On Saturday morning the light flooded the room. I opened my eyes feeling excited and energized, but it took me a few minutes to remember why. Today Lina was coming, and I could officially start getting the house ready for the party. It was precisely one week until the big day. I lay in bed staring out the windows into the backyard. I could see glimpses of fall foliage out the window which added to my happiness.

Thanks to Coal, I could officially check costumes off my list of things to do. I smiled to myself at the thought of him, thinking that with all the bad luck that I had endured, he seemed too good to be true.

Lina would help me with cleaning and hopefully locating decorations, and I had to figure out what to do about food and cocktails. These were all welcome distractions from regular life.

I jumped out of bed thinking I had better clean up before Lina got here at 12 pm. I knew that her job was to help me clean, but I didn't want her to think I was too messy.

I padded down the steps in my slippers and bathrobe. Feeling my robe pocket, I wanted to be sure that I brought my cell down as well. I breathed in a sigh of contentment as I reached the downstairs and looked around. After nearly two weeks in the house, it was beginning to feel a little bit like my own. When I looked at things that reminded me of Aunt Virginia, I didn't feel sad, I felt like a piece of her was there looking after me. My heart was beginning to feel a little fuller. I guess this is what people meant when they say if you loved someone, they never fully leave you. They remain alive in your heart and mind. The impact they've made shaped you into who you are, and that won't disappear, just because they aren't physically there anymore.

I surveyed the kitchen. I was pleased that I had done a thorough job of cleaning up on Thursday night, and last night I went to happy hour with Fiona and ate out. Going into the glassed room, I spotted a stray cup that was left on the table by the window. When I went to collect it, I noticed Lila in the yard again. I walked out, my slippers crunching on the leaves as I walked. The trees had begun to drop more leaves; I would have to get out here and rake soon. Lila was casually strolling towards the actual back of the house, so I followed her.

Bending down to get on Lila's level, I began to softly call to her, "Hi Lila, come here baby."

I caught her attention as she turned and looked at me. Her blue eyes were shining in the sun. "Nooooo," she called as she sauntered over to me.

"You never say what you mean, do you?" I asked her as I stroked her ears. "You're a very complicated woman." She plopped down in a small pile of leaves and began to purr. My heart leapt. I couldn't wait until I could see my baby again.

As if reading my thoughts, I heard Adelaide calling, "Ava is that you back there?"

I walked to the back of the property, and Lila followed at my heels.

"Yes, it's me. I was just talking to a friend," I chuckled.

"Oh, that's nice dear. I don't want to bother you if you have a friend over..."

"Nooooo," Lila called loudly. I think she was mad that I stopped petting her.

"Is that Lila back there with you?" she asked.

I stood on the tree stump and popped my head over

the fence again. "Yes, she came for a visit, and I was just this minute thinking of my baby. How is she doing? Can I visit her soon?" I asked excitedly.

"Of course, dear, anytime," she responded. "I know how busy you are." Her voice trailed off as though she didn't quite believe it.

"You're still coming on Saturday, right?" I asked.

Her face brightened. "I wouldn't miss it for the world. Still thinking of a costume, but I'll work something out," she finished brightly.

"Awesome, I have someone coming over today that's going to help me get the house ready, so I have to go, but we'll talk soon," I finished as I waved goodbye and began walking back towards my house. Lila must have gotten bored waiting for me to finish talking because she was now nowhere to be seen.

I headed back to the side of the house and returned inside. I collected the cup that I had originally seen, before Lila distracted me and made my way back into the kitchen. So far, the house wasn't really in that bad of shape.

I visited the downstairs bathroom off of the kitchen. Pulling my cleaning spray out from under the sink, I sprayed under the rim of the toilet bowl and let it sit for a while. That's the nice part of living alone. You have no one else to come and mess up the work you're doing. I also sprayed down the sink countertop and used a red rag I kept under the sink to wipe it down until it sparkled.

The sitting room was in perfect condition. I never ate anything while in it. It just needed to be dusted. I kept moving, the formal living room I hadn't even used yet. I spotted a pair of Aunt Ginny's diamond earrings sitting on a little marble topped table. She had left them there and never had a chance to bring them upstairs because she had died first. For a minute the reality of the situation hit me, and I felt nauseous. I looked at the mirror across from where I was standing. When I peered in the mirror, I swore for a minute that it was Aunt Ginny's reflection that I saw and not my own. I felt shivers down my spine. I looked down and the hairs on my arms were standing on end. I glanced back in the mirror a second time, but just my frightened face was staring back at me. I really needed to apply some makeup if I wasn't going to scare Lina.

At precisely 12 pm, the front doorbell rang indicating Lina had arrived. I was impressed by her promptness. I had dressed in high waisted dark wash skinny jeans and a cotton v neck burnt orange three-quarter sleeved tee. I wore Aunt Ginny's key around my neck to keep her close. I applied makeup but left my hair in a high ponytail, finishing my look with dark brown knee length riding boots that I found in the hall closet. I never knew it, but it turns out Aunt Ginny and I had the same shoe size.

I opened the door to a fresh-faced blonde woman of about forty, dressed in light blue jeans and a dark blue sweatshirt. She was wearing a pair of low top Converse sneakers in dark blue. Lina had cheerful smiling eyes and looked surprised as she first saw me.

"Ava," she said going in for an immediate hug, "it is so nice to finally meet you. I've heard all about you from your aunt. You are just as beautiful as she always said."

I ushered her inside, out of the cool air and into the cozy house.

"Thank you so much for making time to come," I said as she walked instinctively towards the kitchen. It was obvious that she had spent a lot of time in this house.

"So, you are having an event of some sort?" she asked with a hint of an accent. She put her black purse down on the counter.

"Yes, a Halloween/housewarming party," I started. I knew there was something else I wanted to ask her about. "I know Aunt Ginny used to have some great Halloween decorations. Do you have an idea where these would be? I looked in the library, but I didn't search too far when I knew you were coming."

Lina didn't miss a beat. "Yes, I put them away for her last year. I can show you where they are."

"Would you like something to drink Lina? Some tea or coffee maybe? Let's sit and talk a minute before we get to work."

"Some tea would be very nice," Lina answered politely.

I filled the white enamel tea kettle with enough water for two, and I took out two white saucers and tea cups. I stuck a tea bag in each and found a tin where sugar cubes were stored. As I set them up at the kitchen table Lina sat patiently and watched me.

"I feel like I should be helping," Lina said with a hint of uncomfortableness in her voice.

I waved the comment away with my hand. "Nonsense, I am very happy to have company, especially someone who knew my aunt. Not to mention how grateful I am that you agreed to help me get ready for the party. You really are a lifesaver."

At this Lina smiled and relaxed into her seat a little.

When the tea kettle went off, I poured steaming water into the cups and carried them to the table.

"Do you take it with milk?" I asked before I went to sit down.

She smiled shyly, "No, I am perfect with just a little sugar."

"How long have you known Aunt Ginny?" I asked while using those little metal tongs to place a sugar cube into the cup.

"Virginia and I met probably five years ago now. As you know, she was often traveling for work, and she needed someone to look out for things here." She patted at the corner of her eyes with her napkin. "She was very kind and introduced me to her friends who offered me jobs. I have a very nice stable income now, thanks to her. Before I met her, I was struggling. I will be forever grateful." Her voice caught in her throat, probably at the thought of the hardships she had endured.

I smiled sympathetically. I understood completely. Life was not kind to everyone, up until now, it certainly hadn't been kind to me. "So how often did you come to clean? I want to keep the house up the way that Aunt Ginny did. I want her to be proud of me." I finished choking up a little myself.

"Oh Ava, she was so very proud of you, always talking about her beautiful strong niece. She admired you, said you were so strong when your parents died. You finished college and built a career for yourself with no support."

"It's not true that I had no support," I retorted. Lina was leaning in listening intently. "Aunt Ginny pulled me out of my despair. She wouldn't let me wallow. I am so thankful for that. The ability to keep moving when things are in turmoil all around you is not easy." I stopped for a minute to take a sip of my tea which had cooled enough to finally drink.

"This I know," she said solemnly. Her eyes held compassion and wisdom. I had a feeling that Lina was a fellow warrior.

Now that we had both shared a little, the communication ways had opened. It felt like we were old friends, perhaps kindred spirits.

"This tea really hit the spot," Lina said, placing her cup down on the saucer delicately. "Well now let me think. When Ginny was in town, I would come every other week to do deep cleaning. The tub, refrigerator, baseboards, take down all the sconces to be washed. As you know, there are a ton of things that need to be polished and dusted in the library. Your aunt took care of the day-to-day stuff. I would come and do everything else. When she was away, I would stop by every week to pick up the mail and dust. She didn't want to come home to a dirty house."

"That sounds like exactly what I would need," I said with a smile on my face. If you're available that is."

"For Virginia's niece, I would make the time, even if I didn't have it."

We discussed her hourly rate, which was surprisingly affordable, so I put on a second cup of tea for the two of us to seal the deal.

"After tea, why don't I show you where the decorations are," Lina suggested. "Then I can start the deep cleaning that we discussed. It might take longer than usual since the house was sitting empty for a bit."

Following tea, just as we discussed, we ended up on the third floor, in the spare bedroom with access to the attic. Lina reached up and pulled the string for the trap door. As the door opened, a musty smell filled the air. I could see up into the dark hole in the ceiling. It looked like a black hole that might swallow me up. She maneuvered the ladder down.

"I'll go first," Lina insisted. "I know where the light switch is located.

I nodded my head in agreement. Lina climbed the ladder with ease, turning on the light when she reached the top. I tentatively followed her, taking one step carefully at a time, not sure what I was going to find in that old, dark attic.

As my foot stepped up onto the floor boards, with the help of the light that Lina turned on and the lights streaming in from the windows, I saw that it was nothing like I expected. Although unfinished, the exposed wood rafters and beautiful leaded glass windows were actually quite beautiful. Like the rest of the house, the attic was tidy. There were piles of boxes strewn along the corners of the room, but it looked like it had a sort of organization of its own.

Lina walked to the left of the room and went directly to a very specific box, obviously aware of what she was doing.

"This is where all the decorations are," she explained, "there are fall decorations for Halloween and Thanksgiving, several boxes for Christmas, and of course Valentine's Day. You know how much Virginia loved Valentine's Day."

Remembering that fact about her brought a smile to

my face. Fond images flooded my mind. Aunt Ginny's birthday was on Valentine's Day. In addition, when she married her late husband, their ceremony took place on Valentine's Day as well. It was a really big deal to her, and her favorite day of the year. I can't believe that she and her husband are now both gone. We really don't know what the future will hold for us, so we really should be smart and embrace each moment that we have. I got lost in thought for a moment until Lina's voice broke me out of my reverie.

"There is only one Halloween box, but it's big. How about you go down the ladder first, and I can hand it to you," I admired the way that she quickly came up with a plan. I had been married to Michael for so many years that I just let him handle stuff like that. I hadn't given it a second thought. I would have to retrain myself to be like Lina, independent and a critical thinker.

As I carefully descended the rickety stairs, I made a mental note to come back up to the attic and really explore what was up there. I'm sure there were many hidden treasures just on the verge of being discovered. Pieces of my family's history were up there waiting for me. Now that I knew my worries were unfounded, the boogey man wasn't anticipating my arrival. There were no rats or dead bodies. I was eager to be lost up there in Aunt Ginny's memories.

"Here you go," Lina strained as she handed the bulky box over to me. I struggled for a minute, but then maintained hold of the box. I placed it down on the hardwood floor of the bedroom.

The top of the large carton wasn't sealed with tape. The cardboard was folded with one of the flaps under the other to keep it somewhat closed. I easily opened it. Immediately spotting the spiderweb tablecloth, I eagerly pulled it out.

"You're a lifesaver Lina," I said beaming at her. "I knew these things existed. I remembered them from years ago, however I had no idea where to begin looking."

"It's no problem at all..." Lina hesitated for a minute. Her mouth was turned down. Her eyebrows were knitted together.

"Everything ok?" I asked, feeling concerned by the sudden change in her demeanor. "Did I do something to upset you?"

"No, no. Not at all," she shook her head back and forth several times as if trying to shake something away.

"Lina," I prompted trying to get her to divulge what was bothering her.

"Let's take some of the downstairs decorations with us. No need to carry this whole big box," she suggested. Now I noticed the whitened pallor of her skin.

I gently grabbed her arm. "Please Lina, I don't want you upset. I certainly don't want to be the one..."

She interrupted me before I could finish talking. "I promise it's not you. Let's bring these down, ok?" she asked me. Her voice sounded genuine and despairing. I didn't have the heart to push her any further.

We went through the box and took out as much as we could carry. I pulled out the black wooden cat, the creepy crow, and the spiderweb tablecloth. Lina grabbed an assortment of other things to adorn the house for the party.

We made our way down the spiral staircase into the library. I went to open the door into the hallway when Lina's expression grew even more grave. I stopped and put the decorations down on the writing desk.

"I need to tell you something." The words rushed out of her mouth and then suddenly stopped, like shutting off a faucet. She placed her own hand over her mouth as though trying to stop the words from escaping. Her pale blue eyes grew wider.

I grabbed her hands, desperately wanted her to talk, but I waited patiently for her to continue, even though it was killing me.

"It's about Virginia, your aunt," she finished.

"Sit," I insisted, giving up my favorite green leather chair for her. Hoping the comfort of the old chair would coax her into telling her story.

I took a seat in the wooden chair that Coal had sat in just the other night.

"I don't even have anything concrete to tell you; it's more of a feeling, an intuition," she said, nodding her head that she had found the word she was looking for.

"About what?" I asked prodding gently.

"Something wasn't quite right in the weeks prior to her death. There was a breakdown in her spirit," she was struggling to tell her story just right. Although Lina spoke perfect English, it was her second language, and she didn't have the exact vocabulary to convey her thoughts as she wanted.

I breathed deeply, as a means to calm my racing thoughts. Glancing up at the wall of books, I thought of all the stories contained in them. Everyone had a story to tell. I wished whatever it was that Lina wanted to share could be simply handed to me to be read.

"Ginny had several conversations while I was around, on the phone, so they were one- sided conversations."

Now she really piqued my interest. "Who was she talking to?" I said it aloud but also wondered silently to myself.

She shook her head once more. "That's the thing, I don't know. Whoever it was had really upset her. She spoke in angry hushed tones. Whenever she saw me, she would rush off the phone." She looked down sorrowfully.

"Do you know if it was a man or a woman?" Now *my* heart began to gallop in my chest. There was a thumping in my ears that accompanied it.

Lina seemed frustrated. She lifted her eyes to look at me, like a child who was afraid that they were in trouble. "I have no idea. This is why I didn't want to say anything."

"No, I'm happy you told me," I said.

My thoughts were racing like my heart. If only Lina had an idea about who she was conversing with. I really had nowhere to turn to find answers. I could ask Amber if she knew anything, but I would think that she would have brought it up to me if she felt that there was something strange going on. *Unless* it was Amber who she was having a problem with.

All of the sudden, Lina's face lit up like a student who suddenly remembered an answer to an important test answer that had previously eluded them.

"What is it?" I asked, trying my best not to shout and keep my voice controlled.

"I don't know why I didn't think of it before. Ginny kept a journal. She would write in it often. Sometimes she would leave it laying out. You haven't come across it, have you?" Lina asked hopefully.

"I haven't seen anything, but then again, I haven't been looking."

With a burst of inspiration, I jumped out of my wooden seat and Lina followed suit. We both rushed to the door and burst through it heading to Ginny's room.

"What does it look like?" I inquired as I crossed the threshold.

"It's green leather. It looks very much like the chair in the library."

Well, that would be easy to spot, I thought. I started with her vanity. It definitely wasn't on the top of it in plain sight. The face of the vanity was scattered with various perfume bottles and pieces of jewelry that had been left out. When I was a little girl visiting, I used to sit in the plush chair in front of the vanity and try on her jewelry, spritzing myself with the beautiful expensive scents. I would practice applying her lipstick, trying to get it just right.

Next, I opened each of the drawers. There were 6 in all. I even felt the ceiling of the drawers to be sure that it wasn't somehow hidden there for safe keeping. My efforts were fruitless.

"Listen Lina. I am so grateful that you told me this,

and I promise you I will look for the diary. However, I don't want to waste anymore of your time right now. The party is next Saturday, so we really need to get the house ready."

"Yes, of course," she answered, seeming slightly put off.

"Of course, I hope you can come next Saturday too. It's a costume party, and I know you know Amber. She will be there."

Slowly some of the Lina I saw when I first opened the door returned. She looked relieved that she had gotten her worries out in the open.

"You need me to work next Saturday?" she questioned, unsure if she was invited as an employee or a guest.

"Oh no," I clarified, feeling slightly embarrassed. "I want you to come as a guest. I'm hoping that you and I can become friends."

Now a beatific smile covered her face. I felt relieved that I hadn't insulted her, but I was still anxious about what she told me. If there was a diary, where was it? I would have to get to the bottom of it.

CHAPTER EIGHTEEN

The large majority of my Saturday was spent on the house. I surveyed each room as I walked through, pleased with what I saw. Lina stayed until 5 pm. It wouldn't ordinarily take that long, but the house had been neglected for quite some time. The excitement was building in my body. Gone were the cobwebs that began to form in the corners of the room and a feeling of neglect. A faint smell of wood polish and excitement now filled the air.

Bring! Bring! The urgent sound of the doorbell could be heard as I walked down the hallway on the second floor, passing an assortment of pumpkins decorating the marble topped console table. I wasn't expecting anyone, I thought to myself curiously.

Deciding to try out my app that Coal had installed, I pulled my phone out of my back pocket and hurriedly hit the icon. I switched to the frame with the front door camera and was greeted with a pleasant surprise. There was the image of Coal standing on my porch holding an oversized bouquet of peach-colored roses. He was dressed handsomely in dark wash jeans and a dark brown leather coat. His hair was neatly styled. My breath caught in my throat.

I now quickened my pace and took the stairs two at a time. Spotting the silhouette of the top of his head and bottom of his body through the door. He was partially blocked by the large black rose wreath adorning the front door.

"I see you've been hard at work," he remarked as I opened the door. The cool late October air felt refreshing. The sky had nearly reached its dusk status. A few patches of blue could be spotted amongst the wispy white and purplish ebbed clouds. He stood taking in the large wooden black cat, back arched, that took up residence on the porch. “These are for you.”

I grasped the bouquet of roses that were offered to me. “Thanks, they’re lovely.” I stopped to bury my nose and inhale their scent. "What’s the occasion?” I asked, not being able to stop myself from grinning.

“Us,” he said, simply following me into the house. “Do you have plans tonight?” he asked.

I located the giant white vase that I spotted that day when Coal left the rose on my car. The vase was covered in brilliant fuchsia stoned flowers with enameled green stems. Filling it with water, I laid the roses on the giant wooden cutting board cutting them on an angle, allowing them to take in as much water as possible. Coal stood watching my every move, waiting for me to answer.

“Nothing to speak of,” I answered wondering what he had in mind. “How about you?”

Coal looked shy for a moment; this was a new look for him. “Well, I was hoping to spend some time with my girlfriend.” He shoved his hand in his pockets and looked at me longingly.

I let the flowers lie where they were on the counter and walked purposefully over to where he was standing. I threw my arms around him, forcing his hands out of his pockets, and kissed him hard. My tongue parting his lips. I heard him moan.

“So you *are* available,” he laughed, slipping back into his confident self.

Returning his groan, I took my left hand and pulled at his wavy locks and kissed his eyelids. I inhaled his scent, wood and cinnamon. A wave of desire washed over me.

“I’m wide open,” I answered suggestively. Coal's jaw dropped a little.

He closed his eyes for a brief moment, and I could have

sworn I saw him giving himself a pep talk in his head.

"Are you making this hard for me intentionally?" Coal asked, his eyes mischievous. "The house looks great by the way." He changed direction, taking control of the situation.

Curse Coal and his practical sense. "Thanks, Lina, the woman who used to clean for Aunt Ginny came by today. She helped me get things in order, but she said something very curious."

Coal's face changed to a questioning look.

I continued, "She told me that in the weeks leading up to Aunt Virginia's death that she had seemed agitated. She had mysterious, heated exchanges with an unknown person." I began fidgeting in my spot. I picked at my cuticles, chipping my manicure. He had to be absorbing my anxiety.

"Did she have any idea who it was, or what the tension was about?" Coal asked, taking his seat at the table.

"None, but I could tell that it really bothered her. She was wrestling with the idea of telling me, of whether it was the right thing to do."

Coal blew out breath in a manner similar to air being let out of a balloon.

"I know," I responded, "and the weirdest part, she told me Aunt Ginny regularly wrote in a diary or journal. I haven't found it anywhere in the house though."

Coal's face changed. I could see a light bulb forming over his head. "Remember I was telling you that these old Victorians had secret rooms and compartments?" he asked anxiously.

"Yes," I nodded my head expectantly.

He stood up fervently. "I bet her diary is hidden somewhere in this house." He glanced around the room as if the hiding place would yell out "Here I am!"

"I think you're letting your imagination run away from you," I answered skeptically.

"Your Aunt Ginny lived alone. Things don't grow legs and walk off by themselves. Either she hid it away somewhere or someone took it." His eyes grew wide as he finished. The gravity of what he had said hung in the air.

Now I had to hold onto the counter to support myself, a dizzy sensation overtaking my body. "What are you suggesting?" I asked, afraid but needing to hear his response.

The room grew quiet. We were both lost in our own thoughts. The silence was deafening. Coal must have felt its pressure as well, threatening to take all of the oxygen out of our lungs.

"I think it's here, hidden somewhere. That's all I'm saying," he carefully finished.

I nodded my head hoping that he was right.

"Do you want to search together?" he asked, grabbing my hands. I couldn't help but notice my ragged looking nails. I made a note to see if Fiona wanted to go with me for manicures.

"Yes, let's, but we need to come up with a plan. Do things systematically," I clarified, both excited and terrified at the prospect of what we might find.

"Agreed, why don't we start with her bedroom. It's the most logical place to put something private away."

I hesitated a minute, "Well Lina and I already started scouring the room, but it can't hurt to have another pair of eyes. Maybe you'll see something that we missed."

Coal nodded his head seriously, however I saw a twinkle of excitement in his eyes. Coal should really have been a detective that dealt antiques on the side. First, he double checked through the vanity, just as I had done only a little while before. He pulled the drawer all the way out.

"I already checked the ceiling of the drawers, to see if it was secured to the top somehow," I explained as I watched him.

"Okay, good," he said, as he continued to check the inside carefully.

"I would have seen it," I exclaimed, annoyed that he didn't think I knew how to do a thorough job.

"Hmmm," he said, appearing to be studying something carefully.

"Coal, I was talking to you." Now I was sulking.

"I'm sorry Ava. These old Victorian pieces sometimes have hidden compartments. That's why I was so excited to be searching. I've never seen one in person, but I saw a documentary on them." I could see the passion again in his eyes as he surveyed the vanity.

"Ahh," he announced as he managed to push a wooden piece that revealed a hidden drawer that popped open. He beamed as if it were Christmas morning. I was astonished that he was correct.

Coal moved out of the way, so I could be the first to examine the contents. My heart was beating faster as I joined him to look through the secret drawer. The drawer was small, not nearly wide enough to fit a journal, but there was a single envelope inside.

What could Aunt Ginny have concealed in this drawer? I wondered. My heart was hammering. I stared at the envelope for a good minute contemplating. Coal watched patiently giving me time.

The envelope wasn't sealed. It had been folded in half and placed in this hidden draw for safekeeping. There were 4 single sheets of paper stacked together and folded. I unfolded the pile and saw the top paper. Written in purple block letters it contained only four words: STAY AWAY FROM HIM.

"Look at this," I hissed at Coal.

He moved in several steps towards me to examine the paper.

"What do you suppose that is about?" Coal asked. He kept his voice even, but his face gave away his distress.

"Who is him?" I asked aloud, letting my words linger. I was speaking more to myself than Coal. My whole body was rigid.

"What about the other papers?" Coal asked, hoping

they contained some clues.

I took a deep breath and put the first paper upside down on the vanity in order to reveal the second. The same purple pen had been used. The same block letters, probably in an effort to hide the identity of the sender read this time: HE'S MINE.

"Look at how hard they wrote," I examined the little rips in the paper where the author of the note had ripped through. "Whoever wrote this is seriously deranged."

All at once my breathing began to become shallow. I tried to take a deep gulp of air, but my heart wouldn't stop racing. The room began to spin a little and I grabbed onto the chair next to the vanity.

"Ava, sit down," Coal pleaded with me. The desperation in my face was obviously apparent to him.

"I'm good," I said, making a concerted effort to breathe deeply. No matter how hard I tried, the oxygen didn't seem to be making its way to my lungs.

"Please Ava," he insisted, his voice authoritative this time.

Finally, I conceded and sat on the velvet covered seat. I ran my fingers along the dark gray velvet trying to soothe myself. The letters lay in my lap, an invitation to something sinister.

"Do you want me to look at the other two for you?" Coal inquired. His amber eyes studied me awaiting my response.

I shook my head from side to side fervently. I really needed to get a grip. "I'll do it," I gasped.

I flipped the second paper over on top of the first. The third paper only contained two words that were far more menacing than the first two: OR ELSE.

"What the hell?" I asked turning my head to face Coal, begging him for answers I knew he would be unable to give.

"Did your Aunt Ginny ever hint at a problem? Do you know if she was dating anyone?" he questioned.

I tried to think back. I know that she never told me about any kind of conflict. As far as I knew she led a charmed life. Although her husband died prematurely and she couldn't have any children of her own, she enjoyed her work, traveling, volunteering, and friends. This didn't fit with what I knew of her life. She never dated anyone seriously following her husband's death, but I know she casually dated.

"I don't know. I just don't know," I answered sadly.

I didn't want to look at the last note, but I needed to have a complete picture of what we were dealing with here.

Flipping the third paper onto the other two, I braced myself for what was underneath: YOU'LL BE SORRY!!!! These words were written even bigger and were divided in half by the crease in the paper.

I dropped the last paper as if it burned me. It floated gracefully to the floor like a leaf in the autumn wind. I stood up and Coal embraced me.

"It's an obvious threat," I sobbed into Coal's neck.

"Maybe they're from a long time ago," Coal wondered aloud.

He squeezed me tight, and then let go to pick up the last piece of paper that had fluttered under the vanity. He lay it on top of the other and flipped them all over.

"The ink is still pretty vibrant, and the paper is only worn at the crease where it was folded. I'm not an expert, but it appears these letters weren't written that long ago."

"No," I cried, shaking my head from side to side.

"How did she die again?" Coal questioned.

"Can we go to another room?" I asked, desperate to leave the secrets we revealed behind me.

"Of course," he replied. "Let's put these back where we found them, for safekeeping."

Coal carefully refolded the letters, returning them to the envelope in which we found them. He put them back into the open compartment and pushed it back in, hiding the letters once more.

"Thank you," I managed to whisper. "Let's go into my room."

I grabbed his hand for comfort and led Coal down the hallway in an almost trance-like state. My mind was racing with questions. Disturbing thoughts kept flashing through my consciousness, no matter how much I wanted to lock them away in the drawer with the secret we had discovered.

Sitting on the edge of my bed, I dejectedly removed the brown riding boots and laid back on the cream and rose-colored pillows that dotted the head of my bed. Coal followed suit, taking his shoes off and took his place beside me.

"What do you think it all means?" I asked gazing at the wall in front of me lost in thought.

I was starting to get a tension headache and released my hair from the ponytail that I had made earlier in the day. My auburn locks cascaded around my shoulders. Coal stroked a lock that fell in my face and tucked it behind my ear.

"I don't know," Coal began speaking as he rubbed some of the tension out of my shoulders. "Someone obviously had a problem with her. If we find her diary, maybe we can shed some light on the situation."

I nodded my head in agreement.

"It's just, I feel like I'm in an alternative universe since I've moved here. On one hand, my life has suddenly turned technicolor after so many years of being in black and white. I have you to thank for that," I said gazing up at him. My green eyes caressing him.

"On the other hand, I have never experienced so much drama and weirdness. Lots of strange behavior, the eyeless doll taking the cake. Those letters we found today, those just topped it off."

"Yeah, if it makes you feel any better, my life has never been this exciting before I met you. I was just a regular guy, going to work, refinishing furniture, living my life. Now that I've met you, I've been thrust full throttle into a suspense movie," he chuckled and kissed my cheek.

I turned and locked eyes with him. "I'm really sorry you got tangled up in this whole mess. I don't want to complicate your life."

"I wouldn't want it any other way. What's a little drama when there's a beautiful redhead warrior at the finish line?"

CHAPTER NINETEEN

With November fast approaching, the weather was markedly cooler on Sunday morning than it had been only a few days prior. The day was deceptively sunny and bright. I lay mesmerized staring at my bedroom window from the vantage point of my bed. The cream- colored sheer curtains went from the top of the window and grazed the floor. There was a gold ribbon of thread that ran vertically throughout the entire expanse of curtain. The sun caught the flecks of gold and made it glisten. Gazing outside the window, I became inspired to go for a quick run.

After getting ready and venturing downstairs, I opened the French doors. I was surprised that although 50 degrees and sunny, the air took on a definite chill. I wore a long sleeve pink running shirt and pulled a hoodie over it. At least I could put it up if it was too windy. I was prone to getting earaches with the cold wind. I shook my head to myself. It was hard to believe I was wearing shorts only a week ago.

Deciding to run on the street today, I went around the block past Adelaide's house. I looked for her curly salt and pepper hair in the window as I passed, but she was nowhere to be seen.

Being Sunday morning, the streets were a ghost town. Driveways were stuffed with cars. Everyone was probably still tucked away in their beds with a cup of steaming coffee in hand as they flipped through their apps looking for something to watch.

As I continued past the entrance to the running path, I remembered that it seemed the whole world lived in this direction, yet I wasn't exactly sure where. Marcia's house was only a few houses down from Adelaide's, but I couldn't remember what color it was. I would have to make a point to check from the backyard, as I knew which balcony belonged to her, I thought.

Fiona and Samantha both lived somewhere around here, only I didn't have a clue as to where that was. I cringed remembering Samantha sitting in front of my house in the dark with sunglasses. I would have to face her at school tomorrow and had no clue how to handle the awkwardness of that situation. I knew that I wasn't the one who had something to be embarrassed about, but it didn't make it any easier. I continued down the long winding street, the air both cold and invigorating. My cheeks were stinging from the coolness. I was convinced if I were to look at myself in the mirror that I would see my nose had taken on a reddish color, thanks to my pale complexion.

I made a few turns down side streets but decided it was time to head back when I reached a mile. I didn't want to get lost in the maze of streets, and I had my second dance lesson in about two hours. I wanted to go home and review my steps prior to my class.

As I turned around and began the journey home the sun was warming my face and the wind was at my back. I felt my phone vibrate with a notification.

I was the only person around and there were no cars driving, so I looked briefly down to check it as I continued my jog. Fiona had posted to Insta. I tapped to reveal her post. There was an artsy picture of a couple in silhouette. You couldn't see their faces, but from the bouncy corkscrew curled hair, I could tell that the woman was Fiona. The man was obscured, but they were embraced in a kiss.

You go Fi, I thought to myself. Maybe this would relieve some of the tension between Fiona and Amber. I looked up to make sure I wasn't about to collide into a tree or car. Then I checked her hashtags #theencounter #neverbeenhappier #makemyownhappy. Well, this was certainly a turn of events. I thought about her reaction to my suggestion that she bring a date to my party. Maybe she would reconsider now. I wondered where and when she met this mysterious man. I grinned to myself excited for her.

As I approached closer to home, an idea struck me. I know what Marcia's car looks like. I had seen it at the gym. When I was near Adelaide's house, I spotted a black Jeep tucked neatly into the driveway of a silver house with burgundy trim. I slowed my jog and finally stopped pretending to stretch. The house looked so cheerful with jeweled tone mums lining the entire entrance to the front door; it was hard to believe that it belonged to Marcia. Her porch contained an orange welcome mat, a nod to the university I assumed. An elegant white wicker set for two sat invitingly. I wondered how such a terrifying person could have such a welcoming house.

Back at home, I stood in the mirror dry shampooing my hair and fixing it into a cute ballet bun on the top of my head. I was adding a pink ribbon to match my shirt when my phone pinged.

Hi beautiful!

I beamed as I made my pilgrimage downstairs to the refrigerator. Waiting until I reached the kitchen, before I typed back the message.

Hey yourself! What are you up to?

As I awaited his response, I started to gather the ingredients to make myself a green smoothie. I spotted my red kale, parsley, and mint, but I couldn't seem to locate the ginger. I continued my search while listening for Coal's response.

I'm refinishing an old four panel cherry door for a guy I know. Just thinking of you. Do you want me to text Samantha and ask her why she was at your house? he wrote.

While reading his response, I simultaneously spotted the ginger inadvertently placed in the fruit drawer. I grabbed a pear and green apple while I was at it.

After placing everything on the counter, I paused to think. Did I want Coal to fight my battles for me? Not really, but he's known Samantha a long time, so maybe he could find out what's really going on and smooth things over. Anything I said to her would come out abrasive and cause greater friction.

The door sounds gorgeous! Post pics. Ok, thank you. Maybe you can be nonchalant with Samantha, so there won't be weirdness between us? You're the best! I added a kissing emoji to my text.

Pulling out the butcher block walnut cutting board that stood up by the side of the range, I grabbed a sharp knife. Slicing the pear and apple into smaller pieces, I threw them into the plastic container for blending. I sliced three delicately thin slices of ginger to add some flavor to my shake. After tearing off a few leaves of kale and adding some parsley, I sprinkled in some cinnamon for good measure.

As it was noisily blending, I was startled by the appearance of a figure at my French doors. I sucked in air, nervous for a moment and breathed out when I realized it was Fiona.

Unlocking the door, I opened it and smiled.

"Ava!" Fiona said cheerfully stepping into the warm kitchen. Her curls were hanging loosely at the sides of her face. All the tension I'd seen in the last few days had dissipated. She was practically glowing, presumably from the new man in her life. She left her black running jacket on and continued, "I knocked, but I guess you couldn't hear me. That's why I came around the back. I hope I'm not interrupting. Was just wondering if you wanted to go with me for a run?"

"First things first, I saw your Insta post this morning.

New man?" I asked my eyebrow shot up and a smirk was displayed on my face.

"Yes, but it's all very fragile, so I don't want to jinx it. Going to see how things go," Fiona smiled mysteriously. "I really like him though."

"That's awesome. I'm so happy for you," I said, pouring my green smoothie into a mason jar. I had a good portion left still in the plastic container.

"Do you want some?" I asked, remembering my manners.

"Sure, thanks," she answered enthusiastically as I poured hers into a glass.

"Let's go sit in the glass room," I suggested leading her into the room on the side of the house.

We took our seats. I chose my usual place on the wicker loveseat, while Fiona settled in on a chair across from it against the glass panels to outside.

"It's chilly in here," I said, shivering. I crossed the room to examine the cast iron potbelly stove situated in the corner of the room. I first checked to make sure that the flue was open. I didn't want to smoke us out. I opened the bottom door to allow air flow into the main chamber, the metal creaked as it opened. Aunt Ginny had a pile of newspapers, sticks, and logs stacked up beside it. I began by wadding up newspaper in the main chamber and adding some small sticks. Finally, I placed two smaller logs to the top. I completed the task methodically.

"You're a regular Girl Scout," Fiona laughed, "I'm impressed."

I chuckled, "My dad taught me how to do it when I was a teenager. We used to have early morning coffee dates in the glass room in our old house. We would sit, just the two of us, before mom would get up, and spend time together."

"That's beautiful," Fiona said. A look of sadness flooded her face. "I wish I had memories of my dad. I feel like I really missed out." Regret seemed to make her shoulders slump.

I finished by using a match to light the crumbled newspaper on the bottom of the pile. "It lights quickly and easily and will spread the fire to the sticks and wood," I explained as Fiona sat gazing at the newspaper being consumed by flames.

Now that the fire was beginning to blaze, the room was beginning to feel immediately toastier. A beautiful amber glow emanated from the stove. Reassuming our positions, I spoke, "Do you talk to your dad?"

Fiona began to fidget in her seat. She unfolded her right foot under her and replaced it with her left, not yet speaking, I worried that I upset her.

"I'm sorry Fi; I just thought maybe you wanted to talk about it, but it's ok if you don't," I waited, glancing at the vista behind her.

"No, it's ok. It's just, I don't even know who my dad is," she looked at me, her brown eyes looking like a lost baby deer in the woods. I truly felt for her. "My mom refused to tell me. It's not that she wouldn't tell me his name, she wouldn't tell me anything about him. What he liked to eat. Could he sing? Was he right-handed or left? Even if she didn't want to divulge his identity, why wouldn't she tell me about what type of person he was? Don't I have a right to know where I came from?" she finished. I felt badly; all of the excitement over her new relationship was lost. She looked crestfallen.

Taking a sip of my smoothie, I thought carefully before I spoke, "When's the last time you spoke to Amber about it? If you were only a kid, she probably didn't want you to go and get you upset and confused. Now that you're an adult, I bet you could explain that it's important to you. I mean it's your dad. You kind of have a right to know, and your mom is a very reasonable and compassionate person."

Fiona looked thoughtful. I could see something shift, the gears in her head going round. "You know what, you're probably right. I think I will bring it up again. I'm a thirty-something year old woman; I don't need protection."

Fiona got up and hugged me in my seat; it felt good to

help her, like talking to a sister. "Thanks for the pep talk."

She sat back down and finished the smoothie. "So how about that run?" she asked hopefully.

I laughed. I had totally forgotten that's why Fiona stopped by.

"I'm so sorry. I already went this morning, and I have to leave in about an hour for my tango lesson," I explained regretfully. I would have definitely preferred to complete my run with a partner. We could have kept each other company.

The room was super cozy, from the fire, and my stomach was full. I laid back on the couch happy for the company and moment of peace. Happiness can be captured in the little moments. Bad things are inevitable. They are a force that can't be stopped, even with all the planning in the world. I knew from experience. However, I had also learned that the secret is to appreciate the spaces in between, to find the beauty in the moment. All the rest was life happening to you. The spaces in between were you making life happen.

"Oh, ok," Fiona answered, flipping her raven locks. "I already had my other lesson yesterday. I guess I'll finish my run when I leave here."

"Show me what you learned," I exclaimed, clapping my hands together, excited to acquire knowledge about another dance.

Fi sprang out of her seat, obviously excited to show off her new skills. She paused to pull her running jacket over her head and drape it over the arm of her chair. She was sporting bright yellow leggings with a matching sports bra. I think this was perhaps the first time that I ever saw her wearing a non-neutral color. This new relationship was obviously good for her mood and confidence.

"Come, stand," she said, grabbing my hands and tugging me up. "I'll show you, and you can do it with me. She was in total teacher mode.

Turning to face me she began to explain the dance. "The basic step of the dance is described as a rock step, triple step, triple step. Here, let me show you."

Fiona used her right foot to step diagonally behind her left. "That's the rock. You step by lifting the left foot slightly. There is a slight bending down to the ground which creates a bounce."

She smiled widely, enjoying teaching me her new dance.

"The next part is the triple step. You move to your right with the rhythm, triple step, triple step. Then again to the left." She threw her bare arms up in the air as if saying Ta da!

I stood behind her and copied her actions. The two of us were chanting, "Rock step, triple step, triple step." We collapsed into a fit of giggles. Now I was hot from all the dancing. We resumed our posts in our chairs. The room even looked like it had a happy glow that matched our moods.

"That was fun," I exclaimed, genuinely pleased with the direction that the morning had turned.

"Now you get to be the teacher," Fiona announced, turning the tables on me.

It was now my turn to shed my hoodie that I had worn earlier to combat the wind. I carefully removed it, not wanting to wreck the bun that I fixed earlier.

This was the perfect opportunity for me to get prepared and warmed up for my lesson. Although it was beautiful practicing here in the glassed-in-room, with the pot bellied stove and autumn leaves setting the stage, I was excited when I remembered the exercise room upstairs.

"Fi, next time you come over, we can use the exercise room on the third floor to practice our dances. It has wall to wall mirrors and a stereo system set up. This way we can watch ourselves in the mirror and see just how bad we look,"

We both laughed at that.

"I've never been to the third floor, the few times that I've visited with mom," Fiona answered, "but that sounds like a great plan."

"Here, come stand behind me, so you can see exactly

what I'm doing," I instructed.

"Usually in dances, the woman always steps backwards first to begin, but not in tango," I announced, retelling the information that Demitrus had imparted on me. "Go forward with your left leg, to the side with your right, back with your left, back with your right. Then you will cross your left to the side of your right, back with your right, then close." I performed each step slowly, so she was able to mirror each movement.

"The timing goes slow, slow, quick, quick, slow, as you do each movement."

We practiced the movements over and over, switching between tango and the jive. I glanced at the clock on the end table. I couldn't believe my eyes, nearly 40 minutes had passed since we began.

"I'm sorry, Fi, I really have to get going to make my lesson on time," I frowned that I needed to leave so abruptly.

"This was so much fun," Fiona exclaimed. Much to my delight, her demeanor had returned to how she was when she arrived at my house.

"Yes, I'm so happy you came by. We'll have to make plans once a week to practice our dances together,"

The parking lot was barren. There was an old beat-up white Chevy pickup that I recognized as belonging to the head custodian Henry. The only other car was a new model silver BMW. As I pulled into the closest space to the entrance, I saw another two cars pulling into the lot. I didn't wait to see who they belonged to, as I didn't enjoy being late. It always makes me flustered if I 'm rushed or ill prepared.

I used my key card to get into the building and walked down the long corridor. When the building was nearly empty, it seemed expansive. The halls echoey, as if I was in a big cathedral.

On cue, the door to the gymnasium clanked when I opened it. It seemed extra loud thanks to the absence of people. Chloe was waiting in the gym. She was dressed in black leggings and a black v neck jersey shirt. She looked very much like a dancer. When she looked up and saw it was me, she gave a big wave and grin.

"I guess we have our lessons at the same time on Thursday and Sunday," I said. I felt awkward and didn't know if I should give her a hug, so I did, just so I wouldn't appear rude.

She was nonplussed and hugged me back.

"What dance are you working on?" I asked as I lowered myself to sit on the wood floor to change into my dance shoes. Coal wasn't here to save me today, so I prayed I would be able to get them on by myself and not have to ask Demitrus for help.

"I'm doing salsa," Chloe answered, seeming so carefree. It was refreshing compared to all of the intensity I had been dealing with. "It's fun; I like it. Plus, it's a dance I can use if I go to a club with friends."

"That's true," I said, stretching the shoe strap diagonally across. With a lot of effort and probably five attempts, I finally got it buckled.

I looked down at Chloe's feet. She also was wearing a pair of dance shoes, but hers were black with a t-strap across the middle of her foot.

"Oh yeah, I actually ordered them from the car on Thursday after leaving the lesson," she laughed.

"Do you have plans for next Saturday?" I casually asked. On a whim I decided to invite her to the party. She was very easy going, and we'd be spending a lot of time together while preparing for this dance show. We might as well bond a little to make our time more enjoyable.

"Nothing important," Chloe answered with a laugh.

"I'm having a Halloween/housewarming party, if you're interested in coming. A bunch of people from school will be there. It will be fun!"

"Sounds fun! Would I be able to bring my boyfriend? I know it sounds lame, but we always spend the weekends together," she smiled, the smile of a girl who was obviously smitten.

"No, not lame. Of course, he can come. I'd love to have him."

At that moment Demitrus and a guy, I assumed was Chloe's dance partner, meandered in.

I glanced at my watch and noticed they were about seven minutes late, even though I had seen cars pull into the lot directly after me.

"Ava," Demitrus said, going in for the double kiss on my cheeks. "I hope you have been practicing." He smelled of cigarettes, the probable explanation for his tardiness.

CHAPTER TWENTY

Coal texted me during my lesson to see if I wanted to meet up in the evening. He finished his latest refinishing project and sent me a photo of it via text. He was grinning wildly beside his refinished door. It was done in a black cherry stain, and he finished it off with a gold round crystal faceted mortice door knob. It really was beautiful, especially with its companion in the picture. I, of course, agreed to meetup with my boyfriend. Yes boyfriend, I finally was able to use the title without retreating into myself. I recently decided it was ok to give myself permission to be happy.

We agreed to go out to a nice steak dinner to finish off the weekend. We had so many nights that we stayed in recently, that it would be nice to go out on a proper date. Coal met me at my house at 6 pm donning gray dress pants and a black turtleneck sweater. I dressed in a gray turtleneck sweater dress, dark gray tights, and knee-high black leather boots. We both laughed when he came to the door, and we noticed our matching outfits. We were beginning to even think alike.

The steakhouse was only a twelve-minute drive from my house, and when we arrived, we were seated right away thanks to the reservation that Coal made. The hostess led us to the left, in the room that contained the bar. I would have been disappointed not to be in the dining room, which I would ordinarily consider more sophisticated, but this room was special. In the center was a huge round firepit which bathed the entire room in a warm embrace and a golden glow. Coal and I were seated just to the left of it. I both felt its warmth on my skin, and the beautiful ambiance which it exuded.

"Well played Mr. Blake," I said gazing into his soulful eyes. "This place is perfect."

"You deserve nothing less than perfect," Coal said, partially standing to lean over the table to kiss me.

I was holding the menu in my hands, but I was having trouble concentrating. The waitress approached us, and I shot Coal a panicked look, as I was nowhere near ready to order.

"Can I get you something to drink?" The light brown-haired waitress asked. She looked at both of us, however her gaze fell heavily on Coal.

"Wine?" Coal asked, consulting me before placing the order.

I nodded my head.

Looking at the menu briefly, Coal responded, "We'll have a bottle of your Tango Malbec." He raised an eyebrow at me, looking very pleased with himself.

I was now full-on beaming at him.

"Very good," the waitress said and retreated to help the table behind us.

"So," Coal said, reaching across the table to grab my hands. They had previously been like ice cubes, but they were slowly heating up with our proximity to the fire.

"So," I repeated looking at him and laughing.

His face got serious, which gave me pause. I was unsure how to read him.

"How would you feel about going with me to visit my parents next Sunday?"

I felt a pang of panic, followed by a warm feeling in my heart. I was so conflicted. Meeting the parents was a big deal, however thanks to all of the weird business I'd been dealing with since my arrival in Syracuse, our relationship had been put into a pressure cooker. The intensity had sped up things. Honestly, I don't know how I would be dealing right now if it weren't for my relationship with Coal.

The waitress had temporarily rescued me, as she showed up with the bottle of wine for us to taste. "Who will be doing the tasting?" the vixen asked. I noticed she had unbuttoned the top button of her dress shirt since last visiting our table. She gazed longingly at Coal.

To his credit, he kept his eyes on hers, and then switched his gaze to me, "My beautiful girlfriend will be doing the tasting," he answered, looking at me with a wicked grin.

The waitress answered with a muted, "Very good," as she poured a small amount for me to sample.

I made a big show of swirling it in my glass, pressing my nose into it as though sampling the bouquet, before taking a small taste. I nodded my head as though it were satisfactory.

The waitress gave a tight grin, took our order for food, and retreated with haste.

Coal laughed as she walked away. "I love you," he casually remarked. Then he stopped, realizing what he had just said.

My heart galloped in my chest. Our eyes met. I didn't reciprocate verbally, but I prayed that my face conveyed the message.

Coal raised his glass, and I quickly followed suit. "To life," he said.

"To life," I repeated. We both took a sip of our wine.

"To our happiness," he followed.

"To our happiness," I agreed, eyes locking with him. This time we followed with a healthy sip to seal our fate.

Coal pulled into my driveway and parked. The night was dark and cold. We didn't park close enough to set the motion lights off.

"Thanks for the dinner," I said as he shut off the engine. "It's only eight, do you want to come in and help me search some more."

"What do you think?" Coal asked locking eyes with me. "Nothing I like more than a good adventure." He raised his eyebrows to emphasize the point.

I paused, staying rooted in my seat. "I just want to thank you for... for everything," I started. Embarking on a completely new life after ten years is a hard thing to do. It was exciting and scary. I was so cautious with what I revealed to Coal, not wanting to make a misstep.

True to form, Coal did not push me to say more, but his gorgeous golden eyes shined with emotion. He had received my message.

Coal got out of his car and walked over to the passenger side door. I gathered my purse off of the floor as he opened the door, offering his hand to help me out.

My front path was illuminated as we approached the porch.

"Ava," I heard my name being called from the night. Peter came walking across the lawn. "So happy to see that your lights are working."

"Hi Peter. Yes, they are, thank you," I offered him a smile.

"Coal, how are you?" Peter asked, extending his hand out to Coal. I felt like he was my dad coming to check on me. "Hope you are taking care of Ava," he interjected.

"I wouldn't have it any other way," Coal answered with a smile while shaking his hand firmly.

"So," Peter spoke, he was dressed casually in dark wash fitted jeans and a mint green polo shirt. He was wearing a dark green wool jacket over his ensemble, "has anyone bothered you since the lights were installed?"

I shivered, probably as a result of the cold night air and the creepiness, and frowned, trying to remember when I received the second box.

"Yeah, the night the lights were installed, another package showed up, but there was also an Amazon box waiting for me on the porch when we found it. Did you notice anything after you left?" I asked, wondering why it never occurred to me before to ask him.

Peter looked thoughtful for a moment, "No, but when I left your house, I went to cook that chicken that I had marinating. I was in the kitchen, so I wouldn't have noticed. I'm so sorry," he apologized.

"No, not at all. I was just wondering," I responded.

"I put in cameras at all the entrances after that night," Coal informed him, shifting his weight.

"I thought you didn't want cameras," Peter said looking somewhat accusingly at me. "That's what you said."

"I didn't want them in my house, watching my every move, but I don't mind them outside. Then they are watching everyone else's moves," I laughed. "Honestly, cameras in the house are creepy, anyone can hack into them."

"True," Peter said, looking less hurt, his face returning to normal with my explanation. "I wouldn't want an invasion of my privacy either. Well, I'm glad you got them outside. What was in the package? If you don't mind me asking." He gazed at me intrigued, waiting for my response.

I gulped, locking eyes with him while I answered, hesitant to even say it aloud, "A doll with my exact shade of hair, only it was eyeless. Around its neck was a note that read: Why can't you see me?" I whispered the last part as though I were afraid that if I voiced it aloud, whoever sent it would appear in front of me.

Peter looked faint, as if his knees might give out at any second. This was the first time that I saw him looking anything less than fully composed. "You're kidding me, right?"

I shook my head no sadly. I had begun to feel better about this whole thing since putting in the cameras. There had been no strange packages or feelings of being watched, but now that I'd said it out loud to Peter, the doom crept right back in.

After promising Peter that I would look after myself and keep him updated if I had any more problems, Coal and I headed into the warm house. I headed directly for the alarm pad. I was a pro at turning the alarm system off quickly and smiled satisfied with my skills.

"You're getting better," he responded with a wink.

Coal and I took off our coats, and I hung them in the closet in the hallway.

"Do you want me to make coffee, and we can come up with a plan for our search? The diary has to be somewhere in the house," I said confidently. We had searched her room and found those creepy messages. Were there secrets hidden all over this house? I wondered.

"Perfect," Coal answered, grabbing my hand. We walked side by side into the kitchen.

I headed towards the counter where the coffee was kept when Coal gently guided me to the kitchen cabinets that went from floor to ceiling. It was a pantry of sorts that was flat with no protruding handles. He pressed my back gently but firmly against them.

"You are so beautiful," his husky voice whispered in my ear. "And you feel amazing in this dress." He ran his hand down my sides.

Where was this coming from? I wondered before I sighed, as he kissed the back of my neck that was exposed thanks to my ballerina hairdo.

I remained pressed up against the cabinets, Coal's body was crushed up right against mine. I could feel his strong pecs and tight stomach through his sweater. My body responded, flooding with heat.

"Are you in this one-hundred percent?" he murmured in my ear, his voice both firm and demanding.

I nodded my head yes urgently.

"I need you to say it," Coal commanded.

"What?" I gasped. My breathing was ragged. I wasn't used to his insistence, this urgency.

"I need you to tell me you are in this. That you can handle it. I've tried not to press you, but I have to look out for myself as well," his voice nearly cracked, overflowing with emotion. "I don't know how I'd survive if you pulled away now. I'm not being a hero waiting for you. I'm protecting myself as well. I know that no one can predict the future, but I need to know if you are in this with... with everything."

Never in my life had I ever had an exchange this raw with another human being. He laid his needs before me and asked if I could reciprocate. Tears began to fall from my eyes, and I couldn't stop them. They were surely making Coal's sweater damp. It was a release. I knew that Coal couldn't see them, as our bodies were nearly glued together. Surely, he felt them, as I felt the beating of his heart through our clothes.

"I love you," I whispered in his ear. My voice sounded strange to my own ears.

To my astonishment, Coal pulled away a little so he could see my face. His own eyes were wet as well. "Do you mean it?" He looked astonished that I had spoken the words.

"Yes," I gasped. "I will try to be more open with you. I'm trying." My green eyes were pleading with him to believe me, to be patient with me.

"I know," he nodded his head vigorously. "I just needed to be sure. I felt it, but I just needed to know it wasn't one sided." He lifted me up and placed me down on the counter. His lips met mine and connected. Waves of electricity were jolting through my body. Time and place seized to exist. It was only Coal and me.

"Do you want to go upstairs?" I panted, the full extent of what I meant obvious.

"If we can make it there," he groaned in response.

With his response, I fumbled with his sweater and began wildly pulling at it. He lifted his arms to aid my efforts. His eyes contained the intensity of a feral animal.

The sweater came off in the sitting room. I clawed at his bare skin. The feel of his muscles more than I could bear.

When we reached the landing for the stairs I lifted my arms, and he grabbed my mid-calf dress off in one fell swoop. I was left standing in my black stockings, boots and bra to make the ascend up the stairs.

The dress lay on the landing as he followed behind me. “You are amazing,” he uttered. When we reached the second floor, Coal picked me up. The skin of his bare chest burning my naked stomach.

Coal burst through the bedroom door and released me onto the bed. I kicked off my own boots. He laid down next to me, and I straddled him. My strong legs coiled around his body. He unhooked my bra and grunted loudly as my breasts were out in the open.

“You are everything.” Coal pulled me to him, and we laid together. All the hurts in my life were washed away. My parents' early deaths, my failed marriage to Michael, Aunt Ginny’s death, he washed a cleansing over me. The past was important, but it didn’t define me. Us, here together in this moment made everything worth it.

He reached to my head and took the ponytail holder out of my hair, leaving my red locks to cascade down around me. They were a stark contrast to my porcelain skin. We never stopped to turn on the light, so the only light to enter the room emanated from the moon outside.

“I don’t know how I got so lucky?” Coal said, stroking my bare skin.

“I’m the lucky one,” I gasped.

“No,” he insisted. “I knew the moment that I spotted you that first day at school. I saw you walk in the building with that black and cream polka dotted shirt. Your hair was all loose around your face. Your eyes were mesmerizing, a stormy sea of green. You looked so fucking smart, hurt, and intense, all at the same time. I think I fell in love with you at that moment. It’s like Cupid came and shot me with his bow.

I never had a chance."

I leaned up on my elbow to look at him. "Get out of here," I said laughing.

His eyes became wide. "I've heard people talk about love at first sight. I always thought it was bullshit. You can't love someone you don't know, but then I met you. I think you have been what I've been waiting for my entire life. I was so drawn to you that it scared me and now this."

"What do you mean, this?" I asked.

"Being here with you now. Together." He finished his last word and I lay back down on his chest. We both closed our eyes and listened to the beating of our hearts as one.

"I want you to know," Coal said, "whatever all this weirdness is that's going on, I will help you get to the bottom of it. I won't let anyone hurt you. You've been through enough. You are not alone anymore."

He couldn't have known how much those words meant to me. The contrast between my relationship with Michael and this was so far off that it was like comparing a plastic crystal to a diamond. I thought that the plastic crystal was good enough. It looked nice enough on the outside, but if you stepped on it by accident, it would shatter into hundreds of shards that were sure to cut you. If you stepped on the diamond, it would remain intact, undamaged. It had integrity.

I pulled at the waistband of my stockings. Coal saw me do this and took the cue. He delicately pulled them off, and I lay naked on the bed. He kissed my stomach, making me groan.

I climbed on top of him, and we rocked together. Our bodies and worlds colliding in the biggest fireworks finale that I've ever experienced. Purple, silver, gold, and red exploding in my brain in a show stopping finish.

We both lay breathless. It was so much, and it spoke for itself. I finally unclothed my feelings and laid them all out there for Coal. God, I hoped he chose to be careful with them, but either way at this point it was a chance I was willing to take.

Coal grabbed my hand and pulled it to his mouth to kiss it. "Can I stay here with you tonight? I don't want to leave you."

"I guess we could arrange that," I said coyly. "I'll have to check with the management."

Coal gave me a sideways look.

"Yep, I checked with her, and she says you have to. She won't let you leave." I kissed him passionately.

"Let me go home really quickly to get a change of clothes, and I will be right back. This way we won't have to rush in the morning, and we can drive to school together." He gave me a suggestive look.

"Can I come with you?" I asked, excited about the prospect of seeing his house, having a window into his private world.

Coal grinned like a little boy, "I would love that. I just didn't want to drag you out of the house into the cold, but if you want to come, that would be awesome."

Coal got up and put his gray trousers on. While he was searching for his shoes and socks, I walked over to the dresser to find something to wear.

"Wow, you really are magnificent," Coal remarked, looking up from his shoes.

I pulled on a pair of charcoal leggings and a purple and gray flannel. I added my old black Doc Marten boots. I felt like a young college girl again, excited about new love and the prospects of the future.

"Voila, I'm ready before you," I teased. He linked his arms around me. I couldn't stop myself from admiring his physique. I didn't realize he kept such a strict workout regimen, is all I could think as I caressed his sinewy bicep.

"I would be ready if you hadn't thrown my sweater on the sitting room floor," he chuckled as we made our way down the stairs. I leaned down to pick up my sweaterdress off the landing as we went by, evidence of our passion.

CHAPTER TWENTY-ONE

I will go to ridiculous lengths to avoid driving in a cold car at night. In college I'd stay over at a friend's house overnight only to avoid the cold drive home, however driving in the cold car seemed to be the most exciting prospect in the world to me at that moment, basking in the glow of our night. I felt like I was on vacation in Paris, the lights of the Eiffel Tower glowing around me instead of the dim street lights in Syracuse. Let's be honest, I could have been walking through a blizzard, and you wouldn't be able to get rid of my smile. It turned out Coal was only a ten-minute drive from my house. We pulled onto his street, lined with Tudor style houses, and I was so excited to have a glance into his private world. Since I dove in with both feet, I was anxious to find out everything about him.

The front lawn gave way to a stunning brick Tudor house. It was small, in comparison to the Victorian mansion that Aunt Ginny had bequeathed me, but magnificent. The front face was half red brick and half gingerbread style Tudor. The base was painted a cream color, and the detailing and trim were decorated in an antique green. A red Spanish tile roof adorned the top l ike a beautiful hat.

"Your house is amazing," I gasped as we pulled into his driveway.

I didn't think his grin could get wider, but it did. He smiled ear to ear, obviously proud of his home.

"Thanks," he said, now looking a little shy. "When I

bought it, it was in disrepair. The owners had passed away, and it sat for quite a while before it was put on the market. I had to give it a makeover, breathe life into it."

"Well, you did an amazing job," I leaned over the gear shift, and gave him a long lingering kiss. "You're one talented man."

"Let me give you the tour," he emerged from the car quickly, anxious to show off his handy work.

I swiftly followed suit, and we approached his hand carved front entry door stained in hues of brown, yellow, and green. It was scrolled out in a Celtic style design, complete with a Celtic cross. It was a masterpiece in its own right worthy of being displayed at the Cloisters Museum in the Bronx. The front of his house, I noticed, was brightly lit. There were no strange packages or people lurking around or on his porch, such a welcome sight.

"You have to plant some beautiful flowers in the spring in these flower beds. This house deserves to be decorated," I exclaimed as I stood on the front steps surveying the empty dirt surrounding the front of his house. "Flowers are accessories for a house."

"Yeah, it is missing a woman's touch I'll admit," he said, kissing me on the nose. "I was so focused on the actual house, that I haven't taken the time to do the landscaping. That's where you come in." I felt both excited and nervous that he was talking about our relationship in the future.

When he opened the door, Coal immediately flipped on the light switch, the room was illuminated by a 1920's Georgian Style Cut Crystal chandelier. It was gorgeous. I surveyed the area around me. Much like my house, it was packed with antiques only instead of being Victorian style, his house boasted a steeply pitched roof. Thick dark stained decorative beams ran the course of the ceiling and the tall windows had diamond shaped panes and leaded glass. It looked like something out of a storybook.

"Wow Coal, this is really impressive," I said gazing

around the room, "but I'm not surprised."

"Well maybe you want to wait here while I grab my things. I wasn't...hmmm," he cleared his throat, "expecting company, and I want your first time seeing the rest of the house to be as equally impressive." He winked at me. His eyes crinkled in the corners, only making him more handsome.

"Wait, what happened to my tour?" I asked with a deadpan face.

Coal appeared to panic, so I let him off the hook.

"I'm just kidding. I totally understand," I laughed, plopping myself down on his antique leather Stickley Mission Oak Arts and Crafts couch. It was hard to believe that a man who was a bachelor his entire life had a presentable living room with not even a stray sneaker on the floor. I was sure that the rest of his house must have been at least somewhat presentable.

My heart swelled with pride knowing Coal had picked out all of the pieces in this house and restored it to its former glory. It made me feel more confident that he was authentic. Surely only a beautiful soul could invest the time necessary to make things this gorgeous. I shook my head, unable to believe that I had gotten so lucky. When things went wrong with Michael, I thought my chance at a fairy tale ending was over. I almost felt that a happy ending wasn't in the cards for me. My parents had left me, I had a failed marriage, Aunt Ginny, my only remaining relative, had died. Maybe I was destined to an unhappy existence. I almost believed it and then this amazing man swept me off my feet.

Coal came down the stairs, catching me deep in thought. "Everything ok?" he asked, a look of concern creeping into his expression.

"Better than ok," I assured him, getting up to throw my arms around him.

Coal didn't look so sure, "You looked so forlorn." He studied my face, waiting for my response.

"Do you believe in second chances?" I asked him seriously.

"Second chances with what?" he asked before answering the question.

"At happiness?" I clarified.

"Yes, second, third, and as many times as it takes. Good people deserve to be happy," Coal said seriously. "You deserve to be happy," he took my chin in my hand and nuzzled my face, his stubble gently scraping against my skin.

I didn't say anything in response. I just breathed deeply and closed my eyes, enjoying the smell and the feel of being in Coal's arms.

"Let's get out of here," he said. "Next time you come over you'll get the full tour AND a candlelight dinner."

"Sounds perfect," I finally answered. "Did you get everything you need?"

Coal pointed at the black gym bag that he had slung casually over his shoulder. "Yep, clothes for tomorrow are all set."

I nodded my head, and we headed back out to the car. Coal secured his front door. We walked in silence to the car, but after Coal let me in, closed my door, and got in himself, he didn't start up the car.

"I want to know what you're thinking," he kept his voice even, but stared at me intensely. I felt as though he could see through me.

I didn't say anything, afraid to even breathe, afraid to say the wrong thing, and afraid that he would become tired of all the drama that came with me.

"Do you mind if I ask you what happened in your marriage? If you're not ready to tell me yet, I understand, but I want to know everything about you."

I nodded my head. "I want to tell you. I want you to really know me, and I want to really know you."

"I'm glad," Coal responded, bobbing his head in affirmation. Now he looked nervous. "I just hope... never mind," he trailed off.

"No, you hope what?" I asked.

"I hope we didn't rush things. I was worried you might have doubts. I wanted being together to..." He looked out the window. With the cold night air, his breath was visible as he was breathing and even began to fog up the window. He didn't finish what he was saying. I felt a pang of sadness in causing him any pain.

About this, I knew I could provide comfort. "I have no regrets. We didn't rush into anything. I promise you one hundred percent that this has been the best night of my life. You have given me the gift of being loved and seen in a way that I never have before. I'm sorry if I made you feel anything less." I didn't realize I had a tear coming down my cheek until Coal reached his hand up to it to wipe it away.

With that Coal started up the car and began the short journey back to my house.

It was nearly quarter to ten when we got settled back at my house. I chuckled to myself remembering that in my twenties, we didn't leave the house to go out for the night until ten. I was very content being in for the night with Coal. There was nowhere else in the world that I would have preferred to be, I thought as Coal took off his shoes and placed them neatly next to his duffel bag by the closet.

"Yes," I said to him as he walked toward me. I was still dressed in my jeans and Doc. Martens.

Coal looked perplexed, "Yes what?" he asked.

"Yes, I want to go with you to see your parents," I declared, grabbing his hand.

A look of understanding crossed his face when he realized I was answering the question that he had posed at the restaurant. At the time I was torn about how I felt. After our night, I felt sure.

"That's awesome. You make me so happy," he declared.

"I'm just sorry that I can't introduce you to my parents. They would have loved you," I said thinking of how excited mom would have been for me to have such a genuine boyfriend. Dad would have loved the way that he looked after me and how handy he was fixing things. He would have called him a real man. "Aunt Ginny would have loved you too."

Across the room I spotted my bejeweled key, and I was struck with inspiration to find out what it opened. I ran over to the vanity and grabbed it, placing the ribbon around my neck.

"Are you too tired to do some detective work?" I asked him pointing towards the dangling key.

"Never," he answered enthusiastically.

He lifted the key to get a better look at it. The ribbon wasn't super long, so his face was right next to mine. He moved his face closer and his long eyelashes fluttered against my cheek. I had to catch my breath.

"I wonder," Coal said aloud, "if this key is for a lock on a piece of furniture, or if it locks a secret compartment in the house." He stared at it for a long moment.

"Did you ever text Samantha?" I asked, as I suddenly remembered his promise to contact her.

"Yeah, she said she was driving down the street when she remembered that Fiona said you lived on the block. She was trying to see if she could spot your car in the driveway."

I looked at him skeptically, "What about the sunglasses at night?

"She claims that she didn't want to get discovered around your house because she didn't want you to think she was creeping on you. She was just curious."

"What do you think?" I asked.

"I think she's weird but harmless. I told her next time to just text you and ask if she can stop by."

"You're such a guy Coal. You don't understand women dynamics at all." I patted him on the head like he was a little boy.

"What do you mean? Wouldn't that be the normal

thing to do if you wanted to see where your friend lives?"

"Yes, but we're not exactly friends, are we?" I retorted.

"You invited her to your party on Saturday. I thought that would qualify her as your friend."

"We are acquaintances," I gave him a look of disbelief that he did not get this. "I don't think she likes me at all, but we are coworkers, so I want to be friendly. To be honest, I don't know if I really like her."

Coal chuckled.

"Oh, by the way. I saw Chloe at dance practice today, so I invited her to come to the party too."

Now Coal really laughed, "You didn't even know who she was three days ago."

"Well now I do, and we have dance practice at the same time on Thursdays and Sundays. I don't want things to be weird," I explained, annoyed that he didn't get it.

"I love you," he said in response and pulled me out of the bedroom door to the hallway. "I don't understand, but I love you. Let our search commence. Come on." He was prodding me out of the room.

Once in the hallway I asked, "Where do you think we should begin?"

Coal answered promptly, "The library of course. If this was a movie, it would definitely be in the library. If not in the bedroom, where you would keep personal items, it makes sense that you would keep a book in the library."

"Oh, I didn't even think of that. Maybe it's hidden in plain sight on a shelf. How are we ever going to find it then?" As we stepped into the library, my eyes went up and down all of the book lined shelves, I felt overwhelmed.

"Did Lina tell you what it looked like?" Coal asked, trying to piece together the situation.

"Yeah, it's green leather, like my favorite chair," I said motioning towards the writing desk where the chair was tucked in.

"Have you checked the writing desk yet?" he asked,

not waiting for me to answer but moving swiftly towards it.

"No," I silently wondered how it hadn't occurred to me to check there.

He opened the wide middle draw. It wasn't super deep, but it was long and wide and could hold a lot. Thinking better of it, he turned to me. "It's filled with her personal belongings. I don't feel right going through it. Here, you come look," he patted the chair motioning for me to sit in.

I sat and opened it up. It was filled with pens, envelopes, and ledgers. When peeking inside, the first thing that caught my eye was a photograph. It was of Aunt Ginny and her arm was embracing a man. It was Peter. Her smile was wide. There were Christmas lights behind them in the background, and she was clad in a puffy white coat. She had a silver hat on her head, and her cheeks were flushed pink from the cold. It was hard to tell how long ago this was taken. She looked so young and alive.

I held the photo up for Coal to examine closer.

"Were those two involved?" Coal asked me seemingly confused by the photo. He took the photo from me to examine it closer, furrowing his eyebrows in concentration.

"I have no idea. I thought they were just friends. Although in this picture it looks like there may have been more to their relationship. Look at Peter. He is practically glowing. Maybe we should ask him," I pondered.

"Maybe we should look for the journal first. It might shed some light on their relationship, and let us know if she was involved with anyone else. If you do want to ask him, please don't confront him without me. Just in case. "

I nodded my head in understanding.

"I'm serious," said Coal sternly. His concern was endearing.

If someone did hurt Aunt Ginny, I didn't want to put myself in a position where I could also get hurt because of it. In movies people always confront the person they know is guilty, without letting anyone else know, and almost get themselves killed. They never bring backup. Forget once a cheater, always a cheater. Let's worry about once a killer, always a killer.

"Well, someone was definitely threatening her, and my bet is that it was a woman. With the letters we found, all fingers point towards a woman. The question is why?"

I pulled out the contents onto the green leather top. There were countless pens, a journal where she kept track of her finances. There was a picture of Amber and Ginny. They were on a sailboat together. They were both smiling dazzling smiles and dressed in all white. The white showed off their late summer tans. I put the picture to the side on the desk and decided to give it to Amber when I saw her at the party on Saturday. It would probably mean a lot for her to have it.

There was nothing else in the drawer that provided any answers. I neatly put everything else back in.

"Ok well it's a process of elimination," Coal said. "Let's scan the shelves and see if we spot any green leather bindings.

I systematically started to the far left of the room on the very top shelf. I moved the ladder over, so I could climb up to the top shelf. My Doc Martens made climbing easy. I quickly scanned and didn't spot any green. I moved down to the second shelf. Nothing there either. When I got to the fourth shelf, there was a book in dark green, but it wasn't leather. This was tedious, but if we went shelf by shelf, we'd be sure not to miss anything.

While I was busy examining all the books in the room, Coal was walking around examining the walls. He spotted the storage area that I had previously discovered. He opened the latch and yelled to me, "Hey look at this."

At the time I was on the sixth shelf down and looked over to him.

"Yeah, I found that already. It's storage, but I didn't look through all the boxes. You're welcome to look in them if you want. Maybe she put it away in a box."

"It's possible," said Coal skeptically, but I firmly believe if she hid it, she really hid it. It's somewhere that a person couldn't just happen upon it. Either that or someone took it. Either way is suspicious, especially if she used to leave her journal lying around, like Lina said."

Coal pulled out the boxes anyway, opened them up and did a quick cursory scan. In the one box were little boxes of light bulbs. Coal spotted them and took one out.

"I noticed one of the bulbs is out on the sconce between these two bookshelves. I'll fix it for you," Coal informed me, always considerate and making himself useful.

At this point I had made it all the way down the bottom shelf in the first column of book shelves. I spotted a few green books, but none of them were her diary.

"Thanks babe," I said. "It's nice having a real man around." I said it half joking, but it was true. Michael thought he was a man. He acted macho, but he never wanted to do anything that made him uncomfortable, especially emotionally. He only was concerned with my feelings if it directly affected him. If he had nothing to gain, I wasn't even an afterthought.

As Coal took out a bulb that was pinecone shaped, it was textured, so the light refracted when illuminated, he spoke to me, "Tell me about Michael, please."

"Where to begin?" I asked moving the ladder over to climb to the top of the second column of books. The room looked expansive and beautiful from the top of the ladder.

"The beginning of course," Coal said practically, looking up at me. "I don't know anything."

"Are you sure you want to hear this?" I asked hesitantly. "I don't want to hurt you."

"Unless you're going to tell me you are still in love with him, then you won't hurt me. I just want to understand your relationship and what went wrong."

"Definitely not still in love with him. When I married him, I believed I was, but I had a very limited perspective and experience at that point."

Coal moved over to the sconce with the burnt-out light.

"I'm sorry to interrupt your search," Coal said looking over at me scanning the books, "but can I borrow your ladder for a minute, so I can fix the light?"

"Of course," I said, walking back down the ladder and sliding it over, so he could climb to fix the light.

I watched Coal as he ascended the ladder in stocking feet. He reached the light, and I stretched up to hand him the acorn light bulb.

"I might need a screwdriver to tighten this sconce," Coal noted. The sconce was somewhat askew, leaning to the right. "I don't want to leave it crooked."

As Coal fiddled with the sconce and pulled it farther to the right, to see how far it would go, the wall of books pushed forward slightly.

"No way," I exclaimed. My mouth was agape. I couldn't believe my eyes. The bookshelf had moved away from the wall about two inches. It was dark beyond it, but moving the sconce had actually moved the bookshelf.

"What happened?" Coal asked, still on the ladder replacing the broken light bulb. He was busy concentrating on the sconce.

"When you moved the sconce, the bookcase opened up about two inches," I exclaimed, not quite believing it myself.

"What? Really?" Coal rapidly made his way down the ladder. He almost slid down the final two steps. I'd never seen him move so quickly. He jumped off the ladder and looked at the wall. He grabbed hold of the portion that pulled away from the wall and pulled. The wall of books pulled away to reveal a room that was about 9 feet by 7 feet. It was dark, but he felt around on the wall until he located a light switch.

"OMG," I exclaimed when the light had gone on.

"Wow," Coal stood standing in awe, obviously unbelieving about what he had discovered. "I've heard all about these secret rooms, but I can't believe that we actually found one." He looked absolutely flabbergasted. "This is the coolest thing I've ever seen."

The walls of the secret room were paneled in dark burled maple wood from floor to ceiling. The floor was just a continuation of the hardwood flooring that was used in the library. There was a supple luxurious wine-colored leather armchair in the room. A small mini bar also took residence in the right corner. It was stocked with red wine and vodka. Next to it was a globe on a stand with wooden feet. When it opened up, it held wine glasses on the inside. Aunt Ginny obviously knew about this room and used it.

Then I saw something which gave me pause. There, on the minibar was a martini glass placed on a cocktail napkin. The napkin was monogrammed with VZ in gold lettering. A toothpick and olive pit lay resting in the bottom of the glass. It gave me chills. It looked like it was waiting there for Aunt Ginny to come and retrieve it at any minute. She never returned before she met her fate. It laid there where she left it abandoned, hopeless. Around the rim on the martini glass, the imprint of her lips remained stained in her trademark Gucci 25* Goldie Red lipstick.

CHAPTER TWENTY-TWO

I audibly gasped.

"What's wrong?" Coal asked after he heard me call out. He could tell I was worried by my pale pallor and the sudden change in my demeanor. He had been busy inspecting the walls, so he did not have a chance to witness my discovery.

I pointed accusingly at the tumbler.

He glanced at the lone glass on the table. "Wow, it's like she was just in here and stepped out to use the bathroom," he looked thoughtfully at the glass.

Out of nowhere, I was struck with a thought. "Maybe we should put all of Aunt Virginia's personal items from the desk in here for now. I'm going to be having a houseful of people on Saturday, and I don't want to risk anyone going through her stuff." I furrowed my brow and realized the implication of what I was saying.

Coal nodded in agreement. "We don't know if there was anything untoward involving Ginny's death. "He finished my thought and sent a shiver down my spine. I was not yet willing to accept the fact that my beloved Aunt Ginny, my only remaining relative that I actually had a connection with, had been stolen from me prematurely.

We exchanged a knowing glance and went over to the writing desk. While Coal pulled out the long drawer, I began to remove the contents. I made a tidy pile of her ledgers and mail and brought them into the hidden study. There was a wooden ledge on the wall opposite the door. I laid her belongings there for safekeeping. All that remained in the desk drawer in the library were various pens and a few stray paper clips and the two photos.

Coal joined me back in the little room. "This is the coolest thing I've ever seen in real life," he exclaimed. His mind was racing. In his head, he was caught up in a spy novel. His golden eyes were wide in wonderment. "You know you could use this room as a safe room. All we would need to do is put a lock on the inside to bolt the door shut. If there was ever an emergency, you could lock yourself in here and no one would be able to get to you."

I gulped at the thought of having to lock myself in a little room, a feeling of claustrophobia immediately setting in, however I guessed he had a point. If there was an intruder in the house, it would be better to be able to lock myself in the room and call for help rather than risk getting hurt.

"I wonder if anyone in Aunt Ginny's life knew about this room," I said aloud. "Nobody's ever mentioned it to me. She never personally told me about it either."

"I don't know, but you shouldn't mention it to anyone. This way it will be a safe place for you, just in case."

I involuntarily shivered.

I again found Coal examining the inside walls.

"What are you looking for? You already found the secret wall," I asked perplexed why he was still searching for something we had already found.

"Bingo," he pronounced, pointing to an area to the side of the bar cart. It was located about two feet from the ground and to the left of the bar cart.

I bent down to inspect the area he was pointing to. I was openmouthed when I saw there was indeed a keyhole.

Coal stood looking like the cat who swallowed the canary.

"What is that? I dumbly asked, knowing full well it was a keyhole.

"You have that skeleton key that Amber gave you with

you, right?" Coal inquired, glancing down to my neck. The key was concealed by my flannel. It was obvious that he was trying not to jump out of his own skin.

I didn't bother to answer him,"Here," I said, as I reached into my shirt to retrieve the key. I removed the ribbon from around my neck and thrust the key into Coal's eagerly awaiting hands.

He took his time putting the key into the keyhole. I felt myself holding my breath as he turned the lock. It turned easily and a portion of the wall dropped down.

"No way," Coal shouted out. "I knew it was a possibility that the key would unlock it, but I still can't believe it."

"I'm beginning to feel like it's not me you love but my house," I pouted. I quickly recovered and nearly knocked Coal out of the way as I approached the open wall.

I put my hand in and to my surprise pulled out something flat and soft.

Coal came up right next to me, waiting in anticipation. "Well?" he asked, nearly shouting at me.

"Oh my God," I pulled out the item to reveal a green leather-bound journal. "I can't believe it!" I was truly astounded as I held the diary in my trembling hands. I was conflicted. On one hand I was excited to have a piece of Aunt Ginny back. Reading her words, I would be able to hear her thoughts, as if she were present talking to me. On the other hand, I was terrified that she would reveal something terrible, something that I would be forced to confront and deal with. I guess that's life though. We needed to deal with a lot of scary things, so I sat down in the wine leather recliner and leaned back.

"Here goes nothing," I said to Coal as I opened the book.

"Aren't you going to start from the beginning?" Coal asked as he saw me flip to the back of the book.

"No, this isn't a novel. It's not like I'm going to ruin the ending for myself. I want to find out what's going on. I'm looking for a spoiler."

July 30, 2021

He wants to meet again. I told him this was an impossible situation, but he doesn't want to hear it. Us reconnecting has caused problems from all angles. I've received another series of notes, but I'm not sure which person sent them. I feel like I'm being watched. I did NOT go looking for this trouble, but it seems to be haunting me at every turn. I feel like I am the fox in a fox hunt, and that the hounds are coming for me. Maybe it's my own fault. I should have told him from the beginning. I should have faced up to reality and let the chips fall where they may. Now it is my turn to pay for my duplicity. I am being charged with withholding information, and I'm afraid I will have to pay the ultimate price.

My chest tightened; my breathing felt constricted. The pinging of my smart watch informed me that it was time to take a minute out to breathe. I felt annoyed as it was stating the obvious. It was like telling a man that was being held underwater that he was drowning.

"What is it?" Coal asked, watching in horror at my struggle to breathe. "Take it easy Ava. Put your head between your legs and breathe deeply." He spoke gently, taking the book out of my hands and helping me into position.

I took three deep breaths. In. Out. In. Out. In. Out. my heart rate began to stabilize.

"What did it say?" he asked finally when he saw the color return to my face.

"You have to see for yourself," I whispered, not knowing what to think. "Read the final page. She wrote this only five days before she died."

Coal quickly opened the book and read. A worried look spread across his handsome face. The fine lines around his eyes seemed to instantaneously deepen. "The ultimate price?" he reiterated. "This is messed up Ava."

I nodded in agreement, my eyes meeting his in a knowing glance, but I couldn't bring myself to speak.

"I think you need to start at the beginning and maybe we can figure out what your aunt is talking about. Someone was definitely threatening her. We just don't know who or why. Until we figure that out, there isn't much that we can do."

"Agreed," I finally answered. "Is there anything else in that hidden compartment?" I glanced over to where I had retrieved the diary. From my vantage point, it looked like a black pit in the wall.

Coal stuck his hand in the compartment and pulled out something small and shiny, a little key. This one wasn't an elaborately decorated skeleton key, like the first to reach my hands. This key looked more like a safe deposit key. It was plain and gold colored. Although non-descript, it was yet another mystery to be solved.

"Let me put the diary and the key back in here. I can't risk someone else seeing it. I think I should only read the diary in this room. I better keep it here for safekeeping. I don't want anyone to know that I found it, not even Lina, who originally told me about it. Tomorrow after work, I am going to start from the beginning and try to piece together what is going on. Once I know for sure what's going on I can let Lina know I found it."

"Definitely sounds like a plan," Coal answered, kissing me on the forehead. "It's getting late. Why don't we get ready for bed? Unfortunately, we have school tomorrow."

I placed the diary, the new key and some loose mail of Aunt Virginia's, from the desk, back into the wall compartment and locked it with the key. I then replaced the key around my neck. The ledger was too wide, so it remained on the ledge. Tomorrow would require a return trip, another attempt to find out the truth.

After making sure the secret room was yet again concealed, and the library was in order, we retired to my bedroom. Although Coal had slept over before, this was different. This was intentional, I felt a stirring in my heart as I closed the bedroom door.

"We've certainly had quite a day," Coal said, taking my hands and pulling me onto the bed.

"Yes, we have," I agree, my head laying on my soft pillow. I felt like I had spent the last few weeks on a roller coaster with all the ups and downs and terrifying turns. It was no wonder that anxiety attacks were creeping back into my life.

Coal laid down right next to me. Our faces were nearly touching. A feeling of warmth radiated from us. I wished I could capture the feeling I had at that exact moment, never to be lost. It was this feeling that made everything I had been through worthwhile.

"What are you thinking about?" Coal asked, stroking my cheekbone.

"I'm thinking I've waited all my life to feel like this," I sighed, "but the wait was worth it."

He was grinning like an idiot. He kissed me on the eyes and cheeks.

"Do you want to hear about Michael?" I asked rather abruptly, my eyes locking eyes with his, wanting to get it out of the way. My hope was that if I could share my past with Coal that it would strengthen our already growing bond. Maybe my resistance to getting emotionally closer would drift away.

"Yes," he answered eagerly.

I took a big breath, getting ready to bare my soul. He watched me intently, truly interested in what I was going to say.

"When my parents first died, I was so young and eager to make a connection with someone, to feel that I had someone to depend on."

"Understandably," Coal added, urging me to go on.

"I embraced our relationship because it gave me direction and a sense of security."

Coal nodded his head. I felt lame that that was my reasoning for being in a relationship with him.

"Us getting married seemed like a logical progression to me. I was eager to start my own family, to rebuild what I had lost," I explained, getting choked up thinking about how hard that time was emotionally.

"So why didn't you ever have children?" Coal interrupted, obviously confused that we were married for ten years and no closer to my goal.

"Actually," I said seriously, "that's where our trouble began and ended."

"How?" he prodded, wanting to hear the whole story.

"Well at first I was understanding about waiting to have a baby. We were young, and once you have kids you are tied down... Michael's words. I remembered thinking at the time that it made sense. All our friends were going out and traveling, so I didn't mind waiting a little while."

At that Coal's eyes narrowed slightly.

"After five years, that excuse didn't work for me anymore. I was frustrated. Our friends were beginning to settle down. He tried to convince me that I didn't want to have kids yet. He would tell me that I would get fat and neither of us wanted that."

Now Coal sat up on his elbows, "What an ass," he blurted out. "Momentarily gaining weight is a small price to pay to bring another human being into the world, and he's not the one who would have to do all the work."

I chuckled. Coal was getting so worked up. "It's ok Coal, no one really looks forward to the gaining weight part."

"Of course not, but you also don't make your wife feel bad about it." Now Coal was obviously pissed. "What a jerk."

I was hesitant to continue seeing as I didn't even get to the bad part yet. I dreaded the idea of Coal and Michael ever coming face to face. My stomach was in knots at the thought of it. I ceased telling the story, locking eyes with Coal.

"Please continue," Coal pleaded. "I promise to behave myself. I just don't like the idea of anyone hurting you after you've been through so much."

My knight in shining armor, I swooned.

At his request I continued, "When I assured him the weight gain was temporary, and I didn't need to be out on the scene, as I was married already, then he got really weird." I coughed nervously. I emotionally wasn't ready to continue.

Coal caressed my chin.

"He told me that he didn't want to share me with anybody else," I could feel my shoulders tensing at just the thought of that time. "He didn't want to compete for my affection with a child. If I had to spend so much time tending to a baby, who was going to pay attention to him."

"Wow," Coal responded, "what a weirdo."

"The worst part was that he didn't even value me as a person. He didn't care about my feelings, thoughts, wants, or needs. He only wanted me to be there for him one hundred percent." I struggled for a minute trying to find the right words to explain. "He wasn't obsessed with me; he was just obsessed with the idea of someone dedicating all their thoughts and actions to him. He wanted someone to meet all of his physical and emotional needs. It made him feel powerful, validated. Michael is a complete narcissist."

Coal motioned for me to lay back on his chest between his arms. The warmth of his body and the beating of his heart caused me to immediately relax a little. My breathing slowed, and I could feel some of my tension melting away. He had such a soothing effect on me, the polar opposite of Michael.

"Well, what you told me only confirms what I already knew about you. You're an extremely wise woman," Coal spoke and nuzzled next to my head. "You recognized that he was toxic and you got out. Some people confuse a person's obsession with love. They get wrapped up in the drama and feed off of it. You saw it for what it was."

"Yeah, but it got really bad before I got out. He finally

agreed we could try for a baby. I think he knew I was at the end of my line, but at that point he was following me around. If I was going to a class at the gym, he would mysteriously be in the parking lot checking up on me. If I had to stop at the supermarket to pick up something for dinner, he would end up there. Sometimes I wouldn't even tell him where I was going, but he would miraculously be there. I didn't have a minute to breathe, no time to think about myself and what I wanted."

"Tracking your phone?" Coal guessed.

"Yeah, that's what I assumed anyway, and that's when I knew it was time to get out. I decided that that kind of relationship was not the best example for a child anyway, and I was also afraid of Michael passing his genes on to our child. Does that make me a bad person?" I asked, sitting up and looking at him seriously.

"No, it makes you smart, but now I am wondering if your mysterious packages are from Michael. Maybe he's fixating on you. He's spiraling because you've moved on. I'm not going to lie; it really concerns me."

I nodded my head lost in thought for a minute. I had really been trying to convince myself that it was something else. One of the reasons I left Binghamton and moved here was to create some physical distance between us. I hoped since his obsession was about him and not me that he would find a new person to fixate on.

"Thanks for sharing with me," said Coal earnestly. "I know it's not easy for you to trust right now. I can't blame you for that after hearing your story."

"Thanks for listening," I replied. "Now I don't want to talk about Michael anymore."

I got out of bed feeling lighter from sharing my tales and padded to my ensuite bathroom to wash my makeup off and brush my teeth.

While I was in there flossing, Coal came in and picked up the toothbrush I had given him to use the other day. We continued to get ready in peaceful silence. The prospect of such normalcy leaving me complete.

CHAPTER TWENTY-THREE

I woke up Monday morning with a smile on my face. I felt Coal's warm body next to mine, the gentle rhythm of his breathing and instead of feeling panic, as I did the previous time he spent the night, I felt a thrill. Coal slept peacefully, and the alarm didn't go off yet, so I took my cell phone off of the floor on my side of the bed. Grabbing my forest green velvet robe, which hung on the bedpost, I crept out of the room quietly closing the door behind me.

The house felt so much less lonely with Coal sleeping in my bed. I went into the kitchen to get a glass of water and make coffee. After turning the fire on under the percolator, I decided to check my notifications on my phone. Yesterday was such a busy day, I didn't have time to even glance at my phone.

There was one new text from Fiona. She sent it about five minutes ago. She was obviously also a morning person like myself.

Good lesson? So much fun practicing together. Plans next Sunday morning?

Everything about yesterday was perfect. She was right; it was fun. It was so good to spend time with friends and not feel so stressed. I thought for a minute then fired off a text.

If we do it early. I have my lesson again, and then I'm

meeting Coal's parents. I added a yikes face to demonstrate my nervousness.

Oh, sounds serious! Fi teased me playfully.

Previously I didn't want to make it public that Coal and I were dating, but I suddenly wanted to shout it from the rooftops for everyone to hear.

Yeah, he's great. I added two red hearts. I blushed, even though she obviously couldn't see me through a text message.

The . . . appeared like Fi was writing and then disappeared. She was probably trying to figure out what to say.

I checked my other notifications, nothing of dire importance jumped out at me. Thinking about the pictures that I took at the restaurant, I tapped my phone app. I found it hard to believe that our dinner date occurred only the night before.

I smiled to myself as I reviewed the photographs from the restaurant. Coal had been trying to be a good sport and took our photo the way I showed him where you can't see the screen as you take it. It took so many tries. He kept cutting our heads off or only getting one of us in the picture. In this one picture, my favorite, my head was turned slightly to the side and I was laughing. It was a genuine laugh, the pure joy was depicted on my face, and Coal wasn't looking at the camera. He was looking at me. A look of adoration occupied his face. This was the one. I set to work cropping out a photobomber and brightening up the photo. The light from the firepit made our skin glow. I posted to Insta, *#sundaynight #adventurepartners #steakandmalbec #joy.*

Hearing a ping, I knew Fiona had finally responded.

Yay! So happy for you guys. Do we have a date tonight for the gym? I can't go on Wednesdays anymore, so I'd really like to go tonight.

Not having to think about it, I immediately responded. I looked forward to our classes together, and I wouldn't fall into the trap of spending every minute of my spare time with my boyfriend. I couldn't go down that road again after the way things turned out with Michael. My whole life revolved around him and look how that turned out.

Of course, I can't wait!

With the sound of the boiling coffee being pushed through the percolator, I stepped away from my phone and turned off the stove. Picking a mug stating *Dreams Do Come True* out of the cabinet, I fixed my coffee. My phone vibrated with more notifications. Taking my cafe, I walked to the kitchen table to continue checking my messages.

A new Insta notification popped up, so I checked it. Fiona liked my post and wrote:

Two of my favorites! She followed with two hearts.

My coffee tasted particularly good this morning. The rich caramel taste danced in my mouth. It smelled extra good too as I took in a breath and inhaled deeply. Isn't that the way it is when you are in love? All your senses are heightened, and anything seems possible. Why can't life always be like that?

From watching my mom and dad growing up, I learned some important lessons. Their relationship was a love story for the ages. They had a relationship of mutual love and respect. They fought yes, but they listened to each other and worked through their problems. Keeping love and passion alive is hard work, but they did it. After working, they spent special time together each and every day, coffee dates in the morning, working together in the garden, or an after work run. Just like anything else, if you ignore love it will die. It will wither away slowly while you're busy not noticing. Then when you go back to find it, it's not there anymore. Left in its place is only a void.

You can't expect to keep a plant alive without giving it sunlight and water daily. If you just leave it alone without care, it will start to dry out, droop, and die. To the contrary, if you overwater it, the roots will rot and die. It is a precarious situation. People want love, but they don't want the work that comes with it. It is a delicate situation that only works when both people are doing the work. Love is a two-way street. One way love is toxic. That's why I decided to end my marriage of ten years. I know I felt like a failure, but it was an impossible situation. You can't love someone who only loves themself.

At that moment, sitting at the table sipping my cafe, I had an epiphany. Suddenly it was clear to me that I made the right decision walking away from my marriage; I exhaled as if finally being able to breathe. I had been holding my breath for so long it was no wonder that I had been having anxiety attacks. Now that I truly acknowledged this fact, I could begin to heal.

Walking to the stove, I decided to put on another coffee for Coal and bring it to bed for him. While I waited for it to be done, my thoughts turned to my party coming up. It was now T minus 5 days until the big day.

I checked my email notification and saw that our Halloween costumes were due to arrive today before 8 pm. With that exciting prospect, I took our two coffees and climbed up the stairs to my bedroom.

Quietly opening the door, I crept into the room placing a mug of steaming coffee on the bedside table nearest Coal. I was careful to place it on the marble coaster, so as not to leave a condensation ring on the delicately stained wood.

I went to my side of the bed and climbed in, precariously holding my coffee and gathering the goose down comforter around me. The bed never felt more comfortable, I thought, closing my eyes and sipping the coffee. I felt like I was sitting on a cloud.

I immediately heard a welcome husky voice, "Now *this* is a sight to wake up to."

My eyes flew open, as I turned to a sleepy-eyed Coal grinning.

"Morning sleepy head," I leaned down to kiss his forehead.

"I know I always ask you what you're thinking, but it's usually because I'm worried about you." Coal said, looking up at me propped up with the plush pillows behind me. "This morning I'm happy to ask you what you're thinking because of that peaceful look on your face."

"This is right," I simply stated.

"What is?" Coal asked for clarification.

"You and me."

"Can you put your coffee down for a minute?" Coal asked.

I turned to the right and placed my coffee down on my nightstand.

"Ok, now what?" I asked playfully.

Coal nearly tackled me. I felt the weight of his heavy muscular body on mine. He gently held my wrists and kissed me passionately. I felt it down to my core.

The short journey to work was better than usual as Coal and I drove together. I told him we should take two cars since I was going to my exercise class after work, but he insisted he would drop me back off at home straightaway.

It's amazing how much your life can change in just a few short weeks, for better or for the worse. Lucky for me in this case, it was for the better. I've had it the other way my fair share of times, probably why I'm always waiting for the other shoe to drop.

"What should I do about food for this party?" I wondered aloud as I was relaxing in the passenger's seat, while Coal navigated the way. It was so nice to be able to make casual conversation on the way to work and have someone to bounce ideas off of.

"It's a Halloween party. Just get appetizers. It's a junk food kind of day, right?" he asked.

This was not the response I was looking for, but I didn't want to hurt his feelings. "Well, I figured since it's a house-warming party, as well as being my first solo party ever, I wanted it to be a little fancier." I frowned trying to think what I should do.

As we pulled into the parking lot, as luck would have it, both Samantha and Fiona were getting out of their cars. When they spotted Coal's car, they both stopped and waited, smiling and chatting with each other. From the angle we were at, they probably couldn't see that I was occupying the passenger's seat.

"Here's your greeting committee," I said with a genuine laugh.

Coal smirked in response. "*Our* greeting committee."

After parking, I emerged from the passenger side door. I was wearing my pleated burnt orange accordion skirt with my cream Victorian necked blouse. I finished the look with a long wool camel colored wrap coat to keep me warm. Both of their faces changed as they watched. Fiona's eyes grew as wide as saucers while Samantha's mouth was hanging open.

"Morning ladies," Coal said in the way of a cordial greeting. He looked extra handsome today in a crisp white dress shirt, navy blue straight legged trousers, and a black pea coat. I couldn't blame the women for swooning when they saw him.

Their pairs of eyes darted back and forth from Coal to me, to Coal, and then settled on me. It looked like they had practiced it for a play.

"Hi guys," I said cheerfully, meeting their eyes as I spoke. To her credit, Fiona pulled it together rather quickly, but Samantha still hadn't closed her mouth.

"I can't wait for Saturday," I started. "Our costumes are

arriving tonight." I added nearly jumping up and down.

"Our?" Samantha asked, taking a currish tone. She had now regained her composure and switched gears. Her superior attitude had returned

"Yes, Coal's and mine," I answered not letting her snide tone affect me in the slightest.
"How about you guys?"

We walked as a unit into the building, stopping in the office to sign in and collect our lunch counts.

"Yeah, mine is arriving tomorrow," Fiona answered, ignoring the weird tension that Samantha had attempted to create. "What time is the party again?"

We all walked down the hallway towards our rooms. "Six, but you can come early if you want," I added looking at Fiona. "We can have pre-party cocktails."

"How about you Samantha?" Coal asked, a wry smile taking shape on his face. "Did you get your costume yet?"

Samantha suddenly became uncomfortable. She understood by Coal's tone and face that he was annoyed. She couldn't care less how I felt, however Coal's opinion of her obviously mattered.

"Oh, yeah I'm not sure yet," her pale skin had reddened from embarrassment. "I just didn't know if Ava got costumes for everyone."

"Oh, no. We just got couple's costumes. That's why they're arriving together," he clarified, giving me a wink.

I winked back and Samantha couldn't hide the annoyance on her face. I wanted to tell her that she shouldn't make that face, or she would cause her skin to prematurely wrinkle.

"Is your car in the shop?" Samantha asked, turning to me, daring me to tell her more.

"No," answered Coal before I had a chance to respond. "I slept over at her house last night, so we came in together." He squeezed my hand as he said it.

The ladies were obviously shocked that he brazenly

announced this information. Fiona kept a tight-lipped smile, and Samantha looked like an angry tomato. I almost laughed out loud.

Fiona's face looked worried all the sudden.

"What's the matter?" I asked Fiona.

"It's just, do we still have a date for the gym tonight? I was really excited about it."

"Of course, I wouldn't ditch you," I looked at her warmly. "Coal is going to drop me back at my house, and then I'll meet you there with my car."

The stress fell away from her face. "Oh great! Maybe we can get dinner after?" she asked.

"That would be perfect. We can either get food to go, or we can go out. We'll see how we feel."

We had been carrying on this conversation lingering outside my classroom. Samantha was the first to break away.

"I have to go get things organized for my day," Samantha stated, suddenly all business. "See you guys later." She abruptly left, looking at no one in particular.

When Samantha had departed, I said goodbye to Coal and pulled Fiona into my classroom.

"OMG," Fiona said the second that the door closed. "Does this mean what I think it means?" she asked.

"What do you think it means?" I asked innocently, widening my eyes and trying to register confusion on my face.

"You two totally hooked up," she nearly screeched.

I laughed and responded, "A lady never talks."

Fiona playfully hit me on the arm. "I'm really happy for you. I know it was hard for you when things didn't work out with Michael"

"Thanks, Fi," I said, touched by the sentiment. "How are things going with your mysterious man?" I raised my eyebrow as I questioned her.

"Surprisingly good," Fi answered giggling. She seemed so young at that moment.

"Are we going to meet this mystery man soon?" I asked. "Has your mom met him yet?"

"Yes and no. You will meet him when I'm sure it's going somewhere, and no, mom has not met him. She was thrilled however when I told her I started seeing someone."

I nodded my head. "See, she just wants you to be happy," I affirmed.

Fiona bobbed her head, in agreement, however her eyes told a different story. I guess I couldn't judge. I haven't had a mom on the scene since I was a teenager, so who knows what type of relationship we might have had.

"Well, I guess I should go," she said hesitantly. We both were obviously not eager to get this week going. "I'm doing a lesson on texture today and need to get my materials ready."

"Ok, well, I'm looking forward to tonight," I said waving to her as she went to exit the classroom. I suddenly remembered Samantha stalking my house.

"Wait," I said as she reached for the door knob.

"What's up?" she asked, surprised by my sudden outburst.

"I know you have to go, but I just wanted to tell you something about Samantha." Now I had caught her interest. She moved back towards my desk and waited for me to speak.

"I caught her sitting outside my house the other night. It was the night Coal was putting up my cameras. I looked outside for my mail, and she was sitting in front of my house looking at her phone, so she didn't see me approaching. When I got up to the window, I could see she had on sunglasses, and it was already dark out."

"What? Are you serious?" she asked in disbelief.

"Weird, right?" I asked her for confirmation.

"Um yeah." Fiona totally agreed as she stood there playing with one of her corkscrew curls.

"You should go," I said. "I didn't mean to hold you up. I just wanted to see what you thought about it. Coal talked to her, and she said she just wanted to see where I lived. Coal thinks it's legitimate, but I don't."

"Of course, he believes her. Men don't understand the dynamics between women. Women act very differently with men than they do with other women," Fiona explained.

"Exactly, that's why I wanted to get a woman's opinion. Why do you think she would have done that? Has she said anything to you?" I knew that Fiona and Samantha were friends for much longer than she and I were. However, we seemed to have an instant bond, probably because of our moms, so I felt comfortable asking her. I didn't want to say too much though because I didn't know where her allegiance lie.

Fiona shook her head. "She hasn't said anything per se. She asks me questions about you, but she's never said anything negative." She was quiet for a minute, probably contemplating how to phrase her response. "I think that Samantha is just used to being the alpha female."

"So, let her be who she is. What's that got to do with me?" I was perplexed by Fiona's statement.

"She's used to being number one. Your kids love you so much that the kids in her class all say they wish they were in your class. She used to flirt with Coal all of the time, and now that you're here, she probably feels invisible."

"Oh," I said, "I had no idea."

I stood quietly for a moment lost in thought. Maybe I should do something nice for her.

"Just a shot to her ego I think," Fiona said, "but it doesn't justify her stalking your house."

"Yeah, but now I feel bad. I'm sure she's an amazing teacher," I said brightly." I wouldn't want her to think that I would try to make it seem like she wasn't. What I do has nothing to do with what she does, but I don't want her to see me as a threat."

Now I had a feeling of dread in my gut. I know what it's like to feel bad because of another person. Whether they did it intentionally or intentionally, it still hurts.

"Sorry to run, but I really do have to go. We'll talk more tonight," said Fiona running out the door, her curls bouncing behind her.

As soon as Fi left the room, I received a text from Coal.

Lunch date today?
Yes please!

We made sandwiches this morning from the cold cuts that I had at home. Nice turkey sandwiches with provolone cheese on Portuguese rolls, very domestic of us.

Your room or mine? He asked suggestively, adding a wink with a kiss after it. I felt my cheeks warm.

Yours. I'll meet you there after I drop the kids off for lunch. Make it a candle lit lunch!

I placed my phone on the desk and walked away from it, not wanting thoughts of Coal to distract me any further from the task at hand. It was fruitless, but I had to at least try.

After dropping off my students in the cafeteria, I swung by my room to pick up my lunch bag and water bottle. I knocked on Coal's door before entering. I was venturing into uncharted territory.

His room was so much cooler than mine. I took in my surroundings before even looking at him. He had an antique stained rocking chair in the corner where his students could sit and read books. Carved wooden mahogany bookends sat on his shelf that held treasured books that were lovingly worn with time. He had a wall hanging with carved raised wooden letters that spelled out Mr. Blake.

"Well done Mr. Blake," I said, finally locking eyes with him. He had a rectangle table, probably utilized for his writing conferencing, set up with a tablecloth. He placed an unlit candle in the middle of the table. Coal folded two plain white napkins in half into neat rectangles. Two red solo cups were placed in front of where our food would sit.

"I've reserved our very best table in the place," he said walking with me over to where we would have our lunch. "I can't light the candle, fire codes and all, but I found a candle in my science kit!" He stopped for a minute looking proud of himself. "Who said fourth grade wasn't romantic?"

Grinning, I took a seat right next to the bookshelf where Coal's guided reading books were stored. At least in his room the chairs were more regular sized. When Coal sat down too, we locked eyes, a fire was immediately ignited in my belly. Oh no, I thought Maybe lunch alone wasn't a good idea at school.

"I never thought school could be romantic, however you've managed to make it happen." I reached my hand out and locked fingers with him. "Is this even allowed?"

"If no one is here to see it," he said with a wink.

We ate our lunch side by side, both of us grinning like idiots.

"I'm going to the gym with Fiona tonight, and then maybe dinner," I informed Coal.

Coal's face turned a mini frown. "Oh ok. Have fun." Then he made puppy dog eyes at me.

"I think our costumes are arriving today," I said cheerfully.

"Maybe we can try to put our costumes together tomorrow?" Coal asked hopefully, his eyes once again dancing.

"Yes," I reached for his hand once more. "I would love that."

At that moment Coal's classroom door flew open. I quickly released his hand as Samantha barged into his room.

"Oh," she said, making no effort to hide the fact that she was disgruntled that I was there.

"Hey Sam," Coal greeted her. "What's up?"

"You two look cozy."

"Not cozy enough," Coal retorted, "but as cozy as is permitted in an elementary school."

Samantha did not laugh. Her gaze was steely. Now we

just waited for her to tell us what she wanted.

"I was just wondering if you had that yardstick that I lent you? I'm teaching a measurement lesson today," she explained.

"Of course," Coal said, getting up and going over to a shelf where he kept all of his math manipulatives. Samantha tracked him with her eyes the entire time. She smoothed out an imaginary wrinkle in her plaid skirt and touched her curled platinum locks. She seemed hypnotized watching him.

"I was thinking of doing a class play with the kids for Christmas," I announced to Samantha, trying to make the situation less awkward.

"What?" she aggressively asked, her head snapping to gaze at me.

"A play, I'm thinking of having my students do a class play. Do you want to do one with your class as well? Then we could invite the kindergarteners and first graders to come watch us. It would be fun!"

Coal now joined us again and nodded his head in agreement.

Samantha contemplated what I said for a minute. I could see she had stopped herself from giving the knee jerk no response. She weighed her options in her head before begrudgingly nodding her head, "Yes, I think we could do that."

"Awesome, it's going to be so much fun. I have a book of plays for second grade, if you want to choose one from there, or you could just do your own thing. It's up to you."

She grimaced. I was really making an effort here, but she wasn't making it easy.

"Ok, I'll look at them. Thank you for my ruler," she said to Coal in a professional tone. "We'll talk about the play later. I don't want to interrupt your little lunch."

Samantha cast one last look at us and left, slamming the door abruptly before we could say goodbye.

"Ok, you were right," Coal admitted.

"About which thing?" I asked.

"She obviously has some sort of thing with you."

"Are you sure you weren't involved with her?" I asked, casting him a skeptical look.

"I told you before, I most definitely was not. We have always been friends. Whether her interests in me were more than platonic, she never said as much."

I remembered what Fiona told me about the kids. "Fiona said she's professionally jealous because some kids in her class were saying they wish they were in mine."

Coal looked at me knowingly, "Oh, that could definitely explain it at least partially. She takes great pride in being a good teacher. Seriously, she spends a crazy amount of time preparing and researching."

"That's why I suggested she do the play too. I knew that if I just did it, it would add fuel to the fire when her kids found out."

Coal leaned over and sneaked in a quick kiss. He moaned quietly when I reacted and kissed him deeper. "Just another reason why I love you. You're smart and sweet, and did I mention one hell of a kisser."

Coal pulled into my driveway at 3:45 pm. At least the daylight hadn't run away yet, but the minutes were limited. I spotted two packages stacked on my porch.

"Oh, those must be our costumes," I quickly jumped out of the car as soon as he parked.

Coal followed, "Well I want to see too."

As our shoes crunched on the falling leaves scattering the path, I spoke, "Definitely come in; I don't have class until 5:30."

Coal waggled his eyebrows up and down. I hit him on the arm. "You don't want to injure these arms, or I won't be able to carry your packages in for you," he pronounced, scooping up the packages while I fished around in my pocketbook for my keys.

"Let's bring them into the living room. I've never actually sat in there. It's kind of weird," I said as I headed to the left of the staircase rather than my usual route to the right.

This room was actually quite beautiful, I thought as we entered. It contained a berry red velvet sofa and two pink and berry red sitting chairs with extensive wood carving around the base of the seat.

Coal put the packages on the coffee table, and Coal sat in the middle of the couch. I placed myself directly on his lap.

"I thought you needed to go to the gym?" Coal said, looking at me seriously.

"I do," I answered innocently.

"You're not going to make it if you don't get off my lap. I'm only human," he nearly growled nibbling at my ear.

"Ok, Ok," I pouted, grudgingly extricating myself from his lap. "You're no fun at all."

I picked up the first box. "Do you have your handy knife?" I asked.

"Do I have my knife? Humph, what do you take me for?" he reached into his pocket, but came out empty handed. Coal looked at me sheepishly, "Actually I can't believe I'm saying this, but I don't."

"And you call yourself a man?" I teased him.

"Hey, that's a low blow and you know it," he pretended to be annoyed with me, but his eyes gave him away and were gleaming mischievously.

Coal got up and was going to go in search of something to open the box when his eye caught sight of something shiny in a basket on the book shelf across from the couch.

"I think that's a letter opener," Coal said, going to grab the item out of the container. He accidentally knocked it over sending the contents sailing across the room.

I got up and went over to help him collect the various items. There were four sheets of paper folded together. Before placing them back in the basket where they were previously, I unfolded them.

These were very similar to the ones we found in Aunt Ginny's vanity, only this time there was only one word written on each page. The top page read GET, the next YOUR, the third OWN, and the final MAN.

Coal stood there over my shoulder watching as I read each.

"Wow, there really was someone out there that your aunt managed to make angry. Look at that erratic lettering." He pointed to the jagged edges and non-uniformity in the forming of the words. "That's a special kind of rage."

"Her journal," I remembered. "Tonight, when I get home from going out with Fiona. I will begin reading from the beginning. I'll text you as soon as I find out anything. I really need to get to the bottom of this."

"I don't think you should leave those letters laying around, just in case. Let's bring them upstairs and put them in the secret room," Coal suggested.

"You've always wanted to say that, haven't you?" I said seriously. "Put them in the secret room."

"Shut up," he said, kissing me, and it worked. I remained silent as he pulled me down on the couch and lay on top of me. I felt the weight of his body bearing down on me. If we didn't stop this, I really wouldn't make it to my date with Fiona, and I didn't want to let her down.

"I really love you," I spoke hoarsely, taking a deep breath to slow my heart down, "but I really do have to meet Fiona. I'm so sorry." My feelings for him were becoming all consuming, like a fire that threatened to burn down a whole forest. It was so intense and scary. I was afraid it might become too strong and consume me as well.

CHAPTER TWENTY-FOUR

After Coal left, I went upstairs to get changed for the gym and to secure the letters in the hidden room. I went into the library and moved the sconce, just as Coal had done before when he tried to change the lightbulb. The wall popped open a crack, and I manually opened it the rest of the way. The room made me feel safe somehow. I felt like I had a secret with my Aunt Ginny. I was hoping I would hear her voice through these walls, like she would personally communicate with me.

After securing the room again, I brought our forgotten costume boxes into the kitchen for inspection at a later time. Meeting Fiona with five minutes to spare, she had our spots reserved and greeted me with a big smile.

"Ava," Fiona wrapped her strong, thin arms around me and hugged me tightly. "I was getting nervous with the time, but I knew you wouldn't let me down."

I scanned the room in search of the troublemakers. I saw the one mom; the one who asked about Fiona. I wanted to ask Fi about her, but she was in such a good mood that I thought better of it. The woman was so engrossed in something on her phone and wasn't paying the slightest bit of attention to us.

I looked toward the door and on cue, in sauntered Marcia. She was wearing head to toe black Lycra, her black glossy hair pulled in a low ponytail. She looked very ninja-like.

"Ladies," she said as she passed by our spot. Was that

just a smile I saw? I wondered to myself.

That was the most amicable I had ever seen her. Guess someone was having a good day, or perhaps my invite to the party had actually paid off. I smiled to myself.

"Hope everyone came ready to work," she shouted as she attached her voice amplifier around her waist and put the headset on. "Let the Journey begin!" she screamed like a Viking warrior.

Class was extra good. There were no weird looks, no pointed comments, and I felt like a champion upon finishing. When we were walking out of the class, Marcia strode by us, "See you ladies on Saturday."

Fiona spoke as soon as she walked out of the glass doors. "Wow, you almost wouldn't know that she was the same person. She must be in love or something. Or perhaps she is a robot clone."

We both chuckled, and I nodded my head in agreement. Whatever the case, I was just happy that she wasn't taking her lousy mood out on me.

"What do you want to do about food?" I asked leaning on the table by the leather stools that we sat on, our first day at the gym together.

"I want to get something healthy," Fiona stated, patting her fitness model flat stomach. "Do you want to order salads, to go, from the diner?"

"Perfect," I answered. "Your house or mine?"

"Definitely yours. Your house is much nicer than mine," she said bluntly.

"I'm sure it's not," I said in response, "but who cares anyway."

"It's easy not to care when you have the nicest," she said firmly, but not unkindly. I guess she was right. It's like when you go out to dinner with a rich friend, and they are ordering a bottle of wine exceeding one hundred dollars and expecting to split the bill. Money's no object if you have it, and if you don't, it's a very big deal.

"It's not like I bought that house with my own money," I reminded her. I was no more accomplished than her. I wanted Fiona to know that, to know that I didn't think that I was better.

"*Exactly*," she said. "Let's go to your house."

That *exactly* seemed slightly hostile. I really didn't want to know what she meant by it, so I didn't ask her. People never gave me special considerations when I was met by tragedy. It was just my lot in life, so by the same token, I shouldn't be judged for the bits of good fortune I did receive.

We brought up the menu for the diner on our phones. I scanned it tentatively trying to find just what I wanted. After browsing, I decided on an arugula salad with grilled chicken, avocado, cranberries, and no dressing. I'd put balsamic on it myself at home. It's great to hang out with friends who are health conscious, I thought. If I had been hanging out with Coal, I'd be eating something that contained no less than 900 calories, I was sure.

I placed the order via Grub Hub to have it delivered, this way we could go right to my house.

Fiona followed me, parking right next to me in the driveway. As soon as I heard the resounding thud of my car door as it closed, I felt a freezing wind hit my body which was still damp with sweat from the class.

"Let's hurry, it's freezing," I said, clutching my coat to my body. The wind sent a chill through my body. Prior to this we've had a very mild autumn, even warm, but it seemed tonight like the seasonal weather was coming for us. It felt like a harbinger of harsher things to come.

I shut the front door with a sigh of relief and quickly disabled the alarm.

"I forgot that you were getting an alarm," Fiona said, watching me. "How is it working for you? Has anybody bothered you lately?" she inquired.

"Not really, it's been pretty quiet," I said, the relief evident in my voice. "I won't set it right now because they will be delivering our food shortly."

I hung Fiona's and my coats in the hall closet, and then led the way into the kitchen. I saw the boxes sitting there where Coal and I had abandoned them. With the second set of notes we had found, we totally forgot about checking out our costumes.

I gestured to the boxes on the counter, "Those are our Halloween costumes."

Fiona approached wanting to take a look. She was waiting for me to open them.

"Sorry," I said, shaking my head, "I can't open them yet. I promised Coal that we would do it together."

"Of course," Fiona said in response and settled in comfortably on a chair in the kitchen.

"I'm not sure what to do for food for this party," I said for the second time that day.

Fiona looked at me thoughtfully; her eyes lit up. "Why don't you make a buffet with Italian pasta dishes? It's easy to make, and it feeds a lot of people. I can make a nice salad on the side." She seemed excited at the prospect.

"That sounds like a good idea," I said, happy to get another person's perspective.

"Are you a good cook," Fiona asked me seriously.

"Actually, I am," I paused while taking a sip of water. "I haven't lived with my parents since high school, so I really didn't have a choice but to learn."

Fiona picked up her phone and began tapping. "I'm writing to mom to ask if she can help out and make her famous chicken francaise."

"Oh, you don't have to do that," I insisted, not wanting to put anybody out.

"She wouldn't have it any other way. She actually asked me if you needed her to do anything to help."

My phone buzzed on the kitchen counter.

I'm making chicken francaise, the message read. *No arguments.*

I laughed and shook my head, "You two are too much."

"That's what family does," Fiona said, eyes twinkling. "They stick their nose into your business by setting up an alarm system for you, that you didn't ask for, and they cook food." She laughed. "I know I complain when my mom is in my business, but this doesn't bother me. It's your business. She is just being helpful." This time she threw her head back and laughed really hard. Her shiny straight white teeth gleaming.

"Brrring, brrring." The bell rang, and I walked to the front door. Fiona was on my heels.

A probably eighteen-year-old teenager with light brown hair and freckles sprinkled across the bridge of his nose was waiting on the other side of the door. He handed me the brown paper bag that was stacked with our two salads inside. It was stapled on the top to prevent them from falling out in the car. I handed him the money with an extra five-dollar-bill for his tip, in exchange for the salads.

"Thanks," he grinned wildly, pocketing the money and walking off with a bounce in his step.

"I didn't get to pay," Fiona said, holding money in her hand. "Here's a ten." She insistently tried to place the money in my hand.

"Family buys you food," I retorted, smirking and refusing the money.

"Do you want tea with dinner?" I asked as Fiona opened the brown paper bag and sorted out our salads. "I need some to get warm from that cold chill," I finished, shivering.

"Ok, that sounds good," she said brightly. I handed her two forks and put on the kettle.

I took out two random mugs and plopped one of the

round teabags down in the bottom of each. I put the sugar bowl and a teaspoon on the table and gave us each a mini spoon to stir with.

"So, I'm planning to do a Christmas play with my class," I announced as I sat for a minute taking a bite of my salad.

A look of worry slowly crept into Fiona's face.

"Don't worry, I already told Samantha about it and asked her to do it with us."

"See, I knew you were a smart one," Fiona replied, her smile slowing returning.

"Yeah, she came into Coal's room at lunch to get her yard stick and was really weird to both of us. That's when I decided to broach the subject of the play. At first, I thought she was going to say no, but in the end, she said OK."

"I hate feeling like I'm tip-toeing around her," Fiona admitted. "It's not as bad for me because I don't have the same kind of job as her, being the art teacher and all. I feel for you. Especially at the same grade level, that's rough." She finished with a sympathetic smile.

The tea kettle began to emit a high-pitched whistle, and I got up to shut it off. I poured the boiling water over the tea bags and placed them on the table.

"Thanks so much," Fiona said, grabbing the mug in front of her. She looked at it as she held it in her hands, probably for warmth. "Ah, Miss. New York 1994. Mom was always really envious of your Aunt Fiona for this. She never said it, but I saw the way her mood would shift whenever it was brought up, like a sudden unexpected storm. Her demeanor would change, a black cloud forming over her head that would take some time to go away."

"Really?" I asked, surprised. "I would never have guessed that. Your mom is probably the most confident woman I have ever met."

Fiona pulled a face, as if she didn't agree with me or it annoyed her.

"She's a very good actress," Fi finally said.

"How are things going with Peter?" I asked, sipping my tea. I could feel its warmth finally seeping into me and doing its job.

"Good, I guess. They hang out a few times a week. She gets really giggly when he is around, so I take that to mean she likes him." She said, rolling her eyes and stopping to take a big bite of grilled chicken from her salad.

I nod. "That's good. Do you think she'll ever settle down and get married? It must be lonely for her now that you aren't living there?"

"Well, she better, otherwise I don't know why she's pushing me so hard to find someone and settle down."

"She probably wants grandbabies," I laughed.

"She'll never tell anyone she's a grandma. She'll probably have them call her glam mom,"

We were both bent over laughing now. I caught my reflection in the glass of the windowpane. It looked so right to be here laughing with Fiona. It felt so normal. My days being married to Michael were nothing like this. There was a lot of loneliness, tension, and resentment. The days filled with laughter were scarce even in our dating

"So glad you came over tonight," I said genuinely.

Fiona looked a little embarrassed, like she's not used to a compliment, but then said, "Me too."

Fiona left about an hour later, and I was so tempted to call up Coal and tell him to come over. I stopped myself three different times from reaching for the phone. I busied myself with grading the papers in my bag from our science lesson about the character traits of scientists.

You wouldn't think being inspired by a second- grade science lesson was possible, but I had been thinking all day about what we discussed. It was going around and around in my mind. In order to be successful in life, in all areas, you needed to have a growth mindset, not a fixed mindset. During our lesson, we were particularly discussing how a scientist or engineer needs this mindset to be successful with problem solving and inventing new things.

Some traits of a growth mindset include: embracing challenges, learning from setbacks, being inspired by others' success, knowing that learning is a process that you don't always get right the first time, and knowing that success takes hard work and time.

On the contrary, for a fixed mindset you ignore criticism, give up easily, have negative thoughts that you are a failure, think you can never improve, and you think that intelligence and talent are fixed.

Ever since my parents' accident, I had been trying to be perfect. I was afraid of making a mistake. Mistakes lead to failure, in their case death, and I felt alone. I had no one to help me pick up the pieces if things failed. No, failure was not an option for me. My quest for perfection led me to be successful, despite my circumstances, however it left me emotionally challenged. It dawned on me that I was trying to accommodate Samantha because I saw a lot of myself in her. We both had a fixed mindset but different aspects of it haunted us.

She had an idea of who she was and saw anyone that was successful as a threat. She was linking her success to mine, meaning if I was successful, then she couldn't be. Thinking from an outside perspective, this is obviously not true. When you are emotionally involved, it is not that obvious.

I was not like Samantha in that way. Other peoples' success made me happy. However, I had a problem accepting criticism. I was not ok about not getting it right the first time. I felt like I had one chance, and if I messed it up, it was over. If someone criticized what I did, then obviously what I did wasn't good enough. When you're trying with all you have, not good enough is crushing. If it wasn't good enough, then I might as well not even try. From the outside it is clear this is not true. We all have room to grow. No one is perfect, and just because you might need to work on one aspect of something, it does not equate to being a failure. If scientists took on this attitude, we wouldn't have three quarters of the inventions that we have now.

As I sat there grading, I wrapped it all up in my mind. If we can learn to change the way we think, we can be more successful in the future. I can't do anything about the last ten years other than learn from them. I resolved that, that was what I would do.

I shook my head realizing the wisdom that was imparted to me from an elementary school lesson. The thing about life is the information is often there, but we are just not in a place to receive and apply it. Leaving Michael and removing myself from a bad situation put me in a place where I could now see clearly.

Although I resolved to not call Coal, I did want to check my phone, so I located it in my coat pocket. There were two messages from him. I couldn't help but smile. I felt like I had telepathically sent him a message, and he had in turn responded.

Hope you're having fun with Fi. Tell her I said hi.

Twenty minutes later there was another one.

I miss you so much. P.S. We never looked at our costumes. It was followed by a sad face emoji.

My heart tugged in my chest, but I couldn't resist teasing him as I wrote back.

Fiona and I tried on the costumes. They look great!
Coal sent back a sad face.
Why did I insist on torturing him?

Just kidding. The boxes are on the kitchen counter waiting for you. xx P.S. I miss you more.

The longing to see him was physical. Never in my thirty-something years have I felt like this. My heart ached for him.

Tomorrow???

Yes, definitely tomorrow. I'm going to go read the diary now. I will text you in a bit. xx

With that I put all my papers neatly back into my brown leather bag in preparation for school tomorrow. I wanted to wash my face and change into bed clothes before settling down with Aunt Ginny's diary. I pulled out a pair of gray cashmere pants that were warm, cozy, and way too big for me. On top I adorned myself with a giant blush colored fleece that looked like cotton candy. My red hair was wild and curly all around me. I spread Noxzema on my face and removed my makeup from the day. After applying a generous amount of moisturizer, I was ready for my task at hand. I remembered to fetch the skeleton key out of the jewelry box. I looped the ribbon around my neck. The key danced around my chest ready to do its job.

Taking a deep breath upon opening the door to the library, I shivered. It was quite cold in this room filled with the tales of hundreds of people. Their silent stories quietly occupied the room waiting to be given a voice. I glanced at the fireplace and saw that there were some wooden logs stacked on a black metal rack alongside the hearth, along with some old newspapers.

Nervous about the impending task at hand, I decided the chore of making a fire might calm my nerves some. I opened the flue and crumbled up sheets of the newspaper, placing them under the metal grate that the logs were then situated on. Locating a box of long wooden fireplace matches, I lit the newspaper under the logs.

The room was immediately bathed in the glow of the fire. I stood for a minute mesmerized by its gleam. My stomach was in knots. I knew I had to go read Aunt Ginny's story and give life to it, but I was scared. I wasn't even precisely sure why. I knew if I called Coal or Fiona, they would gladly have sat and read with me, but I knew this was something that I needed to do alone.

The smell of the fire began to fill the air, giving the library a cozy feel. I crept over to the book ladder and moved it over to where the sconce was. For the second time that day, I opened the secret passage.

Although I left the bookcase door open for the warmth of the fire, I immediately turned the lights in the little room on.

The room was warming at this point. I was no longer shivering, and I braced myself as I put the key into the lock and opened the hidden compartment that housed the leather-bound journal. It was right there where we had left it. I placed the new series of letters, that Coal had accidentally found, into the compartment. I had left them on the ledge in the room in my haste to meet Fiona. It was only appropriate that this secret room contained all the undisclosed details of Aunt Ginny's life. In a way it felt wrong prying into matters that weren't mine to know, however if someone hurt her, I needed to get to the bottom of it.

I sat down in the wine-colored leather seat and held the book in my lap. I glanced at the bar cart and decided to pour myself a glass of malbec for courage.

From the vantage point of my chair in the secret room, I could see the fire burning, I had my glass of Argentinian wine, and I sighed as I opened to the very first page of the diary.

Friday January 1, 2021

Happy New Year! Last night was beautiful. What better way to ring in the new year than in the City of Lights?! We danced the night away. The party was located in a building on the Seine. I glanced out at the river and the white lights below as the tango music swooned around us. It was like being in a dream. As the clock struck midnight, I was doing ochos. We then stopped to make a champagne toast and wish everyone around us happiness in the new year. This year my resolution is to find love and embrace it. I've lived a beautiful life. I was blessed with a happy marriage, but it ended much too soon leaving me empty. Since then, true love somehow managed to elude me like a butterfly that doesn't want to be caught. I have been in my own way. I am ready to be caught.

I wonder who she was with in Paris? How sad that she was ready to open her heart again, and her life was cruelly snatched from her. I felt a profound moment of sadness for all that was lost too soon, for life that was not lived.

Saturday January 2, 2021

Tomorrow we fly home, but today we enjoy one more day in Paris. Spent the morning drinking cafe au lait and croissants at a little bistro table in a cafe. We had window seats and watched the snowflakes fall as we sipped our coffee. Is there anything more romantic? We were by the carousel by the Eiffel Tower when I stopped him and let him know about my resolution. I let him know that I was ready to open my heart. He was so happy he actually cried. I saw actual tears forming in his eyes, and my heart was happy thinking about the possibility for the future.

CHAPTER TWENTY-FIVE

I read a few more days of diary entries and became very invested in Aunt Ginny's life, intrigued really. I stopped when I finished my glass of malbec. I didn't find out anything that would help our investigation, but I did get a lot of insight into her as a person. She was always my lovely glamorous aunt, however the adults in a family don't often share the personal details of their lives with younger family members. My only wish in this whole thing was that although she was no longer with us, that she wouldn't see me reading her diary as an invasion of her privacy. I wouldn't even be doing it if there weren't urgent questions that needed to be answered.

I wondered, who was her mysterious love interest? Where was he now? Did they break up before she died? Was he at her funeral? I probably brushed right past him and didn't have an inkling of who he was. Instead of getting answers, I had so many more questions.

I closed up the library tightly and went back downstairs to double check that the house was secured and that the alarm was engaged. The front motion detector light was on, so I stood for a minute looking out the front window, but there was no one in sight. Not even Lila slinking around the bushes.

Climbing up the stairs, I couldn't get my mind off of Aunt Virginia. She had no idea when she wrote that diary entry on New Year's Day of this year that in August she would be gone. It was spooky. I guess that's why we need to live life to the fullest. We really have no idea from one day to the next. Tomorrow is not promised to anyone.

I called Coal as soon as I settled into bed. I propped up the pillows so I could sit in bed comfortably. It was lonely without him by my side. He picked up on the first ring.

"Hello love," he said before I had a chance to say anything.

"Hi," I answered, excited to hear the sound of his voice on the other end. I stretched out in bed and wished I could reach over and touch him.

"So, did you find out anything?" Coal asked curiously.

"Not really. I did find out that she was either interested in someone or perhaps more seriously involved with them. She was very sketchy about details, but I do know that she was looking for love." I got quiet for a minute thinking to myself. "I wonder why she never told me. We spoke often. She was always discussing work or asking how I was." I felt slightly wounded that she didn't confide in me.

"I wonder if Amber knew, I mean they were best friends. Surely she told her. Maybe you should bring it up?" Coal suggested.

I was quiet for a minute. "I want to read more. I want to keep her diary private, just for me. I'm afraid if I tell Amber, she'll want to see it. I don't think that's what Aunt Ginny would have wanted."

"No, I totally get it," Coal said.

Then his voice changed, it was lower, huskier, "Completely unrelated but I really, really miss you. I know that I'm probably totally losing cool points right now telling you this, but I do."

"I almost called you on three separate occasions after Fiona left and asked you to come over," I admitted.

"You should have," Coal answered. "I would have been right over, without even thinking."

He couldn't see me, but I smiled happily to myself.

"Oh, by the way, when I went downstairs to make sure

the house was locked up and alarms were set, the front motion light was on. Is there any way to check the video footage? It was probably just Lila again, but is it possible to do?" I asked.

"Of course," Coal said. "How long ago was it? Write the time down and tomorrow I'll show you how to check the footage on the app."

I glanced at the clock. It was probably ten minutes ago now. I wrote down 11 pm in the notepad on my phone, as I spoke to Coal on speakerphone.

"Well, as much as I hate to leave you, we better get to bed," I announced, longing in my voice.

"I know," returned Coal.

I should have just asked him to come over earlier I thought but didn't say. I don't know what I was trying to prove by torturing myself.

"So tomorrow we'll check out our costumes and peruse your video footage. Should I come over right after school?"

"Well, I have to run tomorrow. I should probably do it first, while there is still at least some light out," I announced.

"I'll come with you," Coal suggested, sounding excited at the prospect.

"I didn't know you ran," I said, surprised at Coal's suggestion.

"I do now, if I can be with you and keep you safe."

"You don't have to do that. I know that running is torturous for nonrunners," I laughed out loud. "It's even torturous for runners that run on purpose."

"It's my pleasure, really," he insisted. "I'll bring clothes with me and change at your house. You can't see me, but I'm wiggling my eyebrows right now."

I laughed. "You can't feel me, but I'm hitting you right now."

The next day at school I arrived bright and early, excited to have some quiet time in my room to catch up on grading and set up for the day. I was stunned to find Samantha standing by my classroom door awaiting my arrival. I almost felt she was a mirage, as I couldn't fathom why she would be waiting for me.

"Hi," she said brightly. Her hair was curled into waves down her back. She was wearing a long-sleeved v neck purple dress with ruching around the center. She paired it with silver high heels and dangling silver earrings. I did a second glance at her because I was wearing the exact same dress only in dark pink. My hair was also down in waves, only I had black heels and earrings instead. She didn't seem fazed though because I had yet to take off my coat, so she couldn't see my outfit in its entirety .

"Samantha, what's going on?" I asked, trying to appear friendly. I was carrying my heavy bag and wanted to go in and put it down. "Come in," I said, motioning for her to follow me into my room.

"I wanted to see the book with the Christmas plays. If there is something good in there, I want to start right away with my students, so we can put on a star performance." She tossed her blond locks for effect. "Otherwise, I am going to get busy searching for something else," she explained.

I deposited my big leather bag and pocketbook on my swivel chair, and I took off my coat and hung it on the back of it. That's when she got a full scan of my outfit. Her eyes raked over me, and I laughed.

"Yeah great minds think alike I guess," I said, handing her the book of plays that I had on my desk.

She took it and smiled sweetly, "Thanks." She didn't even comment on the identical outfits which made it kind of weird.

"I'm doing the third one with my kids," I said, leaning next to her to show her, "*The Christmas Reunion*. I already made copies of it, so you are welcome to borrow the book and give it back when you've decided." I was desperate to get her to leave my room.

"Ok, thanks. By the way, I got my costume for the party. I'm really excited about it. Do you need me to bring anything?" she asked, pretending to be a normal person.

"No, I think I have everything taken care of," I lied, but at least thanks to my conversation with Fiona, I at least had my ideas in place.

"I'll get this back to you as soon as possible," she said, pursing her lips together. "I told Mrs. Avery that you and I were going to do the plays, and she was very excited. She said it was a great idea and that the little kids would love it," she practically shrieked that last bit. "She also likes to see collaboration between colleagues."

"Oh good," I said, trying to keep my voice even. I had to force myself to keep my face neutral when what I was thinking was, how dare she tell Mrs. Avery when this was my project?

The second she left I picked up my phone, but I held it in my hand thinking. I couldn't decide if I should text Coal or Fiona, but I eventually decided to write to Fiona.

OMG, are you here yet?

I didn't get an immediate response, so I decided to take out my pile of ungraded spelling sentences and get to work. I flew through the papers, leaving comments as I went. Then I signed into my grading website and entered the grades.

My phone indicated I had a message. I picked it up anxious to talk to Fiona.

Hey, just got here! Sorry, Samantha ambushed me in the hallway. I'll be right there!

I took a deep breath and clicked on the app for the Bundle Board. Then I brought up my attendance page, so I could take care of it as soon as the students arrived.

I heard the door click and looked up to see Fiona walking through. She was still wearing her dark navy pea coat and silver hat. Her curls were trying to escape out of it.

"Morning," she said, handing me a jumbo-sized cup of steaming coffee.

I got up from my chair and greeted her. Carefully taking the cup, I gave her a hug, "You're the best!" I exclaimed.

"So, what's going on? Your text sounded desperate."

"Did Samantha say anything to you about me?" I asked already on the defensive.

"Like what?" she asked, clearly confused.

"You mentioned that you saw her in the hallway, didn't you? She was waiting for me at my classroom door when I got here, and she was coincidentally wearing the same dress as me. It is just a different color."

Fiona looked at me more closely. She laughed tilting her head back. "Twinning?"

"No, it's not cute," I responded.

Fi didn't look convinced.

"She went and told Mrs. Avery about our Christmas plays, and the way she said it, it sounded like she led her to believe it was her idea."

"Oh," her eyes widened, and her face took on a more serious expression. "So, what did you say to her?"

"Nothing, she didn't outright say she told Mrs. Avery that it was her idea, but you know she did," I pouted, sitting back down at my desk and taking the lid of my coffee to help it cool.

Fiona nodded seriously. "Yikes, I'm sorry. I don't know what to do with her. If you don't invite her, you're wrong, and when you do invite her, she steals credit."

I nodded at her assessment. This is why I called Fiona instead of Coal. He would probably say that she didn't mean anything by it. He had a way of trying to see the best in people that sometimes made me crazy. I knew that Fiona would understand.

"I can't believe we have to go pick up the kids already," I snarled, looking at the clock.

"Just make sure you take a selfie of the two of you twinning when you go to get the kids," she laughed as we made our way down the corridor.

Besides my annoying early morning run-in with Samantha, the rest of the day went quickly. I forgot all about the drama, as I was too busy wrangling twenty something second graders who were amped up for Halloween.

Coal and I walked down the hall at exactly 3:10 pm together, both of us anxious to start our day together. We opened the doors to reveal a cool, but still sunny fall afternoon. It was probably fifty-five degrees, but the sun made it feel like sixty.

"You look gorgeous today," Coal said, eyes sparkling, as we walked through the still packed parking lot to my car. "I love your dress." He kept his glance on my legs for an extra few seconds.

"Yeah," I asked, stopping to face him, "did you love it on Samantha too?"

"Samantha? What do you mean?" He was clearly confused and afraid he was in trouble with me for some unknown reason.

I let him off the hook and began laughing. "She was wearing the same EXACT dress only in a different color. Can you believe that?"

"Unlucky coincidence," Coal said, his sweetness not understanding my annoyance at the situation.

"Yes, it is an unlucky coincidence, but that's not the real reason I'm annoyed at her. I'll explain on our run. It's a beautiful afternoon. Let's get out quickly while it's still nice out.

Coal followed me to my house, and Peter was arriving home precisely the same time as us.

"Good afternoon," he called from his yard. He was dressed smartly as usual, and he was carrying an attache case.

"Hi Peter," Coal and I called in unison. We turned to

each other and laughed.

"Everything good?" he asked, a look of semi-concern on his face.

"Yeah, how about you?" I questioned.

"No, I'm good. It's just I saw a man I didn't recognize coming up your walk last night, when I was dragging out the garbage cans. Then I turned, and I didn't see him. Was it a friend of yours?" he asked.

"What time was this?" I asked, panic obvious on my face.

"It had to be around 11 pm. I was going to get ready for bed after I brought the trash out."

Coal and I looked at each other remembering our phone call last night. There was someone out there. My instincts told me that last night. I felt it in my gut.

"I didn't have anyone over then, but I also came downstairs to lock up, and I noticed that the motion lights were activated. I assumed it was a cat or some other animal."

"We're going to check the video footage as soon as we get back from our run," Coal said, looking at me sternly. "Please no more running alone until we get to the bottom or this."

I wasn't going to argue with him in front of Peter. I knew they would team up on me, so I just nodded.

"Please Ava," Peter joined in, I saw him make eye contact with Coal. "We don't want to see anything happen to you." He was so earnest that a sudden shot of fear overtook me.

"Don't worry you sweet men; I'm ok. I won't take any unnecessary risks," I finished.

Peter and Coal both looked at each other knowingly.

The minutes of daylight left were slowly slipping away, so we swiftly apologized and slipped inside to get ready for our run. I sent Coal to the downstairs bathroom to get ready, while I went up to my bedroom. I was worried if we went up together to change, that we would never actually make our run, and I seriously was in need of decompressing.

When I came downstairs, I was fully dressed in a matching chocolate brown long sleeved running shirt and leggings. I put my hair in a ponytail near the top of my head. My auburn locks spilled halfway down my back. Coal was standing in my kitchen in forest green athletic joggers and an oatmeal- colored thermal shirt. His pecs were obvious through the shirt. His biceps threatened to rip out of the material.

"You are the cutest runner I've ever seen," Coal said, coming to wrap those finely sculpted arms around me.

"You should talk, but I wouldn't use the word cute for you." I grabbed my pocketbook and keys and quickly ushered Coal out of the house.

"Who's driving?" Coal asked as I locked the front door.

"I will; I know where we're going," I reminded him, as I leaned over to unlock the passenger's side door from the inside.

I drove the ten-minute ride to Armory Square and found a parking spot in the identical spot that we parked on our first date. I figured it was good luck.

We crossed the street to where the Creek Walk began. Rather than parking a car at the end, I decided we would just run until we got to a mile and a half and then turn around and run back.

"Now I'm a new runner," Coal said with a smile, "so please take pity on me. None of your Navy Seal training."

"I appreciate your vote of confidence in my abilities," I laughed as we ran on the path along the sidewalk, "but I'm not really that fast of a runner. It took me a long time to work up any kind of endurance, and every time I start a run, I always feel terrible. The first mile is always the worst. After that it gets easy."

"So why do you do it then?" Coal asked sensibly.

"I do it for the end goal. I feel amazing when I'm done. It reduces my stress and also keeps my weight in check."

We kept following the path around, crossing over streets. Last time I went with Ava we did it from the other directions, and that way the path is more obvious. When you start this way, you are running down a lot of city streets first. You have to keep checking that you are going the correct way.

Coal stopped dead in his tracks on the corner of Erie Boulevard and Franklin Street.

"Are you ok?" I wondered if he was having trouble breathing.

"No, I'm good. Look," he demanded, pointing to an old art deco building.

"Oh yeah, that's the power company," I said casually.

"I know it is. It's also the most beautiful building in all of Syracuse. I have to stop and look at it every time I go by, especially on foot. Then you really have time to admire it. I appreciate things of great beauty. How do you think you caught my eye?" he asked, grabbing my hand and kissing it.

"The sun is about to go down. Let's just keep running a little longer, and then we can turn around," I suggested.

By the time we reached the amphitheater by the Inner Harbor signs, the sun had officially gone away. We stopped to admire the water and took a minute to breathe.

"This is a beautiful path," Coal said, "you see the city through such a different perspective."

I nodded in agreement. "You really do, when Fiona brought me here, I felt happy to be back in Syracuse. We both stood watching all of the water fowl that were on the grass near the water. You could see the mall in the distance.

Speaking of Fiona, I saw a couple running ahead. The girl's bouncy hair looked reminiscent of Fi.

"Fiona," I called out. It was dark, but I could have sworn I saw the girl's head turn slightly, but she kept going.

"Was that Fi?" Coal asked.

"I don't know," I shrugged. "I thought it was, but I guess not. We better turn around and head back. It's getting chilly."

Coal threw both of his arms around me in a bear hug. I felt momentarily warm.

"You were right, you know," Coal said.

"What about this time?" I asked, my voice muffled by Coal's chest.

"That first mile was awful," I pulled away and hit his arm, "but the last five minutes were easy, and this, this I could do my entire life."

He pulled me back for a kiss. This kiss was slow and magical, and just like that, the cold ceased to exist.

"Let's get back," I announced, watching one of the birds skid across the water.

Turning around and coming back the same way we had just gone we had to follow the signs for the path diligently. It was dark and easy to make a wrong turn.

"Please don't ever do this by yourself at night," Coal said. "We're having a hard time with the two of us watching."

I didn't say anything. Although I appreciated his concern, after the relationship that I had spent the last decade in, I wasn't making that promise. I just kept my eyes peeled for signs, and we ran.

Finally arriving where our car was parked, we decided to go to our bar. The one from that first night. It seemed like it was forever ago, when really it was only a matter of like two weeks. So much had changed in that short time. Being a Tuesday night, when Coal opened the door for me, there were several open tables to choose from. We sat at a high top in front of the window.

The waitress came over right away and took our drink order, and then we were left alone.

"Do you want to check the door camera while we're here?" Coal asked. "Or would you prefer to do it back at your house?" He watched me quizzically, awaiting my answer.

I thought for a minute. My eyes glanced around the restaurant. It was fully decorated for Halloween with witches, pumpkins, and zombies. It would probably be slammed this weekend. There was music playing, loud enough to give you privacy, but not so ear piercing that you had to shout. "Ok, let's do it here," I decided.

"Do you want to have dinner here as well?" Coal asked.

"Ok, this way we don't have to figure out what to do when we get back," I answered.

Coal waved the waiter down and asked for the food menu with a smile and a wave. The attentive waitress came right back and handed each of us a menu.

"I'll give you a few minutes," she said with a smile and walked back over to the bar.

"I'm getting shepherd's pie," Coal announced triumphantly. "What about you?"

I continued to scan the menu as Coal was speaking. "Well, I had a girly salad with Fiona last night, so I'm going to pretend I'm ten and order chicken fingers and fries." I laughed, delighted at the prospect.

Our waitress came back over with my martini and Coal's beer. We placed our order, and she walked away.

"I'd like to propose a toast," Coal said, holding up his beer glass. I followed suit and held up my martini glass. "To the most beautiful girl in all of Syracuse and to the luckiest guy that is bestowed the honor of witnessing her life."

We clinked glasses. My heart leaped at his proclamation.

"So, let's get down to business," I said after taking a sip of my dirty martini. I pulled up the app on my phone for the outside cameras and handed it to Coal.

He had me sign in, and then hit a few buttons.

"What time am I looking for again?" he asked.

I remembered what Peter had said. "Between 10:50 and 11:00 pm. "

Coal nodded and looked back down at the phone. I moved my chair closer to him, so I could get a better look at what he was seeing, a whole lot of nothing. It must be very boring to be on a stakeout and wait for something to happen,

I thought, feeling my mind wandering.

"Wait, there!" I shouted as I saw something akin to a shadow start to come into view and then disappear just as quickly. The motion light flickering on almost simultaneously.

Coal rewound it probably 5 times. It was hard to tell what you were seeing, but there was definitely a disturbance in the forcefield at 11:03 pm. We watched on. There was nothing else. We even watched as far as 11:20 pm, but the light never came back on.

We managed to finish our drinks during this whole process. The waitress came back carrying our food.

"Another round?" she asked, motioning towards our empty cups.

"Just water with lemon for me please," I answered somberly.

"Same, thanks," Coal said acknowledging the waitress then turning quickly back to the phone.

"What do you think?" I asked Coal, very frustrated.

"I think whoever it was saw the lights coming on, so they changed their mind about approaching the house any further." Coal looked at me grimly.

"Shady business," I responded, shaking my head, agreeing with his assessment.

"Let's eat, despite everything I'm starving," I announced, picking up my battered chicken finger and dipping it into the ranch dressing they provided. I always got hungrier when I was happy. I definitely wasn't a stress eater. When I was stressed, I simply ate to survive. When I was happy, I felt I could relax a little and enjoy myself.

"Well, I'm glad whoever it was, that they were deterred by the lights. However, I don't like that they were there to begin with, especially at 11 o'clock at night."

"Agreed," I said between mouthfuls.

Coal just sat there smiling, not eating his food.

"Is something wrong?" I asked, shoving a French fry in

my face.

"Nothing at all, I just love seeing you happy. I know it's a funny thing to say with all the drama going on in your life right now, but you seem . . . ok." He shook his head and grinned. "You amaze me, that's all." He lifted his hand and brushed my cheekbone.

"Do you want to hear what happened with Samantha?" I said, suddenly remembering my weird encounter with her this morning.

"Only always," Coal answered, finally taking a bite of his food.

I glanced around the half empty bar to make sure that no one I knew was there. The music was still on to disguise our conversation, but I didn't want to take any chances. There were two biker guys in the corner who appeared to be on their fifth beers. A young couple of barely twenty-one were on a date, sitting at the bar. Four women who were what would have been my mom's age were huddled together gossiping. No one here was listening to anything I had to say.

"So, when I came in this morning, she was standing in her matching dress," I couldn't help myself, "waiting outside my room. I don't know how long she was standing there, but she was just waiting for me to arrive."

"At least you didn't find her nosing around in your desk," Coal pointed out.

"Well, I didn't catch her doing it at least," I said skeptically. "So anyway, she wanted to look at my play books to pick one for her class to do, and she went and told Mrs. Avery all about how we are doing the plays together."

"Ok, why is that bad?" Coal asked densely.

"She made it seem like it was her idea." I was exasperated at this point.

"Oh, yeah that's not right," Coal stated, but I could tell he didn't quite believe it.

"Let's change the subject," I grumbled. "We still need to go try on our costumes after this. Also, Fiona and I decided on Italian food for the party."

CHAPTER TWENTY-SIX

Upon pulling into the driveway my phone pinged. It was Fiona, and I was happy for the distraction. My imagination had begun to run wild picturing an unknown assailant looming by the old growth foliage waiting for me to arrive so they could pounce.

Hey girl! Am I still able to bring a guest to the party on Saturday?

I typed back quickly,. *Of course you can! Are we finally going to meet the mystery man?*

I was excited at the prospect, thinking how nice it would be to go on a double date.

Ignoring my question Fiona writes,

Even after I gave you such a hard time for asking me the first time?

Yes, even then. You know how family can be. I added a winky emoji for good measure.

. . . She was in the process of writing, but apparently changed her mind because the dots disappeared.

Coal remained quiet as he waited for me to finish.

"Fi," I said, sensing his eyes on me. "She wants to bring a date on Saturday."

"Really?" Coal replied, his eyebrows shooting up. "I

didn't realize she was dating. Is it anyone we know?"

"Not sure, she's been kind of mysterious about it. I can't say anything, as I didn't want anyone to know that we were dating at first."

"Thanks a lot," Coal answered, feigning being insulted.

"When you've been burned," I looked around at the darkness surrounding the car, "you are reluctant to trust. Telling someone about the person you're interested in feels like you might jinx it."

"You're not into voodoo, are you?" Coal asked, chuckling and going to grab my hand.

"It's not funny," I retorted, pulling back my hand. "This is the way that it feels to me, and I don't appreciate you belittling my feelings." I wasn't feigning anything. I was straight up annoyed.

"I'm sorry," Coal said softly. "I wasn't laughing at you. I was just trying to lighten the mood, but it was stupid."

Glancing sideways at him, I narrowed my eyes, but my words came out nicer than my face looked, "It's fine. All I'm saying is, I understand where Fiona is coming from."

"Hopefully she's bringing someone cool," Coal said offhandedly as we got out of the car and tread the path to the house.

We settled in at the kitchen table with mugs of coffee that Coal offered up as an apology. While he was doing that, I fished around in the junk drawer of the kitchen and found a little blank silver journal and pen. I began to compose notes for Saturday

Guest List
Fiona and date
Samantha
Tabitha and fiance
Marion
Adelaide
Amber and Peter

Marcia
Lina
Chloe and date
Coal and me

That was fifteen people all together. Basically, all the people that I actually knew in Syracuse, but it was a good amount for my first party. Enough to seem like a party, but I was grateful that it was a manageable number of people to prepare food for.

I was lost deep in thought thinking of what needed to be done when I felt Coal's gaze fall on me, studying me intently.

I looked up. "Can I help you with something?" I asked, my eyes locking eyes with his.

"I don't like when you're mad at me," he bluntly said.

I sighed deeply, "I'm not mad at you, it's just I want you to try to understand what I'm saying." I knew this was too good to be true. We were already in the mists of our first fight.

"What are you so angry about anyway?" Now his voice became defensive.

I felt the tension ripple through my body like a shock wave. I stood up by the table, and Coal seemed shocked by my reaction. If my body and face looked anything like I felt, then I understood his panic.

"My feelings are not a joke," my voice came out clear and steady. For all the shakiness I felt inside, I was as still as a statue. "You don't have to agree with them, but you don't get to ridicule me."

Although I hadn't moved an inch, I was glued still in my spot by the table, Coal looked like he had been slapped.

"Listen Ava," Coal said, attempting to close the physical distance between our seats. It was only a few feet, but it might as well have been an ocean.

"Don't," I said, putting my hand out in a gesture to stop.

Coal looked as crestfallen as I felt. He was smart enough to heed my warning and not try to touch me, but he continued to speak in a soft voice, "I know you have been through a lot since you moved here. I understand that your marriage to Michael was tumultuous. I appreciate that Samantha is a weirdo with a lot of hang-ups. I'm sorry if I made it seem any other way."

I felt my body's rigidness soften with Coal's words. The fight went out of my body like the air out of a balloon, in one big whoosh leaving me deflated. I sat back down in my chair and all of my strength left me. Putting my head in my hands, I began to cry. Not little tears, great big sobs that wracked my body. I cried for all that I had lost. I cried for all the fear that I've lived with for the last two weeks but never really dealt with. I cried big ugly tears, so many that I was afraid I would flood the downstairs of my house.

When the crying ceased, I began to worry about how crazy I must have seemed to Coal at that moment. He was probably thinking that he didn't sign up for the crazy mess that sat before him. I slowly looked up at him, my mascara smeared across my face. My cheeks and eyes were red and puffy.

Coal now cautiously took the plunge and closed the gap. He kneeled before me. He didn't speak; he simply wrapped his arms around me. I let him, and we melded together.

"I'm sorry for being insensitive," declared Coal.

I said nothing. I felt hollow. Coal must have seen it in my face because he grabbed my chin and said, "You deserve for good things to happen for you because you are a good person. I will do everything in my power to be sure that you get what you deserve. Life is not always fair, but I plan to make sure that my love makes up for that."

He leaned over and kissed my lips. This time it wasn't a hungry passionate kiss, but it was a kiss that sealed his promise, both soft and strong.

I would be lying if I said I wasn't touched by his words and gestures, however I was not willing to move on like I wasn't hurt. Instead, I said, "Let's open our costume boxes, they are annoyed at us that we've taken so long."

We opened the first box, and it contained Coal's accessories. I pulled out the fedora and tossed it to him, "Try it on," I said, finally softening a little.

Coal put it on and pulled the hat down over his one eye. His other golden brown eye peered out, no supermodel had anything on him. I might be biased because of my feelings for him, however in my opinion Coal was the most handsome man I had ever encountered.

Reaching in the box, I pulled out the rest of the contents and handed them to him.

I grabbed the steak knife and sliced down the center of the brown tape on the second box. Excited because I knew this one contained my accessories, I happily pulled out my charcoal gray wool beret and did the best job I could of putting it on with my red hair spilling wildly around me. I then pulled out the scarf that I had acquired to wear with my costume. Since I didn't have to buy a lot for my costume, I splurged on the scarf. I knew I would be able to wear it long past Halloween. It was an unusual antique and artful floral 100% silk scarf dating to the 1930s. It evoked the era of the Great Gatsby, featuring a beautiful, subtle floral pattern in soft blues, red and pale green. It would really highlight my hair and eyes.

I quickly tied it around my neck and turned to Coal.

"Wow," he gasped. "You are gorgeous."

My mood suddenly shifted as we stood there in my kitchen playing dress up with our Halloween costumes. I watched Coal attach his suspenders to his pants and walk around toting his money bag. Despite my best efforts to be miserable, I laughed.

"Do you need help shopping and cooking for Saturday?" Coal asked. "I know how hard it is with school to get things done during the week." He waited, looking at me, not wanting to push it so soon after our first fight. I wasn't even sure if it was over yet.

I leaned against the counter. "Let me think," I said. "Tomorrow I have my class at the gym and Thursday is my tango lesson, but I have nothing on Friday. Do you want to go shopping after work on Friday? You can help me get things prepared. Maybe even sleep over. Maybe," I added for clarification.

"Sounds perfect," he said.

"How about I make us some hot toddies, and we go read some more pages of Aunt Virginia's journal? Or do you have to leave?" I asked, not wanting to assume anything.

"That sounds perfect," Coal said looking hopeful.

The two of us worked in tandem, quietly preparing the drinks. Coal turned on the kettle to boil water, while I procured the honey and sliced some lemon. Coal rummaged around in the liquor cabinet and found the brandy. When we were all done putting the concoctions together, we went up to the library.

Today upon entering the library, the smell of the fire from the other night lingered in the air making the room seem cozier than our previous visits.

I turned on the lights, placing my hot toddy down on a coaster on the writing desk.

"Do you want another fire?" Coal asked, glancing in the direction of the hearth.

I was reluctant to ask him for any favors. Obviously, I was perfectly capable of starting my own fire, but it would be nice. I finally agreed.

"Ok, while you do that, I'll start reading."

Before I could say anything else, Coal whizzed past me, opening the bookcase door, so I grabbed my hot toddy and began to walk towards the opening. I realized I forgot the key and stopped in my tracks.

"What's wrong?" Coal asked, noticing my hesitation.

"I forgot the key in my room. I'll be right back."

I turned on my heels to go to my room. I noticed Coal struggling whether to follow me or not, but he ultimately decided against it. When I returned to the library, he was already lighting some newspaper to get the fire started.

Sunday January 10, 2021

Things have been going beautifully since New Year's, so why did I have to run into him again? The second he brushed his hand against mine, all of the old memories came flooding back. Silly, simple things. Carefree times flooded my mind. I have a particularly strong memory of walking on a cold gray November day around the lake. I was transported. I can still feel what I felt at that moment. The cool wind whipping around my hair, tangling it in knots. The sting of the cold on my cheeks, turning them pink, but the thing I remember most was the joy. The pure unadulterated happiness I felt at that moment. It was unparalleled in my life. Although I've lived an extremely lucky and happy life until this point, I've never managed to recapture that feeling. My marriage, although cut short, was amazing. I really don't have room to complain, but my times with him were different, magical. I know we tend to romanticize the past. I've managed to leave that time in a little corner of my mind where I don't visit often. It's necessary in order to move on. I didn't want my future relationships to be tainted by comparison.

"Wow," I said aloud, looking up from the green leather book. I spotted Coal gazing into the now blazing fire, adjusting a log that was glowing along the border of the wood, with the fire poker. He turned around at the sound of my voice.

"Something interesting?" Coal asked, striding towards the entrance.

"Yes, nothing solid, maybe even nothing to do with anything, but to hear her internal dialogue means so much to me. How much do we ever really know the people that we love?" I wondered aloud.

"I want to know everything about you," Coal interjected, really making an attempt to connect with me.

"Are you sure you won't make fun of me when my ideas don't line up with your own?" I asked. I knew I was making a big deal over a silly incident, but I wanted to make a point, so we didn't have a repeat performance.

"Please don't judge me too harshly. My brain doesn't pick up on subtleties like yours does. I can be a little dense. I don't know an accident happens until I'm in the back of an ambulance with an oxygen mask on. You are the type who sees it coming and swerves out of the way before the car hits you, missing the accident all together."

I nod my head considering this.

"The thing I'm seeing," I say wanting to open back up to Coal, "is that everyone has a story. We think that our escapades and heartache are special only to us, and in a way, they are because it's our story. No one else has your specific story, but we need to remember that everyone has a story of their own. The whole time I was worried about my parents dying and my life falling apart, I realized I was failing to see that Aunt Virginia had her own story. I feel bad that it took me this long to see, too long for me to actually be there for her." I looked down, ashamed at this realization.

"Ava, you need to give yourself a little leeway. You were trying to cope the best way you knew how. You were just a kid trying to not drown in your own sorrow. Aunt Ginny was older, wiser, and she was able to throw you a life raft, so she did."

I took another sip of my drink and felt my insides warm up.

"Thank you," I say sincerely, ready at last to let our little tiff go. "Do you want to sit by the fire for a little while?" I ask in an attempt to reconcile.

"That sounds awesome," Coal exclaimed. He grabbed the journal and placed it in its secret compartment. I came over and secured the lock, just in case we didn't make it back tonight to read more. Coal turned my green leather chair around so it was facing the fire and pulled up the wooden chair for himself.

I happily sat down, cradling the rest of my drink in my hands.

"I think we need to buy you a leather chair, so you can be comfortable too while we sit in here," I said. I realized the promise I was making in my statement. I felt I owed him.

"I think that's a great idea," Coal answered smiling, showing off his beautiful straight white teeth.

I leaned over and rested my head on his strong shoulders. The hardness of his muscles changed my already mercurial mood again.

"That chair is too hard to be comfortable," I said, standing up and patting the soft green leather. "Sit."

Coal stood up from his seat in the hard wooden chair and exchanged it in favor of the soft leather one I offered. He then in turn patted his lap urging me to get comfortable.

I didn't have to be told twice and crawled right into his lap, I snuggled up on his left shoulder and stared at the fire.

"You know, I pictured you and me sitting in here just like this," I admitted.

"Really?" he asked, sounding surprised by the statement. "When?"

I felt my cheeks redden.

"When we first started talking." I hoped I didn't freak him out with my confession. We really barely knew each other at that point.

"Don't be embarrassed," Coal retorted, feeling brave with my proclamation, "I already had us getting married, thinking how beautiful our children would be." Coal didn't blush though. He said this like it was simply a fact that was being stated.

I didn't answer this bold statement but instead decided to revel in the feeling of sitting by the fire watching the crackling of the logs, finishing my hot toddy, and enjoying the company of this man.

CHAPTER TWENTY-SEVEN

Waking up Friday morning I had both butterflies in my stomach and excitement charging through my body. I was filled with anticipation for the party the next day. There was so much to do still, so I was also nervous. While still laying in bed, I texted Lina to see if she could come by today to help me with finishing touches instead of her usual Saturday. I wanted her to be here tomorrow at the party strictly as a guest, so I wanted to get all the actual work done today. I knew it was early, so I didn't anticipate her immediate response.

Wanting to get the actual clothes for my costume sorted out, I went to my closet but was dissatisfied with my findings. I had finally sorted through the clothes that I brought with me from my previous life, hanging up and storing clothing in my mirrored armoire.

The idea to look in Aunt Ginny's closet struck me. We had been roughly the same size, and God knew she had beautiful things. I hadn't been back in her room since my time with Coal, but after reading a little of her diary I felt better about going in her room. You can't have a more intimate look into someone's world than reading their actual thoughts. Going through her clothes was not such a big deal to me now.

Opening the door into the hallway, the house was eerily silent. Who was I kidding? My house was always silent, so I couldn't wait for my kitten to come home to live with me. Then the sounds of scampering feet in the house would be heard. It was nearly November, but I still wouldn't be able to get my kitten until December. Just as I thought this, as if on cue, the sounds of the heat kicking on began, the banging and whistling of the water moving through the old pipes and into the ancient radiators filled the house breaking the deafening silence.

I opened the door to her room and flipped the light switch. I no longer felt the room was filled with ghosts. Now I had Aunt Ginny's voice in my head. I could feel her thoughts and dreams swirling around in my conciousness.

When Aunt Virginia moved in with her husband Franklin, they wanted to leave the entire house original. It made them so sad when people bought Victorians and gutted them. Throwing all the history in a dumpster destined for a landfill, in favor of a condominium like home. They didn't even remove the lathe and plaster walls in favor of sheet rocking to make it more energy efficient. The only thing she did do to alter the house was have a walk-in closet constructed in the master bedroom. It was the most luxurious thing I've ever seen.

I went over to the closet and walked in. The delicate crystal and chrome chandelier sparkled as I flicked on the lights. It twinkled as if winking at me. I took it as a sign that Aunt Ginny approved of me being there.

Lina must have come in here and cleaned the crystal. It surely would have been dusty and dull by now. I had to remember to thank her when I saw her, hopefully later today.

The room looked like an upscale boutique that you would find in New York City. All of the beautiful designer clothing was displayed as if for sale. The floor was white marble with gray streaks occasionally streaking through it. All the shelving and walls were white washed. I located the rack that held skirts. I picked up a gorgeous navy blue pleated accordion style skirt that I had never seen before. I understood why as I saw that there were still tags on it. I shook my head sadly and returned it to its place amongst the skirts. As

I scanned the rack, my eyes landed on a tweed pencil skirt. I took it off the rack and held it up to myself.

The tweed skirt, in varying shades of gray, had a slight plaid pattern running through it. It landed right below the knee and had a very slight flare on the bottom. I got excited thinking that it might just work. Taking it off the hanger, I placed it on the quilted white leather bench in the middle of the room and returned the hanger to its rightful place.

I went to the right of the skirts, to the section of the closet that contained blouses. A periwinkle blue blouse caught my eye. It was the exact shade that was in my silk scarf. The shirt was a silky material and sported three quarter length sleeves and a very slight puff on the shoulder, enough to make it more stylish than a plain ordinary dress shirt.

Stripping down to my panties and bra, my feet felt cold on the marble floor, so I slipped the skirt and blouse on quickly. I pulled on the skirt at an awkward angle and adjusted the placement of the zipper on the skirt so it was in the correct place. Tucking in the blouse to the high waisted shirt, I peered at my reflection in the massive mirror. It was perfect. The clothes looked expensive, because they were. Aunt Ginny was a fashion writer, so she was gifted high end clothing all the time. Not to mention, she wasn't a teacher like me, and she had a budget that could afford nice things.

My eyes glanced at the shelves on the right wall of the closet. This was where Aunt Virginia had her purses. They were all in pristine condition and displayed as if in a showroom. There were at least twenty on display. In my old house, mine were thrown in a box. The insides of the purses were never properly cleaned out when they were switched out, and were littered with tampons, old lipsticks, and pens without caps staining the inside of the bags. Perhaps I could do better in this life.

Amongst the other handbags, I located a dark blue 1930's retro glass carnival glass seed-beaded purse. I gasped happily. This would be perfect to go with my Halloween attire.

About to change back into the original clothes I entered the room with, I spotted a deep purple sweater dress hanging on the rack with dresses. I folded the pencil skirt and blouse, and laid the purse on top in a neat little pile, a smile of satisfaction was on my lips. I had procured the perfect Bonnie outfit. Hopefully Coal had as much luck with his Clyde attire. I then tried on the sweater dress and it clung to me perfectly.

My steps felt lighter as I walked back to my room with the clothing. I deposited the pile on the red chaise lounge. Glancing at the clock I silently cursed, as it was time to get ready for work. Now that I had a dress to wear, I located a pair of black tights and pulled them on under the dress. I wore a pair of high heeled black suede knee high boots.

After getting dressed I thought to myself that in hindsight, I should have taken off work today in preparation for the party. I retrieved my phone before heading back downstairs to have a quick cup of coffee.

Surprisingly, Lina already texted back. She said she had an opening at 1 pm today, but she was busy besides that. I could leave her a key to the house, it's not like she hadn't been here a hundred times unsupervised, but then I would have to give her my alarm code. Was that a good idea? I wondered to myself, going back and forth in my mind. Finally deciding it would be ok, Aunt Ginny had trusted her with her home, and she was the one who tipped me off about her diary. I texted.

I will leave the key under the stairs by the side door. Please enter through the front. The code for the alarm system is 14343. Please arm the alarm before you leave. Thanks again.

Satisfied that I made the right decision, I went about preparing a salad to take for lunch. A cherry tomato went rolling across the kitchen counter, and my cell pinged indicating I had a message. I stopped to look at my phone.

Sounds good. I'll text if I have any problem. Should I just go through and do a dusting?

Yes, that's perfect. I know you usually come on Saturday, but I'm looking forward to you being here as my guest. xx

. . . She was taking a minute to answer back, so I rescued the tomato and completed my salad by storing it in a Tupperware container.

I pulled into the parking lot later than usual, it was three quarters full, and as I got out of the car feeling harried. Tabitha was exiting her black convertible at the same time.

"Hey," I said in greeting. I rarely saw her most mornings as I tended to arrive super early. She probably tended to arrive on the later side.

"Morning Ava," she greeted me cheerfully, pulling her red wool coat close to her for warmth. The morning was on the chilly side. The grass was frosted over and crunchy. "Looking forward to tomorrow. It will be nice to hang out outside of school, plus I'd like you to meet my fiance. He and Coal get along, so maybe we can go on a double date sometime."

I was blown away by this conversation as Tabitha had never said this many words to me ever. Maybe she was just that type of person that required some warm up time before getting too friendly.

"Oh, that's awesome. I didn't realize that they knew each other," I returned as we approached the door to the school.

"Yeah, we've been dating a long time, so he's been to after work functions with me."

"I would love to plan a double date," I said, at that moment Fiona was walking by with her lunch count.

"Where are you guys going?" Fiona butted in sounding hurt.

"Nowhere yet," Tabitha said with a laugh, "but we want to set up a double date."

Fiona gave her a look I couldn't decipher, and I didn't have time to worry about it, as I only had five minutes until I had to pick up the kids.

As we approached the hallway where my classroom was, both Fiona and Tabitha paused outside my door, luckily Samantha was not lurking there today.

"Oh, I'm going to make a bowtie pasta salad as well as a green salad for tomorrow. Does that sound good?" she said cheerily.

"Awesome," I appreciate it.

"Oh, I'm so sorry," Tabitha interjected, looking embarrassed. "I didn't even ask if you needed anything."

I blushed not wanting to impose on anyone. I wished Fi hadn't brought it up in front of anyone else. "Don't be silly. Just bring that fiance of yours."

Being Friday and test day, work flew by in a blink of an eye. I was grateful seeing as my mind was preoccupied all day. I received a text from Lina right before 3 pm telling me she was leaving the house, and she had rearmed the alarm system. I was grateful that it went well, as I was picturing receiving a call from the police when the alarm was triggered. After reading Lina's text, I was busy checking the weather forecast for the next day, when Coal tapped me on the shoulder.

"Ready to go beautiful?" he asked as I looked up and met his warm eyes. He was wearing a chocolate brown jacket that highlighted his eyes and hair.

"Yeah, I was just checking the weather, and it's supposed to be kind of warm tomorrow. Do you think we should make a fire in the firepit?"

"Absolutely," Coal sounded enthused by the prospect.

"I'll chop some wood tonight."

"Let's just stop at my house, and we'll take inventory of what we need. Then we can go together in one car."

"I brought a change of clothes with me and my costume for tomorrow night, just in case you needed me to stay," he said with a wink. "No pressure, I just like to be prepared."

I nodded, but my insides went gooey at the idea of him staying over.

After arriving home, we got out of our cars and leaned against Coal's car. We basked in the sun for a moment. The cold morning had given way to a beautiful afternoon. The grass had softened, and the remaining leaves on the trees were lit up in the sun.

"Yeah, it definitely feels like it's warming up. Tomorrow will be a beautiful day for your party," Coal said, intertwining his fingers with mine. He began to lead us to the front door, but I pulled us towards the side of the house.

"Lina was here, and I left her the key under the side steps. I'm assuming she left it in the same place," I said as I approached the side door. "I just want to get it now; I don't want to leave it there for anyone to find."

"Of course," Coal said. "Wait, did you give her the code to your alarm system?" he asked, looking concerned.

"Well, I really didn't have a choice," I said, sounding defensive. "She could only come during the day. Plus, she's been in and out of the house all the time when she used to work for Aunt Virginia. To be honest, I debated whether it was a good idea, but in the end, I decided it was ok."

I reached under the steps but did not feel the keys, so I bent down to take a closer look. My eyes scanning the area and even moving leaves around, the keys were not there.

"I immediately stood up and began texting Lina.

"What's wrong?" Coal asked, noticing my instant panic.

"The keys aren't there," I answered curtly, continuing

to text.

Hi Lina. Thanks so much for coming today on short notice. I was just wondering if you hung on to the keys. Please let me know. Thanks. xx

While I awaited Lina's response, Coal spoke, "Maybe she still has them since she's going to see you tomorrow, or maybe she thinks since she's going to be cleaning for you, you meant for her to keep the spare."

"You could be right," I said, relaxing a little. "Either of those situations are plausible and could explain it."

The phone pinged.

No, I left them right where I found them, under the steps. Did you want me to keep them?

"This can't be right," I said aloud. "She says she left them here."

"Let me take a look," Coal responded, "before you write her back again.

Coal crouched down and searched the whole area.

"There's nothing under here," Coal said definitively.

My heart began to race again. I punched out another text to Lina.

Are you sure you put them back? It's ok if you didn't remember to. It's just that I looked, and so did my boyfriend, and they aren't there. Just a little worried.

... I know for sure I returned them exactly where I found them. Since you didn't tell me to keep them; I didn't want to assume. I'm so sorry.

"She insists she put them back. I don't know what to think. Should I have the front door lock changed?" I asked, trying to problem solve.

"Let's not be hasty. There is probably a reasonable explanation for where they are. In the meantime, you have the alarm system, so if anyone had them and tried to get in, the alarm would go off."

"That's true," I said, agreeing with his logic. "Let me just write her back quickly. Sorry."

Ok, I don't see them, but they couldn't have just disappeared. I'm sure I'll find them, no worries.

I led Coal back to the front of the house and stopped to locate the keys in the bottom of my purse. I had intentions of using the spare keys to open the door.

"Don't panic," Coal said gently, picking up on my nervousness as I searched my bag.

"I'm not," I insisted as I heard the jangle of keys and pulled them out.

I pressed the alarm code and disarmed it upon entering.

"Well, she armed it the right way anyway. Maybe she thought that she put them back, but she'll actually find them later in her coat or something," I said.

"Let's go to the backyard," Coal said, leading me into the kitchen. I want to see what you have in the way of wood. If there is nothing there, we'll have to pick some up while we are out."

I unlocked the back French door and we stepped outside. I had been neglecting the backyard the last few days, and I noticed that the leaves had really piled up. They were deposited in colorful little lumps all around the backyard.

"I think the wood is piled in the back of the yard," I said, leading the way as we crunched through the leaves.

"Ava?" I heard Adelaide's unmistakable voice over the fence. "Is that you?"

Standing on the tree stump, as had become customary now, I leaned my head over the fence. "Hi Adelaide," I smiled at my elderly neighbor.

"I thought I heard you. Everything alright dear?" she

asked me, her voice filled with concern. Her eyes watery from the cold weather.

"Yes," I said, remembering to be patient with her, "just getting ready for the big party tomorrow. My boyfriend is here," I added gesturing for Coal to join me on the tree stump.

Coal chuckled silently and joined up on the stump, "Nice to meet you Adelaide," Coal said charmingly.

"My, aren't you handsome?" Adelaide said, giggling as she took in Coal's Roman sculpture face over her back fence. She placed her hand to her heart and turned pink.

"Why thank you. You're quite the beauty yourself. I look forward to speaking together more tomorrow night," Coal finished, being the consummate gentleman.

At that moment, I felt eyes on me. I looked up and to the right, and sure enough Marcia was looking down at us. This time instead of her usual ice queen scowl, Marica was dressed in a fluffy white coat, her eyes sparkling, as she gave us a warm smile, waving furiously.

I managed to plaster a tight smile on my face and wave back. Adelaide tutted, and Coal just looked confused, as he had no idea who she was.

"6 o'clock tomorrow, right?" Marica called down, her voice strong but friendly.

"Yes, see you then," I confirmed.

Marcia nodded and headed through her sliding door.

"I can't imagine why you would invite that woman," Adelaide hissed quite loudly. She shook her head as if it were the most preposterous thing in the world.

Coal looked amused and said, "Who was that?" His eyes sparkled mischievously.

"That is my instructor at the gym. I'm trying to be nice, so she can stop being so...," I struggled with how to finish the sentence in Adelaide's company.

"So bitchy," Adelaide finished the sentence for me with fervor.

I chuckled, "I was going to say difficult, but the sentiment is the same."

"Well, it was a pleasure meeting you," said Coal, trying to keep me on track. "We need to finish getting ready for the party, but we are looking forward to catching up with you tomorrow."

"The pleasure was all mine," replied Adelaide, patting her curly hair.

I gave a wave, but she was too preoccupied with Coal to notice.

We stepped down from the stump, and I put my finger to my lips indicating that we should remain quiet. She had eagle hearing apparently, as she heard me practically every time I was in the backyard.

"Here are some logs that can be chopped," Coal announced, pointing to a pile of wood decorating the back of my house. "Do you have an ax?" he asked.

I remembered seeing one in the garden shed where the lawnmower was kept, so I led him that way.

After sorting out the ax and wood, Coal carried them up to the patio area saying he would deal with them later. We entered through the doors into the kitchen.

"Those are some interesting neighbors that you have there," Coal proclaimed finally as we shut the French doors. "Your exercise instructor seems nice though. She seems sweet."

"Sweet?" I asked incredulously. "She has been nothing but nasty to me since I met her. I don't know what was going on today. Perhaps she found out she won the lottery, or the man of her dreams asked her to marry him. All I know is that woman you saw out there is not the same woman I know. Maybe she's a cyborg," I suggested chuckling. "Or maybe she fell under the spell of Coal Blake, like every other woman in this town."

"Oh please," Coal said, rolling his eyes. "I just hit it off with the over 60 crowd, but seriously why did you invite her to your house if she's not nice to you?"

I felt a little embarrassed, but I answered him honestly, "I know if she got to know me that she would like me." I felt like a little girl who needed the approval of the teacher.

Coal pulled me to him, "Her not liking you, in all likelihood has nothing to do with you and everything to do with her. Unless you've done something really bad to her, which I know you haven't, then it's about her issues. You can't fix that. You can only work on yourself."

"When did you get so wise?" I asked him, breaking away to pour myself a glass of water. "Well, I can't disinvite her now, so I'm glad she's acting nice at least."

"Yeah, but be careful. People don't change that drastically. If she was rude once, you can choke it up to a bad day. If it happened multiple times, her feelings didn't magically go away. Be nice, but be weary. I wonder what her intention was wanting to come."

Coal's last comment left me wondering. I never thought about it before, but why *did* she agree to come? What was her motivation? I hope it was that she wanted to be friends, but Coal was probably right. It was unlikely.

I glanced down at my phone and saw I had a direct message from Samantha. I rolled my eyes, even though she wasn't there to see me do it. I couldn't fathom what she could possibly want.

Hi. I am going to bring my famous pasta with Bolognese sauce. It's my grandma's recipe and is to die for.

I could see that Fiona had pricked Samantha's competitive side. She had a need to outdo everyone in everything, but at least it was one less thing I had to cook. I wrote back.

You really don't have to.

No really, it's my pleasure, besides I already started, so you can't say no.

Ok then. Thank you so much! Looking forward to trying it. I ended with a smiley face.

Coal handed me the silver book that I was using to comprise the Guest List. I turned to the next page and made a new heading

Food

Green Salad (Fi)
Veggie Pasta Salad (Fi)
Chicken francaise (Amber)
Pasta with Bolognese Sauce (Samantha)

I looked up from my silver notepad and showed Coal my list. "What do you think?"

Coal held the list in his strong, rough hands. "I think you're having all of your food cooked for you. That's awesome."

"I have to make at least one thing, plus I'll buy appetizer type things. I want there to be plenty of food." I furrowed my brow in concentration.

"How about sausage and peppers? I can grill the sausage, and you can saute the peppers and onions tonight. Then tomorrow you'll just have to heat them in the oven."

I smiled brightly, "That's a great idea. Let's get out of here. We need to get to the store." Now that I had a plan, I was anxious to execute it. I searched on the counter for my purse, locating it, Coal and I were on our way.

CHAPTER TWENTY-EIGHT

Returning home with an armful of supplies, and Coal carrying a box stuffed with bottles from the liquor store, I lowered the bag to the floor, ignoring the thump it made as it hit the ground. I was in a panic to disarm the alarm. We had to make two trips to the car to bring all of the groceries, but when I placed the last bag on the counter, I felt accomplished. Everything was really coming together.

"It smells nice in here," Coal noticed, taking a big loaf of Italian bread out of the bag.

I looked around the room. "I completely failed to remember that Lina actually came and cleaned. That was all forgotten with the key mishap. I was so consumed with the missing key." I continued to empty the contents of the bag out on the stone counter. I had gouda, cheddar, and fresh mozzarella sitting in front of me. "P.S. I'm still worried about the key." I bit my cuticle as I spoke.

Coal nodded in agreement, his brown wavy hair moving as he did it. "That's why you need to make sure to set the alarm, and as a side note, one in two police officers recommend that I stay over to protect you." With this he comes from behind me and circles his arms around my waist.

"Is that a fact?" I ask, chuckling.

"Sorry, it's not my rule," Coal added.

I spun around so I was facing toward Coal. His face was warm. I inhaled him and sighed. "Did you bring your costume for tomorrow?"

"As a matter of fact, I did, since I was contracted to be your guard." He kissed the top of my head.

"That doesn't make any sense; we just found out about the key after work. I think you're lying about being contracted," I teased.

Coal feigned an innocent face and leaned down to kiss me for real this time. He lifted me up on the counter.

"We have things to do," I protested, laughing as the gouda fell to the floor.

"I'm sorry," Coal said, "you're right." He bent down and picked up the gouda and I lowered myself back down to the floor.

I continued to empty the bags, placing the sausage to the side for Coal. "Here, do you want to start grilling, and I'll start with the vegetables?" I pulled out the peppers and onions and put them on top of the cutting board on the counter.

"Of course," Coal said, springing to action. "Do you happen to know if you have any gas left in the grill tank?"

I pulled a face. That's one thing I didn't think of, as I never personally grilled anything in my life. Michael was in charge of that.

"Don't worry, I'll check," Coal said, disappearing out the back door in search of the grill.

I continued to work putting away all of the perishables. When that was complete, I made quick work of peeling the skin off of the red onion. As I began to cut, my eyes began to tear.

"Don't cry," Coal said, reentering the kitchen. "There's gas left."

"Oh Coal, how could a person tell so many dad jokes when they aren't even a dad?"

"Not yet," he said, raising an eyebrow to me, "but I'm practicing so I'll be good. I'm hoping to get the position soon."

My heart did a backflip. I wasn't sure if he was kidding,

and I knew it was way too soon for him to be making proclamations regarding us being parents together. All the same, my heart ached. That was all I had wanted from the time that Michael and I got married, and he refused to give it to me.

I was so lost in my thoughts that I failed to notice that Coal was back out the door with the sausages already on the grill. I looked out the window and saw that while he was watching them, he was chopping wood for our firepit too.

I quickly finished the onions and started on the red peppers. Inspired by Coal's multitasking, I located a saute pan and put it under the flame. Remembering what my old high school Home EC teacher used to say "Hot pot, cold fat, food don't stick", I waited for it to heat up before adding the olive oil. Once that got to temperature, I added the onions and the peppers that were ready. I sprinkled some garlic powder on the vegetables for good measure.

"Wow it smells good in here," Coal said for the second time that afternoon, only instead of the lemony smell of furniture polish, the air was aromatic with garlic and vegetables.

"How are the sausages coming along?" I asked while using the spatula to turn over the peppers.

"Almost done. Just needed to get this," he said, holding up the silver tin that the sausage and peppers would be stored in.

Coal went to complete his task, and I set about making the garlic butter paste that I would use on the garlic bread. I wanted to prepare it and leave it in the refrigerator for tomorrow.

Once again Coal burst through this door, this time carrying the tin with the sausages in it.

"That exercise instructor was out on her balcony looking down into your yard," Coal announced, putting the food down on the counter. "She has a light on, on her balcony, so she was illuminated. She was up there in a fluffy white robe drinking a martini, just staring into your yard. I don't think she realizes how visible she is from the ground." He shook his head, and I was waiting for him to tell me how creepy it was that she was staring into my yard, but it never came.

I added the cooked vegetables to the tin and covered the entire thing with aluminum foil.

"We need to go back out to the car and get the pumpkins," Coal reminded me. "Plus, I'll bring my bag in, just so you can see my costume of course," he finished with a wink.

I left the garlic butter paste for a minute to assist Coal with the pumpkins. We stopped at the farmer's market while we were out and picked up 6 jumbo pumpkins. My plan was to have a pumpkin carving contest at the party. It took two trips because the pumpkins were enormous. On our last trip back in, I engaged the alarm system, just in case.

Seeing me dutifully press the numbers on the pad, Coal watched with a grin. "Does this mean what I think it means? Are we in for the night?"

I was about to tease him when I saw a smoldering look in his eyes, a dangerous look. "As far as I know," I answered instead.

We finished up in the kitchen and stood side by side washing up the kitchen. It felt like we'd been together for years instead of weeks. The ease between us was equally as important to me as the electricity. I had neither of these things in my marriage. There was only tension and nothingness. I don't know which was worse.

"Let's put on some tea, and then we can bring the pumpkins to live in the backyard until tomorrow," I said. "Oh, I guess I'll have to disengage the alarm for that."

Without another word, Coal took it upon himself to put the kettle on. I took out two of Aunt Ginny's special matching tea cups and saucers. They were brownish red, gold, and white and had an Asian theme. I have always loved them since I was a little girl. She would set up a tea party for me and use these cups. I also grabbed the matching teapot, sugar bowl, and tiny spoons to dole out the sugar with.

The sky was now completely black, but we had the motion lights in the backyard that would suffice for light. I went into the hall closet and grabbed my coat, and an oversized navy-blue hooded sweatshirt that said George Washington University on it in gold lettes. I gave that to Coal to wear.

While we waited for the water to boil, we put on our jackets.

"Did your aunt go to GW University?" Coal asked, glancing at the hoodie that adorned his body.

"No, she went to Syracuse like me," I said. "I'm not sure where it came from, but I'm happy she had something that could actually contain those huge muscles of yours." I gave him an admiring glance.

I went over to the pin pad and disengaged the alarm in preparation for our trip outside.

"I'll start bringing the pumpkins out, if you want to wait for the tea," Coal stated, grabbing two of the biggest pumpkins, they completely filled his arms to capacity as he headed for the door. I went and opened it for him.

Coal made two more trips as I placed the tea bags into the pot and refilled the sugar bowl. When the whistle of the kettle finally pierced the silence, I turned the stove off, pouring the steaming hot water over the tea bags. I glanced outside to see how Coal was doing, when I noticed an amber glow.

Grabbing the teapot and sugar bowl, I headed for the door and precariously opened it, while being sure not to drop anything. There was an artistic glass table made out of what appeared to be an old fire pit near the black iron rocking chairs. I placed my items down.

"Nice fire you have going Mr. Blake," I remarked.

"There's always a fire burning when you are around you," he retorted.

I laughed and went back inside for the cups and saucers.

This time Coal was waiting at the door to open it for me. I was grateful, as I was worried about holding the saucers with one hand. I placed those also down on the table. The little fire had now caught and was a full- blown blaze.

I sat on one of the rockers that was placed at exactly the right distance from the fire to feel its warmth but not get burned.

"This is nice," I said watching a log that was glowing orange around the edges.

I fixed myself a cup of tea and held it in my hands as I sat mesmerized.

"It really is a perfect night for a fire. I know we're going to do one tomorrow, but this is the one I can really enjoy. Just me and my girl."

"Yeah, it is nice to have a little calm before the storm." The fire was now warming my face, and the hot tea was warming up my body. "Thanks for coming to help me tonight. I've never hosted a big event like this myself."

"Oh please, no trouble at all. Do you think I would ever say no to the opportunity to spend time with you?" he asked. The joking look had left his face was replaced with a look so serious, it made me jittery.

I sat frozen in my seat, not saying anything, both scared that he would go on and scared that he would stop.

Coal continued talking, "I have never even dreamed of meeting someone like you. Someone who can light up even the darkest day. I didn't think that you existed." He paused, all that could be heard was the crackle of the fire. I saw an errant piece of glowing wood float with the wind right past me. I watched to make sure it wouldn't set dried leaves ablaze, but it landed on the stone and quickly fizzled out.

I remained quiet, just waiting.

"I know you are not great with compliments, but you are going to just have to get used to it. I know I scared you with what I said in the kitchen before, but I want you to know I'm all in. I hope to make you Mrs. Blake one day, when you're ready."

I was blown away with emotion. I took a sip of my tea before speaking.

"Coal," I began unsure how to respond.

"Don't," Coal said looking at me seriously, "I don't need you to say anything. I understand that this is all hard for you. I just want you to hear it, so you can consider how you feel. I mean not your immediate reaction, what you really feel. Then you can tell me when you're ready."

We sat in silence for a minute when I heard what sounded like the crunching of footsteps around to the right of where we were sitting, between Peter's house and mine. Coal must have heard it too as his head whipped in that direction. Suddenly, the motion light by the side door went on illuminating the area in front of it. There was nothing to see but the stones on the path and a few stray leaves, but the definite sound of fast footsteps, someone fleeing, could be detected.

Coal jumped out of his seat and ran over to the side of the house. I was right behind him on his heels. Coal darted to the front of the house, but there was no one in sight. My heart was racing, not from the run, but from the bomb dropped on me and the prospect of a trespasser skulking around my house. The darkness was a curtain for the intruder. It hid them, but I could feel their presence. Coal jogged down the street to the right, passed the house, and jogged down the street to the left. He looked like a guard dog protecting his property. At least whoever it was knew I wasn't alone.

When Coal came back to where I was standing, he was out of breath and livid.

"Come on out," he shouted in vain into the night, an attempt to taunt the prowler, "if you have something to say to Ava, come and say it." His attempts were futile. Whoever was sneaking around my house was long gone. I couldn't help but wonder if it was something menacing. Could it be the person who took my key? Or was it something completely innocent, a kid about to cut through my yard to get to the street behind me?

"Can we put the fire out and go inside?" I asked, turning to Coal nearly in tears. My hands were actually shaking.

"I *am* going to get to the bottom of this," Coal said, his sweet romantic demeanor completely erased. In its place was a man enraged. He reminded me of a tiger in the zoo who was being taunted by a kid, only the glass stopping him from pouncing.

"I appreciate it," I said quietly. I was afraid to speak loudly in case anyone was listening.

Coal went and put the top on the fire to snuff the oxygen out of it. Coal and I both grabbed the china and made our way to the house. I couldn't get inside fast enough. I began to hyperventilate as I locked the door and engaged the alarm.

I immediately ran to the light switch and flipped it off. We were now standing there in the kitchen in the dark.

"What are you doing?" Coal asked gently, probably afraid that I was really losing it.

"Let's go upstairs," I urged him, pulling at his arm, "please?" I begged.

"Of course, Ava, anything you want, but I don't want whatever this is to steal your peace."

My eyes had now adjusted to the dark, and I could see the outline of Coal. His eyes were now filled with a mix of rage and sadness. I didn't want him to pity me.

"I just want to go upstairs," I managed to say, taking deep breaths and calming myself.

"Then that's what we'll do. Hold on a minute," Coal said walking to the side door, I knew he was checking to see that it was locked. He put the chain on the door for added security. Then he finished the job by walking in the glass room to be sure that that door was secure.

Coal finally joined me back in the kitchen where I stood in the middle of the room in the dark, not wanting to be seen by anyone.

"All set," he said, grabbing my hand and pulling me into the sitting room. We stopped at the front door, the chain was already fastened. I double and triple checked that the alarm was set. The house was dark and quiet. All I could hear was the thumping of my heart in my chest.

We ascended the steps to my bedroom. I originally wanted to read a little more of Aunt Ginny's diary, to try to get a little closer to the truth, but I just didn't have it in me. As we walked down the hallway, I noticed that it smelled nice up here too. I would like to thank Lina tomorrow, I thought, a temporary distraction from my sorrow.

Coal twisted the crystal knob on my bedroom door, as we walked in and closed it, I desperately wished I had a dead-bolt to lock Coal and I away from the rest of the world. He went to flip the switch when I smacked his hand.

"Don't!" I hissed, "I don't want anyone to know where in the house we are."

I heard Coal sigh. He took a deep breath, but he didn't say anything about my erratic behavior, he just pulled me on the bed and wrapped his strong capable arms around me.

"It's going to be ok," Coal whispered, even though we were the only two people in the house. The moon was nearly full outside, and luckily the beams flooded in bathing us in pale light.

"What if this never ends?" I gasped. "I knew this was too good to be true." I began to sob gently.

"What's too good to be true??" Coal asked quietly.

"When I met you and saw what a genuinely good person you were, and you wanted me. I knew it was too good to be true."

"I don't understand," Coal said. "What does any of this have to do with me?"

I broke away from him and my gentle sobbing turned into hysterical tears. "I don't know, I don't know, I don't know," I felt broken. I couldn't stop myself from repeating the same phrase over and over again to myself.

Coal grabbed me and embraced me, like he was trying to comfort a hysterical child. He didn't say anymore but just held me. I probably cried for a half hour before I finally fell asleep from sheer exhaustion.

Coal didn't get a wink of sleep that night. He stood guard, listening for any sounds. He dozed off here and there. I know because every time I woke up, he was up either standing guard at the window or lying on the bed staring at me. All I knew was it was time to put an end to all of this. I felt like I've been terrorized since I've moved to Syracuse, and that night was the final straw. I wished I knew who to congratulate because I was broken.

CHAPTER TWENTY-NINE

I practically jumped up out of bed at the crack of dawn, a cold sweat coating my body. The sun wouldn't be up for at least another two hours, but it reached that time in the morning that the sky was a shade lighter than the middle of the night. I knew that look well, and my body woke me up nearly every day at this time. The second I moved, Coal spoke, as if he was poised all night just waiting for me to stir.

"How are you?" Coal asked. I turned to look at him. He was turned on his side, his cheek lay on the pillow, his eyes were wide and alert. His hair was tousled from a long night.

"I'm fine," I answered. I realized my shoes were off. I spotted them tossed to the side of the bed. They looked so out of place in the otherwise perfectly neat room. Coal must have taken them off me once I fell asleep.

"No, really," he asked seriously.

"Actually, I feel a lot better. I'm sorry about the way that I overreacted last night. It just hit me all at once," I said my voice strained.

"Ava," he started, the weariness obvious in his face, "this whole thing is messed up. I don't blame you for reacting, for having feelings. It would be hard for anyone to handle. To be honest, I wondered before this how you were just taking everything in stride."

"We just need to solve it," I said with resolve. "Let's lay out all the parts and see how they fit together. Then we can resolve this and make it go away, for good."

Coal nodded, his brown eyes red rimmed from lack of sleep.

"It started with the dolls. The first one and then the doll with no eyes," I involuntarily shivered while saying it.

Coal grimaced. When I said it aloud the reality of how bad it was really hit home.

I glanced out the window into the still darkness. "The letters," I finally say, Coal watching me, waiting. "We found two sets of letters warning someone, presumably Aunt Ginny, to stay away from someone. It's all so vague," I concluded.

"Do you think that the dolls were meant for Aunt Ginny and not you? I mean you two do look stunningly alike." Coal asked, trying to make a connection. "I know she's not with us anymore," he checked my face before continuing, to see if I was alright,"but if someone was that obsessed, maybe they're not internalizing that fact."

Now I nodded. He had a point. It was one theory. This might not be about me at all. This might be about Aunt Ginny, which means we needed to finish reading her diary. We had no other way of knowing what was going on in her life. What information we were not privy to.

"Well let's try to enjoy ourselves tonight. This is your big party, and I don't want it to be ruined for you."

I smiled, my face relaxing a bit for the first time since before we found someone creeping around in my backyard. "Yeah, we need to prep the house, food, and ourselves. We'll leave the detective work until tomorrow, after we see your parents."

Coal looked surprised and sat up in bed, "If it's too much, you don't have to go with me tomorrow. We can do it another day."

"No, I'm looking forward to it," I answered and surprised myself because I really meant it.

Coal's eye shone with happiness at the prospect,

I jumped up out of bed determined. "I just have to

get out of these clothes from yesterday," I said looking down at my plum dress which looked pristine yesterday and now looked rumpled after a night of laying in it.

I went to my dresser and pulled out a pair of high waisted skinny stretch jeans so dark blue that they almost looked black. I found a burgundy sweatshirt with puff sleeves to wear with it. We wouldn't be putting our costumes on until much later, but I wanted to look cute since Coal would be here with me getting ready.

"I'll be right back," I said, giving Coal a wink as I proceeded to the bathroom and closed the door.

"I guess I'll get ready in here," he shouted so I could hear him through the door.

I quickly changed, brushed my teeth, pulled my hair into a ballerina style bun, and washed and moisturized my face. I didn't want to leave Coal waiting any longer and rushed back into the bedroom to join him.

The sky was a shade lighter, and Coal was changed into a fresh pair of black jeans and navy sweater.

"I'm just going to use the bathroom, and then I'll meet you downstairs," Coal announced.

"Sounds good, I'll get the coffee," I grabbed my phone off of the night stand and strood down the hallway confidently.

I wondered to myself as I descended the stairs, what I was so afraid of last night? Honestly, I was embarrassed by my display. I supposed it was good that Coal saw me at my worst, and he stayed. Anyone can love you when you're strong and optimistic, when you are your own cheerleader. There is no work to be done then. It's those terrible moments when you can't bear the light that you need someone to stick by your side and hold your hand and get you through the night. That's just what Coal did for me.

As I walked through the house into the kitchen, I felt a warmth of appreciation. This beautiful house was mine. I got to call it my home. That man up in my bedroom was also mine. I had the privilege of calling him my boyfriend. I had successfully pulled myself up from my lowest point, and I was making the climb up to the peak of the mountain. Sure, there were obstacles blocking my way, but I took out my machete to cut clear the path and kept moving up.

The bubbling of the percolator happened in tandem with Coal entering the kitchen.

"Good morning beautiful," Coal said, as he was rooting through the box from the liquor store and was pulling out the white bottles of wine to be chilled in the refrigerator in preparation for the evening's festivities.

"I'm putting the white wine on the door," he said, gesturing to where the wine would take up residence. The refrigerator was still widely vacant, cooking for one was really not much of a thing I did. There was a spacious amount of room to store everything we needed to have in there for the party.

"Perfect," I said, preparing our cups. Although still dark, the sky began to brighten just the slightest amount. "Alexa, what's the weather like today?"

"The current weather is 43 degrees. You can expect a high of 54 and a low of 40 degrees with ample sunshine. Enjoy your weekend." Alexa's mechanical voice finished.

"The weather does sound perfect," I said. "I'm glad that we can make a fire and do the pumpkin carving contest outside. I really didn't want to make that mess in the house. I just hoped we didn't have any uninvited visitors lurking around tonight."

"Well, if we do, we will have plenty of people here for backup to help us," Coal said, trying to put a positive spin on the situation.

"Very true," I responded, "but I don't think we need any help. We can use our ninja skills to rid the world of evil."

Coal approached me and kissed me sweetly. "Yes, we will."

"Should we have our cafe in the glass room?" I asked

him.

"Of course," he answered. We took our mugs and made the short journey to the glass room. I turned on the wall sconces on the sides of the couch. Remembering the soft navy-blue fleece blanket stored in the hassock, I pulled it out.

As Coal and I arranged ourselves tangled in each other on the couch, I draped the cover over us, and we sat the mugs of coffee balanced on our laps.

"This is a beautiful way to have our morning coffee," Coal said, a huge grin spread on his face. "The rainbow after the storm."

"After coffee, let's try on our costumes together to see if we need to make any last-minute adjustments." I looked pointedly at him.

"You don't trust my costume judgment, do you?" Coal asked with a wicked smile.

"I most certainly do," I replied, "just wanted to make sure we're on the same page. We do after all need our costumes to complement each other. "

"Yes, we do," he kissed me again.

"Did you leave your costume in the kitchen or in the bedroom?" I asked, feeling impatient to get this day rolling. I started going to stand up. Coal tugged me back down to his lap.

"No, I want to surprise you. Let's just finish our coffee, then we can do a big reveal."

I nodded happily agreeing to the plan.

"You know," I began. Laying my head on Coal's chest, "I was thinking, Amber had to have known who my aunt was involved with. They were best friends, after all. They were practically family."

"True," Coal murmured, stroking my neck. "So why don't you ask her?"

"I think I will, maybe tonight, if we can find a private moment." I took the final sip of my coffee and lowered my legs down to the floor to stand up.

"You rushed the coffee on purpose," Coal teased. "You just can't sit down and enjoy the moment, can you?" he asked. He said it in a joking voice, however it was the truth. If I had something on my mind, the only way I knew to get through it was action. With the party and my concerns over the strange happenings, sitting on the couch doing nothing was the farthest thing from relaxing that I could imagine. If there was one thing I've learned, problems don't fix themselves, so while I sat there doing nothing, I imagined the problem growing exponentially until it suffocated me.

I didn't want to scare Coal away with my thoughts, so I simply answered with a wink, "I just want to see what you put together."

Coal chased me playfully into the kitchen, through the sitting room and up the stairs.

"I bet you wish you were as quick as me," I taunted him, as I took the stairs two at a time. He smacked me on the butt and twisted me into his arms at the top of the stairs.

"Oh, you are good, but I am better," he said, embracing me.

"You wish," I returned, wiggling out of his grasp and sliding in my socks until I reached the slate gray floral patterned runner that went the length of the hallway.

At that point, Coal swept me up in one fell swoop and lifted me completely off my feet. He twirled me around, and I let my body go limp to make it harder for him to carry me. My head hung down, tendrils of red hair escaping on the sides.

We both collapsed into a fit of laughter as Coal tossed me onto the bed. I literally bounced and he wrestled me, both of us out of breath from laughing so hard. I managed to make my way to the top and coiled my legs around him. The strength of my legs, from all those squats and hundreds of miles run, actually managed to hold him down.

"One, two, three," I called dramatically, hitting the bed with each number called out. "Victory is mine," I bragged while holding him in place.

"You win," Coal said, surrendering to me. "You are always the winner to me."

We laid on the bed kissing, a tangle of body parts. I reveled in my success. Looking back, I wished that we could have a snapshot of that moment. Two souls connected, together in the fight for life. The fight for us. Neither of us knew that our victory would be so short lived. As I saw only days before, life could unexpectedly change at any moment, for better or worse.

CHAPTER THIRTY

The doorbell rang at 5 pm. Dusk was already descending on the day. The sky was filled with a smoky mix of dark purple, vibrant orange, and pink. The colors were all muddled together as if an artist took their finger and smudged them, a perfect Halloween party night. The hours of daylight were filled with throwing up some last-minute decorations, cutting and preparing food, and putting myself together for the party.

I took the time to blow dry my locks straight, then putting in curls from halfway down my hair until the ends. I finished by placing the steel gray beret on my head at an angle. I answered the door with the entire ensemble together, complete with the purse slung across my body, fake money and prop gun spilled out. Lina's face was smiling at me.

"Ava," you look amazing," she said, hugging me with one arm. Her other arm was carrying a tray of food in a silver tin with aluminum foil covering the top. "I prepared some homemade golabki. It was your Aunt Ginny's favorite."

I took the tray and glanced at Lina. She looked stunning. Unlike last time I saw her she was done up to the nines. Her blond hair was obscured by a black wig. Her well-toned body was on display in her Wonder Woman costume. She had a golden lasso attached to the side of her costume. The sweet girl next door was turned into a brunette goddess.

"Lina come in," I said, ushering her into the house. "You look fabulous,"

"You're too kind," she answered. She took the jacket she wore and hung it in the hall closet herself. "You have plenty of hangers for guests," she observed.

I took my hand on the small of her back and gently guided her into the kitchen. I put the golabki on the table and peeled the tin foil back. The aromatic smell of the stuffed cabbage wafted into the air.

"Those smell amazing!" I announced. "Maybe you can teach me how to make them someday? I miss my mom's cooking."

"Of course I will," Lina said, her eyes darting around the room to see what needed to be done.

"Lina I wasn't kidding when I said I wanted you here as my guest. I want you to relax and enjoy yourself."

"I promise you I will. I just wanted to get here early and make sure everything was ready." Lina's face changed as she spoke, lines of worry began to appear on her forehead, "Did you find the key?"

Trying not to show concern on my face, I took a deep breath and shook my head, "No, we looked, but it wasn't in the house or outside."

Lina appeared deep in thought when her face brightened, "Wait, you put cameras at the doors, yes?"

Knowing I was going to crush her hope, I reluctantly answered, "I did but only at the front and back doors. I didn't do it by the side door because it is facing my neighbor's house. I figured no one would be so bold when they are so visible."

"But I know I left the key there," Lina insisted. She looked like she was going to cry.

"Honestly, don't worry about it. If the key doesn't show up, I'll change the front lock. It's really no big deal," I assured her.

At that moment Coal came walking into the kitchen from the direction of the dining room. I was happy for the distraction from talking about the key.

"Lina, I want you to meet my boyfriend Coal," I said smiling as Coal came over and extended her hand to Lina.

Coal was also dressed in his full costume, and he did

not disappoint. He was going to give Peter a run for his money in the James Bond department. His black suit pants were tailored to his body, showcasing his athletic build. He wore suspenders over a crisp white buttoned up shirt. His black shoes were polished within an inch of their life. The black fedora tilted to the side brought him right out of a black and white gangster movie. A dark gray patterned tie hung from his neck. The overall effect was perfect.

"It's a pleasure meeting you, Lina," Coal said, shaking her hand. "Ava has had such nice things to say about you."

I was so thankful for Coal's ability to put people immediately at ease, as I saw the worried look drift away from her face as they spoke.

While Coal was introducing himself, I took the opportunity to scoop some of our signature drink out of the punch bowl on the table using a huge silver ladle and into a cup for Lina.

"Here you go," I said, placing the drink in her hand.

Lina looked down at the cup and giggled, "What is this?" she asked with delight.

"It's an eyeball martini. Those floating eyeballs are made with lychees stuffed with blueberries. The main drink is vodka, lychee juice, blood orange liqueur, and a green tea simple syrup. Try it, tell me what you think?"

I watched Lina delicately take a sip, making an effort not to smear her perfectly applied red lipstick.

Based on her smile, I knew we had a winner. "It's delicious," she remarked.

"I'm so glad. To be honest, the drink was Coal's idea, and I was a little skeptical. It does look really cool when it's put together," I finished squeezing Coal's hand.

"I'm just going to put the stuffed cabbage in the dining room where I'm setting up the food," I announced, leaving Lina and Coal to chat.

As I went off to deliver the cabbage to the dining room, the sounds of Monster Mash filled the air. Coal must have set up the Alexa to the Halloween Station.

The ringing of the old crank doorbell could be heard. At this point it was only about 5:30 pm, the party wasn't officially due to start for another half hour. It was probably Fiona at the door coming early to help me get set up.

I opened the door and was startled to find a man and a woman wearing full masks. The woman wore a cotton candy pink, knee length cocktail dress. Her face was adorned with a beautiful Venetian mask. There were cat-like eyes cut outs. The lips were painted the same cotton candy shade of pink as her dress. The right side of the face contained a chess board in white and pink, while the left side had a composition of music note adorning it. The man was dressed in a deep plum suit. His mask looked like a patchwork quilt in tones of gold and black. The eyes were an opaque mirrored purple color that obstructed your view of the wearer's eyes. I stood there just staring at them, not sure what to make of it.

"Ava, darling, you look lovely," Amber said, leaning over to hug me. "I brought the chicken francaise, just as promised." She lowered her eyes, the only part of her face that was visible, to the tray she was carrying.

"I guess that's you under there Peter," I said with a chuckle. He lifted the mask up onto his head to reveal his smiling face.

"Thanks so much for having me," Peter said, carrying two wine bottles wrapped in silver foil and tied in a bow with an orange ribbon.

"Come in, come in," I said happily ushering my guests into the house.

"Everything looks wonderful," Amber said as we walked through the parlor into the kitchen. "Where would you like me to put the chicken?"

"I'll take it into the dining room where I set up the rest of the food," I said with a smile. "I really appreciate you making it."

"No trouble at all," she said, her smile brightening even

more when she spotted Lina, who despite my best efforts, was busy wiping the kitchen counter down.

Lina stopped what she was doing and went over to Amber and Peter. "Hello Amber, Peter," she said, extending her hand to them. She still had a warm smile, but I noticed a note of formality in her greeting.

"I'm so glad that you and Ava connected," Amber said, ignoring Lina's hand and going in for a hug. "It's nice for her to make more friends in Syracuse, since she is living here now."

Lina smiled, "Yes, she is a lovely girl."

They were speaking as though I weren't standing right there next to them.

Coal came over and gave Peter an effusive handshake. Peter took this opportunity to introduce him to Amber.

"Amber, this is that lovely young man who I was talking about that's been looking out for our Ava."

"Nice to meet you," Coal said, smiling warmly at Amber. "You are Fiona's mom, right?" he asked.

"Yes, I've heard all about you from both Peter and Fiona, the pleasure is mine," she returned. I noticed the tone of her voice change slightly, and then it went away. With her mask still on, it was hard to tell if I imagined it.

"Well, there's an eyeball martini punch on the table," I said motioning toward the kitchen table where we had set it up. "And of course, I have white wine in the refrigerator and red wine on the bar cart. Oh, and there's beer too. What would you like?" I asked, taking their orders.

Coal and I got their drinks. An eyeball martini for Amber and cabernet sauvignon for Peter.

"Those masks are beautiful," Coal said, admiring them.

"They're authentic Venetian masks from Italy," Peter said proudly. "Actually, Ava's aunt Virginia brought them back from Italy for us on one of her many trips. I saw Amber's when I was over at her house. That's when I got the idea for us to wear them for your party. Do you know in Venice, at one time, that wearing masks around the city was a daily occurrence? It was a common practice."

"That's very interesting," said Lina, sipping her second martini. She seemed to have relaxed a little. I wanted her to feel comfortable at the party, so I was relieved when she added to the conversation.

Amber slipped her mask off and put it on the top of her head. She grabbed a napkin off of the table and dabbed at her eyes.

"Are you ok Amber?" I asked, slipping my arm around her. I was concerned by the tears.

"I'm just fine Ava. This is just a little emotional for me, so I'm sorry that I'm not quite myself. This is my first time back in Ginny's house. It's just stirring up a lot of memories for me."

"Oh, of course," I said, now pulling her in for a full embrace, which was awkward with my fedora and her mask piled awkwardly on her head. "I totally understand."

The bell rang for the third time that evening. I let go of Amber and saw her slip her mask securely back into place.

"I'll hold the fort down," Coal said. The kitchen was now filled with the sounds of Michael Jackson's "Thriller" and happy chatting.

I could see the silhouette through the door. It was obvious it was Adelaide, as she was on the small side and slightly hunched over. The outline of cat ears on her head could be seen through the glass.

"Ava darling," she said as the door swung open. She was precariously holding a covered tray with her and a bottle of wine.

"I can hold that," I said, reaching for the bottle of wine. I was trying to recover it before I ended up with the deep red liquid splashed over the entrance of my house.

"Is it ok that I blocked your car in?" she asked, looking worriedly back at the driveway, the tray that she was holding was teetering precariously.

"That's perfect, I'm not going anywhere tonight," I said happily. "I love your costume by the way." I patted her ears as I closed the front door.

"It certainly sounds like a party," Adelaide sounded delighted as she heard the commotion coming from the kitchen.

Adelaide took in the house, eyes wide. She looked delighted to be out. I felt happy that I had included her in my party. I would never have wanted my own mom or grandma to be left alone with no social life, no family to visit. No one to make her feel important or alive. I hoped that Adelaide would feel like a princess at a ball. I collected her coat and hung it in the closet. A little black tail could be revealed now that the coat was gone.

"Everyone, this is Adelaide, my wonderful neighbor who lives behind me. She is giving me one of her kittens from the litter that her cat had a short while ago. I can't wait until she comes home, so I can have some company." I took the tray from her hands to free her up.

"Good evening, Adelaide," Amber said, her voice seeming suddenly lively. "It's so nice to meet you. I am Amber."

"Nice to meet you too Amber," Adelaide said, doing a little bow thing.

"Would you care for a drink?" I asked Adelaide, wanting to get her settled before anyone else arrived. "I have white wine, red wine, and there is a martini punch on the table." I motioned towards the floating eyeballs.

"How fun!" she stated, clapping her hands together. "I'll take a glass of the eyeball punch. It's been so long," she said, staring dreamily into the corner of the room. "My husband and I used to throw such grand parties in our time."

"Perfect," I said ladling the liquid into the gold cup and passing it to her. "Would I be able to come by this week and spend some time with my kitty?" I asked genuinely.

"Of course! She's been waiting for you," Adelaide answered.

At that moment, Coal came over as if on cue. "Hello Adelaide, remember me from this morning?" he asked.

Adelaide looked back and forth between Coal and me. "How could I forget such a charming man? Let me guess, Bonnie and Clyde?" she asked anxiously.

"Yes!" I said, excited that she knew who we were without asking. I also gave myself a pat on the back for pulling off the characterization.

"You two are perfect!" Adelaide declared, glowing triumphantly at her win. She clapped her hands together enthusiastically.

Adelaide took a sip of the martini. "Oh, this is divine," she announced.

The bell rang yet again, I looked at Coal pleadingly. He nodded and headed for the door. Things were really starting to heat up now. It was 6:15 pm, and the party was in full swing.

"I just want to thank everyone for coming," I said. "Feel free to roam the house. You don't all have to stay in the kitchen. Later on, we'll head outside for some fun."

Everyone in the room raised a glass to my speech and drank. I never knew that hosting a party could be so much fun.

A minute later Tabitha and a very handsome tall Italian man walked in, trailed by Coal.

"Tabitha, thanks for coming," I said, going in for a hug. Tabitha was dressed in what appeared to be some sort of dessert costume.

"Nice to meet you, I'm Enzo, Tabitha's fiance," said Tabitha's man who spoke with a strong Italian accent. He leaned in for the double kiss on the cheek. "I'm a cannoli, a true Italian treat."

Normally I would have rolled my eyes, but I was high on the adrenaline of the night. I laughed. "Nice to meet you Enzo!"

"She's a puff pastry," Enzo explained, "Her sweetness is

on the inside." He winked as he said this.

That sent me into a fit of giggles. I was grateful when Lina jumped in to ask them about drinks. I gave up trying to tell her to relax and be a guest. She was obviously happiest when busy.

The next time the bell rang, I figured I should be responsible and answer it. I was still chuckling to myself about Enzo. I was thinking that opposites really do attract when I pulled the door open. I was hoping it was Fiona; I couldn't believe that so many people got here before her.

On the other side, I found Marion in a very short nurse's uniform. She was standing in fire engine red five-inch heels. Even though her costume was tissue paper thin, she wasn't wearing a coat.

"The temperature is about to get hot in here," she announced, pushing her way in the door. To her credit, she did stop right inside the door to actually greet me.

"Hey girl, thanks for the invite. Amazing house," she said, not bothering to wait for me but instead walking toward the sound of the voices. I let her keep walking, watching to see if she will topple in those ridiculously high heels. She was going to be sincerely disappointed when she saw there were no single men here. I was about to follow her when I heard the sound of footsteps approaching.

I didn't wait for whoever it was to ring the bell. Instead, I swung the door open to find not one person but three people chatting amicably. Even though I invited them, I was still somehow shocked to see them standing there on my front porch.

Marcia was dressed as exercise Barbie, complete with matching blonde hair with bangs. She wore hot pink Lycra leggings with a turquoise leotard on top of them and matching leg warmers. I almost didn't recognize her with the blonde hair. The weird part was that she was chatting with Chloe, who was dressed as a fifties-girl donning a pink poodle skirt. She was accompanied by who I presumed to be Chloe's boyfriend, who looked suspiciously like John Travolta in Grease. In the weeks that I've known Marcia, I've never seen her act that friendly towards anybody. That's what made it so disconcerting.

For this group, I prayed that my real feelings were not plastered all over my face. I got my party hostess game face on, "Hi guys, thank you for coming!" I said leading them into the foyer.

"Thank you for having us!" Chloe said cheerfully. She seemed to be the spokesperson for the group. "By the way, this is my boyfriend, Russ."

"Nice to meet you Russ," I said smiling at him. "You can hang your coats right in here," I said, gesturing to the big closet directly in front of us.

"Your house is lovely," Marcia said graciously. I was happy for her response but did not quite trust it.

Chloe and her boyfriend were busy hanging up their coats first which, lucky me, left me to make conversation with Marcia.

"Have you ever been here before?" I asked, not sure what to talk to her about. I didn't know if Aunt Ginny had known her. It's possible that they ran in the same circles.

She seemed to bristle before answering, "No, I've only seen it from behind." She had even put in blue contact lenses making her eyes an artificial turquoise color. The whole exchange seemed surreal.

Finally, they were done hanging their coats and came over to talk to me while Marcia hung hers.

"Your house really is beautiful," said Chloe. "Everything looks so great!" She looked around at my decorations and peeked her head to both sides to see both the living room and the parlor.

I extended my hand to Russ. "It's so nice to meet you! My boyfriend Coal will be thrilled that there is another guy in the mix," I said cheerfully. He had a nice strong grip and his eyes were an unusual shade of green.

"All done," Marcia said, joining our little group. I ushered them all into the kitchen and luckily Coal caught my panicked face and came over to take care of drinks.

Brrring!!!! The bell went off yet again, this time I was grateful for a chance to slip away. I went right back to the door. My shoe slipped off and I momentarily paused to fix it. I caught the silhouette of two people in the smoked glass door. This was probably finally Fiona. She had some nerve leaving me to greet Marcia alone. I couldn't wait to give her a piece of my mind regarding her late arrival.

I opened the door and stood there with my mouth agape. It was as if time froze. I was sure we had stood there frozen long enough for a painter to replicate an accurate portrait. Nothing could have prepared me for what was waiting for me on the other side of that smoked glass.

CHAPTER THIRTY-ONE

I narrowed my eyes, fixing my gaze on Fiona. She was adorned in a medieval style dress in cream, green, and burgundy. It had long billowy sleeves. A gold headband was placed amongst her raven corkscrew curls. She even had a little makeup on for a change and her face looked glowing. Her date, a tallish man with brown hair and eyes was wearing what was obviously a Robinhood getup. It was complete with a quiver on his back to hold the arrows. He was holding a bow in his hands and looking intently at me.

"Is this a joke?" I spit out, not caring how rude I sounded. I felt as if my anger could shake the buildings around us. I wanted to yell to the other guests to run for cover.

Fiona looked completely confused. Her face was crestfallen. She had never seen or heard me be anything but completely polite. "What do you mean? I'm sorry we were late," she fumbled with what to say, not wanting to make me any angrier than I already looked. "Michael wanted to make sure that he got his costume exactly right."

"Michael," I said, my voice holding the ice of a hail storm in it. I turned to him. He pasted an innocent yet amused look on his face.

"Nice to see you again Ava, you look well."

"Wait, you know each other?" Fiona asked. Her eyes were two brown saucers and her mouth remained in the shape of an O. She looked back and forth between Michael and me, not knowing where to fix her gaze.

"Michael," I repeated again, this time staring at Fiona, waiting for a reaction. Something that would explain away this whole ridiculous situation.

"No!" she nearly screamed, "It can't be." She covered her open mouth with her hand. The realization of what was going on just dawned on her. A myriad of emotions crossed her face all at once. Michael's expression didn't change at all. He stood there looking smug.

"Everything ok?" Coal suddenly appeared at the doorway. "You were taking a while, and I thought I heard shouting." He looked a little concerned. His eyes went back and forth between Fiona and Michael. I could see the confusion in his eyes. "Ava?" he asked again.

"Everything is fantastic," I said snidely. "Coal, you already know Fiona of course, and this is Michael." I stressed his name when I said it and Coal immediately got it. I saw his body language shift. Coal crossed his arms over his chest. Michael spread his legs farther apart and thrust his hips slightly forward. I felt as if I were watching a couple of male turkeys trying to intimidate the other.

"I didn't know that you knew Fiona until we were pulling into your driveway, and by then it was too late," he said innocently. "I swear."

I laughed inside at the thought of his words holding any value. I was wondering if he could actually believe I was dumb enough to believe his feigned innocence, as if his words could actually mean anything at all to me.

"This can't be!" Fiona shouted, tears falling and soaking her face.

"Let's move this inside. We can straighten everything out, in there." Coal was trying to save Fiona from unraveling in front of the entire neighborhood. He pointed to the door. He seemed to have cooled down; his body language toned down at last. He better not have believed Michael's sad story. His alleged innocence in being brought to a party at my house. Now I was angry at Coal too for being so naive. I turned my fury down to a simmer, only because I was afraid if I didn't someone was going to get hurt.

The four of us went in the door, just as we were going to close it, I heard, "Wait, don't forget me." At last Samantha arrived. She literally stuck her heeled foot in the open space to stop us from closing it. All the guests were here and the party could officially begin.

Fiona did not wait for me to give further instructions, she took Michael's hand and dragged him into the kitchen. She went straight to the bar cart, took out tequila and poured herself a shot, all without saying a word.

Samantha, who was dressed as a dazzling mermaid with a red wavy-haired wig was oblivious to what was going on. She was busy pouting because nobody told her how beautiful she looked. Little did she know that she had unfortunately walked in on our own personal shit storm.

Amber walked over just as Fiona had slammed down her shot glass. She saw her mom standing there and audibly groaned.

"Fiona, you look beautiful," she gushed. "Just love your makeup!" She turned to look around her and saw Michael. Looking alarmed she looked from me, to Fiona, to Coal. Her head kept whipping around. Amber had met Michael on more than one occasion, and she wasn't sure what was happening.

"Are we doing shots?" Marion asked, coming up next to Fiona. "Pour me one, will ya?" she demanded.

Fiona, not knowing what to do, obliged and poured Marion a full shot and another for herself.

"One, two, three, shoot," Marion yelled and they both poured the shots down their throats in one quick motion. Marion threw her arms in the air triumphantly. Fiona looked as if she was trying to escape.

"*Fiona*," Amber's voice took on a warning tone that

sent shivers down my spine. Fi put the shot glass down and looked earnestly at Amber. I think it was probably good she did the two shots, because I didn't know how else she was going to make it through this.

"Yes," Fiona said calmly, the regular color had returned to her face. There was just a trace of dried tears that remained.

"Can I speak with you for a minute? Ava, can you join us as well?" Amber was so calm and spoke as if she were an employer addressing her employees.

I panicked. Was it ok to leave Michael alone here with Coal? It would have to be. My stomach lurched. We needed to get to the bottom of this.

Fiona and I both followed Amber up the stairs. I watched Fiona's curls bounce as she walked each step. Amber led us into the library and closed the door.

"I hope you don't mind Ava," she said, turning to me apologetically, for taking control in my house during my party. "Please have a seat, girls. "

I quickly sat down in my green leather chair being sure to claim it as mine before Fiona had a chance.

"Excuse me for being a busybody, but what is going on?" Her luxurious Venetian mask was now balanced on her head, and her normally serene face was filled with confusion. Her beautiful gray eyes were all business.

"Fiona brought Michael as her date to my party," I finally said, as Fiona had declined to speak. I felt like a kid tattling on her classmate to the teacher.

Amber's eyes turned to Fiona; they were filled with an almost rage mixed with disappointment. "Is this true Fiona? Did you really bring Ava's ex-husband as your date to her own party?" She fired the words at her as if she were the district attorney trying to rattle the witness on the stand.

Amber started crying again, but this time she was not hysterical. It was a gentle, calm cry "You have to believe me Ava; I had no idea that my Michael was your Michael."

I took a deep breath and looked at her, willing her to continue.

"We just met a few weeks back. He said he wanted to take it slow, so that's why I never introduced any of you to him. I swear."

I tried to think back. I only met Fiona a few times throughout the years. I don't think that she ever met Michael. Amber was a different story. She knew Michael pretty well. It was possible that she was telling the truth. She probably was just as side swiped by this whole thing as I was. She finally met a guy that she liked only to find out that it was my ex-husband. If I were her, I'd feel devastated.

"Fiona, I believe you," I said finally, grabbing her hand and squeezing it.

"You do?" she asked with tears in her eyes.

Amber just stood there watching the interaction between the two of us. Her beautiful face tense as she waited to see how it would unfold. I think we were all afraid to breathe.

"Yes, did you ever mention me to him by name?" I asked carefully and watched her face for an authentic reaction.

Amber sat thoughtfully for a minute, trying her best to remember exactly how it went down. "I asked him if he wanted to go with me to my friend's costume party, and he said it sounded like fun. No, no I don't think I ever mentioned your name to him." Her face lit up. I saw hope stirring in her.

"Well then this is just one terrible coincidence." I put my fingers to my forehead and began massaging my temples, attempting to soothe the dull ache that had threatened to take over and rock my head.

Amber looked somewhat relieved, "Why don't we go down and have a good time. If you want him to leave Ava, I can tell him for you." She gave me a motherly look, that I certainly appreciated. It was nice to have someone to count on. She wasn't just looking out for Fiona's interests but mine as well.

"No, it's ok," I started, taking a deep calming breath. "He can stay. I'm here with Coal. Fiona is here with Michael. It's ok."

Before anyone could say anything else, I was up and at the door. "You can leave it open," I said to Amber and Fiona. "I want people to come upstairs eventually to hang out in the library." I asked my upstairs Alexa to play Ella Fitzgerald and strode away quickly, leaving Amber and Fiona whispering behind me.

As I went down the hallway, admiring all my decorations and work that Lina and I put in, my head was spinning. Exiting the stairs and going by way of the living room this time, I rejoined the party. Everyone seemed to be having a great time. I watched from the side, remaining undetected for a moment. Michael seemed to fit right in. Marion even wormed her way so that she was directly by his side. He didn't look the slightest bit disturbed by being in his ex-wife's house, uninvited.

The only person who did not seem at ease was Coal. He was by Adelaide's side listening politely, attentively to a story she was telling, but it was there in his face. A slight tick by his right eye gave away his tension, the pull of his shoulders. No, Coal was not happy, and I couldn't blame him. My much anticipated first ever solo party slipped out of my hands like dust in the wind.

Amber and Fiona made their reappearance back into the party before I had a chance to slip out of the shadows. Fiona went by Michael's side, but Marion wasn't moving over, so she stood there lamely. Amber had put her mask back down and slipped in next to Peter giving his hand a squeeze. I just had to make it through the night, I reminded myself.

Coal looked relieved as I reentered the room. He excused himself from Adelaide for a minute, and he wrapped his arms around me.

"Are you ok?" he asked, whispering in my ear. He didn't even need to whisper as the music and the cacophony of voices made it impossible to hear.

"I'm ok. From speaking with Fiona, it seems she had no idea that Michael was who he was. In fact, I kind of feel bad for her," I sighed.

"What about Michael?" he asked skeptically. "Did he know he was coming to your house?" His voice took on a hard edge, and Coal couldn't help but glare in his general direction.

"That remains to be seen, but Fiona doesn't think she ever mentioned my name. Come to think of it, I wasn't friends with Fiona until I moved here, so it might just be some type of sick coincidence. Whatever the case, I told her he could stay."

Coal let go of me and dropped his arms by his sides. I didn't have time to deal with his annoyance. I had my own tribulation to deal with, so I walked away, turned down Alexa so the Ghostbusters song wasn't thrashing around in my brain.

"Thank you so much for coming, my friends," I announced loudly, capturing everyone's attention. People stopped their side conversations and turned their attention to me. "I hope you are having a wonderful time. You all look great. Your costumes are amazing!"

"Here, here," Peter cheered. Everyone raised their glasses and took a sip of their varied drinks.

"Please help yourself to the food. It's set up in the dining room," I pointed to indicate where that was for the people that had never been over before. "If you need anything, don't hesitate to ask, but please feel free to help yourself to food and drinks. Happy Halloween my friends." I was proud of myself for my acting job and felt it could have won me Best Actress. Only the key players knew that anything was wrong, and I hoped I fooled even them into thinking that I didn't care.

Everyone raised their glasses in unison a second time. I turned the volume on the music a little higher. Some people made a beeline for the food while others poured themselves a second drink. I made myself a dirty martini and stood back watching.

It's interesting the things you see when you stand still and everyone else is moving. I saw Adelaide staring down Marcia who was chatting animatedly with Chloe. I still didn't understand that connection. I saw Marion setting her sights on Michael once again, as Fiona slipped her arm possessively around his waist. Peter put his mask up on his head as he took a sip of his red wine, his eyes glancing in my direction and quickly diverting once he realized I was watching.

Only Lina even noticed that I was standing by myself. She came up to me and whispered, "Are you ok?"

"I'm good," I said, trying to produce a smile that reached my eyes.

She looked at me intently and tilted her head.

"We can talk about it over tea the next time we get together." This time I gave a genuine smile. I was happy I invited this lovely woman. The only person that seemed to realize that the bricks were falling one by one around me. I gave her an A+ for being perceptive.

"Yes, we will," she nodded in understanding. Then she walked over to Amber who was beckoning her to come speak with her.

Coal came back over to me. "Do you want me to start the fire outside now?" he asked, doing his best not to look annoyed.

"Yes, that would be great; it looks like almost everyone got some food already."

Coal nodded and headed towards the French doors. Just as he was about to head out, Tabitha and Enzo stopped him. Coal broke out into a wide grin and shook Enzo's hand genuinely. Enzo patted him heartily on the back, and Enzo and Tabitha happily followed Coal into the backyard.

I turned the volume down once more, looking out at my party guests.

"Sorry guys," I'm not one for making speeches, so I felt the need to apologize. I was not used to being Master of Ceremonies. "Coal is setting up the fire pit in the backyard. We will be having our pumpkin carving contest shortly. Let's meet in the backyard in five minutes. I'll give you your team members when we get out there. Then you can come up with your design and get right to work."

The air was abuzz with conversation, everyone talking excitedly.

"I know just what to do," Samantha bragged to Fiona.

"I don't want to carve a pumpkin," Marion protested. "The insides are disgusting! Have you ever felt how slimy they are?"

I began to relax a little. I had finished my first dirty martini, and I saw how engaged all the guests were at this point. Little by little, people began to file outside onto the patio. Coal and I had strung twinkle lights out earlier that day. Together with the fire Coal started, and everyone in costume, the night looked magical. I spotted my phone on the counter and reprimanded myself for not memorializing the event yet. I stood at the French doors and took some pictures of the partygoers scattered around the fire.

After snapping off several pictures, I went in search of the large purple index cards that Coal and I had made earlier that day. We had bought 6 pumpkins, so we divided the guests into teams of two, with the exception of one team that would have three participants. Funny enough, I didn't know that Marcia knew Chloe, and I had put them together, along with Chloe's boyfriend.

I gathered together 6 knives that were suitable for carving, 6 Sharpie markers, along with plastic bags from the supermarket that people could use to dispose of the pumpkin guts. I shooed the final lingering guests out the door before making my departure with the knives and bags in hand.

With everyone gathered round, my heart filled, despite the earlier awkwardness. The backyard looked like a movie set. Everyone's faces were aglow bathed in the light of the fire. The antique hydrangeas were lit up by the fire. The costumes added to the magic. Without the music that was present inside, it was much easier to hear each other.

"Okay, so I will hand each team a Sharpie, index card, and knife. You can discuss with your team member your idea for your design. Then you can sketch your idea on the back. When you are ready, start drawing your design on the pumpkin and carve away. There is a prize for the winning pumpkin."

"Yes, Ms. Z," Marion said in a child's voice.

That got a laugh from the crowd. I wasn't going to deny that I sounded like a teacher in action, but it was much easier instructing a group of adults than it was a group of second graders.

"Team One, Fiona and Michael," I announced, handing the necessary items off to Fiona. Michael beamed at her; I witnessed Marion scowling.

"Team Two, Tabitha and Enzo."

"Team Three, Marion and Samantha."

"Fine with me," Marion muttered. "At least I know you'll think of something," she said under her breath as Samantha eagerly claimed her tools.

"Team Four, Adelaide and Lina."

"Team Five, Amber and Peter."

"And finally, Team Six, Chloe, Marcia, and Russ." I saw Marcia and Chloe smile conspiratorially. I really would have to find out their connection.

As the teams spread out and got to work, Coal and I joined together, finally a chance to take a breath.

"I'm sorry about before," Coal whispered, his face looking extra handsome by firelight. "I know this must be hard for you, and can I say you are handling it like a real lady." He grabbed my hand and kissed it.

"Thank you, Coal. I know it's not easy for you either. This situation is weird, but really what do we care about those two dating? We have each other. If they are happy together, good for them," I finished stealing a glance to where Fiona and Michael laughed together while sketching on their pumpkin. Coal saw them in action and seemed to relax a degree more.

"Besides that nonsense, I think the party is going swimmingly well," Coal said, glancing at our friends scattered around the yard hard at work. We set up several stations on the patio and scattered around with a little table and chairs for our guests to work on their pumpkin designs.

Coal stole a kiss from me. My knees began to buckle slightly, my pulse quickened.

"Bonnie and Clyde, get a room," Marion shouted across the yard where Samantha was hard at work, and Marion was busy nursing her beer. "How come you two get to have fun while I have to scoop pumpkin guts?"

A few people grinned and returned feverishly to their work.

Coal and I began to circulate to be sure that everyone was doing okay. Although the teams were at various stages of being complete, everyone was moving along. My eye caught Adelaide's and Lina's pumpkin. An outline of a cat, complete with pointy ears and intricate whiskers, was sketched in black on their rotund pumpkin. I assumed and hoped that Lina would be doing the carving as Adelaide professed her blindness to me on more than one occasion.

"Ow," I heard someone shout. I turned to see Chloe holding her finger. Marcia was hovering over her.

"Everything ok?" I asked, rushing over to them to see what happened. Now Russ was holding up her hand to examine it.

"Do you have bandages?" Russ asked, a worried crease across his forehead.

"Oh no, you got cut?" I asked moving closer to examine her pointer finger on her left hand.

"It's only a little cut," Chloe insisted, brushing off all of the unwanted attention.

"No, come with me," I insisted. Her entourage got up and filed into the house behind me. I didn't know these people too well and wasn't looking to be sued.

Coal hung back in the kitchen with Russ and Marcia, while I took Chole into the bathroom on the first floor to fix up her hand.

I flipped on the light and the two sconces decorating either side of the mirror came on. Feeling unnerved, I quickly opened the medicine cabinet in search of supplies. Locating a bottle of hydrogen peroxide, Neosporin, and bandages, I placed them on the marble countertop.

Grabbing two tissues out of the purple tissue box, I drenched them in hydrogen peroxide and applied pressure to where the cut was on Chloe's finger.

"Sorry if this hurts," I said in a motherly tone. "I just want to make sure it's clean, so it doesn't get infected." The tissue had a crimson stain seeping onto it.

"It's fine really," Chloe insisted. "Thanks for taking care of me though." She smiled and her spiky hair glimmered in the light of the sconces. It looked like she just got fresh highlights.

"It's no problem. I'm just sorry you got hurt." I squirted a dab of the ointment on the cut now and struggled to open up the bandage.

Chloe smiled, "Russ told me not to cut the way I was doing it, but I knew better," she said with a laugh. "Guess I showed him!"

Now we both laughed.

"So how do you know Marcia?" I asked. "It was just a coincidence that I put her on your team for the pumpkin decorating contest. I didn't realize that you knew each other."

Chloe looked at me for a minute before answering. I had her cut all cleaned and wrapped up now, and I was putting all of the supplies back into the cabinet. "She's my sister," she answered. "Actually, my half-sister. We have the same mom but different dads. I was the result of a second marriage for my mom. It was funny because we didn't realize we were both coming to your party tonight until we showed up at the door at the same time."

"That's so funny. What a coincidence," I said, flipping the light off and walking with Chloe back into the kitchen to join the others.

"You ok baby?" Russ asked, going up to Chloe and kissing her on the head as soon as we entered the kitchen.

Chloe smiled and nodded.

"Then let's get back outside to finish that bad boy off," Russ insisted enthusiastically. Marcia just rolled her eyes. "I've got a contest to win."

"Does anyone want to get a drink before we go back outside?" I asked the trio.

Coal automatically went and got Russ a craft beer out of the fridge.

"I'll take one as well," Chloe spoke up before Coal closed the refrigerator door.

"What about you Marcia?" I asked.

She smiled, but it didn't quite reach her artificial turquoise eyes, unlike her sister whose smile was genuine.

"I think I saw you drinking a dirty martini before. Would it be possible to get one of those? Less calories," she said, eyeing her sister's beer disapprovingly.

"Of course," I answered. I pulled the vodka and ice cubes out of the freezer. I located my container with olive juice, and grabbed a jar that had olives stuffed with blue cheese. Measuring two shots of vodka into the shaker, Marcia narrowed her eyes and watched me closely.

"So, how long have you and Coal been together?" Marcia asks. She flips her wig as though it were her own hair.

"Just a few weeks," Coal said before I even had a chance to respond, "but they've been the best weeks of my life." He looked dreamily at me.

Russ spoke up, "Chloe and I have been dating a few

months, but I feel exactly the same way." He gave her a peck on her lips.

Marcia smiled at the four of us politely.

The French doors opened and Marion came bounding through, "Need to get reinforcements," she said, grabbing a beer in each hand and heading back out the door.

I finished off Marcia's drink by pouring it into the martini glass and spearing two olives on a toothpick, dropping them in her drink. I had doubled the recipe and poured myself another one as well.

"There you go," I said, handing it carefully over to her.

Marcia took a long sip, "You've got skills, I must admit." This time she smiled approvingly, and the five of us made our way back out to the party. The inky night aglow with excitement.

CHAPTER THIRTY-TWO

The rest of the party guests were so engaged in their pumpkin designing that it barely registered that we rejoined the party. The trio went back to finish off their pumpkin, with promises to be more careful cutting. Coal went and added some more wood logs to the fire. It was nice and hot now and burned evenly, no smoke ruining the ambiance. While he was doing that I mulled around to see if anyone needed to have their drinks refreshed.

"This party is just lovely," I heard Adelaide exclaim to Lina. She looked more alive than I'd ever seen, eyes bright, cheeks flushed. I felt happy that I had included her, but my heart ached for her and her estranged family. "That Ava is such a lovely girl to have invited an old lady like me." I didn't want her to know that I heard, so I continued to walk by them nonchalantly.

I didn't want to ask Fiona and Michael how they were doing. As I walked by, I looked down at their Jack-o'-lantern. They had cut out two hearts that were connected. Michael must have felt my presence, he looked up at me and sneered. A mean vengeful look filled his eyes. Then Fiona noticed me and looked at me trepidatiously, so I stopped.

"Just checking to see if you guys need your drinks re-filled?" I asked as sweetly as possible. I really wasn't jealous; I would swear to it. It's just that I finally got Michael out of my life, and now here he was sitting in my backyard, completely at ease, like he belonged there. It's like he was a boomerang that I kept throwing but would find its way back to me.

"I'll take a beer, as long as you're asking," Michael replied, happy to have an opportunity for me to serve him yet once again.

"Oh, I'll get it," Fiona piped up right away insistently. "I want to get some more of that eyeball martini punch anyway. It's delicious."

"Ok," I said and began to walk away from them, happy to leave Fiona to it. He was her problem now.

"Wait up," Fiona said. Inwardly I groaned, but I waited for her just as she asked.

"Thank you," Fiona said, matching my stride as I made my way to the house.

I didn't respond. I opened the door and grabbed my previously made martini off of the counter.

"This means a lot to me Ava, that you let Michael stay." She used the ladle and filled the orange sparkly plastic cup with the eyeball punch.

I nodded, at a loss. If Fiona didn't know that Michael was who he was, I couldn't fault her for that. It didn't change my feelings of outrage, but I would not misplace my outrage. It didn't belong to Fiona. However, surely, she must understand how awkward and terrible this was for me. It should have been awkward for him as well, but glancing back out the window seeing him flirting with Marion in Fiona's absence, he looked completely at ease. He hadn't changed a bit. I wasn't the problem, he was. I told Fi so many stories about him, I couldn't possibly see how they wouldn't be playing in her head on loop now that she knew who he was.

"I mean, I understand this is a weird situation," she began twirling one of her loose curls nervously around her finger, "but we just really clicked. You know, like you and Coal. You just know that it feels right."

At the mention of Coal's name, I began to thaw a little. I mean one girl's frog is another girl's prince. Who was I to deny her a chance at happiness?

"I get it," I said, "I'm just going to need a little time." I exhaled, not realizing that I had been holding my breath the entire time.

Adelaide came ambling into the kitchen. "The ladies' room is calling my name my dear," she said, giving me a wave as she shuffled through, her cat tail waving behind her. She was definitely spry for her age.

"Well, I think most people are close to being done with their pumpkins. I'm just going to make an announcement to everyone, so they know what is happening next," I said, grabbing my martini and nearing running away. I left Fiona standing at the counter, her drink in one hand and Michael's beer in the other.

I took a detour and walked through the glass room. I had lit a giant orange glass pumpkin in the center of the table. It created an eerie vibe in the room, orangish bits of light refracting on the walls. I shivered and walked out the door, ending up on the right of the house instead of the center of the back by the French doors. Coal was standing to the side of the yard chatting quietly with Enzo. I wondered to myself why they didn't hang out more, when I instinctually stopped and stood for a minute. I heard my name spoken.

"Wow, that is crazy!" Enzo exclaimed in his excitable Italian accent. I almost laughed. His cannoli costume really added some humor to the situation. "Fiona showed up with Ava's ex? That is really bad luck. I hope she is not too upset."

"Maybe," Coal said, not sounding so sure. "If it was an accident, it was bad luck, but if it was planned, it was evil." They stood quietly for a moment. Enzo nodded in agreement and took a sip of his red wine before he continued.

"Does she know that you used to date Fiona?" he asked in a hushed tone. He glanced around the yard and at the French doors in an attempt to make sure that their conversation went unwitnessed. Their backs were to me, so I was the only one who went undetected.

Dated Fiona? I couldn't have heard him correctly.

Dated Fiona, as in, was her boyfriend? Boyfriend? The word swirled around and around in my brain. Rather than go over to Coal and ask him why those crazy words were coming out of Enzo's mouth, my body filled with heat. A red flash of color sliced through my brain. The immediate heat enveloped my body from my ears down to my toes. I felt like I had been given a shot of adrenaline. I couldn't think. I darted back inside the glass room, I peered around the corner, and it appeared that the kitchen was vacant. I made my move, going quicker and quieter than I had ever moved before. My actions were as seamless as a ninja. I moved in silence taking the stairs two at a time headed for the library. Not sure what I was going to do when I got there but just needing to move. As I reached the top, I heard an old jazz singer crooning from within the walls of the library. I reached the library without anyone seeing me, I quickly and quietly secured the door, so as not to alert anyone to my whereabouts.

I wasn't sure how much time I had before someone came looking for me. Pulling the skeleton key from beneath Aunt Virginia's shirt, just to be sure that I had it, I quickly climbed the ladder, moved the sconce and made my way into the secret room. I pulled the door completely shut and turned on the light. My heart was beating so rapidly that I became frightened. I opened the bar cart and pulled out the vodka. Finding a shot glass, I poured myself a hefty shot and tilted my head back. I didn't even like shots back in my college days, but I needed a way to slow down my brain and body. Coal was right. This did make a good safe room, I thought ironically, to keep me safe from him.

I sank into the wine-colored chair. Ideas jumped around in my brain. Maybe I heard wrong. I probably should have stuck around and listened to Coal's response. Then everything would have made sense. Right? The two martinis and the shot of vodka that I just drank worked their way through my system. My brain slowed down a fraction, enough to lower the rate of my rapid beating heart.

Coal and Fiona? Fiona and Coal? No. It was impossible, but that is what Enzo said. I heard him with my own ears. Does she know you dated? It was crazy because the crushing feeling that was hitting me, making it hard to breathe, tearing my heart out, sucking the very life out of me, was worse than what I felt when my ten-year marriage burned out. That was like a firework that you lit that was past its expiration date. It just smoked and fizzled. I was more disappointed about not being able to start a family. Just when I trusted that I got my second chance, it was cruelly snatched from me. I thought in Coal I had finally met someone who had my back. He was someone who made my heart sing. He comforted me when I was sad. He was both practical and reliable. Coal was the devil dressed as an angel, and I would never forgive him.

Bang, I heard the sound of the library door closing and voices murmuring, interrupting my wallowing. I silently thanked God I was hidden because I was not ready to face anyone. In fact, I wondered how I would make it through the rest of this party. Perhaps if I stayed hidden everyone would just go home when I didn't reappear. Not likely, I thought feeling defeated.

"I always loved this room." It was Amber speaking. I heard her sit down, probably in my beloved green chair. "There's something really special about it." Her voice sounded despairing. It held a longing.

"Yes, it's beautiful," a man's voice agreed. She was obviously with Peter.

"What's this?" Amber asked. I obviously couldn't see her, but I pictured her finding the photograph of Aunt Ginny and her that I left in the left corner of the desk, holding it in her hands and running her fingers over it. "Oh my, I remember that day so well." Her voice was filled with melancholy. She went quiet for a moment. I pictured her sitting there with tears in her eyes.

"I think you need to tell her?" Peter said seriously, probably interrupting her thoughts. "I think that it's eating you alive."

"I'm not so sure," Amber said, her voice weary. "I don't know if it's my place. I don't know if it will help anything, make anything better. I don't want to cause any more pain. It isn't just."

"If not you then who?" Peter asked gently. "Is it fair that she never knows the truth? She loves you. She deserves to know. You will help her through it. You are a wonderful strong woman."

Now Amber was audibly weeping, "No I'm not. I'm a terrible mother. I handle everything wrong with Fiona. I'm not so sure I can do it. I'm a hypocrite after all. Aren't I?" She asked. I pictured her looking up at Peter with her big blue eyes. Even crying she probably still looked gorgeous, unlike me who looked like a mottled, tear-stained mess, probably thanks to my red hair and fair skin.

I was grateful for the momentary break from my own disturbing discovery. For a minute I could forget my tragedy. My heartbreak could wait because I knew that it wouldn't go away for a very, very long time, if ever. I thought I found the stuff in the storybooks, and it was actually a big con.

My head was swimming with questions that I couldn't ask right now. Who was Amber talking about? Who should she tell what to? I was so intrigued and had so many questions, but I knew I had to lie in wait and be patient. I couldn't even emerge until after they left. Even then, I couldn't tell them I was sitting in a secret room listening to their private conversation. Their business was personal and was not meant to be heard by me.

"Amber love, I don't mean to rush you, but Ava is going to be looking for us since everyone's finished their pumpkins. Let's not ruin her party. It's been tough for her." His voice was still gentle and kind.

"I know," Amber said, her voice filled with regret. She blurted out, "How could Fiona do that? How could she show up here with Michael? What was she thinking? That poor girl was just starting to heal. She lost her parents, her marriage, and Virginia. How could she be so thoughtless?" Amber's voice was now filled with anger. She was condemning her daughter for her selfish behavior on my behalf.

Wait, what? Did Amber know something I didn't? Was there anyone that I considered close that wasn't lying to me? Did Fiona bring him here purposely? No, I had to believe that wasn't the case. I obviously was the worst possible judge of character. I couldn't trust my own judgment.

"Chin up," Peter said. I heard them stand, the chairs scraping against the wood. Billie Holiday was serenading me in the background. The sound of the door opening and then closing again, leaving just me hidden behind a wall.

They were gone. Now what? I knew the right thing was to march back downstairs and put on a good face for my visitors. It was something I was good at. I could deal with Coal later. I would think about the conversation that Peter and Amber had when everyone had left. After all, I had nothing left but time by myself now. It was another mystery to solve. It would distract me while I stained my pillow with tears. There were no second chances at love, only heartbreak.

CHAPTER THIRTY-THREE

I calculated in my head. I waited a solid five minutes before leaving the room, just in case they came back looking for me. I didn't want Amber to know that I had witnessed such a raw private moment that was not meant for my ears. I also needed those five minutes to compose myself in solitude. The heat in my body had dissipated and was replaced with weariness, a tiredness that penetrated my bones entering every cell of me. I almost longed for the heat. Anger could keep me going. This just left me hollow.

When five minutes had passed, I pressed my ear to the door. I listened for any evidence of footsteps, conversation, or breathing. None could be heard. I quickly opened the door, as I was climbing up the ladder to straighten the sconce, the same song that played the first night Coal and I danced began to play in the walls of that old library. You had to be kidding me. It was the universe's way of giving me a big slap in the face.

Opening the door of the library, I glanced down the hallway both ways, no one was there. Turning to the right, I opted to go to my room and fix myself up before facing everyone. Entering my bathroom, I looked in the mirror and couldn't recognize the face that was looking back at me. I looked like a ghost of the person who got ready with so much excitement just that afternoon.

I dusted some purple eyeshadow on and reapplied my eyeliner. Pulling a piece of toilet paper off the roll, I swiped off my remaining lipstick which now felt dried and caked on. I re-lined my lips and applied a fresh coat of red lipstick. I looked a little better. Reaching into the cabinet, I found my absolute favorite perfume. It was expensive, so I didn't wear it every day. It had some fancy French name that I could never quite remember or pronounce correctly for that matter. I inhaled a deep breath and felt ready for battle. Counting to ten backwards, I made my way down the hallway and marched down the stairs to what felt like my death.

There was not a soul in sight as I crept through the house. The party in the backyard was still rocking. I could see out the window by the kitchen sink. The fire continued to burn, everyone chatted loudly. By the looks of it, you would have never known that my life was falling apart. Isn't it funny that no matter what travesties are going on in your life, the rest of the world continues to turn? That should be proof enough for anybody that our life is just a blip on the radar. It is both depressing and relieving at the same time. It takes a little pressure off.

Deciding to come out the door in the glass room, so I could go undetected until I was ready, I noticed that the door was wide open. I backtracked into the kitchen and saw that the French doors were also opened, as was the side door on the side by Peter's house.

Instead of coming back quietly and going undetected, I went directly out the open French doors. "Does anyone know why all the doors are open?" I asked loudly, making my best attempt not to scream. Peter and Amber stopped and looked at me.

Lina came walking up to me cautiously. "I'm so sorry. Are you mad? I left them open; I was not thinking it was a problem. It is an old Polish tradition. You leave the doors and windows open to let the spirits in for Halloween."

At the word spirits, I shivered. I wished the spirits of Aunt Ginny and my mom and dad came right now and chased all of these people away.

I took a deep breath, not wanting to take my problems out on Lina. She was an innocent bystander. "No, no worries. Let's just shut them now though, ok," I said, softening my tone. We both went in through the French doors into the kitchen.

Lina looked down sadly, "I'm truly sorry." She looked like she lost her best friend.

"It's no problem, Lina. I'll shut the door of the glass room, and you can close the side door."

When we were done, we met back at the kitchen counter.

"Adelaide, your neighbor from behind you was looking for you before," Lina said softly.

"Oh, I had to use the ladies' room. I guess I'll go find her now."

"I would like to stay after the party and help you clean up, as a friend," she added for clarification and put her hand on my shoulder. She understood I didn't want her here as an employee. She obviously noticed that I could use a friend.

"That would be great," I said. Although I wanted desperately to be alone, I had absolutely no one left to confide in. It would be nice to have Lina around, a real friend. I wished I could borrow that Lasso of Truth that's been attached to her costume all night and wield its power. Maybe I could finally get some answers. Her being here would also serve as an excuse for me not to be left alone with Coal.

Entering the party again, my eyes did a quick scan of the yard for Coal. I figured he would have been looking for me at this point. I guessed wrong. I finally found him playing darts with Enzo and Russ. We set up an old dart board on the giant tulip tree near the back of the yard.

Adelaide was busy chatting with Peter and Amber by the fire, Fiona and Michael were snuggled up on the oversized bench towards the left of the yard, nestled by my rose garden, and the rest of the ladies were in a group chatting by the summer house to the back right of the yard.

Remembering what Lina said about Adelaide looking for me, I reluctantly approached her.

"Hey Adelaide, are you having fun?" I asked, forcing a smile on my face.

"Oh yes dear. I was just speaking with Peter and Amber. I am having a lovely time. I just wanted to thank you again for inviting me," she smiled. "I'd also like to invite you around to mine, to spend some time with your kitten, get to know her before she comes home to you. I know you mentioned it before. Are you available tomorrow afternoon?"

I thought of all the plans that I made for tomorrow. They were now just dreams dashed. "Well I have dance practice tomorrow for that Dancing With the Teachers event, but when that's over, I can definitely come by."

"Dancing With the Teachers, dear?" she questioned, her painted on whiskers moving up and down with each movement of her face.

"It's a fundraiser for an after-school program for school. A bunch of the teachers are dancing with professional dancers from the area. People come to watch and the money goes to the school for the arts program. "

Adelaide puts her hands together. "Oh, how exciting! I just love dancing. When I was a girl, I had dreams of being a ballerina. I would dance all around the house," she looked like a little girl on Christmas morning reminiscing.

"We're going," Amber interjected, when she saw Adelaide's interest. "Both Amber and Ava are dancing. Tickets are a bit steep, but if you're interested you could go with us. The money goes to a good cause, after all."

"Oh, the money part isn't an issue," she said waving her hand, "but you really wouldn't mind an old lady like me cramping your style?" Adelaide asked, eyes still sparkling, lost in a dream of her childhood.

"Of course not!" Peter answered, always the gentleman. "It will be a fun night and what a lucky guy I will be to have two lovely ladies to escort."

"Great, it's settled then! I'll pick you up a ticket tomorrow," Amber said excitedly.

"Around what time dear?" Adelaide asked,

All that could be heard was the crackle of the fire, as Adelaide was looking at me this time, awaiting an answer.

I was still lost in thought, mesmerized by the bottom burning embers of the fire. They were the hottest part. They didn't burn with giant flames, like a fire does when it first catches. Although they burn the hottest and take the longest to go out. Those embers represented the feelings that Coal stirred in me.

"Ava dear?" Adelaide says waiting for my answer.

"I'm sorry?" I asked, snapped out of my reverie.

"What time do you think you'll be 'round tomorrow?" she asked.

"Oh, I can probably be there at 2 pm. Would that work for you?" I ask, finally looking away from the fire and into Adelaide's blue eyes.

"That would be just fine dear," she said, satisfied with my answer.

With Adelaide settled, I guessed it was time to get the voting for this pumpkin contest over and done with. When I originally planned for this evening, I was filled with such excitement. Now, I just wanted everyone one step closer to going home.

I stood at the edge of the patio, so I could be heard by all of my guests. "Please bring your pumpkins up to the table on the patio with the tablecloth. This is where we will present them for voting."

It took a few minutes; I wished they responded as quickly as my second graders, but everyone finally got it together and brought their pumpkins to the table. Well, the women did at least. My gaze went over to the tulip tree where the men were still occupied with their rousing dart game.

I spaced them apart and turned them so the design was visible to everyone to choose their favorite. Coal and I had pre-made oak tags bent in half so they would stand on their own. They were numbered 1 through 6. I assigned each pumpkin a number.

After getting them numbered, I lit tea candles and placed them inside each of the pumpkins. The table looked so cool in the dark of the night. Only the jack-o'-lanterns, twinkle lights and the fire giving off light. I was so angry I couldn't truly enjoy this moment, but for a minute when I stood back taking in the scene, I felt a flash of happiness. Then I remembered, and it evaporated as quickly as it came.

Number one was Adelaide and Lina's cat.

Number two was Fiona and Michael's hearts. The sight of it didn't even bother me when I thought about Coal. Perspective is a funny thing.

Number three was a witch's hat. I wasn't quite sure who it belonged to. In the confusion, I didn't see who brought up which pumpkin. I laughed to myself; I didn't know which witch was which.

Number four was an intricately carved spider. I was impressed that whoever made it was able to carve the skinny legs without breaking the pumpkin.

Number five was a dumb bell, which I could only assume belonged to Marcia, Chole, and Russ.

Number six was a wine glass.

Each pumpkin was unique. I just loved them.

"So, here's the rules," I said as everyone came and stood to ooh and aah over the presentation. The boys had finally joined us. I felt Coal come behind me and put his arm around my shoulders. I reflexively shrugged him off. Even though I wasn't going to create a scene, the thought of him touching me made my skin crawl. "Everyone picks their favorite one, but you cannot vote for your own. Please write your own name in the top left corner, so I know I have everyone's vote. When all the votes are tallied, I will announce the winner. I have a little prize for first place."

A cheer could be heard when I said this. "That's right

witches, bitches," exclaimed Marion. I chuckled to myself. I guess we figured out who the witch pumpkin belonged to.

Coal stood there looking at me strangely. He obviously noticed my reaction to him touching me and didn't know what to make of it. I handed him the notepad, with the skeleton design on the top, for him to hand a piece of paper to each person. We had spoken about it prior to the party, so no instructions were needed. It saved me having to talk to him. At the same time, I handed out pens to everyone.

There was excitement in the air as everyone scurried around gazing at the table, trying to choose the most-worthy jack-o'-lantern of all. I saw Samantha nudge her way to the front examining each pumpkin critically. When Coal was done passing out the paper, he came over to me and tapped me on the shoulder. I pretended to be absorbed in picking my favorite.

"Ava," Coal said, looking at me wide eyed. "What's wrong?"

It hurt me to even look at him.

"No," I simply said, holding my hand up like a stop sign.

Now his face looked panicked. I could see him running through his brain, trying to figure out what he had done to evoke this reaction from me. To his credit, he took a hint and backed up a little though. He must, I thought to myself, be aware that if he pushed me, it wouldn't end well.

One by one, each person handed me their paper. As they did, everyone made a beeline for the French doors. Coal dutifully put the lid on the fire to help contain it. The party officially moved back into the house. Everyone gathered in the kitchen and dining room getting second helpings of food and fixing fresh drinks.

Going into the glass room to count the votes, no one even approached the room as I calculated the winner. I wrote each number (with a description of the pumpkin next to it) and made tally marks to keep track of how many votes they received. I double counted. I had fifteen votes and fifteen people. I had my winner and would only announce first place. I had a thing about not wanting to hurt anyone's feelings. I knew that if I was the person who came in sixth place, I didn't want to know. Exiting out of the glass room door, I approached the fire pit, lifting the lid using the fire poker, I threw the papers into the fire. I watched as they disintegrated into nothingness. Then I reentered the house the way that I came.

Rejoining the party, I made myself a new dirty martini, spotting Marcia right next to the kitchen table, I asked her if she would like a refill.

"Yes please," she said with a soft smile. She actually looked prettier and younger. I guess the first martini had mellowed her a little, brought down her guard. I wondered for the first time what made her so hard. Has she been through a bad marriage like I had? Was her fate going to be mine as well? It was disconcerting to me. I didn't want to end up like Marcia, rude and suspicious to people I didn't even know.

"Having a good time?" I asked casually as I topped off her drink. I forced eye contact, trying to make a connection with her.

"Yes, I am Ava. Thank you for inviting me," she paused for a moment trying to find the words for what she wanted to say. "I guess I had you wrong," she said casually and turned her back away from me and began a conversation with Chloe.

I guess I had you wrong? What did she mean by that? What a backhanded compliment! I honestly didn't understand why she would have any opinion about me at all. I only knew her in the context of my exercise class and over the fence talking to Adelaide. My faith in humanity was waning.

Sipping my freshly made cocktail, I wondered where my phone was. I chastised myself for losing it again. I barely took any pictures of the night, caught up in my own drama. I didn't truly know how much I actually wanted to remember this night, but I figured other people would like to have the memories. I tapped the find your phone button on my Apple Watch and heard the beeping but couldn't quite pin down where it was coming from. I continually tapped the icon and traveled throughout the rooms. It definitely wasn't in the kitchen or dining room. At last, I found it between the cushions in the living room which was bizarre, as I hadn't sat in the living room ever since Coal and I found the poison letters hidden in the basket.

Thinking that the alcohol was clouding my memory and judgment, I grabbed my phone without thinking too much of it and headed back to the party to capture some images of the night's festivities. For better or worse, this was my reality.

"I'm going to have to get home soon," Adelaide said, yawning while glancing down at her watch.

"Would you like some coffee or tea first?" I asked, remembering my manners.

Adelaide seemed to consider it but finally said, "If I have caffeine too late, I'll be up all night and won't make our date tomorrow. Don't get old Ava, stay young and lovely."

"We're all getting older by the minute Adelaide, but you are always lovely." I gave her a little hug. "Let's just get a few pictures before you go though."

The sky was extra dark, but bright stars seemed to peek out of pockets of clouds. Honestly weather wise it had been a perfect Halloween party night. I guess the series of events suited Halloween as well. I corralled everyone out the door to the patio one more time. Standing at the end of the group, I took a selfie and got everyone around the glowing Jack-o'-lanterns. It only took about five tries. Next, I tortured everyone a little more getting a picture of them with their carving partner next to their creation.

. "Are you going to announce the winner of the contest?" Samantha asked, eager because she always figures that she will be the winner.

"Yes, just give me a moment to gather the prizes." I retreated to the house. The room was beginning to shift slightly as I walked. I better grab some water on the way back outside, I thought. I found the gifts I bought secured in the hutch in the glass room. Pulling them out, I had to sit back on the loveseat as the room began to spin. I would just sit for a moment. I took three deep breaths and closed my eyes. It helped a little. I thought it was just for a minute, but I'm not sure how long it was as Lina came in and found me sitting up rigidly against the couch.

"Are you ok Fiona?" Lina asked.

"Fiona?" I questioned.

"No, it's Lina," she said, now her face changed and she looked panic-stricken.

"I know you're Lina," I said, not understanding what was going on. "You called me Fiona."

"Perhaps you misheard," Lina said. "Why don't you hand out the prizes? I will prepare dessert and coffee, and then I will send everyone home." Lina was now taking charge, and I was grateful.

"Ok," I nodded in agreement. "It's been quite a night."

"You can tell me all about it when everyone leaves."

"Lina," I said standing up and clutching her hand, "thank you for being a friend and looking after me. Please, can I ask you one very big favor?"

"Of course."

"Please make sure *everyone* leaves." I stared at Lina in her Wonder Woman costume, putting my faith in her that she was the woman to get the job done. I didn't add, even Coal, but I hoped that she had got the unspoken message.

"Let's go," Lina said, leading the way out of the glass room. We entered the kitchen, and it was vacant. I peered out the window and there was no one in sight.

"Where is everyone?" I asked, wandering into the parlor. I heard a cacophony of noise coming from up the stairs. "I guess they took a field trip upstairs?" I was walking perfectly fine, even in heels, but my head was still spinning.

"Do you want me to tell everyone to come down?" Lina asked in a motherly tone.

"No, it's ok. I wanted to show everyone upstairs too. It's fine." I carefully gripped the banister and walked cautiously up the stairs one at a time, being sure to feel the stair beneath my feet before taking the next one. Lina walked closely behind me, probably worried that I was going to fall.

After what seemed an eternity, I got to the top of the stairs. Seeing the door to the library swung wide open, light, music, and laughter spilled out into the hallway. I guessed the party had gone on without me.

"Hey Ava," Fiona said when I stood in the doorway taking in the scene. She was standing next to her mom looking unsure.

"I hope you don't mind," Amber said, "everyone was curious about the upstairs, so I decided to take them on a tour."

"No, I'm glad," I reassured her. "Oh Amber, I have something for you. I found it when I was cleaning out the desk drawer," I said, remembering the picture on the desk that I heard her find while I was hiding out from the world. It was sitting on the upper hand corner of the desk, just where I left. I looked at it briefly before handing it to her. I felt a tugging at my heart.

Amber looked down at the picture as a somber look crossed her face. "I can't believe that she's gone," Amber said, clutching the picture and bowing her head.

Marcia was standing relatively nearby, she was leaning against a bookshelf and watching us with interest. I only noticed because I felt her gaze boring holes into me. When she caught sight of my eyes on her, she looked away pretending to be engaged in conversation with Chloe and Russ.

CHAPTER THIRTY-FOUR

The rays of sunshine were pouring into the room flooding it with light. It was in stark contrast to the dark cloud that was sitting over my head. I sat straight up as soon as I realized how late it must be. I felt disoriented. What time was it? I was used to waking up way before the first traces of the sun, every single morning. How did I get into my bed? I was dressed in a pair of peach colored flannel pajamas. My head felt like someone was playing the vibes on my brain, a particularly jaunty tune that wouldn't stop. A rush of panic hit me. The last thing I remembered was giving Amber the picture of her and Aunt Ginny. What happened after that? I drew a blank.

I tried to think. How much did I have to drink? I had that first martini, definitely a second, and a shot of vodka. Yes, it was more than I normally would have imbibed, but it definitely wasn't enough to warrant not remembering. In my entire life, that has never happened to me.

A thought occurred to me that made me particularly nervous. Was I alone? I looked at the other side of the bed. By the looks of it, I was positive that no one had slept in my bed beside me the night before. Glancing across the room where Coal had left his bag the day before, I noticed that the black carrier bag was conspicuously missing. I breathed a sigh of relief which was immediately followed by dread.

My first instinct was to call Fiona. She would be able to tell me the details of what happened post-picture. I wasn't mad at her per se, however she was right at the center of this whole mess, and I had a lot of thinking to do before I was ready to sit down and talk to her.

The idea struck to call Lina. Yes, that's what I would do. My cell, I reached down to where I usually leave it on the floor, much to my dismay, it was not there. Full-fledged panic coursed through my veins. It could be anywhere, and it hurt so much to think.

Spotting my watch charging on my dresser across the room, I immediately got out of bed and put it on. After entering my passcode, I pressed the ping button. I couldn't hear where it was, but it was in range, thank God. No one had taken off with it.

Feeling hopeful, I pushed my feet into my bronze-colored slippers which were sequined on the top and fluffy on the inside. They lay resting beneath my dresser, and I made my way downstairs. When I was halfway down the winding staircase, I pressed the button again. A low beep emanated from one of the rooms downstairs. In my current state, I was in no mood for a scavenger or Easter egg hunt. It definitely wasn't in the parlor I deduced as I walked through it continuing to ping. Getting warmer, the pinging grew louder as I entered the kitchen. I could tell the noise was coming from somewhere to the right of where I was standing.

First things first, I needed to take some Advil for my throbbing headache. When the pain subsided, perhaps I would be able to think. Locating the bottle in the cabinet above the microwave, I spilled three pills out into my hand and swallowed them down quickly with the help of some water.

Pinging once more, the sound was definitely coming from the glass room. I really had no recollection of going back into the glass room. As far as I could remember, I climbed the stairs with Lina, talked to Amber and gave her the picture that was on the desk. The very next thing that I could remember was waking up. While remembering feeling dizzy, I don't even remember being sick, saying goodbye to anyone, or changing my clothes.

The phone was not visible, but the beeping was loud. I lifted the blue cushion off the loveseat and at last uncovered my cell buried in the crevice between the base and the back of the couch. What on earth?

I looked at the locked screen and saw that I had 10 text messages. I was frightened to look at them and didn't quite know why. I stared at the screen without unlocking it. Sinking into the cushion on the loveseat, I put my feet up and leaned back, closing my eyes to help decrease the throbbing.

Other than the headache, all I felt was numb. When I moved to Syracuse, I didn't have much expectation other than starting over for a second chance. I was blown away by having a built-in support system with Amber, a new best friend with Fiona, and a man that seemed too good to be true and with Coal. Amber was still here for me, but both Coal and Fiona went terribly wrong. The worst part was I worked with them both. There was no escaping their daily presence in my life, other than getting a new job.

Opening my eyes, I took a deep breath and looked at the first text message.

Hi Ava, thanks for a wonderful party. Thanks for not throwing Michael out. He even remarked how cool you were about the whole thing. Are you still up for running this morning? Let me know.

That message was at 7:30 am. Well, it all sounded pretty normal, not as if I had done or said anything crazy last night that I had to feel ashamed about.

I hope you're not mad at me. Please let me know if you want to go. It would be good to get a chance to talk. I don't want things to be weird between us. 7:40 am.

Hopefully you're still sleeping, or maybe busy. winky face. Maybe we can catch up tomorrow after class. xx Fi.

The final message from Fiona came in at 7:50 am. I had to stop and take a deep breath. I tucked my auburn hair, which was falling in my face behind my ear. Well, it appeared that Fiona was at least attempting to keep things real between us. I really couldn't blame her for dating Michael when she didn't know he was Michael. The Coal thing was different though. I was having a hard time moving past that. I could forgive the Michael thing, but why didn't she tell me she dated Coal? I flip flopped in my head between totally understanding and feeling outraged. I was not in a good place.

Going back to my notifications, the next message was from Amber.

Thank you for inviting Peter and me to such a lovely party. We truly had a wonderful time. I hope we can share many more memories together. Thank you for the picture; it meant a lot to me. xx Amber

Not being able to hold Amber responsible for Fiona's actions, my heart felt a little less heavy. At least I still had someone on my team.

I felt as though I was punched in the stomach as I looked and found the next few messages were from Coal.

Ava? The first message simply stated.

The second,

What's going on? It was sent only two minutes after the first.

I inhaled a deep breath. This wasn't going to be easy.

If I did something to upset you, I wish you'd tell me so we can work through it.

This one was about a half hour later than the first two.

No one says the right thing all the time. This made me weary of Coal from the beginning. Anyone who was too smooth and always said the right thing had an angle. They didn't get tripped up because their emotions weren't really involved.

Ava dear, thank you for the spectacular party! It made me feel so young again!!! Looking forward to our date today. See you at two!

I must have given Adelaide my cell number last night. What else had I done? At least I did have a recollection of making plans with Adelaide.

The next text was from a number that I didn't have saved in my phone.

Thanks for the invite last night! Sorry, that we got off to a rocky start. I'd really like to be friends xx, Samantha.

Wait! What? I gave Samantha my number, and she apologized for her behavior. This was all too weird. I had to get to the bottom of what happened last night.

There was one more message, again from a number I didn't have in my phone, only this one was from a blocked number, my heart thumped loudly.

Let this be your warning. Stay away from him!

I dropped the phone, and I watched as it plummeted to the floor and spun around.

Get a hold of yourself Ava, I told myself. There was no time to feel bad for myself. I had to find out what happened last night. I had to find out what secrets Aunt Ginny had been hiding and why it was affecting my life. Then, I needed to find some new friends.

The doorbell rang a half hour later. I had put a chocolate brown velvet robe on top of my peach pajamas. I brushed my hair and put it in a ponytail, not wearing a trace of makeup on my face. Although I had slathered it in moisturizer, just in case I neglected to do it the night before.

Panic surged through my body. I wasn't expecting anyone, not that I knew of anyway, but that didn't mean anything since I apparently gave my phone number away to anyone who wanted it. What if it was Fiona wanting to run? I just couldn't face her quite yet. What if Coal refused to accept my silence and came here to speak with me? Suddenly remembering the cameras, I pulled my phone out of my robe pocket and hit the app that Coal had installed on my phone for me. Pulling up the front door camera, I breathed a sigh of relief when it displayed Lina dressed in 90's jeans, a quilted coat and her blonde hair pulled into a ponytail.

I quickly went to the door to answer, afraid that she might leave. Just as I was about to open the door, she turned the knob from the other side.

I stood there shocked. How did she get a key? I hastily went to the pin pad and entered the code.

"Lina," I said, "where did you get that key from? I thought you said you left it by the side door. Remember I couldn't find it and was really freaked out about it." Now my voice had turned accusing, but could you really blame me?

Lina's face looked completely confused. "You gave it to me last night? You don't remember?"

"Gave it to you last night...," I started, this whole mess was getting too confusing. Did I give her a key last night? I don't even think I had an extra one besides the one that was missing.

"You gave it to me in case you were not home to clean. Remember you asked me to come today to help you clean up after the party. You also said you had some things you wanted to speak with me about." She sounded a little defensive now. Was she telling the truth?

"Come," I said, ushering her into the parlor. "Sit down."

Lina followed my orders but sat stiffly on the purple couch like she was at an interview.

Not wanting to ruin things with Lina too, I sat down on the leather chair across from her and rested my head in my hands. "Listen Lina, I'm sorry. I don't remember anything that happened after you and I went up to the library last night. Nothing. It's like it didn't happen. I feel like It was a film and someone cut out the whole end portion of the film. It's as if it didn't happen for me." I knew my voice was shaky and my sentences were choppy and confusing, but I couldn't help it.

Now Lina's back softened a little but her eyes got wide," What do you mean don't remember? Were you very drunk?"

I was exasperated, "I don't know. I don't think so. This wasn't like being drunk. I don't have a hazy memory. I have a black hole. I really need your help," I pleaded.

Lina looked at me, seeming to consider for a moment. "What kind of help? I will help in any way I can Ava. I don't want to see anything bad happen to you."

"Why would something bad happen to me?" I asked. I knew that things were strange around here, but I didn't fear for my safety, only my sanity.

Her eyes turned sad, "This reminds me of Ginny." Grief was evident on her face. I felt bad for having doubted her.

I finally came out with it. "Do you think someone could have slipped something into my drink?" I asked. I know I sounded paranoid, but it was the only explanation. Giving my phone number out to people and the loss of a big section of the night, this was not like me.

"It is definitely possible. There were a lot of people at your house walking around. It could have been anyone."

To hear her affirm my suspicions both reassured me and made me panic. Was someone really trying to hurt me? What could they gain from me not remembering the end of the night? I needed details of everything that happened from the time I gave the picture to Amber until everyone left. Lina was my only hope.

"Please start with the key. Where did I get the key from that I gave you? Did you see where I took it from?" That was a good starting point.

"Wow, you really don't remember, do you? When you came into the library, after you gave the picture to Amber, Peter came up to you."

"And...," I said wondering where this was going.

"He handed the key to you saying that he saw me put it under the steps, and he didn't think it was safe to do that considering everything that was going on. He went and took it after I left, with the intention of giving it back to you that evening."

I thought for a minute. That sounded like a plausible explanation. Maybe, but why didn't he give it to me sooner? That was on Friday. Why not ring the bell on Friday night and give it back to me?

"I was standing there, and you said that I should keep the key so I could get in when I needed to."

It all made sense, but it was super scary to hear about things that you did and had no recollection of doing.

I nodded my head. "Thank you, at least we solved the mystery of the key and some random person isn't walking around with it, having access to my house anytime they wanted." My immediate reaction was that Coal would feel better knowing this, but then I remembered that Coal was no longer a part of my life.

"Yes, I was so relieved when Peter gave it back to you. It was weighing on my mind since Friday afternoon when you called. I felt so guilty. I did not want to be responsible for something bad happening." This was the second time that she had mentioned this, and it was really starting to freak me out.

"I never blamed you, Lina. I'm the one who left it outside to begin with, not you. Why wouldn't you think it was ok to leave it there when I did it first?"

"I understand that," Lina said, "but when people are

upset, they don’t always think of things this way. We are all guilty of it.” She shrugged her shoulders. Lina was not someone who had an easy life, and that is what gave her character. She didn’t live in an imaginary world. She knew bad things happened, and people weren't always fair.

Lina didn’t know it, but she had given me a gift. She was giving me the night back piece by piece.

I felt guilty over my initial reaction to her entering the house. “I’m sorry; I’ve been so rude, Lina. Would you like a drink? Water or tea perhaps?”

“I will take some water, but let’s go into the kitchen,” she suggested standing up. She obviously felt comfortable with me again. “I will get it myself.”

We stood in the kitchen. Lina poured two glasses of water, one for me and one for her. I glanced around the room remembering the night before. I was trying to conjure some details that previously eluded me. Nothing would come.

“What else happened while we were in the library?” I asked, taking a sip of the water that she had poured. It tasted so good. I was terribly thirsty, but at least my throbbing headache was dulled down to a gentle thud.

“You brought your guests up to the third floor to see the dance room. Everyone had a wonderful time showing off their dances for the big show. Your tango looks beautiful by the way,” she said seriously.

I was mystified. We danced? How could a person not remember dancing? It actually sounded like a fun time. I was sorry that I couldn’t remember it.

“Did everyone dance?” I asked curiously, sorry that I had missed it.

Lina nodded her head, “Yes, all of the teachers. It looks like it is going to be a fun show. Perhaps I should purchase a ticket as well. Amber invited me to sit with her, Peter, and Adelaide.”

Hmmm, I was trying to think. Who would want to slip something into my drink? “Do you remember anything strange happening? Anyone acting weird to me? You didn't see anyone go into my or Aunt Ginny's bedroom, did you?"

She shook her head sideways. "After you were all done doing your dancing, I ushered everyone downstairs. Then you presented Tabitha and Enzo with the award for the winning jack-o'-lantern. You gave them crowns and capes. You took pictures of them. You can see for yourself on your phone," she said.

My phone! Maybe I took some photos that would give me some better insight. I couldn't wait to look through them later when I was alone and really had time to contemplate.

"Thank you so much Lina, you've really been helpful," my voice lingered. There was one final thing that I needed to ask, but I was reluctant to say. Lina obviously picked up on it as she got to it before I could.

"Oh, there is one thing that you might want to know," she hesitated seeing my tense face. "I'm sorry to bring it up, but it is important seeing as you don't remember. After you announced the winner of the contest, you turned to Coal and said to him that he better gather his things, as he was not welcome in your house any longer."

Now my mouth was hanging open. Did I really do that? It would explain his text messages this morning. One thing didn't make sense though.

"Lina, was Fiona there when I made this announcement?" I remembered what she said about me being busy this morning.

Lina closed her eyes for a minute, obviously deep in thought, "Yes, wait no, she went to use the bathroom, so she didn't hear this. Everyone else was there though. You would think that Michael," I heard the disgust in her voice as she said it, "would have told her though."

"Do you know about Michael?" I asked her curiously. I hadn't said anything to her, so I wondered how much she actually knew.

"You mean that he was flirting with every girl, including me, every chance he got?" she asked, displeased by the memory. "Fiona was hanging on his every word. Men like that make me so mad."

"He's my ex-husband," I announced.

"What? No," she stood there, her mouth hanging open in disbelief. She shook her head back and forth.

"Yeah, we were married for ten years. He wasn't a creep like that when we were married, just very obsessive and controlling. A fact that I've told Fiona about," I added.

"I didn't even think about that part. How could your friend go out with your ex-husband?" she tsked and shook her head once more. "It's shameful."

"She supposedly didn't know. I wonder where they even met. So many unanswered questions."

"If you don't mind me asking, and if you do just tell me to mind my own business, what happened with you and Coal? You both seemed so... in love," now her voice was gentler, her eyes held compassion. I think she was a romantic at heart. I had to remember to ask about her story.

"I overheard last night that he used to date Fiona. Neither of them ever said a word to me about it." It was a sucker punch to my stomach saying it aloud.

"Do you think she knew about Michael and dated him to get revenge?" she asked, taking a broom out of the closet and beginning to sweep the floor. She moved all of the chairs out of the way and swept all of the crumbs into a neat pile.

"I hadn't considered that, as I just found out about her and Coal. Somehow I don't think so." I took the glass cleaner and several sheets of paper with me over to the French doors. I began to clean all of the finger prints off of them from the night before. Then I opened the doors and wiped the outside surface as well. It was amazing all the cleaning you did right before a party and then had to redo immediately after.

"You don't have to do that Ava, that's what I am here for," Lina said as I reentered the kitchen.

"No, it's good, it's helping me calm down talking

to you and keeping busy," I assured her, smiling warmly. "Thanks for talking to me by the way."

"It is my pleasure. Your Aunt Ginny was like family to me, my own family doesn't live here. They are back in Poland. Ginny *always* treated me like family, unlike other clients. I can tell that you are kind, just like her. She would want me to treat you well."

Lina and I went through the house, her with the broom, me with paper towels and cleaning supplies, and we made quick work of the party mess.

"Do you have someone special in your life Lina?" I asked, both wanting to get to know her better and happy to not talk about my own disaster for a while.

Lina was quiet, so I looked over at her and saw a small Mona Lisa smile on her face.

"Is that yes?" I asked, teasingly.

"Yes, I have a very special man. We have been dating for a half of a year now. He is part of the Polish community here in Syracuse. His name is Aleksander."

"Why didn't you bring him to the party?" I asked. "I would have loved to meet him. We could double..." I trailed off realizing what I was saying. In my excitement for her, I had momentarily forgotten my own troubles.

"I did not know if it would be ok," she stated simply. "I did not want to assume."

"Well, he is always welcome with you; this is an open invitation," I announced.

She nodded and smiled, "I really appreciate it."

We finished the sweeping and polishing of the first floor and made our way to the second. The only place people really were was the library.

"People are pigs," Lina said, spotting crumbs on the hallway floor. "Who would bring food into the upstairs of another person's home?" She stopped for a minute staring. I halted, to see what she was looking at. There were crumbs right in front of Aunt Ginny's room.

I opened the door and we both gasped as there was an obvious gap in Aunt Virginia's photo collage on the wall. Someone had taken one of her pictures off the wall.

"No, it can't be?" I said in disbelief. "All those people were here as my guests. Who would steal something from my house?" I was rooted to the spot, unable to move.

"This is terrible," Lina agreed, but she was not in disbelief. Her pretty pale face was flushed with anger, furious rather than surprised.

"Which picture was it?" I asked out loud to myself.

Lina focused on the wall.

"I know," I said suddenly, putting my hand up to my mouth. "The one of her in the convertible when she was Miss New York." My shoulder slumped realizing it was gone.

Now Lina looked outraged, her blue eyes were wide and nostrils were flaring.

"You must be careful who you trust," Lina said evenly but with ferocity. "People are often not what they seem."

"Do you know who did this?" I asked, scanning the rest of her room for anything else that might be missing.

"No, but I do know it was someone you trusted enough to invite into your home," she answered bluntly.

"This is all just too much," I said as we exited Aunt Ginny's room and pulled the door tightly closed, unfortunately the damage was already done. "I never thought anyone would go into rooms that they weren't invited into. I left the doors closed for a reason." I was naive.

We went into the library to tidy up there. Lina found a wine glass drained to the bottom. Only the red remnants stain the bottom. It was balanced precariously on the book shelf, if the wind blew, it might fall over. She shook her head and placed it on the desk for us to take when we left the room. While Lina swept the floor, I went around polishing the table and bookcases. When the room was returned to its former glory, we both smiled. This was exactly what I needed. Talking to Lina and helping clean was therapeutic in a way that I couldn't have predicted.

I opened my mouth to tell Lina about the hidden room, when I stopped myself. Hearing her own words in my head, I needed to be more careful until I knew exactly what was going on and who I could trust. I would hold the information about Aunt Virginia's diary close to me and not tell anybody else. Sure, Coal knew about the room and the diary, but his sins were in not disclosing his relationship with Fiona. I knew he had no prior knowledge of Aunt Ginny. He wasn't tangled up in the rest of this mess and therefore not a threat to me.

We were going back downstairs, passing through the living room, which remained largely untouched by the party, when my phone buzzed that I had a message. Dread filled the pit of my stomach and slowly moved through me. There was nobody that I wanted to talk to.

CHAPTER THIRTY-FIVE

After moving through the rest of the house, satisfied that everything was in its place, I suggested that Lina stay and share a pot of tea with me before I had to go to my tango lesson. She happily agreed, so I took out the fancy French teapot that I found in my first days living in the house.

We took the steaming pot of tea into the glass room. The sun was shining brightly through the large window panes both beautifully lighting it up and warming us in tandem. I felt like a cat bathing in the sun. I sat with my legs tucked under me on the loveseat, and Lina took the chair that Fiona had sat in last week. I felt a wave of sadness ride through me at the thought that Fiona and I were supposed to go for a run today and then hang out before my dance lesson.

"Do you live close to here?" I asked, taking a sip of tea from the cup in my hand.

"Yes, probably fifteen minutes. I live in Liverpool. I've lived there since I moved to the United States. My chopak lives only a few minutes away," she smiled, the smile of a woman in love. "If things go well, we hope to get a place together." A dreamy look I've never seen before on her usually serious face appeared.

"That's awesome," I said, genuinely happy for her. It seemed like life hasn't always been easy for her. She deserved a chance at happiness.

Lina's eyes suddenly grew serious, looking like a storm in the ocean, "I am so disgusted that someone came into your house and stole that picture of Virginia. No decency." It was amazing how quickly she went from nothing but sunny skies to a storm rolling in.

"I know," I was quiet for a minute thinking over the guests that had been present. "I can't imagine who it was that would actually do that."

I quietly berated myself for not getting the cameras in the house like the creepy instillation eye suggested. I never thought I would need them inside my home. I guessed that I was wrong once again.

"Do you take any exercise classes or run?" I asked. I am thinking that I have an opening for a new exercise buddy, just posted as of last night.

"Well, all day I'm scrubbing things and walking around. It keeps my arms nice and toned.," she answered.

I nod my head in understanding. "I'm so sorry to cut this short, but I need to go to my tango class to practice for the show. I still have to get ready," I said looking down at my pajamas. "Are you really going to come and watch the show?"

Lina smiled, the sunshine coming back, "Yes, I will go. I'd love to see you, and I love dancing. It is good to support the program for the children." She nodded her head emphatically.

"Awesome, I'll send you the link for tickets," I said getting up. Lina took the cue and followed me. We deposited our tea cups on the counter. "Leave them Lina, I'm going to take care of them later."

Reaching for my pocketbook to take money out to pay Lina, she waved her hand away. "Don't be silly. Today there were just two friends hanging out. You did at least half of the work. I insist. When I come next Saturday, you pay me for deep cleaning."

She was standing by the living room table, and I went up to her and gave her a big hug. "I'm so glad we met Lina, truly." Feeling like our friendship was cemented, I at least had something to be thankful for.

After Lina left, my phone buzzed twice indicating messages. I didn't even take it out of my pocket to check. The second she left, so did any traces of a positive mood. I put on a black bodysuit with a pair of stretchy black jeans. I was in mourning. I left my hair in the messy ponytail I had previously made. The effort to fix it was more than I could muster.

Arriving at the school, I found Chloe already sitting on the gym floor. She was clad in a pair of tangerine joggers and a yellow fluffy sweatshirt. A matching tangerine headband decorated her head.

"Ava," Chloe said, waving as soon as she spotted me. "Great party last night. Thanks so much for the invite. Russ really liked..." she trailed off hesitant to finish her sentence. She must have realized something bad had happened between Coal and me. Probably witnessing my embarrassing act of telling Coal to leave. She waved her hand away and finished, "he really liked the party. Had loads of fun. He was even talking about it this morning."

I smiled but didn't comment on the party. "So, do you know your routine so far?" I asked changing the subject to something less emotionally delicate.

"I think so," she said half-heartedly. After fastening the final buckle around her ankle, she stood up. Here, let me show you." She stood up and announced to me what she was doing as she was doing it.

"I start with two counts of eight, doing the basics. Following that, I do a cross body lead where I spin, like this." She perfectly executed her moves looking far smoother than I believed I looked. "Then I do two cucarachas followed by a grapevine."

"Wow, you look great," I said enthusiastically. "I mean it."

Chloe grinned, "Thanks, I just need Russ to learn the men's part, so we can dance together. I know a great bar where they have salsa on Thursdays." She smiled enthusiastically.

"Sounds wonderful," I said as both our teachers came waltzing in the door.

"Ava," Demetrius announced as he sauntered across the floor, "You look ravishing today, like a sexy black cat. I wish you had worn some ears and a tail," he said, looking me up and down. "It is Halloween after all."

Chloe, who had been chewing a piece of gum, nearly choked swallowing it and had to suppress a laugh.

Today Demitrus was carrying a big cylinder-shaped speaker that he must have hooked up to his cell phone via Bluetooth. Without saying a word, he started our song on his cell phone. The hypnotic notes of the Argentine tango flooded the air. With all that was going on, I really felt the music today. I took all of my pain into my body as I took my two counts of eight and walked toward him feeling every beat, and we assumed our position. I took my time doing lapiz on the floor with my right foot. Each embellishment poured my pain out. He held me in a tight embrace as we did a basic, and I swiveled into ochos. Next, he led me into back ochos, his cheek pressed against mine. We moved as one.

When we came to the end of our routine, Demitrus let out a wolf whistle. "Damn girl, what was that?" he looked at me differently than he ever had before, a twinkle in his eye that made me nervous.

I didn't know what to say, so I took a little bow and both Chloe and her partner clapped.

"Seriously, that was poetic. *That* is what you need to do on show day. You've always been technically good, however you made that your own. I'm feeling bothered after dancing with you." He made a big drama of fanning himself off. I laughed it off.

Chloe and my lessons ran simultaneously. I felt a little excited, a little fluttering of butterflies in my stomach, like this dance show was going to be something special. I was so grateful that I had this to concentrate on during this crappy time.

At the end of the lesson, Demitrus lingered longer than necessary, and I felt a little trapped. Thank God Chloe took notice and pulled me aside.

"Wow, you looked amazing," Chole said, eyes wide. "I'm not just saying this. The two of you had chemistry on the dancefloor that blew me away. I was waiting for the flames to ignite."

I felt my pale cheeks redden. "Thanks, guess I'm just channeling my inner turmoil," I said honestly.

"Are you ok?" Chloe asked seriously. "You seemed pretty upset with Coal last night."

"I'm ok," I said, not really wanting to get into it with her. "Just some things need to be sorted out," I explained, shaking my head sadly.

"Are you broken up?" she asked probing a little farther than I was comfortable with.

"I really don't know what we are," I said looking down at the scuffed gym floor. Our dance shoes had left errant marks. I wished the lesson wasn't over, and I could continue to dance the tango for another hour or so, becoming lost in the music.

"Ok," Chloe said, reading my reluctance, "well if you need to talk, I'm here."

"I appreciate it," I said, making eye contact now and smiling, not wishing to burn any more bridges.

Chloe and I both sat on the floor and changed into our regular shoes. I pulled on my knee- high black leather boots. Chloe unfortunately finished before me and basically ran out of the gym with a wave, leaving me lagging behind with Demitrus.

"You nearly gave me a heart attack back there," he said, grinning like an idiot.

I laughed it off, not wanting to send him the wrong message. I had seen my future with Coal. I imagined the children we would have, growing old together, and it was all taken away in one overheard conversation. If I could go back and unhear the conversation between Coal and Enzo, I might do it. This was so unlike me. I was never one to live in denial, to bury my head in the sand. Things were what they were, for better or worse. However, if I could unhear that Coal and Fiona were involved in a relationship, I think that I would do it in a heartbeat.

Luckily for me, I had secured plans for that afternoon. Keeping busy was the key to me staying out of a black pit of despair. I stopped at the farmers market on the way home and picked up a gigantic bouquet of sunflowers. I couldn't help but feel happy looking at them. It was too late to bake anything, so I figured the flowers might brighten Adelaide's day.

As my Mustang pulled in the driveway, I felt my phone buzz yet again. I realized I had never looked at the texts from earlier that day. I took a deep breath and looked around at the bright orange and red tree in my front yard. I could feel tears welling in my eyes. I closed them and breathed again. I couldn't avoid it forever. Tears now gently rolling down my face, I pulled out my cell. The first, most recent, message was from an unknown caller and was blocked. A trickle of fear now replaced the tears.

Doesn't feel good, does it? I'm going to enjoy this. Stay away from him.

I dropped the phone frazzled by that last message, and it fell beneath the brake pedal of my car. What the hell was going on? Stay away from who? Coal? Who the hell was writing to me?

Bending down to retrieve my phone, it was just out of my reach. Finally, I stretched my fingers an inch more and secured it.

Breath in. breathe out. Don't let fear control you, I told myself. I decided to look at the other two messages. One was from Fiona.

Hope we're still on for tomorrow's class at the gym!

Doubtful, I said aloud to myself. I read the final one.

We need to talk. It was followed by a broken heart emoji.

I'd never seen the broken heart emoji before, but it was perfect. That basically wrapped up my feelings. I was broken-hearted. I was being terrorized and my new best friend and boyfriend lied to me. I had no family left. I was on my own where it felt like everyone else around me was guarded and protected by people who loved them. I was a lone woman on an island all by myself in the middle of the ocean.

I only had forty minutes until I was due at Adelaide's house. I glanced out my windows, a sense of uneasiness was grasping at me. The wind blew. I breathed. In and out. In and out. I began counting backwards from 20. When I reached zero, I would go in.

Turning the corner to Adelaide's house with two minutes to spare, I hustled a little quicker, not wanting to be late. She must have been watching out the window for me; the door opened precisely when I reached her front steps.

"Ava! Come in, come in," she insisted.

In the entryway of her house, she had had a table fashioned out of an old Singer sewing machine. An antique lilac vase decorated the table. It was quite unique and beautiful. The layout of her house was remarkably similar to mine, probably built by the same builders. Adelaide took my black quilted coat and hung it in her hall closet.

"These are for you," I said, extending my hand with the bountiful bouquet of sunflowers in her direction.

"Oh my, they are just beautiful!" she exclaimed, holding them in her arms like a baby. "Won't you grab that vase Ava dear? The purple one," she added pointing at the table where I had just admired it.

I grabbed the vase and followed her into her kitchen. The kitchen was done in a buttery yellow that made the whole room glow.

Grabbing a cutting board that was resting against her tiled backsplash, Adelaide set to work cutting the bottoms of the flowers at a diagonal. Where I would have cut them with one slice of the knife, she took care to cut them one at a time.

"These are just gorgeous," she said in delight. "They will brighten up my entryway for sure!"

"I'm glad you like them. So sorry I didn't have time to make anything," I said apologetically.

"Don't be silly dear, you hosted a party just yesterday. You have such good manners though dear, so refreshing to see," she tutted. It seemed she was speaking primarily to herself.

"Thank you," I said self-consciously.

"Meow," Lila came curling around my legs in an S formation. "Meow."

Bending down, I brought my head to meet her face. "Hi girl," I exclaimed, meeting her blue eyes. "I missed you too."

"Noooo," Lila exclaimed.

Both Adelaide and I laughed.

"Have you given any thought to what you will name your little one?" she asked as the miniature of Lila came skulking into the room to see what all the fuss was about. Adelaide looked delighted that she had made an appearance on her own.

Very cautiously, she made her way over to Lila and me. I put my hand out for her to smell me, get used to my scent. I knew better than to approach her, I didn't want to scare her away, let her come to me. Cats are very cautious creatures. They aren't like dogs, who will lick anyone who comes their way. They are choosy. Once they trust you, they will adore you. Before they trust you, they won't bother in the slightest. As the tiny cat approached my outstretched hand, I thought to myself that I needed to be more like a cat. I should keep my group small. Better to have a few meaningful relationships than embrace just anyone that comes my way.

The kitten had grown a lot, but she was still tiny in comparison to the other kitties that were milling around. Finally, she sniffed my hand and licked it. I felt the texture of her sandpaper tongue on my hand. I was patient though. I still didn't make a move to touch her, I just spoke to her in a soft motherly voice, "Aren't you an absolute beauty?" I said to her, "I can't wait for us to get to know each other better."

I was lost in the moment with this little creature. I was brought back to reality by Adelaide's voice. "Ava dear, I hope you don't mind me saying, I don't want to be a busybody, heavens no, but what was all that fuss with you and Coal at the party? He seems like such a nice man. I can tell that he genuinely cares for you. Why did you tell him to leave?" Her eyes were wide awaiting my response. I waited a minute, looking down at the kitten. I met Adelaide's eyes. It was as much a surprise to myself as it was to Adelaide, I began bawling like a baby.

I forgot for a minute that I was at a virtual stranger's house. I just let the tears fall. A few of the big fat tears fell onto the kitten making her fluffy fur wet.

"There, there," Adelaide said, patting my back. "Whatever it is, I'm sure you can work it out. My husband and I were married for 50 beautiful years, but they weren't all easy. Beauty isn't all pretty, but it is real. No, not at all, you need to fight to keep things good. When things are tough you need to fight, don't retreat."

Her kindness reigns me back to reality. I am grateful to have this wise woman to confide in.

I take a leap of faith and reveal to Adelaide that I overheard that Coal used to date Fiona, a fact that no one bothered to mention to me.

"Whatever he did before you met him is none of your concern dear. He only has eyes for you, just like my dear Jack only had eyes for me. I can tell these things believe me," she said, her eyes becoming dreamy, probably remembering back to her own love story.

I don't say anything, but I take a deep breath and stand up. The kitten nudges her head into my legs. "Do you think it's ok for me to pick her up?" I asked Adelaide.

"She seems to want you to do it dear," she said, encouraging me. I moved very slowly, bent down, let her smell my hand, lick it, and finally, gingerly, I scooped her up in my arms and she licked my face.

A moment of pure joy filled me.

"How did your dance lesson go today?" Adelaide asked as I cuddled with my kitten. Taking a chance, I placed my lips on her soft fluffy head for a kiss.

"It was actually amazing," I told her with a real smile. "I think all my real-life anguish is translating well into my tango."

"I am so looking forward to the event dear," she said. "It will be great to see everyone"

I put the kitten down, not wanting to push it. She meowed as I placed her on the floor.

"Why don't you come into the dining room now for tea?" She led the way and motioned for me to sit.

The table setting was breathtaking. White filigree placemats were set in six places. I felt sad thinking that she probably hadn't had a table of guests in quite some time. There were settings for two set up with crisp white linen napkins and silver ring holders around them. The tea cups and saucers were stunning. They were fine bone china with a hand painted floral motif. Gold gilding surrounded the scalloped shape. She had prepared scones fresh out of the oven. There were two bowls, one with clotted cream and the other with lemon curd. She had really taken care in preparing a proper tea party.

Ding, dong. The bell rang. I looked at Adelaide expectantly. "Are you expecting anyone?" I asked, my heart jumping.

"No dear, my guest is already here," she said with a chuckle. "It's Halloween you know."

I kept forgetting. While Adelaide shuffled to the door, I lingered right behind her. Sure enough, she opened the door to reveal a tiny ballerina with pale skin and golden hair, her mom was smiling at us from the sidewalk. Luckily it was a sunny warm afternoon and her costume wasn't covered up by a bulky winter jacket.

"Trick or treat," the beauty said in a tiny voice. She couldn't be more than five, and she was adorable.

Adelaide held out a black plastic candy bowl. It had a cat's face painted on it along with protruding triangle ears. With shaky hands, she extended it out to the girl and said, "Choose any two, dear."

The little girl's face lit up as she chose a lollipop and a Reese Peanut Butter Cup, a girl after my own heart. "Thank you," she said sweetly as she turned and walked back to her mother.

The two of us retreated back to the dining room table.

"Nothing so precious as small children," Adelaide said.

"Yes, she really was adorable," I agreed sitting down.

"Do you want to have children one day dear?" she asked, while putting a scone on my plate. There were orange brown chips in it which I discovered were butterscotch pieces.

I nodded solemnly, "I do. That's one of the reasons things didn't work out with my ex-husband."

Adelaide looked shocked for a minute, "I'm sorry Ava; I didn't realize you were married." She looked at me obviously scandalized by the idea.

I felt a need to defend myself. "He was a very self-indulgent man, only loved me for what I was to him, not because he loved me as a person. He was a true narcissist."

Adelaide looked thoughtful for a moment, and I realized I was on pins and needles. I shouldn't have cared how

Adelaide felt on the subject, but I did.

"Well, I don't really approve of divorce, but I say good for you for recognizing your own worth. I knew you were a smart girl."

I relaxed a bit, thankful that Adelaide showed some compassion. I realized that she was from a different generation, so I shouldn't be particularly offended by her position. I just didn't want her being cross with me.

I spooned some lemon curd and two big dollops of clotted cream on my plate. I dipped my scone into the cream and took a bite. "These are heavenly," I said after my first bite.

Adelaide was back to looking delighted and my kitty cat came over to the table and rubbed against my legs. Perhaps I would have to form a new sort of family, less conventional, but it would be my own.

Returning to school on Monday kicked my anxiety into high gear. I was at least happy that I hadn't done anything embarrassing, save throwing Coal out at the end of the night. Both Coal and Fiona's calls went unanswered. I needed to take the night to decompress. I would deal with them when I was ready.

I ran into Tabitha in the hallway on my way down to pick up my students in the morning.

"Ava, I just wanted to say thank you for the party on Saturday," she approached me looking as glamorous as ever. She was wearing silver dress pants that flare out at the bottom. She had a shirt that had a funky pattern in purple and silver that she told me she got on her trip to Italy. Her glossy black hair was worn pin straight. "Enzo and I had a wonderful time, and we were extra excited about being the winners of the jack- o'- lantern contest. I brought in my crown and cape to show off to the kids."

I managed a smile, not wanting to be rude. "Oh, that's awesome." I realized I hadn't posted any pictures of the party on social media. I was happy that the party was such a hit with everyone, even though it sent my life into a tailspin. "I'll post pictures later today, so you can show your kids your winning pumpkin."

"That would be great," Tabitha responded as we walked down the stairwell to the cafeteria.

Fiona was down in the noisy cafeteria. She was picking up one of the first- grade classes, so I assumed she was covering for someone today. She was clad completely in gray. It was not a silver gray like Tabitha. It was a drab depressing gray, and she had scraped her hair back into a bun. Not a trace of makeup could be found on her face. She seemed to look through me as I passed her. I wasn't too keen on talking to her either, but this was an interesting turn of events. What could *she* possibly be mad at? She's the one who showed up with my husband at my party, and I'm the one who didn't throw her out. She's the one who failed to tell me that she dated Coal, so she had no ground to stand on regarding me dating her ex. Fiona exited the cafeteria, and I felt like I was a ghost. It was like she never saw me.

"Oh Ava," Tabitha said watching the whole exchange, or lack of exchange I should say. "Do you happen to do Pilates?"

"As a matter of fact, I do," I said smiling.

"I'm taking a class today after work, and I was wondering if you'd like to go with me. It's a very small class, and you get to train on the Reformer machines."

"Oh," I said, my mouth forming an o. I had always wanted to try out the machines. "I would love to go."

"Great," she said grinning, "I'll email you a link. You can sign up for the six o'clock time slot, and I'll meet you there. It will be fun."

As I went to greet my kids, I felt conflicted. I had a bad feeling in my gut about Fiona's strange behavior, and I was excited about plans with Tabitha. She never showed interest in hanging out solo before, but perhaps she felt more comfortable now that she had been to my house. I also appreciated that she didn't mention anything about Coal and me at school. I didn't want to get emotional when I still had the whole day to get through.

As I lined my students up, I noticed that Coal's class was gone already. I thanked God for small miracles that I wouldn't have to come face to face with him this morning. By the time my class got upstairs, his class would already be settled in their classroom.

During my break, my phone buzzed. It was Tabitha, and she had sent me the link for the Pilates place, just as promised. I noticed that it was sent in a text rather than Instagram, which was odd as I didn't remember ever exchanging phone numbers with her. Yikes, I must have given the entire party my cell phone number. It was unnerving. I typed back thanks and went onto the website. I saw they still had four openings for the six o'clock class, so I immediately booked and typed out a message to Tabitha to tell her that I secured my spot. The place was only a five-minute drive from school. Although I loved my class at The Journey, I had plenty of reasons not to go there tonight. Marcia gave me a weird vibe at the party, and I didn't want to take any chances that Fiona might show.

Glancing at the black and white clock above my white board, I saw that I still had fifteen minutes until I had to pick up my second graders. I might as well find that picture I promised Tabitha. As I began to look at the pictures, I realized this was the first time that I had gone through them. I meant to yesterday morning, but then I was distracted by Lina. By the time I got back from Adelaide's house, all I wanted to do was put on a pair of pajamas and watch TV in bed. In all the excitement of getting ready for the party, I never bought candy to give out, so I had to hide out upstairs anyway. When kids see no lights on, they usually don't bother ringing the bell.

The first picture of the night was of Coal and I dressed

in our Bonny and Clyde costumes. We stood on the stairs with a big black spider in the background looming on the right of us. Coal was posed with one hand holding his gun and his other arm slung over my shoulder. He was trying his best to make a menacing face, but his good nature was still shining through. How was it possible that this was only two days ago? Two days ago, not only did I see a future, but it was a bright shiny one. It was actually a fairy tale future. Now all I had was this picture. Not allowing myself to lament here, I moved on. I found various photos throughout the night that I remembered taking. Finally, I came to the photos of the finished pumpkins. They really did look pretty all lined up on the table outside, glowing with the light of the tea candles. I found an up-close picture of Tabitha and Enzo's spider jack-o'-lantern and sent it to her. I once again glanced at the clock and saw I had to pick up my cherubs.

As I was about to open the classroom door, my phone buzzed. I looked at the message as I walked down the hall to the gym. I didn't even want to glance at the room across the hall, afraid I might catch a glimpse of Coal in the window. Tabitha sent me a jack-o'-lantern, spider and an orange heart emoji letting me know she received the photograph.

When school let out, I went home. I needed to get exercise clothes, and I had two hours to kill before the class actually started. I didn't see Fiona again for the rest of the day, and I managed to avoid Coal altogether. I knew eventually I would have to face them, but today was not the day.

Upon returning home, I immediately dressed in a pair of light brown leggings and a ballerina pink sports bra and tank top. I put all my hair up in a bun and used bobby pins to make sure that no strands escaped. Satisfied that I looked presentable, I grabbed the skeleton key out of my jewelry box. It was time that I did some reading and tried to find out what was going on once and for all.

I crept into the library and closed the door behind me.

The room both smelled and looked immaculate thanks to Lina's and my handiwork. Once I'd settled into my reading chair with the diary, I started again from where I left off.

Friday January 15, 2021

I met Amber for dinner and drinks. Time spent with friends after a challenging work week makes it all worth it. I was in definite need of unwinding. Especially given his return. After we ate, we sat in the lounge area. There was a band playing, and we sat with drinks talking. I probably had one too many drinks because one minute we were talking about work, and the next minute, I told her. I just blurted it out really. I never meant to tell her, but I did it. She was obviously shocked. Her reaction definitely confirmed that, although she composed herself pretty well afterwards. My biggest fear is that she will judge me. I fear losing her respect, she assures me this isn't the case but only time will tell.

CHAPTER THIRTY-SIX

On the way to meet Tabitha, I tried to think what Aunt Ginny could possibly have done that would make Amber not respect her. It was hard for me even to think up a scenario that made sense. Aunt Virginia was always such a respectable and classy person. What out of character thing could she have done? I also wondered why she was so cryptic in her diary entries. It was after all *her* diary. Amber was the first person that she actually mentioned by name. It was as though she knew someone would find it, and she didn't want her secrets divulged.

The Pilates studio was located in a little wood building tucked back from the street a little. Trees adorned either side of the building in orange and red. A big store front window took up the front of the building and was lit up. Inside I could see the Reformer machines that Tabitha promised. We both pulled into the parking lot, located to the front of the building, within thirty seconds of each other. She got out of her black BMW and was clad in an entirely black workout outfit.

"I'm so glad you could make it," Tabitha said. The sky was inky black but lit up with millions of bright twinkling stars. There didn't appear to be a cloud in the sky. The air was frosty and sent shivers through me.

"Thanks for suggesting it," I said as we walked towards the door and the warmth of the studio. Bells on the door jingled announcing our arrival.

"Good evening," a woman of about thirty with attractive caramel colored skin and beautiful almond shaped eyes greeted us. "Did you make a reservation?" she pleasantly asked us.

After giving her our information, she walked us over to our instructor Kristy who had super fine and straight strawberry blond hair pulled into a skinny ponytail. She was dressed in what appeared to be the uniform of the studio, a black leotard and black leggings. This was something Tabitha failed to inform me. She walked us over to our machines for the class.

"We'll be starting in about 5 minutes," Kristy informed us. "If you have any questions, I will be right over there," she said, motioning towards the left of the room.

"How long have you been coming here?" I asked Tabitha as we waited.

She smiled, "Oh about two years. I was a ballet dancer for many years and Pilates is a great extension of that." That explained Tabitha's lean muscular physique.

I smiled happy to find out that Tabitha was a dancer. This was our first time hanging out alone, so I was happy to learn more about her. "I did ballet when I was little too. I've done mat Pilates before, but I've never used the Reformer. Pilates really helped sculpt my thighs which were too bulky looking for my liking."

"You're going to love it," she assured me.

I smiled and nodded my head. At that point it was almost awkward *not* bringing up the Coal situation. I didn't want her to think I didn't trust her. If I wanted to make new friends, I was going to have to learn to put myself out there and share a little about myself. "I'm sorry I fought with Coal in front of you guys. I ordinarily would keep my private business private."

Amber waved her hand away from me. "Oh please, it was no big deal. Trust me when I tell you that Enzo and I have had our share of fights."

Appreciating her effort to keep me at ease, I decided to confide in her further. "Tabitha, between you and me, I think someone at the party put something in my drink. Ordinarily

I would never think of airing my personal business, especially at a party."

Her chocolate brown eyes widened looking concerned. "Wow Ava. Why do you think that? What happened?"

"That's the thing, I don't really know. I don't remember anything after finding everyone in the library. The next thing I remember was waking up much later than usual in my bed in the morning. I don't have a single memory in between these events."

Tabitha's body became more rigid as the seriousness of the situation hit her. "That is not ok. Do you have any ideas about who could have done it? I mean you didn't have any strangers over." She sounded outraged at the prospect that this could be done to me in my own home.

I nodded my head sadly and my auburn hair waved back and forth.

More women began to filter in. Tabitha waved to a few. They all smiled at me as they made their way to their machines. It was a completely different experience than when I visited The Journey. There I was made to feel like an outcast. Everyone here was very relaxed and inclusive.

Kristy came back to the front of the room, "Good evening, everyone, thank you for joining us for reformer flow. We are going to start with Table Top. Some tips to remember, your shoulders need to be down. You are maintaining a ninety- degree angle. Our goal is to stabilize the lower half of our body."

The class went on for 50 minutes. Since I had never utilized the machines before, I needed to focus on what the teacher was saying and connect to my body. It actually felt like a therapy session. When the time was up, I felt like all the built-up tension had left my body.

After saying thank you to Kristy and waving to the women in the class, Tabitha and I made our way back out into the frosty night.

"Do you want to get coffee?" Tabitha asked.

Glancing at my watch, I saw that it was 7 pm. The thought of the lonely night that awaited me at home filled me with dread. "Yes, that would be great," I said, grateful for the invitation. "Did you have somewhere in mind?"

"There's an independent coffee house called the Eclectic Cafe about five blocks from here. I think they have an open mic night tonight. Do you want to try it?" she asked, zipping her black jacket.

"Perfect," I'll follow you.

As I got in my Mustang and waited for her to pull out, a thought occurred to me. Given the fact that Fiona has been dating Michael, it explained why I had spotted his car in the neighborhood so many times. It doesn't however explain why he's been stalking my house, because I know for a fact that he was. I was so lost in thought, that I nearly forgot I was following Tabitha and almost missed the left turn that she made. At the last second, I cut the wheel and made the turn. The parking for the cafe was behind the building.

"You're like a regular race car driver," Tabitha joked as we got out of the car.

"Yeah," I laughed, "guess I was preoccupied."

We entered the front door. There were mismatched sitting chairs and coffee tables strewn about the entire space. Towards the back of the building, there was a microphone set up, that must be the space where the entertainment takes up residence.

"Two?" a twenty-year-old with dyed black hair and a nose piercing asked.

Tabitha nodded her head politely and the girl led us to a chipped marble coffee table. I sat in a plush purple velvet armchair, while Tabitha sat in a golden leather sitting chair. She handed us two menus and made her way to another table. Open mic night didn't start yet and the sounds of jazz filled the air. The atmosphere was very relaxing and dreamlike.

"I like this place," I said, giving a nod of approval. The cafe was nice and toasty thanks to the fireplace that was lit with blazing flames. I removed my coat and settled back in my seat to examine the menu.

"Yes, table for two please." I heard the deep voice of a man that sounded slightly familiar. Looking up, I noticed at once that Mayor Whitherton was walking, with a painfully thin woman, to a table across the room. The woman had perfectly coiffed blonde hair. It reminded me of the haircut of that Spice girl back in the 90's. She wore dark indigo designer jeans. Even though they were a super skinny cut, they almost hung off of her. She wore a baby blue cashmere sweater that looked so soft, I wanted to go over and touch it.

"Isn't that the mayor?" I asked in my quietest voice. I didn't want to risk being overheard like some kind of paparazzi.

Now Tabitha looked up from her menu unimpressed. "Yeah, and his wife Elise." I was happy that I was with Tabitha now and not Samantha who would have lost her mind.

The mayor and his wife sat at a rectangular antique table. A silvery candle holder held a lit candle and cast shimmery light onto their faces. I saw the waitress approaching us and quickly looked back at the menu, not wanting to leave Tabitha and the waitress waiting.

The waitress stood pen poised looking at us. I was still gazing down at the menu, but I felt her eyes on me.

"I'll have a hazelnut latte with almond milk," Tabitha said.

I looked up, "Americano with French vanilla and oat milk," I said, happy with my quick save, as I spotted something on the menu I wanted.

"Will you be wanting food?" The waitress asked, her nearly black eyes appraising us.

We both looked at each other and in unison said, "Yes."

"Ok, I'll put your drink order in and be back in a minute." The waitress walked over to the coffee bar. I figured

I better get my food sorted out before she returned.

Quickly deciding on a bacon, avocado cheese melt, I saw Tabitha was still searching the menu, so my gaze fell on the mayor and his wife again. This time, when I looked over, he was staring directly at me and gave a friendly wave, so I waved back pleasantly. This was quite a shift in demeanor since my last puzzling run-in with him.

Simon then turned to his wife, and she turned and smiled at us. She was quite pretty when she smiled.

The waitress once more was back standing at our table, depositing our drinks in front of us. She placed them on paper doily style coasters. Tabitha and I placed our orders and then leaned back in our chairs once more.

"So," Tabitha said, turning to me earnestly, "I was seriously considering what you told me about the night of your party. Are you sure you didn't just drink too much?"

I nodded my head vigorously sideways. "I had a total of two drinks and a shot within the span of four hours."

Tabitha nodded her head agreeing. "You're right; it's not possible that you would black out for the rest of the night from that. Have you ever blacked out before?"

"No!" I said, unconsciously raising my voice an octave. I realized Tabitha was just trying to help me sort things out, but I couldn't help getting a little defensive. What did she take me for?

"Believe me, I believe you. I just had to ask. I want you to get to the bottom of this because if someone spiked your drink, that's not ok." She looked at me honestly, square in the eye.

"I understand. I'm sorry for getting upset, and I appreciate your concern." I hung my head a little now feeling embarrassed.

The cafe was now filling out more. There was only one table for two still available. The jazz music was still playing, but it was turned down considerably. A man of about forty with longish blond hair that flopped into his eyes went up to the microphone.

"Good evening," he said, his surprisingly baritone voice filling the room. "Thanks for joining us for our Monday Open Mic Night."

Several people at various tables clapped politely.

"Before we officially open the mic, we have a special treat. Mayor Whitherton and his lovely wife have joined us tonight." At this an uproarious clapping spread through the audience. Their heads were spinning widely trying to locate where the mayor was seated.

Mayor Whitherton stood and encouraged his wife to follow him. They walked up to the mic and stood in the spotlight that was pointed at the mic.

"Good evening, Syracuse," the mayor greeted the crowd. He wore a pair of black jeans that seemed tailored to his body. He had on a button up shirt with a forest green cashmere sweater over it. "My lovely wife Elise and I are very pleased to be with you here tonight."

More clapping followed.

"I'd like you to give your attention to Elise for a moment."

Everyone followed his direction and halted their individual conversations.

"Good evening, tonight my husband and I want to promote a big fundraiser that we have coming up in November. I am working with the elementary schools and teachers to help raise money for an after-school arts program. This program would be open to all students, despite their ability to pay." She paused, her blue cashmere sweater slipping slightly off her shoulder. Her eyes were captivating as she stood there clearly loving the spotlight.

This announcement caused several people to clap and one person yelled, "A mayor for the people!" Then everyone joined in clapping heartily.

The mayor whispered something to his wife and took the microphone from her. "There are actually two lovely ladies that will be dancing for our fundraiser in the house, right now. Come up here ladies!"

A wave of shock hit me. He was obviously looking right at us and both Tabitha and I stayed frozen in our chairs stunned by the sudden request.

"Don't be shy," the mayor said. "Elise and I would like to personally thank you for your contribution. We wouldn't be able to do it without you."

Now everyone's eyes fell on us, including our waitress. I could feel the blood rushing in my ears. The room got hot, and I second guessed my decision to wear my workout clothes out to eat. I self- consciously got up and Tabitha followed suit.

We went and stood by the mayor and his wife facing the audience.

"This is Ava," he said, introducing me to the crowd. I could feel my face and chest reddening.

"Ava why don't you tell these fine people what you will be doing for the fundraiser?"

I took the microphone and took a big breath, breathing in and out. "Hi! I'm Ava and I teach second grade. I will be dancing the Argentine tango with my professional partner Demitrus. I hope you can join us at this fundraiser. We will have a great show for you, and the money goes for a really good cause."

The people clapped as loudly for me, as they did for the mayor. I was flabbergasted. Although I wasn't excited at being ambushed the way we were, it was exhilarating. Elise shook my hand and the mayor smiled happily.

"Nice speech," he said with a wink. He was quite charming. I'll give Samantha that. He patted me on the shoulder.

Tabitha next took the microphone and introduced herself. She wasn't quite as chatty as I was and looked mortified.

"Thank you again ladies," Mayor Whitherton said as

we scampered away to our seats.

Our sandwiches beat us to our table and were waiting for us when we got back.

"We hope to see you all there. Please go to syracuse.org and follow the link to buy tickets for this worthwhile charity event."

"I am so sorry," Tabitha said, despite her olive skin, I could still see her blushing. "When I asked you to come here, I had no idea *that* was going to happen," she finished.

"That's ok. It wasn't so bad," I replied. "The mayor and his wife seem very nice."

Tabitha raised her eyebrow at me. "Mayor Whitherton is quite popular in Syracuse, and his wife is very ambitious."

"She seems nice," I said, taking a bite of my sandwich. Cheese oozed down the edges of the bread.

Tabitha was about to respond when Simon and Elise came up to our table.

"Sorry about that," Elise said, "Simon insisted it would be good for publicity. We are trying to raise as much money as possible." She made direct eye contact, first with me, then with Tabitha.

"It's ok," I said, "it added a little excitement to our night." I laughed, and Tabitha chuckled politely.

"It was lovely meeting you Ava, Tabitha. I look forward to working with you in a few weeks."

Elise headed back to their table. The waitress had delivered their food as well. Elise sat down and dug into her salad without waiting for her husband. She was used to him having to talk to people and didn't look the slightest bit bothered.

Simon paused for a minute, "You girls were very good sports. Ava, I think you might have a future in politics," he finished laughing to himself as he waved and turned to join his wife.

"Ok this night is officially weird," Tabitha said, "but it was also a lot of fun. It's really nice getting to know you without everyone else around." A hint of distaste entered her tone. I wasn't sure who the distaste was for, but I was certain that it was there.

Returning home, I felt much more centered. I was thankful for Tabitha's invitation and kindness, as I pulled in the driveway, I felt at peace.

Getting out of the car, I approached the front of my house when I heard Peter's voice before I saw him. The front lights came on and Peter joined me on the path.

"Hi Ava," Peter said, looking strangely nervous. I had never seen him look anything but confident and casual.

"Oh, hi Peter," I said, smiling at him.

"I just wanted to thank you for the wonderful party yesterday, and I felt like I should apologize as well."

"Apologize?" I questioned, not sure where he was going with this.

"Yeah, I want to apologize for Fiona's behavior." He looked sheepish now.

"You have no need to apologize. You've done nothing wrong."

"Can we speak inside for a minute?" he asked, gazing around as though to check if anyone was watching us.

"Ok," I said a little hesitantly. Peter followed me in the house and stood politely to the side as I entered the security code.

"Let's go in the kitchen," I said leading the way, "would you like a cup of tea?"

Peter nodded his head in affirmation. "If it's not too much trouble," he said, a quiver in his voice.

Patiently I waited as I went through the ritual of making the tea and set the dining room table for two for our conversation. I worked in silence until finally we were ready to sit down for the tea.

Peter sat, his face upon further inspection looked ashen. I poured the steaming tea into our two cups and waited for Peter to start.

"Let me just start by saying Fiona was out of line bringing Michael to your party. I'm assuming this is the same Michael that has been skulking down our street since you moved in?" he asked for confirmation.

I nodded my head using one of the tiny spoons to spoon a scoop of tea into my cup. "In her defense, I don't think that she knew he was my ex-husband. I think she was as surprised as I was," I finished.

"As soon as she realized, she should have made her apologies and left. She should have either sent him away, or left with him. Leaving him to mingle at your house all night was not the right thing to do. Not to mention I saw him ogling every girl that walked past him." He finished the last bit apologetically like he was afraid of hurting my feelings. He was visibly distressed by the entire situation.

"What does this have to do with you though Peter?" I asked, still not understanding why he was apologizing.

I saw him take a deep breath and a sip of his tea, as though giving himself a pep talk before continuing.

"I did something I shouldn't have," he said. His face now was completely ashen. My stomach sank, a sickening feeling filled my body.

CHAPTER THIRTY-SEVEN

I would have been nervous for my safety if Peter didn't look so sick. I actually felt kind of bad for him.

"Start from the beginning," I said, refilling his teacup.

Peter spooned some sugar into his cup and continued. "Saturday night, Amber and I went up into the library to talk privately," now I felt a little guilty because I already knew this, but I said nothing and just waited for him to continue his story.

"While we were talking, Amber spotted the picture of Ginny and her, on the desk. Later on when we were back upstairs, I took something that didn't belong to me."

Was he the one who snuck into Aunt Ginny's room and stole her Miss New York picture right off the wall? I couldn't believe what I was hearing.

"What did you take?" I asked, my voice obviously annoyed although I gave no indication that I might already know what he was talking about. Peter noticed and grimaced.

"I opened the desk drawer in the library and saw a picture of Ginny and me in there. She looked so happy." He had tears in his eyes, and I had to stop myself from going to comfort him. If I did, I might never have heard the whole story.

"I know I had no right going in there. It's just when I saw the picture of her and Amber, I wondered what other pictures she might have. It's no excuse," he chastised himself, so I still remained quiet. I guess I was right to hide all of her other personal effects.

"I took it. I just slid it in my pocket. If Amber knew, she would be very upset with me," he paused. "For lots of reasons."

I finally spoke. "Peter, it's really not that big of a deal. If you wanted the picture, you should have just asked me. It obviously means a lot to you."

He nodded his head, "Thank you for your kindness. Once upon a time, I thought Virginia would be my happily ever after. I was a bachelor my whole life and perfectly happy with it. My friends joked that I was a confirmed bachelor and there was no single woman who could tie me down. It wasn't until I met Ginny that I realized the one thing I was missing in my life, her. She didn't tie me down; she enabled me to fly."

I held my breath for a minute, wondering if he was the man she was talking about in her journal. I didn't want him to realize that I had her diary, so I didn't bring anything up. I just waited for him to share. He obviously wanted to get it all off his chest.

"Oh, I had no idea," I said, "since you and Amber are together, I just assumed you and Aunt Ginny were friends." Peter looked sick to his stomach.

"There was a moment, one beautiful gorgeous moment when we were more. I was the happiest man alive," he paused and squeezed his eyes shut. "It was captured in that photo. That's what drove me to take it," he deflated before my eyes. This James Bond of a man sat at my dining room table weeping openly.

I was in shock; I wasn't sure what I should do. I put my arm on his shoulder, and he turned and held onto me. His hug was more fatherly than creepy, so it didn't bother me so much, it helped diffuse the awkwardness of the situation and for that I was relieved.

"Ginny would hate this. She would hate Fiona flaunting Michael in your face, and she would hate me snooping in her personal effects. That's why I came here to apologize.

I don't know if it's because you look so much like her, I just needed to confess. I *never* wanted to do wrong by her."

"Listen Peter, after hearing your story, I totally understand," I could hear the sincerity in his voice. The state that he was in could hardly be faked.

"Thank you," he said, composing himself. Some color was coming back to his face. "Thank you for listening and being compassionate. Your Aunt Ginny was right when she said you are a lovely girl."

"Do you feel better?" I asked, sitting back down at the table. "Obviously keep the picture, Aunt Ginny would want you to have it, and it must have meant something to her, as she kept it in her desk drawer. All of her other photos are stored away in boxes." I nodded at him in reassurance.

He was still staring at me strangely. Once again, I waited to let him tell me what was on his mind.

"There's just one more thing," he seemed hesitant to say. His eyes darted, nervously around the room. He seemed tortured.

"What is it, Peter?" His hesitance made me feel concerned. Needing to get to the end of this story, I wanted to urge him to continue. I needed to finally move on with my life. Until he finished, I was held captive.

"I've always felt strange about how she just . . . died." His own eyes widened as though he couldn't believe that he actually said it to me.

"What do you mean?" Now my voice went down an octave. I didn't recognize it. Peter was putting to words what I've been feeling since I've moved into this house.

"I don't know. It's just a feeling, a hunch really, nothing concrete. I saw Ginny the night before she died. She went for a run with Amber, then the three of us had dinner together. I remember every detail of that night. It was our last. I can still hear her laughing at a dumb dad joke I made. I can see her red hair tied in braids. There was nothing wrong with her, Ava. She was the embodiment of life."

I paused a minute trying to think about what he was saying, "She did have a congenital heart defect though Peter." I was playing the devil's advocate, but it was important to say. I wanted us to stay grounded in facts.

"I know. I know all of that, but she just had a checkup with the doctor. With you receiving those creepy dolls, I can't help but think it's tied to Ginny's death." He shook his head, obviously distraught and frustrated by this entire situation.

I let out my breath. Now that Peter had said it aloud, I felt validated in my own theories. Before this I felt like I was letting my imagination run away with me, now I had an ally. I trusted him, but not enough to tell him about the diary. Not just yet.

"Have you told Amber? Maybe she has some insight into what happened. She was after-all around and knew Ginny for so long. They were best friends."

Peter was quiet. He sat there staring at me so long that my heart started beating wildly. His silence was deafening. He looked like he was having an internal struggle. Finally, he croaked, "Yes, Ginny considered her to be her best friend. She confided in her and trusted her."

"But...," I said, my voice ragged, not believing what I was hearing. Did he not trust Amber? I felt like I was balancing on a ball, and it was rolling and wouldn't stop. I was about to crash at any second.

"What about Amber?" I asked desperately. Now I was standing on shaking legs at the table pleading with him to continue.

"I don't know," he finally admitted.

"You don't know?" Hysteria had taken over at this point. What he was saying couldn't be true. Could it? A cold sweat began to coat my skin. I was beginning to tremble slightly. Amber and Aunt Ginny were best friends for as long as I could remember. Aunt Virginia would always tell me stories about things they did together. She looked up to Amber and went to her for advice. Perhaps Peter was just grief stricken and looking for answers.

Peter sighed. "I don't know how to explain it. Following Ginny's death, I was so shattered I couldn't think straight. Amber was there for me. We shared our grief together. It bonded us. That's how we ended up dating."

I nodded my head, "I could understand that. Amber made you feel close to Ginny still. I feel the same way about her."

"Yes, but I don't think that Amber was so happy about it. In the beginning she insisted that she understood. Lately she has begun to call herself second fiddle, and I really couldn't deny it." This poor man was torn apart.

"So, what do we do?" I ask Peter. "How do we find out what really happened to Aunt Ginny? I want answers for her, but I also want to stop the terror." I was embarrassed because finding answers wasn't just about Aunt Virginia. Was I selfish because I was investigating to make my own problems stop?

Peter and I both sat there in a deep silence. It was heavy, and finally I broke it.

"I want to go see Amber and get a read from her. I won't mention anything you've said to me, but I have to try to get answers."

Peter looked panicked now. "I'm not so sure that's a good idea, but If you really have to go, then I want to be there too." As protection, he didn't say it, but he believed that Amber might try to hurt me.

I nodded my head, "Ok, I'll text her to see when she's available." I didn't necessarily think that she would try to hurt me, but I wasn't sure she wouldn't either. Picking up my cell off of the table, I typed out a message.

Hi Amber, Sorry about the delay in getting back to you. Things have been a little crazy at work. Do you want to have dinner sometime this week? Let me know! xx Ava

I couldn't slow down the rapid beating of my heart as adrenaline surged through me. "I sent it," I said, taking a sip of my now ice-cold tea.

My phone buzzed and Peter looked at it like it might bite me, a rattlesnake waiting to strike. Picking it up, I read.

Sounds wonderful! You can come by me since you hosted last! How about Friday night? I'll see if Peter and Fiona are available as well. 7 pm? xx Amber

I was about to read Peter the text when his own phone buzzed. He nearly jumped as he pulled it out of his pocket.

"She invited me to dinner with you on Friday. Well, I guess that's settled," he didn't look convinced that it was a good idea.

"Ok good, maybe with some gentle prodding I can get a better idea of what was going on at that time." I turned to him seriously, "Peter, thank you for coming to me. I've been kind of alone in this whole thing, and I truly wasn't sure where to turn."

The next morning, I woke up exhausted. I felt like there were sandbags holding me down. I barely slept an hour the entire night. My brain was spinning. If Amber was going to invite Fiona on Friday, I would have to make an effort to talk to her at work. It would just be too awkward to show up there for a dinner party on Friday without speaking.

I had my opportunity when I got out of my car in the school parking lot, and I saw her pulling in. I stopped and grudgingly waited for her. I might as well get it over with. Fiona spotted me as she was pulling into her spot and looked shocked to see me just standing there waiting. The day was dark and raining, matching my mood and making me feel even more drained.

"Morning," I managed to say as she shut her car door. Yesterday she was dressed in all gray, today she chose all black. Her curls bounced around her face though adding more life to her than her scraped back bun yesterday.

"Hey," she managed.

"So, are you coming to your mom's house for dinner Friday night? For the dinner party," I added. She invited Peter as soon as I texted her, so I assumed she did the same with Fiona.

Her face got a little brighter, "Yeah, sounds good. I wasn't sure if you were talking to me, since you didn't answer my calls on Sunday." Now she looked at me accusingly.

"I just needed a little time. Lots going on, but we're fine," I told her as we walked in the door to the hallway of the school.

I took a left and headed towards my classroom. Fiona followed and entered the door to my classroom right behind me.

Putting my bag down on my swivel chair, I turned and faced her. She just stood there like a statue staring at me. "I never meant to hurt you," she said in a monotone voice. "I didn't know he was your ex-husband."

I nodded my head but didn't say anything.

"It's been a long time since I met someone I could connect with, someone who really understands me. I can't just walk away from that."

Nodding my head once more, I finally spoke, "We are all responsible for our own happiness."

There was a tapping at my classroom door and Fiona and I both whipped our heads in the direction. Tabitha stood in the window looking in with a smile on her face.

"Come in," I called, actually thrilled that she came to rescue me.

"Morning," Tabitha said brightly as she entered the room. She was like sunshine coming into a storm. "Just wanted to see if you were sore today after the class last night."

Fiona's eyes changed, but she didn't say anything.

"Actually, I am," I said, "that's why it's good to change up your workout routine sometimes," I said as a quick save. "Muscle confusion is good for growth." I glanced at Fiona to see if she was buying it.

Tabitha nodded in agreement. "I can't believe the dance show is coming so soon now," she went on talking. "That was crazy last night with the mayor."

Now Fiona's entire face changed. "What are you guys talking about?" Her expressionless face changed to one of anger.

"Oh, we saw him and his wife last night at the cafe promoting the charity event, and he called us up to speak to the crowd. It was embarrassing," Tabitha finished. "Not for Ava though. I think she was made for the spotlight."

"Oh," was all Fiona said. "Well, I have to go get supplies ready for a project we're working on. See you guys later." Fiona hustled out of the room without looking back.

"Thank you," I said in a whisper, afraid that Fiona was lurking outside the door.

"No problem, I really was coming to talk to you. When I glanced in the room and saw the palpable tension, I knew you needed rescuing."

I nodded my head, raising my eyebrows in agreement. "Seriously though, thanks for last night. It was great hanging out, and it really was an adventure," I finished chuckling.

"Yes, it was great. We'll have to go to our class again," she smiled. "Well, enjoy your day. Maybe we can catch up at lunch."

Being as I was exhausted, I was thrilled that the rest of the day was uneventful. There was a close call when I saw Coal's class walking down the hall, but then I saw they were led by some middle-aged women with sandy brown hair.

Once I could breathe, I went to the teachers' room to make copies. Samantha was in the room front and center making a cup of coffee. She wore a knee length chocolate corduroy skirt with buttons down the front. She paired it with a shimmery gold colored fitted tunic. She really was quite pretty, I laughed to myself that I was concerned that Coal dated her, when it was really Fiona he preferred.

"Hey Ava," she said nonchalantly. "How's it going?"

I had to stop myself from grunting my reply, "Not bad."

"I'm thinking of handing out scripts for the play tomorrow. Halloween is officially over, and you know how November is a short school month. What do you think?" She asked.

What I really thought was this was the first time that Samantha was talking to me like I was an equal. I was honestly taken aback. "Yeah, that sounds like a good idea. Since the students will be memorizing their lines and not just reading them, it does take a lot of practice before the performance." I was ordinarily so excited at the prospect of starting play practice. At the moment, I was exhausted just thinking about it.

"Perfect!" she said with a smile. You had to admire her enthusiasm. "I can't believe Coal is out today. Do you know in all the years I've worked with him, he has never taken a sick day?"

"Is that so?" I asked feigning indifference. I wasn't sure what Samantha knew about Coal and me, but she wasn't getting anything from me.

"Hope everything is alright," she said with a frown. I gave no reaction. "Ok, so I'll hand out the plays tomorrow and assign roles. You'll do the same?"

"Yes," I assured her. "I'll start to read through it with the students tomorrow." At least she wasn't trying to go ahead without me. It was something.

"Ok, great. See you tomorrow," she said with a wave as she walked out the door.

I still didn't know what to make of her. I just had my guard up not to reveal anything of importance to her. The fact that she was being nice to me now was unnerving.

Where was Coal? Why wasn't he here? Despite myself,

I began to worry about him picturing a number of scenarios that left him in a hospital bed. I looked back at that last text that he sent me on Sunday.

We need to talk. Followed by the broken heart emoji.

I assumed he meant we needed to talk about our relationship. What if I was wrong? Maybe something happened with his family. He was going to visit them on Sunday, I thought with a pang of regret, as I was supposed to go with him. Dreams of meeting the parents were dashed as quickly as they came. Going over the different scenarios in my head was making me crazy. If he didn't come to school tomorrow, I would call him, I resolved. Then I was angry with myself for caring.

The night turned cold. It was officially November and the beautiful October nights were a thing of the past. It was like a switch was flipped. It was hard to believe my party with its beautiful weather was only a few days ago. The wind was whipping violently, matching my mood, but I was determined to go out for a run. I needed the exercise and to decompress. Even though it was dark by the time I changed into my running clothes, I was going. I wore a pair of opaque tights under my black running pants for added insulation. I had on a hot pink running bra, my pink Pretty Girls Run t- shirt, an insulated purple running shirt, and a deep plum running jacket with a hood. I also wore a cream-colored wool hat, making sure to cover my ears. The unforgiving wind would surely give me an earache if I didn't.

I set out carrying a single key with me to regain entry to the house. I secured it in my plum running top, zipping it into the pocket. After the whole key disaster with Lina, I wasn't taking any more chances leaving it outside. Deciding to run on the wooded path, I turned the corner and headed into the woods. There wasn't a single person in sight. My heartbeat and even breathing was the soundtrack for my run. Instead of being nervous about being alone, it was liberating. I now knew that the green car was Michael's and was primarily in the neighborhood because he was visiting Fiona. This definitely dissipated my apprehension slightly.

The trees formed a barrier and protected me as I ran along the path, shielding me from being spotted on the street. The lights in peoples' backyards, along the path, were giving off just enough light. I took deep breaths in and out, in and out. I was ok. Everything would be ok. The cold stung my face turning my porcelain cheeks pink. My wool cap kept my hair from becoming a tangled mess.

After running my full three miles on the path I headed back to my house feeling like a new person. I just needed a little time on my own to think. At least I had Peter to talk to now. Both Lina and Tabitha had been very kind to me. Everything would work itself out, but I needed to find out once and for all if someone hurt my lovely Aunt Virginia.

CHAPTER THIRTY-EIGHT

Settled in the secret room once more, the design on the sconces cast a pattern on the wood walls. I brought a cup of hot tea with me to make the job less arduous. I used Aunt Virginia's Miss New York cup, in an attempt to channel her strength. With the wall shut, I felt the slightest bit nervous, every little noise setting my nerves on end. The sound of the steam pipes nearly sent me into a tailspin. I should do as Coal suggested and put a bolt on the inside. I promised myself I would definitely look into it.

With the book on my lap, I set about seriously reading, wanting to make some substantial headway. The next several entries spoke mostly of her work and some drama she had with another woman named Megan who worked as a columnist at some fashion magazine that she freelanced at. It was interesting and definitely gave me insight into how Aunt Ginny thought, but it didn't get me any closer to solving my mystery.

Amber and Aunt Virginia spent so much time together; I was really doubting that Amber would have done anything menacing towards her. They spent time shopping, running, and discussing life. They were practically sisters. Surely one sister would not hurt another sister.

The entry marked January 21 caught my attention.

Thursday January 21, 2021

I saw him today. Despite my attempts to avoid getting in-

volved at any level or at any cost, he is finding a way into my life. He says it was coincidental, but I don't believe him, not really. If it is, the universe is strongly conspiring against me. I went for a run on the path around the block from my house. The weather was quite cold, but I love to run in the cold! (It makes me feel alive!) I was just bundled up rivaling any Eskimo. That's the trick you see, dress warm enough and it's a nonissue. That's what I tell Amber, but she doesn't enjoy the cold weather runs like I do. She loves the summer when it's too hot to breathe. I really don't get it. Ok, I'm getting off topic. I was on the path, by myself when I heard footsteps behind me. I felt a little apprehensive because I could hear the footsteps growing closer quickly, like whoever it was, was coming up on me intentionally. I turned my head and there he was. His face looked innocent enough, but I know he is a good actor. I paused for a minute to deal with him. There was a big oak tree on the path, and he backed me up against it without me even realizing it was happening. He leaned in close, just talking, but I could feel his hot breath on my freezing cheek. I felt a different kind of warmness go through my body from my head to my toes. Why does he have that effect on me after all this time? He lingered, his lips just inches from mine. Nothing happened, but something happened deep inside of me.

Wow! Well now there are two men that Aunt Ginny was involved with that I had no idea about. One of them might be Peter. I wondered which. Why was this man so forbidden? Was he married? Maybe he was connected to something illegal. This was turning into a real-life soap opera. A soap opera that ended tragically, and unlike on shows, Aunt Ginny wouldn't magically reappear from the dead. It wasn't really her unknown twin sister that met her demise while she was in hiding. I wish that was the case. I also marveled at the fact that Aunt Virginia ran the same paths as I did. It was all surreal. I decided to read on.

Friday January 23, 2021

My heart is beating so fast that I'm terrified of what might happen. I tried to use the breathing that I learned in yoga. I took long deep breaths and took my time exhaling as well. I focused on my happy place, on the dance floor in Argentina. What is going on here? I came home from a brunch date with Amber to an unwelcome surprise. Crammed in my mailbox was a blank envelope. I thought it odd that it wasn't addressed to me. The envelope was stark white, but slightly rumpled from being crammed in the mailbox, probably in an attempt to do it hastily and avoid being spotted on my front porch. I wasn't nervous when I saw the envelope, just curious and thinking it strange. I opened it, not sure what to expect, but whatever it was that I thought it might be, did not prepare me for the reality. Inside that envelope were four pieces of paper. On each paper, one word was written as though stabbed into the paper. The words were gone over what seemed dozens of times. Jagged and bold. On the first paper it said only a single letter I. On the second paper, saw. The third paper said, you. The final paper finished with the word, yesterday. I started trembling when I saw them. First my hands began to shake, then my body, followed by my heart. Who were they from? Were they talking about my run the other day? Was it something else that I can't think of? Those letters were not written by a normal person. They were written by someone who is deranged. Maybe they got the wrong house, I thought for only a single moment before intuition set in. I don't believe in deluding myself. No, those letters were meant for me. They were about him. I knew before this that he was bad news, but it doesn't stop me from feeling drawn in. I am ashamed to admit this. The pull is strong, like a magnet that I have no power against. The attraction is too great, and I am too weak.

I found myself holding my breath. It was identical in style to the letters that Coal and I had discovered. The actual message was different, but it wasn't, not really. Where were *those* letters hidden and how many more like it did Aunt

Ginny receive? I desperately wished Coal was here to help me brainstorm. Reading her writing, I felt that it was me going through the experience. Probably because on some level, I had. I felt chills run down my spine. At that point I had read through two weeks full of entries. I was no closer to finding the identity of anyone being mentioned other than Amber. It did however make me feel more secure about seeing her on Friday and that was something.

I looked down at my watch. It was late, and I needed to get to bed if I was going to be ready for seven and eight - year-olds first thing in the morning. I sighed, really wanting to read on but knowing it was not practical.

A giant coffee was waiting in the middle of my desk when I arrived the next day. I saw it the second I walked in, like a beacon of hope. It wasn't a Starbuck cup, like Fiona would usually bring me, so I wondered who it was from. It was a tall cream cup with some type of gray printed design that I'd never seen before. There was no note attached. As I was studying the cup, I heard the sound of the classroom door creaking open.

"Oh good, you got the coffee." Samantha stood there wearing a pair of brown trousers and a cream- colored sweater. Her blond hair was in beachy waves. "I asked Fiona what type you like, so it should be good."

I took a sip and was pleasantly surprised that it was delicious. She had gotten it just right. I silently wondered what her angle was. All these weeks in school and she barely spoke to me, and when she did. It was rarely pleasant.

"It's perfect," I said with a smile. "Thank you."

Samantha was full on beaming. I seriously felt I was in an alternate universe. "So, I made a copy of the plays for my class. Here's your book," she said, handing me the play book from the other day. Maybe she really was just happy that I had included her in the play. I patted myself on the back for having the foresight. Imagine what she'd be like if I hadn't included her.

"So, I usually spend two weeks just having them read through with their script at the end of the day. We do it casually, just in their seats. This makes it so they know how to pronounce all of the words and get the lines in their head. After that, I slowly start taking their scripts away and feeding them lines as necessary. Then I start having them do it standing up and acting it out."

"Awesome, thanks for the advice," Samantha said, she glanced up at the clock and grimaced. "Well, I guess we better go get our kids. Thanks again."

I smiled. It was best to keep your enemy close, but what I really hoped was that perhaps in the end we wouldn't be enemies at all.

While going to pick up my students, I got my first glimpse of Coal. He looked pale, gaunt even, his cheeks looking more chiseled than usual. He appeared to have lost five pounds since Saturday. It's frustrating that it never works that way for women. He hadn't seen me yet, and I found myself holding my breath. As he turned around and saw me, our eyes connected, his pleading, mine quickly looking away. My first thought was that he was here, so at least I didn't have to reach out to him. He was at least as ok as I was.

"Good morning, Ms. Z," my little blonde lovebug Jenna said when the class was lined up. "Why does your face look so frowny? Do you have a bellyache?" she asked, touching her own stomach.

Oh, dear girl, you have no idea, "A little," I responded, looking at her cherub-like face, "but I feel much better now that all my friends are here." I made a concerted effort to smile. I was a professional. I had a lot of practice pretending that everything was ok. Maybe if I pretended long enough, it might actually be true.

Sitting in my car, in my driveway, after school, I was trying to decide on my plan of action for the night. I took a deep breath. I would go to The Journey. It was the perfect opportunity to get a class in, especially with the knowledge that Fiona had her dance lesson and wouldn't be there.

Making my way to the front door quickly, wanting to escape the November chill, I stopped abruptly. A box wrapped in craft paper and twine was evident on the porch next to the rocking chair. I felt my heart flutter. It looked identical to the other two boxes I previously received. I stared at it, afraid to pick it up. The night was approaching quickly, getting darker and more ominous by the minute. I probably stood there a solid two minutes when Peter appeared.

"Hey Ava, everything ok?" he asked, strolling up to the porch. He had on a chocolate brown sweater and tweed brown dress pants. He looked a little better in comparison to the night he sat at my dining room table a mess, but he still didn't look like Peter.

I pointed to the wrapped box without saying a word.

"Is that what I think it is?" he asked, his brown eyes widening, his Adam's apple bobbed as he swallowed.

Staring transfixed at the box, I answered him, "I'm not sure."

"Do you want me to come in with you to open it?" he offered.

This time I wasn't hesitant at all. I nodded my head in affirmation. I didn't touch the box, afraid that a snake might slither out of it and bite me.

Peter bent down and picked it up, while I nervously fumbled to open the door. After shutting off the alarm, Peter and I retreated to the sitting room.

"Do you want to open it or do you prefer that I do it?" Peter asked not wanting to assume anything. I appreciated his respectfulness.

I spoke in a small voice, the biggest I could muster, "Can you do it? Please?" I knew I looked pathetic, weak. My hands were shaking, remembering the doll with the missing eyes. I was so grateful that Peter came out of his house when he did. I didn't think I'd be able to do it alone.

Unlike Coal, Peter did not carry a pocket knife in his pocket. He asked me for my keys, which I was still holding in my trembling hands.

Taking the sharp edge of the front door key, he sliced the tape down the middle. The box was packed identically to the other two boxes. He unwrapped the tissue paper to reveal a third doll. This one had a pretty periwinkle dress and boots on. She even had silver earrings hanging from her ears. The face was smiling and the green eyes seemed to twinkle. It didn't look scary. There was nothing menacing in this box. Suddenly I felt foolish. I let my breath out in a big whoosh.

"How odd," Peter said, holding the doll examining it. There was no anonymous message attached to this doll.

"Why?" I asked, dropping my head into my hands.

"I'm so sorry Ava," Peter said, his eyes sincere. "I really wish I had answers for you. What do you want me to do with it?"

"Just put it back in the box please," I responded.

Peter did just as I asked and rewrapped the doll, depositing her right back into the box, just as I requested and handed me the box. He just stood there looking undecided on how he should proceed.

"Have a seat if you'd like?" I finally say. "Or if you have to go, I totally understand."

"I'll sit just for a minute," he answered, taking a seat in the armchair perpendicular to the couch. "Wait, I just remembered, what about the doorbell camera?" Peter asked excitedly. He looked a little less tired at the prospect of finding some answers.

I groped around in my bag until I spotted my phone and immediately pulled up my app for the cameras. I wasn't sure what time it had arrived, so I had to fast forward through footage of nothing until I saw some movement. There it finally was at 3:30 pm, a figure approached the front door carrying the box. They wore a big bulky coat with a hoodie pulled up. On their eyes were a pair of those gigantic sunglasses that I saw my mom and Aunt Virginia wearing in pictures of them in the nineties. A scarf was wrapped around their face covering both the mouth and nose. The person wasn't very tall or very short. They had a very medium build. I couldn't tell definitively if the figure was a man or woman. Whoever it was, they were smart enough to disguise themselves, so they would be unrecognizable to me.

"Peter, come see this," I said, patting the seat next to me. He tentatively sat down, and I rewound the footage to precisely 3:30 pm. Handing him my phone, I let him watch what I had seen. Maybe he would be able to catch something I hadn't. I didn't get the feeling it was anyone I knew, but I wanted to get his take on it.

"Well, one thing is clear," he said, handing me back my phone. "Whoever sent you that doll wishes to remain anonymous. They are definitely not trying to get credit for sending you a gift. *That* lets me know it is something to be worried about."

"At least this one has eyes," I said in an attempt to lighten the mood. Peter didn't look like he appreciated my joke.

"Don't touch it any further," Peter said seriously, "just in case we need to present it to the police." His face was grave.

I stood up and put the box in the hall closet where I stored the other two dolls.

"Well thank you for coming in with me. I don't think I could have faced that alone. I think I'm going to go to my gym class. I really need to get some of this tension released."

Peter nodded and stood up, "I think that's a good idea. Listen, if you need anything before Friday, here is my cell number. I mean anything. If you get scared, or if anything else happens. I know you feel like you are alone right now, but I promise you that you're not." He passed me a business card that contained all of his details. I took it and held it in the palm of my hand.

"Thanks Peter," I said, hugging him. After letting him out the door, I immediately locked it and set the alarm, even though I had plans to leave shortly after. I wasn't taking any chances.

I went upstairs and carefully chose my outfit for the gym. I couldn't explain it, but Marcia was so strange the night of the party. She was half extremely polite and half intimidating. I felt like I was going in ready for battle, but that was another reason I was going. I would not retreat just because she had issues. This thing with Fiona and Coal was different. We had history and real feelings involved. Her issues with me were nonsense. Girl Code dictated that you needed to go in looking your best. I found a matching tank/ legging set that was blue, white, and yellow. Fastening my hair in a side braid, I added a pale yellow ribbon to it. I dusted a little loose powder over my face, touched up my eye liner and added a fresh coat of lipstick. I was as ready as I would ever be.

Rushing, I made it to class with only three minutes to spare. Unfortunately, the class was pretty full and my favored spot was already taken by a fifty-something year old man with ruffled salt and pepper hair. He was stretching down to touch his toes and had his one knee wrapped in a knee brace. Marcia was busy setting up the music as I found a place and put my mat down and took out my weights that I brought with me in my bag.

When Marcia looked in the mirror and spotted me, a look I couldn't decipher crossed her face. I pretended to not even notice. I looked around at the rest of the class. That mom group, that took that picture of Coal and I at the very beginning, was there. The mom, whose husband had supposedly gone out with Fiona, was directly in front of me. To my surprise, she turned and gave me a half wave. I seriously felt like I slipped down the rabbit hole.

Before I had any more time to think or wonder, the music blasted. "Let the Journey begin," Marcia screamed.

Say what you want about Marcia. Her personality was definitely lacking and scoring at about a 3 out of 10, but she knew how to run an exercise class. By the time the hour was up, my mind was clear. I was so busy focusing on getting through the tortuous circuit that she had created that when it was finished, I nearly collapsed onto the hardwood floor. I returned my weights to my gym bag, and I rolled my mat back up. As I put my long black coat on, a mom that I've only seen before but never spoke to came up to me.

"So sorry to hear about you and Coal," she said sarcastically.

"Excuse me," I said, thinking I couldn't possibly have heard her correctly. Was this woman who I had never spoken to before actually giving her fake condolences about the end of a relationship that tore my heart out?

"You and Mr. Blake, so sorry it didn't work out," she reiterated, extremely insincerely. She stared at me with her hazel eyes challenging me. Unlucky for her, I was up for the challenge issued by this big boned woman with ash brown hair and a rather nondescript face.

"Do I know you?" I asked, my voice turning hostile. I was *almost* willing to talk to Coal to wipe that smug look off of her face.

She looked a little taken aback, probably thought I would cower being confronted. This is the reason that you should never assume. When you pick a fight with someone you don't know, it's always dangerous. She definitely had miscalculated and picked the wrong person on the wrong day.

According to her usual routine, Marcia would typically have been out the door by now, but it seemed she caught sight of the confrontation between this mom and me and she made no move to leave. She was occupied fiddling around with CD's at the front of the room as if it were the most interesting thing in the world.

I took a step closer to this woman who was a stranger

to me. She was a good four inches taller than me which could be quite intimidating, but I stood at my full height and looked her dead in the eye. "I couldn't imagine how someone I've never met would have anything to say to me about a relationship that she knows nothing about." As I spoke my voice remained completely even, my green eyes boring holes into her soul.

She took a step back and acted as though I struck her. The other moms all the sudden pretending to be otherwise occupied, as though they were not with her. I looked in the mirror and I saw Marcia watching, she actually looked impressed with me.

I picked up my gym bag and tucked my rolled-up mat under my arm. I did my best Marcia impression and strutted out the glass doors, never looking back.

CHAPTER THIRTY-NINE

The next afternoon meant my tango lesson. I started to really look forward to Thursdays and Sundays. The music and movement made my heart happy. Much like running and my classes, it was like going to therapy without having to talk to anyone. I cleared my mind of any other thoughts for those sixty minutes. It even worked on Sunday when I was newly devastated and raw. My only regret was that Coal had his cha-cha lesson today, the same time as mine. What I once found to be good luck filled me with dread. I managed to avoid him for the rest of the day, but seeing him during my lesson was inevitable. I opted to change my shoes in my classroom, so I could walk in, right on time for my lesson and not have to linger there waiting for it to begin.

I was actually going down the hall at the same time that Demitrus was entering the building. I was certain based on my experience with him so far that he would be late, so I planned accordingly and took my time.

"Oh, hello Ava," he said opening the gym door, he had his other arm across my back. "I was dreaming about our dancing on Sunday." He had a wicked smile on his face, his blue eyes twinkling.

Coal was already standing in hold with his dance partner. They were poised in position, but he was facing the doors, so he saw our grand entry. A dark look crossed his face.

Demitrus brought the same black speaker that he utilized on Sunday. "Hello my friends," he said, speaking to the other dance instructors. "If anyone wants to borrow my speaker to play their music, it is available." His loud voice echoed across the gymnasium.

The other instructors smiled and nodded. Chloe's instructors shouted, "Thanks bro." Chloe made eye contact with me and rolled her eyes. I bit my lip to stop from laughing.

"Ok, why don't we run through our dance with the music," Demitrus instructed me. "Then we will work on more choreography." I was thrilled that he wanted to get right to business.

I stood the appropriate distance away from him, so we could make our dramatic entrance. My eyes were trained on him waiting for the exact cue to begin.

The music filled the room, when I looked around, I noticed everyone's eyes on us. We were the first to dance using music that could be heard by the room, so everyone was excited. Up until Sunday, we had been practicing with a cell phone. We were all taught the beginnings of our routines. We practiced counting out and executing our steps. The introduction of music made everybody turn to take notice. To be honest, I was excited about seeing everyone else's routines to music as well. With showtime looming closer, we were all getting ready for the big event. As I counted the walks in my head, I blocked out everyone around me. We executed the dance with perfect precision. After the back ochos, Demetrius had added in a grapevine with kicks. He led me into a molinete to the right, which is like a grapevine only in a circle. I finished with an enganche on his right side, which is actually hooking the side of his body with my leg.

We finished our choreography thus far and everyone started clapping.

"Bravo," Tabitha yelled.

Marion put her fingers in her mouth and did that obnoxious ear-piercing whistle that I always find so annoying.

Coal looked away and quickly pretended to be engrossed in whatever his teacher was doing.

"Take a bow Ava," Demitrus insisted. "You have not lost it, probably because you are dancing with me." He poked me in the side.

Everyone resumed their practice. Chloe practiced her salsa to music and she looked great. Demitrus fixed some of my footwork that went awry and finished my choreography.

When the hour was over, I bolted to the bleachers to retrieve my things from where I left them. As I bent down to get them, I felt someone standing there. Feeling sick, I turned, thankful to see Tabitha.

"Wow," Tabitha said, face animated. "The tango really suits you. Do you know what you're wearing yet?"

Demitrus must have overheard her because he sidled up behind us.

"Ladies and Gentlemen, I need to make an announcement. I almost forgot," he said smiling boyishly, as though it was charming to be irresponsible.

Everyone was done with their lessons by this point, and I wanted nothing more than to leave, but of course I was stuck rooted in place waiting for the big announcement.

"Saturday morning everyone needs to come by sometime between 8 am and 12 pm. You will have a consultation with the seamstress and your partner, and you'll be measured for your costume. It is very important as the show is right around the corner."

"So important he almost forgot to tell us," Marion said, coming up to Tabitha and me.

Since my exit plan hadn't worked as I anticipated, I figured there was safety in numbers. I relaxed a little as we all stood and chatted amicably.

My entire adult life, the life I had to forge after my parents died, I've always been afraid to relax. In my head I believed, the moment that you relax, something bad happens. That moment proved my point. Much to my dismay, Coal walked right up to our group.

"Can I speak with you for a moment?" Coal asked calmly, politely. He walked up to me like I was the only person in the room. Coal was usually so considerate and polite to everyone. He didn't look around at all the questioning eyes that were staring at him. I however was well aware that I had an audience.

"Ok," I said reluctantly. Taking my time putting on my black coat, I hoped in vain that he would give up and go away. I looped my bag with my dance shoes around my shoulder. "See you guys tomorrow," I said with a wave as we walked towards the gym doors.

My heart was in my throat. I braced myself for what was coming next.

Demitrus smiled as I exited. "See you Saturday Ava," he called.

Coal and I walked down the corridor in a stony silence. I felt like I was walking a march to my death. I opened the main door that led outside and a cold gust of wind hit me in the face.

The night had taken a blustery turn. I hoped that this would shorten the amount of time in which Coal and I would converse. He didn't say anything, so I started walking towards my car. I was now standing at my sapphire Mustang, yet Coal hadn't uttered a word.

Finally, he came up to my driver's side door and leaned against the car. His face contorted into a picture of pain. "Why?" His word came out as almost a tortured cry. It's ferocity tore at my heart.

I didn't know what he was going to say to me, but I never expected this. Why? As if I was the one who was keeping secrets. As if I had secretly dated his best friend and never mentioned it.

Before I could figure out how to answer him, he spoke again, "I trusted you with my heart." He clutched his hands to his chest and turned to look off into the trees. Tears were in his eyes.

Anger began to bubble up in me. "I trusted you," I retorted, spitting the words at him. "Those weeks we had together, I thought we had something real."

Coal turned back to me now, his eyes locking with mine. The wind kept blowing but I could no longer feel the cold. The pounding in my ears was a loud drumming.

The sound of the others coming out the front door broke the silence of the night. Coal and I continued to stand there by my car door. Unfortunately, Tabitha was parked directly to the right of me. She had no choice but to walk right toward us.

"You ok Ava?" she asked, pushing a strand of her long black hair behind her ear. She was obviously taking in this tense scene before her, trying to decide how much she should get involved.

I nodded my head. "Yes, thank you." I didn't dare say more as tears were threatening to fall.

"Ok, have a nice night, guys," she called, getting into her black BMW and driving away.

The two of us just stood there. The only sounds that could be heard were the whistling of the wind and the banging of car doors closing. We just stood waiting for the rest of the teachers to get into their cars.

Just as I was about to speak, out walked the dance instructors. They were talking loudly.

Demitrus spotted the two of us and shouted, "Bye Ava. I count the minutes until I see you again."

That got a reaction from Coal. He finally moved like he was going to attack him. I put my hand on his arm as if to stop him. Demitrus was none the wiser. He was already backing out of the parking lot.

The silence was deafening. I finally broke down saying, "What is it that you want from me?"

Coal looked like I had struck him in the face. "What do I want from you?" He went from looking heartbroken to looking murderous. I actually got a little nervous and took a step back realizing that it was now just the two of us in the very dark parking lot. He noticed my shifting of position. This seemed to agitate him even more. "You really think I would hurt *you*? You don't know me at all," he spat out.

"You're right, I don't." My own anger began to build, and I started to pick up steam. "Come to find out you dated Fiona, the person that I'm closest to in Syracuse. We're practically family, and you never told me. Everyone knew but me. I felt so stupid and deceived." I had to force myself not to let my voice become hysterical.

Coal looked dumbfounded. "Is *that* what this is about?" he asked, clearly confused by this information. He let out a big sigh.

"Well," I said, annoyed by his lack of response.

"Who told you that?" his voice now calmer, which made me get slightly more hysterical.

"I overheard Enzo saying it to you at the party. If Tabitha's boyfriend knows then clearly everyone knows, and no one has said a word. Just so you understand my fairness, I'm equally as furious with Fiona too."

"Ava," he said, touching my arm now, his voice softening.

"No," I said, pulling my arm away. "I really thought this second time around I was going to get a chance to be truly happy.. I'm not having a pity party for myself, Coal. I am no victim. *That's* why I told you to leave. I won't be deceived again. Not ever again." I couldn't help it, the anger turned to tears. They felt cold as they fell making my face wet, leaving a physical trail of my sadness on my face.

"I wish you had talked to me instead of running away," Coal said, the softness of his eyes returning. "I could have saved us both a lot of heartache."

I remained quiet. It was his turn now.

"Fiona and I literally went on two dates, back when we first worked together. She actually asked me out. I really liked her as a friend, but it was *never* more than that. There was nothing to mention. I promise."

I stood there shivering. Was he telling the truth? This was something that I could easily find out. I could ask Tabitha. If I was being honest, I probably should have asked Tabitha to begin with, but with the dolls and the notes I didn't trust anybody.

While I struggled with my internal dialogue, Coal moved closer and put his arm around me. I could smell his scent, I ached. God how I wanted to believe that this was one big misunderstanding. I would give anything, but I didn't want to live a lie like I did for the last ten years.

"Would it be ok if I followed you to your house, and we could talk more there?" Coal suggested gently.

I nodded my head. While I was driving, I would call Tabitha and verify that he was telling the truth. Taking my keys out of my purse, Coal dropped his arm.

"Thank you," Coal said as he stood watching me. I could only imagine how disastrous I looked at this point. I was so cold and so very tired.

Opening the car door, I got in and he closed the door for me. He put his hand on the window. Following suit, I put mine up on my side, our hands lined up together, only a pane of glass stood between us. I prayed that no lies would keep us apart.

As soon as Coal left to walk to his car, I found Tabitha's contact information in my phone. I put it on speaker and began to pull away.

"Ava?" Tabitha's voice filled my car.

"Hey," I said, feeling embarrassed about having to have this particular conversation, but it had to happen.

"Everything ok? We were all concerned about you? I didn't want to bring it up, figured if you wanted to talk about it, you would, but that scene between you and Coal was intense."

"I know, I'm so embarrassed," I said as I made a right-hand turn.

"There's nothing to be embarrassed about. Everyone fights, but God Coal has been a mess, not at all himself. I was afraid to even talk to him."

"At the party, I overheard Enzo talking to Coal about him dating Fiona," I admitted, feeling especially foolish for eavesdropping on a conversation that her fiance was having.

"I wouldn't actually call it dating Ava. Honestly Fiona had a crush on Coal, and he basically had to find a way to make it apparent that it was platonic."

"Do you promise?" I asked, my voice cracking, hope soaring through me for the first time.

"I wouldn't lie to you Ava, there was nothing there," Tabitha said words pouring over me, healing me like medicine. She couldn't possibly imagine the impact of this seemingly simple conversation.

I burst out crying, right there on speaker phone with Tabitha.

"Are you ok?" Tabitha asked again for the third time that night.

"Yes, oh, God, yes. I'm so sorry," I must have sounded like a lunatic to her. I really owed her an explanation. "Thank you for being a friend, Tabitha. I've been so distraught over this. I'm coming out of a bad ten-year marriage. I was so disappointed when I found out that Coal and Fiona were previously involved and they didn't tell me. "

"Well, this explains a lot. I was wondering what the hell was going on with all of you. Coal is a really good guy Ava, and he is smart. I'm not going to lie, he's had a lot of women after him, but you are the only one I've ever seen turn his head. He was smitten with you from the minute you walked in the door, and that's made a lot of women around here crazy."

"I'm on my way home right now," I told her as I turned onto my street. "Do you think it's ok that I agreed to let him come over and talk?" I questioned, really needing reassurance.

"I think it's perfect. Go get your man, and Ava," Tabitha paused.

"Yes?" I asked pulling into the driveway.

"I better get an invitation to the wedding."

CHAPTER FORTY

Hanging up the phone, a rush of adrenaline surged through me. Coal hadn't arrived yet, in fact, I didn't remember seeing his car behind mine when I was driving home. I was so caught up in my conversation with Tabitha that I failed to pay attention. Jumping out of the car, I ran to the front door. Once I got inside and locked it, I took the stairs two at a time. I wanted to fix myself up as quickly as humanly possible.

I didn't want to change my clothes because I had no intention of keeping them on. I sprayed my special perfume, washed my face which was red and blotchy from my crying episodes. My skin was so dry from the cold, so I slathered on moisturizer and quickly reapplied my makeup.

Bring, Bring. My heart leapt; he was here. I ran down the steps at lightning speed. I went so quickly I was afraid I might trip down the stairs. I recognized Coal's silhouette through the smoked glass. My heart was thumping. I fumbled with the lock and threw open the door.

There stood Coal. He was holding a bouquet of flowers, looking unsure. His brown wavy hair fell a little in his face, his sunset eyes looked at me questioningly. I could see him calculating in his head whether he made the right move.

I would leave him in agony no more. I stood on my tiptoes and kissed him on his soft lips. The urgency of our kiss took me by surprise. I pulled him inside and shut the door, not wanting to put on a show for neighbors.

To my surprise, Coal had tears in his eyes. "We're... we're ok?" he asked, not quite believing it was real.

"Yes. Yes we are definitely ok," I cried now too.

"God I was so scared," he admitted, with so much honesty in his voice that I was taken aback. "Ava those days without you, they were dark. Please don't *ever* leave me again."

"I'm sorry," I cried hard now, so much for my newly applied makeup. "I should have talked to you. I should have confronted you when I first heard. This was all my fault. I'm a mess..."

"Shh, you're perfect. None of that matters. I just won the lottery, and I don't want to hear any negative talk about my prize," he said, handing me the flowers. "I would have been here sooner, but I wanted to bring you something. Luckily the farmer's market was still open. I thought they would look beautiful with your hair," The bouquet consisted of gorgeous apricot- colored roses.

"Why are we still standing here?" I laughed looking at the entryway of the house. "We have so much to catch up on."

The flowers in one hand, the other hand in his, I dragged him up the stairs towards the bedroom. He stopped when we reached the table where all the Halloween decorations had once been, the hallway looking a little barren. Coal scooped me up, carrying me into the bedroom. He laid me gently on the bed. I pulled him down on top of me, feeling the weight of his body on mine.

"I understand why you were so upset, especially after seeing your ex-husband in action. What a creep!" Coal was whispering in my ear as he laid on me.

"I don't want you to think he was like that when we were married. He was never hitting on other people, or looking girls up and down. He was actually kind of dull but controlling, a little obsessive. That night he acted like a frat guy. I don't know why Fiona was ok with that," I said. "I don't want to talk about Michael anymore. I am happy things didn't work out with our marriage, if they did, I wouldn't have met you." I traced his lips with my finger. They were a perfect bow shape.

"I went to see my parents the next day, as planned," Coal said. I was listening to both him and the rhythm of his heart beating as he spoke. "I actually spent an hour crying to my mom about you. I mean literal tears. My dad got uncomfortable and remembered something that desperately needed fixing in the other room. I told her how special you are. That I wasn't sure what I did to lose you, so I didn't know how to fix it."

"She must hate me now," I said feeling sad. I really wanted his parents to like me, especially since I don't have my own anymore. Surely, I had no chance now.

"No, she said that you were my once in a lifetime, and that I should give you a little time to calm down. She said everything would turn out ok. I didn't believe her, but she was right. She's always right. Do you promise that we are ok Ava? You're not going to change your mind, are you?" he swallowed hard. I felt like crap for putting both of us through the last few days, but now I felt so sure of his feelings that I could cry from joy.

"My feelings for you have never dulled. They grow stronger every second. That's why I was so scared and angry when I thought you were keeping something so big from me."

Coal rolled me over, so I was on top now. I sat up and leaned down to kiss him once more. He groaned.

"I have so much to catch you up on. Someone stole Aunt Ginny's Miss New York photograph, the one where she was in the convertible," I said sitting up again.

"Stole? From where?" he asked, his face in disbelief.

"Right off her bedroom wall, during the party."

"No way," he said incredulously. "Who would do something like that? Come into your home as a guest and steal something, especially something personal that can't be replaced."

"No idea. That was bizarre, but I didn't tell you the scariest thing yet. Someone slipped something in my drink at the party. I'm sure of it. The last thing I remember was walking into the library, when you guys all went upstairs. I have no recollection of anything that happened after that until I woke up late in the morning. I didn't even know that I threw you out. Lina is the one who told me."

The look on Coal's face scared me. "What?" He used his arms to push himself up now. "This is serious Ava. You could have been seriously hurt or worse, and I should have been here to protect you."

"I know, I was pretty freaked out, and I had no one to talk to because I really don't know who I can trust. I got another doll on the front steps, and a few threatening texts too." Telling Coal everything that happened in the last few days, it didn't seem real. If someone told me all these things, I might think that they were making it up for attention. At the very least, maybe exaggerating things, but if anything, I was actually playing it down a little. I didn't want to scare Coal.

I sat on the bed now leaning against the pillows, as did Coal.

"Please let me stay with you until we get this all sorted out," Coal pleaded with me. He took a deep breath, and we sat our heads leaning against each other. "I know you like your independence, and things are still hard for you, but I could never forgive myself if something happened to you. Please."

I nodded my head. "I guess it would be fine for a little bit. Maybe we could stay at your house sometime too, just so it doesn't get lonely."

Coal grinned widely, "Yes, definitely. I would love that. I was so scared you would say no. I won't let anything bad happen to you. You are after all going to be Mrs. Blake one day." He looked at my face and continued. "I'm sorry if I'm scaring you, but after what we just went through, I'm going to lay it all out on the table. I want no regrets."

I said it before, life is unpredictable. Things change, flip without a moment's notice. I guessed the best thing to do was go with it. I couldn't live my life being scared about what might happen because then I'd be wasting the time that I really had to live.

I squeezed his hand tightly. "Should we go to your house to get a few things, or do you want to start staying tomorrow?" I asked.

"Are you kidding? I'm not wasting a single day without you. Do you have anything you have to get done for tomorrow? If you want, I can just run home to get a few things. Over the weekend I'll have you at my house and make you that dinner I promised you."

I thought for a minute. I did want to have a few minutes to get things settled before Coal was back. "That's a good idea. Tomorrow night I'm having dinner at Amber's house with Amber, Peter, and Fiona," I wrinkled my nose in distaste.

"How did that happen?" Coal asked, putting his coat back on. "I thought you were mad at Fiona too."

"It's a tricky situation," I explained. I told him about Peter coming over and his worries and suspicions.

"Seriously Ava, it's like you're living in a Lifetime movie."

"Do you want me to ask Amber if you can come too? I don't want to just show up with you, but I wouldn't mind asking if you can come."

I picked up my phone and texted. She answered me back rather instantaneously.

Hi Ava. Looking forward to tomorrow. Yes, bring Coal! We'd love to have him! Is 7ish ok for you? xx Amber

"She said you should come," I said as he approached the door. "Do you want to come?"

"Yes, I want to get a feel for things too, and I hope I can help make things less awkward for you and Fi."

"Ok," I said, disarming the alarm, "text me when you get back and I'll let you in and disarm the alarm. I gave my spare key to Lina." He leaned down and kissed me like he meant it.

"Wait, wasn't the key missing from the backdoor when you gave it to Lina last time?"

"Yeah, but Peter saw her put it there and grabbed it. He was nervous that someone else would find it, and he read me the riot act about not being careful."

"Good, I need back up," he said as I opened the door and watched him walk to his car.

While Coal was gone, I started a fire in the library fireplace. I also got two wine glasses ready and poured us each a glass of cabernet. By the time he texted me, I had the fire roaring, and the room was nice and cozy.

I came down stairs and let Coal in. I showed him how to arm and disarm the system, since he would be staying for a little while. Then I led him upstairs, after depositing his bag in the bedroom, we settled in the library.

"I'm impressed you make such a good fire," he smiled, eyes bright. "Not surprised though. You can do anything." He winked at me as he sat in his wood seat. I beamed at the compliment from him.

I sat in my green chair and stared for a minute at the fire. Watching it crackle, I remembered the wine that I poured and reached over to the writing desk handing Coal his glass. I took a sip of mine and held it in my hands. It felt warm in my chest.

We sat enjoying the silence and each other's presence. My mind couldn't wrap around the fact that Coal was here with me. After the party, I truly was finished with him. I thought I was betrayed. The fact that he was here with me was a miracle. I was afraid to accept it because I didn't want him to disappear again.

Coal reached for my hand. He held it tightly as he spoke, "This is a beautiful life, Ava. Being here with you, it makes everything right." I leaned over and kissed him.

"When I awoke this morning, I would never believe that I would be finishing my night like this. I feel as if I'm in a dream. We'll see if we wake up tomorrow morning. I was going to read Aunt Ginny's diary more, but I want to end things on a hopeful note tonight."

"Agreed," Coal said, "however tomorrow, we get right to business."

Morning came too soon. I woke up at my usual time, however I didn't want to get out of bed. I contemplated staying and laying with Coal forever. I did have to get things done though, so I leaned up and kissed his forehead and eyes. I saw him smile but not open his eyes. Tiptoeing into the bathroom, I quietly closed the door.

After brushing my teeth and taking a quick shower, I put my hair in my terry cloth robe to help it absorb some of the moisture. I wrapped myself in my plushest towel and put my thick silver robe over it. Finally, I put on a layer of moisturizer on my face and went down to put on coffee.

The sound of the heat kicking on greeted me as I walked into the kitchen. Although six o'clock already, the yard was clothed in darkness. This time of the year was the worst for the darkness. I hated the fact that I didn't get much time outdoors now. I missed being in the yard with my coffee in the morning.

While I was waiting for the percolator to brew, I started taking out ingredients for my green smoothie. I wasn't sure if Coal would want one too. We still had a lot to learn about each other's likes and dislikes. I took out the cutting board and started slicing a pear into pieces. Next, I sliced the ginger into a few fine strips, but I was interrupted by the boiling of the coffee.

Coal came walking into the kitchen on cue as I took two mugs out of the cabinet.

"Good morning beautiful," Coal said, coming up from behind me and wrapping his arms around my waist. He looked to be fresh out of the shower as well and fully dressed in dark jeans and sweater. It was Friday, so our casual dress day at school.

"Good morning love," I said, spinning around so I would be facing him. "Coffee's ready. I'm preparing myself a green monster, but I wasn't sure if you wanted one."

Coal glanced at my fruits and vegetables littering the counter. "I've never had one before, so what better time than today to try it?"

I smiled and grabbed another container to place his ingredients in.

"What are we going to tell people at school?" I asked, realizing that Tabitha was the only one who knew what was going on.

"Tell? We don't need to tell or explain anything to anyone. Our happiness is for us. If people care about us, they'll be happy for us. If they don't care about us, then they shouldn't be privy to information about us." He held up his coffee mug as if giving a toast.

"Well said. It's funny, but Samantha has been very friendly to me since the party." I de-veined the kale and put it into two separate containers. I'm not sure why, but she actually bought me a coffee the other day and left it on my desk as a surprise."

His mouth dropped open, "Seriously? Things are even weirder than I imagined." We both laughed.

We drove to school together that morning. It was extra cold out and the wind was whistling. I wore my navy-blue goose down coat that goes past my knees. My hair was only partially dry, so I put on my navy and white hat with the gigantic ball on top to protect my head. We walked through the doors of the school together, but no one was around to witness it. As Coal and I approached our classrooms, Samantha was waiting at my door again. Her face fell when she saw Coal and I laughing together.

"Hey Samantha," I smiled, greeting her. "How did play practice go?"

She seemed confused by my question. I wondered what she was waiting at my door for.

"Are the two of you...?" Her question trailed off.

"Are we what?" asked Coal looking at her. I appreciated him fielding this. She liked him much better than she liked me.

"Did you ... make up?" she asked, not even trying to hide the disgust in her voice.

"Yes, Ava and I are together," Coal said bluntly. "I was lost without her," he added.

A stormy look crossed Samantha's face. "Oh, that's great. I'm happy for you both," she turned on her heels and walked down the hall to her classroom, not waiting for a response from either of us.

Coal and I stood in silence, he motioned for us to go in my room.

"Wow," he said, closing the door behind him. I deposited my bag on my swivel chair and hung up my coat on the back of the chair.

"You're positive that you were never involved with her, right?" I said for the third time, instantly regretting it. This wasn't the time for us to turn on each other.

"Ava, I wouldn't lie to you. Nothing remotely like dating ever happened between us."

"I know, I'm sorry," I said remembering what Tabitha said to me last night. She alluded to the fact that there were people that weren't happy about mine and Coal's relationship.

"Please don't let this or anyone else's opinion get in the way of what we have. It's special," he said, kissing my cheek.

"I won't. It's just upsetting."

There was a tapping at the door, Tabitha's face filled the window, and she was smiling.

"Hey guys," she said, coming into the room with a gigantic smile on her face. "I'm so happy to see the two of you worked things out. Enzo was hoping we could set up a double date for Sunday."

"That sounds great," Coal said, "If it works for you Ava." He turned to me to double check.

"Of course, I would love that."

I thought I saw something out of the corner of my eye. I turned my head and saw Fiona at the door. She looked much better today than she's looked all week. She was even wearing some mascara and lip gloss. Her hair was back to being bouncy around her shoulders.

Walking in she immediately hugged me. "Hey Ava, mom told me you were bringing Coal to dinner tonight. I'm so happy," she turned and saw that Tabitha was in the room with us and frowned. She quickly recovered and replaced the scowl with a smile, but it wasn't quite quick enough.

"Coal," she said, embracing him too with a gigantic bear hug. "I'm so happy that you and Ava are ok. You make a wonderful couple."

"Thanks," he smiled, but it was obvious he was a little uncomfortable with this demonstrative display of affection given our fight.

"Hey Tabitha, isn't this great news?" Fiona asked, turning to her at last.

This whole morning since arriving at school was giving me a headache, but Coal was right with what he said. Real friends are happy for their friends when good things happen. This was a good way to sort out where loyalties really stood.

"I'm super excited. I wanted to give you an invitation to our wedding," she said, handing me a thick cream envelope. "I already gave Coal one a while back, but that was before you even worked here. The wedding is actually only two weeks away now, but Enzo and I would love for you to be there."

"I wouldn't miss it!" Now it was Tabitha's turn to get a hug. "Thank you so much for including me. It means a lot."

"I was going to ask her to come as my date anyway," he said jokingly to Tabitha. "So, you really didn't have a choice."

The gesture of inviting me meant so much. I was finally building a new group of close friends in Syracuse. It's all I ever wanted when I moved here.

"Guys, I hate to break up the party, but we have to pick up the kids in like one minute."

Everyone scampered out of the room and off to work.

Friday afternoon couldn't come soon enough. As we walked towards the doors to leave for the night, the afternoon was extra deceptive. The sun was shining brightly. The remaining autumn leaves were lit up, and the sky was cloudless. It looked like a picture perfect day. As soon as we opened the doors, the cutting wind hit us, making it hard to even breathe. I hoped it wasn't foreshadowing of our night to come.

I happily got into Coal's car and away from the wind.

"Well, I'm happy to see that you and Tabitha are becoming better friends," Coal said, smiling hopefully at me. "I always felt she was genuine, and besides I love hanging out with Enzo, an added bonus."

"Yeah, I like her a lot too. We hung out on Monday night."

Coal pulled out of his parking spot. The wind blew the leaves in circles around the lot.

"I only didn't see you for four days, and it seems like a million things happened to you."

"I know, and I forgot to tell you, after we went to a Pilates class we went out for coffee. While we were there, the mayor and his wife were there too. The mayor was promoting the dance show, and he had Tabitha and I go up to the microphone and tell the audience about it."

"I wish I could have seen that," Coal said, grinning while making a left turn. "I'm also glad things seem okay with you and Fiona."

"Yeah, me too. It's just, did you notice she was a little weird when she saw Tabitha was in the room with us?"

"I did notice, but she is probably just a little jealous that Tabitha will take her place as your Syracuse bff." He chuckled to himself.

"I guess," I said, picking at my cuticle.

Coal turned onto my street, going up the gradual incline. "I'm going to drop you off and bring my bag with me back home. I have to get changed for tonight, and I want to straighten up a little, so I can have you over properly tomorrow night for that dinner I promised you. Do you want to stay at my house tomorrow night?"

"I would love that," I said sincerely as he pulled in the driveway.

Peter came walking across the lawn when he spotted us.

"Hey Ava. Amber told me that you were bringing Coal tonight. Hi Coal," he said, reaching across to shake his hand firmly. He paused, probably unsure of how much he should say in front of Coal.

"It's ok Peter, Coal knows everything."

Peter shook his head, "Good. I'm a little nervous. I don't know." He put his head in his hands. "I don't want to be right that there is something untoward, but I just can't seem to shake the feeling."

"Well, I'll casually ask some questions tonight, just see how she reacts. It will be fine. Hopefully we are just having an overactive imagination about the whole thing," I said trying to convince both of us.

Coal nodded. "Either way, we need to get it sorted out, for all of us."

We all nodded our heads.

"Ok," Peter said, "I'll see the two of you tonight." He turned and walked back to his house.

Coal came in with me for a minute to collect his bag and things.

"That guy looks like a nervous wreck," Coal said walking up to the bedroom. I followed in step with him.

"I know, I told you. He was in as bad a shape as I was when I thought things were over between us. We were quite a pair talking the other day."

"He seems genuine though. I'm not getting a bad feeling from him. Are you?" Coal asked putting his clothes from yesterday into his duffel bag. He folded his pajamas, from that morning, and left them on a chair by my vanity.

"No, he seems heartbroken. That's not something that can be faked. I'm going to go read more of Aunt Ginny's journal while you're gone," I went into my jewelry box and retrieved the jeweled key. Ironically Amber is the one who unwittingly gave me the key that would hopefully settle things once and for all. "We are going to get to the bottom of this whole thing, so I don't have to be looking over my shoulder every second."

"Agreed," Coal said. I want nothing more.

"Here, take my keys while you go. Just make sure you set the alarm."

"Don't you worry about that; I will," Coal said, giving me a deep kiss that I felt down to my toes. I walked with him until we got to the library.

I waved and shut the door to the library, hearing the sturdy click of the door. The library, the most amazing room in the house, looked even more spectacular this time of day. Light was streaming in the stained glass windows. Beams of light hit the bookshelves. I felt like Aunt Ginny was in there with me at that moment telling me everything was going to be ok. I was usually in here at night and never really got a chance to experience it this way.

I decided to read the journal at the desk today. I had a pen and paper poised in case I needed to take notes on anything. Coal was right. This needed to end.

I started on January 23rd, where I left off last time. I skimmed the next few entries. I really wanted to read every word, but it was going to take me forever. I could always go back and read it at a later date, once everything was settled.

The next few days didn't give me any new information. When I got to January 30, my mouth hung open. I sat frozen in place. A nauseous feeling rolled through my body. I was in freefall, falling down, down, down.

CHAPTER FORTY-ONE

January 30, 2021

I have always been a goal setter, my whole life. All those plans I made when I was little were practice for the life that I would have one day. Putting on dance shows for the neighborhood, making paper dolls with designer dresses for every occasion, writing stories up in my room, the click clack typing away on the typewriter on those hot summer days. I was destined for great things. That's why I let them convince me that the plan was a good one. I gave away my greatest creation because they led me to believe that all my dreams would be shattered if I didn't. When you're a kid, (I was only 19!), you put your trust in your parents, surely, they would guide me in the right direction. I should have known that I could have done it all and now it's too late. I suppose I just need to accept the role that I have put myself in. Amber always tells me that dwelling on mistakes of the past only leads to unhealthy places, concentrate on your future. That we can help shape. The days that have passed are gone, worry about the here and now. I essentially was given a second chance. I gave myself a second chance.

What the hell? Her greatest creation? Is she talking about a baby? For as long as I remember, my mom and dad would talk about how sad it was that Aunt Virginia had her heart condition and was unable to have a baby. I figured when she married an older man, it was probably because she figured he wouldn't pressure her to have kids. It was actually a viable solution. I sat at the desk and tapped the pen. I had to think. Did I have a cousin out there I didn't know about? That was big news, actual family. Maybe there was someone out there that shared my DNA. It was an exciting prospect. I started to feel a little less alone at the possibility. Did Aunt Ginny know where her child was? Maybe she told Amber. So many ideas were swirling through my mind. When I heard the front door open, I bolted out of my seat in the library and ran down the stairs.

"Coal?" I called anxiously.

"Hey baby," he said coming through the door. He was setting the alarm code just like I had instructed him.

"You're not going to believe this," I said, jumping up and down.

"What did I miss?" Coal asked. He was carrying two suitcases this time around, looking like he was going on vacation. "I brought enough clothes for the next few days." He gave me a dazzling smile.

"It looks more like the next couple weeks," I said, eyeing his bags. "Didn't you hear me? I have big news. I might have an actual blood relative. I can't believe this!"

Coal shifted his weight. The bags were probably starting to get heavy. "Did you find something in her diary?" he asked.

"Let's get those bags upstairs, and I can show you." I went to grab one of the bags from Coal, and he shooed me away.

"I've got these," he said, "you lead the way."

I instructed him to leave his bags in the walk-in closet for now. I didn't want the bedroom to start looking messy. After he put them away, I ushered us into the library.

Coal settled into his chair.

"Tell me already," he said laughing. "I can't take the suspense."

"Here, look," I yelled pointing at the entry in the diary. Coal read it and handed it back to me.

"It could be a baby, I guess," Coal said, scrutinizing Aunt Ginny's words.

"You guess?!" I was getting properly annoyed by his lack of enthusiasm. "What else could it be? I'm going to ask Amber tonight. I've decided." How else was I going to find out? Amber had to have answers. Now at least I knew what to ask.

"Speaking of, we should get ready for Amber's," Coal said. "Rather than change at home, I decided I would do it here, so I could rush back to you.

"Yeah, I need to pick up a bottle of wine or something to bring. Wine is probably a good idea. I have a feeling we'll need it."

After picking up two bottles of wine, one red and one white, since I wasn't sure what we would be eating, Coal and I got back in his car. Giving him step by step directions, we pulled up in front of Amber's house with five minutes to spare. I paused to tie a strip of purple ribbon with gold edging around the border, in a bow around each bottle.

"You don't think Fiona would show up with Michael, do you?" I asked, turning to look at Coal's handsome face. His skin was darker than mine, while mine was porcelain, his was more olive toned. The cold made mine look all ruddy, while he still had a nice even complexion.

"I don't think so. Not with Amber's knowledge anyway. I think she would be really embarrassed if she did that," Coal said.

I tended to agree with him, but I crossed my fingers and hoped that there would be no antics tonight. We were here for a purpose, and that purpose was to find out anything we could about the days before Aunt Virginia died. An audience would hinder Amber from talking. I needed it to be intimate.

We each carried a bottle as we made our way to the front door of her house. Coal was busy admiring the spindles on the front porch as we approached the house. Amber's house was Victorian style as well, but a smaller version of my house. Not even getting a chance to ring the bell, Amber answered as my finger reached out to ring it.

She was wearing a cream-colored ankle length sweater dress with a cowl neckline. She paired it with knee length brown suede boots, and it was belted with the same type of leather as the boots. Today her hair was down and straight and framed her face. Only someone with her height could pull off that length and color dress and look slim, I thought upon appraising her.

"Ava! Coal!" she fussed over us, giving us both a warm hug at the door.

She turned to Coal and said, "I'm so happy you could make it as well. I remember last time Ava came over she had only just gone on a first date with you. Now look at the two of you," she exclaimed beaming at us.

We were standing there holding hands. I chose to wear an emerald green dress that was just above the knee. It had long sheer sleeves, but the rest of the dress was opaque. Right above the scoop neckline, I wore a beautiful emerald necklace that I found in the jewelry box in Aunt Ginny's room. The key to the secret compartment was around my neck too but was safely tucked inside my dress and not visible. I also found emerald green pumps that matched the dress perfectly. My red hair was long and loose hanging down my back.

"You look so much like your Aunt Ginny today. I had to do a double take," Amber said shivering. Peter sidled up to her side. "Doesn't she remind you so much of Virginia today."

Peter smiled sheepishly and nodded his head. He came closer to give us a proper greeting.

"Coal, always a pleasure," he said, giving him a hearty handshake.

"Ava, stunning as ever," Peter said, "green is really a wonderful color for you." He gave me a hug.

"Come in, come in," Amber insisted, pulling us away

from the door. "Peter, do you mind taking their coats? You two can come sit in the living room, and I'll get you both something to drink."

I took off my coat and handed it to Peter thanking him. "Oh Amber, these are for you," I said, handing her my bottle of wine. Coal followed suit with the other bottle.

"How sweet of you," Amber said, taking the bottles we presented her.

"I wasn't sure what we were eating, so we brought one of each," I told her as I settled in on Amber's leather Chesterfield sofa from the 1940's. The living room was extra cozy with a roaring fire going in the fireplace. Coal settled in next to me on the welcoming sofa. There was a woodsy smelling candle burning on the side table. We didn't sit in here last time I came over. It was a very comfortable room, however I was surprised by the manly vibe of it. It reminded me of a man's study, although beautiful not at all what I would expect to be Amber's taste.

"Red or white?" Amber asked both Coal and me.

"Red," we said in unison, turning to smile at each other.

"I just love the two of you together," Amber said. She expertly opened the bottle of wine and poured a generous amount into the two glasses set on the end table.

"Is Fiona here yet?" I asked, listening, for her voice in the other room.

"No, not yet. I...," she looked nervously at Peter and then at Coal and me, "I appreciate your understanding about this thing with Michael. It's very awkward, and I'm hoping she will get sick of him soon. It's just, I think she needs to learn for herself. If I push the issue, she will just push back harder."

"I understand, and honestly I feel worse for her than I do for myself."

Amber nodded her head. "You're so sensible Ava. Ginny always said that about you."

She poured herself a glass of red wine and sat in the high-backed chair with a sueded olive color cushion and brown leather back. She took a sip and Peter still stood by nervously. I wished he would get a drink and sit down. His fidgetiness was making me nervous.

I didn't want to start asking serious questions immediately. I wanted her to have a glass of wine or two, so she would be more likely to talk. If I force it too soon, she might clam up and then I wouldn't find out anything.

Turning to Coal with a pleasant smile, Amber asked, "Does your family live around here, Coal?" I felt conflicted. My intention for being there that night was to find out if Amber was involved with or had knowledge about something menacing with Aunt Ginny, yet here she was doing the job of my mom. It made me feel deceitful.

Coal was more than happy to answer questions about himself. "About forty minutes away, not too bad. We see each other at least once a month, more in the summer when I'm not working," he answered, sliding a little closer to me and grabbing my hand. "I have a sister that lives in the same town as them, so at least it takes a little heat off of me for living farther away."

"Oh, that's nice! It's wonderful having a sibling, someone who knows your story. I always felt sad for Fiona that she didn't have a brother or sister. Sometimes it's just not in the cards I guess," she says with a sad smile.

Ding, Dong. "Excuse me a minute," Amber said, getting up to answer the door. I could see Fiona standing at the entrance holding groceries.

"Fiona, darling!" Amber kissed her on the cheek and ushered her in.

"Hi guys," Fi said.

Peter came over to her and grabbed the bags out of her hands.

"Thanks Peter," Fiona said as she was finally free to hang up her coat. Fiona was wearing a pair of high waisted wide legged black trousers and a navy-blue blouse. The sides of her black hair were pinned up with the curls still down in the back.

"Don't you look lovely this evening?" Amber remarked as she surveyed Fiona.

Fiona beamed, "Thanks mom."

It was one of the more pleasant interactions I'd seen between the two. It had been a long time since I had parents around, I noticed the pride Amber had in her eyes when she glanced at Fiona. It refocused me on what I needed to do.

Fiona took the seat that Amber previously was occupying, while Amber and Peter settled in on the love seat. I noticed that Amber had already refreshed her own wine. It gave me a little courage to speak.

"So, Amber, I was speaking with Lina a little, and she mentioned that something was bothering Aunt Ginny in the weeks prior to..." I got a little choked up on the final word, "her death."

I watched her face closely. Her eyes got wider, but she didn't say anything. Coal squeezed my hand, knowing how hard this was for me. Peter got up and put another log on the fire.

"Did she confide in you at all about what was bothering her?" I gazed at her, waiting for her to speak.

Finally, she composed herself, clearly choosing carefully what she was divulging. "Well, I guess the usual worries that a person struggles with daily. Her job was exciting but a little stressful at times with all that traveling. You could imagine."

Peter stood by the fire and cleared his throat. Four pairs of eyes looked over at him. His eyes pleaded with hers, but he remained silent.

Amber took a deep breath and stood up, walking over to the couch where I was sitting. She took the seat on the other side of me and grabbed my hand. Her own hands felt warm and soft. My heart nearly stopped at her touch. I simultaneously wanted to stop her from saying whatever it was that she was going to say. Stop her from altering my reality and wanted her to hurry up and tell me, so I could move on with my life.

"Ava," she paused, her ice blue eyes locking with mine. I caught myself still unconsciously holding my breath, "Ginny loved you so very much."

"I know," I managed with a lump in my throat.

Everyone else in the room watched silently. I felt like the whole scene was being played out in slow motion. I wanted to be able to fast forward, to get to the part where I knew what was going on, but I didn't have the remote control. Amber was in control.

"She didn't know whether she should tell you or not." She looked at me trying to gauge my reaction, trying to decide if she made the right decision.

"Tell me what?" My calm facade had cracked; it began to have tiny hairline fractures. I was in the middle of a serious melt down. Fiona watched with sympathy on her face. Coal stroked the back of my auburn hair.

"Virginia was actually your mother." She just came out with the words, a simple fact. The words came tumbling out of her mouth and everything in the room spun.

"My what?" I asked, confusion clouding my brain. I heard her but the words weren't making sense. Everyone's faces looked paused in varying expressions of sympathy and confusion. "What are you saying?"

"Ginny got pregnant with you right out of high school. Her brother and wife, your parents, were having a hard time getting pregnant. They were told by a doctor that their chances of ever having a baby were very slim, only about 20 percent. They very much wanted a baby," she paused, taking a big gulp of her wine. Peter came around and topped off our glasses.

I was hearing her, but this couldn't be. There was no way that I had been lied to all my life. Who would do that to a child? My internal dialogue kept going round and round, but I remained perfectly still. I needed her to finish, or I might never hear the truth.

"Your grandmother thought that your uncle and aunt adopting you was the perfect solution. You would still be raised by your family, Virginia would have the opportunity to go to college and pursue her dreams, and she would still be in your life. Ginny wasn't convinced at first, but she thought it was probably the best thing for your future." Amber looked spent at delivering this story to me. This was my real story, the one that I was never privy to.

I finally spoke. I didn't wish to hold Amber in torment. She obviously thought hard and long before delivering my origin story to me. "Thank you for telling me. I know it couldn't have been easy for you."

I looked across the room and saw Peter looking somewhat relieved, a little more like his usual self.

"I realize that this is shocking information," Amber said, tucking her blonde hair behind her ear." I've known Virginia my entire adult life, and she only told me this, the real truth about you being her daughter this year. It's something that has been eating her up since your parents' death."

"I just need some time to process this. You did the right thing telling me. A person should know their own story, for better or worse." There were tears brimming in my eyes. I stood up. Coal stood as well and looked at me for a cue. "I just need to use the ladies' room," I announced, now tears were free falling.

"I'll walk you there," Coal said, Peter nodded his head indicating that this was a good plan.

We walked off down the hall, Coal encased me in his arm, sturdy, reliable, ready to hold me up, support me if I couldn't support myself. I heard hushed talking as we walked down the hall.

"Oh Ava," Coal said, stopping outside the bathroom, leaning against the hall closet, holding me close. "I'm sorry you had to find this all out when they are all gone, and you can't even ask them questions or express how you feel."

I nodded my head. He got it exactly right. I'm not even angry. People are just people. They try to make the best decisions they can based on their experiences and feelings. I just wished that I could tell my mom and dad that I loved them, and that they were amazing parents. They always loved me, always supported me. They put my needs before their own. I couldn't have wished for more. I would also tell Aunt Ginny that I wasn't angry at her. She didn't give me up. She was always there for me when I needed her, giving me the best that she had to give.

"Coal, I'm the luckiest girl in the world," I kissed him and sighed. "Thank you for understanding." I let go of him and went into the bathroom locking the door behind me. I spent a minute taking deep breaths to regulate my breathing. Then I took a few extra minutes fixing myself up. I used a tissue to diminish the smudges under my eyes. Running my fingers through my hair, I felt a little better.

When I opened the door, I was surprised to find Coal was still standing fixed in the same spot, just where I left him.

"You didn't have to wait," I said, now feeling bad about how much time I spent fixing myself up.

"Wild dogs couldn't have dragged me away from you in your time of need," Coal said. His eyes were sincere; they were studying mine for clues about how I was feeling. He intertwined his fingers with mine.

I glanced at a portrait of Fiona and Amber in the hallway. Fiona was just a little girl. She was probably in about 2nd grade, which was apparent to me based on the window in her teeth. She looked so proud that two of her teeth were missing. Her black curls were longer, more weighed down and stretched down her back. She was dressed in a bright blue dress, super frilly, not at all like the Fiona I know. Amber looked just like she looked now. Maybe a little younger, but there was no remarkable difference.

"So, what do you want to do?" Coal asked.

"What do you mean?" I asked, confused by the question.

"I wasn't sure if you'd want to stay for dinner, if it would be too much considering the bomb that was dropped on you."

"No, we'll stay. Amber was good enough to prepare dinner, and honestly it couldn't have been easy to deliver that information to me. I owe her."

Coal didn't look so sure, but he didn't say anything. "Ok, whatever you want, I'm on board with."

We joined the rest of the party in the living room. They were silent when we entered.

"Sorry I took so long," I apologized. "Just needed to fix myself up a bit."

"No problem at all," Amber said, happy that I at least seemed ok. "Are you still hungry?"

"Yes, dinner sounds great," I announced. I could almost feel a collective sigh being let out from the group.

"Let's head to the dining room then," she announced.

The entire group headed into the dining room. The table was set with bone white china. A candle was lit in the middle of the table. I gravitated to the same seat I sat in for my last dinner party with Amber and Fiona. I assumed Coal would be right next to me.

"Do you need any help?" Coal asked Amber, as he placed his wine glass down by the seat next to mine.

"Don't be silly. Sit and relax, keep Ava company. Fiona and I will bring the food in," Amber insisted.

The two of them made their exit, but rather than join them in the kitchen. Peter sat down. I think he was looking for a moment alone with Coal and me.

"Are you really doing, ok?" Peter asked, leaning in to speak to me in a whisper. "I really pushed Amber to tell you. I hope it was the right thing to do. It wasn't my place to tell you." He looked at me with a questioning look. He wanted affirmation that he did the right thing.

"Thank you, Peter, although I'm in shock, it was the right thing to do," I assured him, nodding fervently. "It was something that I needed to know."

"I hope this is the truth," he looked skeptical. "My intention is to help you, not hurt you more than you've already been," he gave me a fatherly look.

Amber came walking into the room with a jumbo-sized serving bowl of delicious smelling meatballs. Fiona followed with a matching bowl containing pasta. After putting down two blue pot holders, Amber placed the tray on top of them and retreated back to the kitchen. She came back with a tray of garlic bread, and Fiona came back with a salad.

After their second trip back into the dining room, they sat down.

"Thank you for having us for dinner," I said at last when everyone was seated. All the guests were awkwardly quiet, and I was bracing myself for something more to come.

"Yes, your house is lovely," Coal added, smiling his usual Coal smile.

Amber took a deep breath and closed her eyes, looking like she was in the middle of a yoga class. Then she spoke, "We're really looking forward to seeing you all dance in the show this month. I know your neighbor Adelaide said she will be joining us too."

Finally, I had an opening for conversation that wouldn't make everyone uncomfortable, "I'm so happy to hear this. Adelaide is on her own. It's great for her to get out and be with people."

Amber smiled warmly, "Yes, she seems so nice, and she kept reiterating what a great time she had at your party. It was really very sweet of you to include her. I hope when I'm an old lady, someone will do the same for me." She smiles. Thinking of her picture when Fi was little, I can't imagine her ever being an old lady. She will probably look the same in another twenty years. Preserved in time.

"Oh, I'll be bringing home my kitten from her soon. As soon as the kittens are old enough, this little baby one is coming home to live with me. She is adorable. I'm looking forward to having another living thing in the house. Something to keep me company." At last, my voice was animated again. Everyone started talking at once about what a great idea that was.

"I can't wait to play with her," Fiona chimed in lamely.

The rest of dinner was similarly stilted, making polite conversation, but the truth of what was revealed hovered over the night like a storm brewing. Amber got out Tupperware and gave me a big portion to take home. Excusing ourselves after dinner, I promised Amber that I appreciated her telling me the truth about Aunt Virginia. I just needed time to process it, but it really didn't change anything in my life. I felt like it was my job to assure everyone else that I was okay. It didn't ever give me time to not be okay. Amber stood at the screen door in her cream dress and waited for us to pull away before closing the door behind her. As I looked through the car window at her, she looked haunted.

CHAPTER FORTY-TWO

Coal unlocked his car with his key fob and let me in the car first. He shut the door for me, and the cold of the leather seats penetrated my skin. Pretty soon I would have to give up wearing dresses until the weather got warmer, I thought. Coal gave me a strange look as he walked around to the driver's side.

"Everything okay?" I asked Coal as he uncharacteristically started the car without uttering a single word. I saw that Amber was waiting for us to pull away, so I didn't want to delay our departure.

"I'm sorry. Just worried about you," he said as he pulled away from the curb. I saw him put on the seat heaters as though reading my mind.

"Well, that was quite a night, "I started, hoping once he saw I was really alright that he would start acting himself again. "I never dreamed that was what was going to come out of Amber's mouth. A confession that she was somehow involved in mom's death seemed more probable to me. Maybe that was the big secret all along, the thing that was bothering Aunt Ginny before her death." Even as I said the words, I was second guessing them. Aunt Ginny, my mom, Aunt Ginny, my mom. How was I to think of her now?

As we pulled in the driveway, Coal shut off the car but made no move to get out. Instead, he turned to me very seriously.

Why didn't everyone see that I needed time? I didn't

want to be pressed to talk about it right now. I just found out that my history was a lie. Once I figured out how I felt about it, then I would want to talk about it. I just sat there looking, what I'm sure looked like, slightly annoyed waiting for him to proceed.

"Ava," he said, his voice trembling slightly.

"Yes?" I asked. Now I felt a surge of adrenaline shoot through me. Something wasn't right.

"I found something at Amber's house?" his voice wobbled.

A huge unease entered my body, I felt my hands shake. "What do you mean?"

He closed his eyes and rested his elbows on the steering wheel, his head in his hands. "When you were in the bathroom, I didn't want to leave you alone, so I stood there in the hallway. I could hear everyone talking in the living room. I couldn't hear what they were saying, just hushed voices. Everyone sounded appropriately concerned."

"Okay," I said, urging him to continue.

"Well, I looked in the hall closet, you know the one I was leaning on when we were talking?

I nodded my head.

"I don't know why, but I had an instinct to look around in there. Something told me to lift up the towels and inspect what was under them. It was just a hunch. I really didn't think it would amount to anything."

"What did you find?" My pulse quickened.

Coal leaned into the back seat and retrieved the bag with the leftovers that Fiona had lovingly packed for me. He pulled out something rectangular. Turning it to face me, I saw that it was the missing picture from Aunt Ginny's photo collage. I gasped. Starting to hyperventilate, I couldn't get air into my lungs.

"Breathe," Coal instructed me, "long, deep breaths."

Breathe in, breathe out, breathe in, breathe out. I heard Aunt Ginny's voice. When I first started training and began running, I would be so out of breath that I would get dizzy to the point that I thought I would pass out. She taught me to take less breaths that weren't shallow. Eventually, I didn't have to think about it, and my body would regulate my breathing on its own. As I sat in Coal's car and heard her voice in my head, I matched my breathing to her words. Finally, I calmed down, much to Coal's panicked relief.

"What does this mean?" I asked, horrified, staring at the picture that was stolen from Aunt Ginny's room.

Coal shrugged his shoulders. "Honestly, I'm not sure. I just wanted to get you out of there, but I didn't want you to know until we were gone. I wasn't sure how you would react."

I took the picture from Coal's hands and gazed at it. I looked at it with new eyes, with the eyes of a daughter. I felt pride swell inside my chest. My mother was beautiful. I was more determined than ever to find out what happened to her.

Finally leaving the car, Coal and I deposited the food in the refrigerator and marched right upstairs to the library.

We went through the ritual to obtain the diary. I decided to break our rule and take it out of the room today. We had too much work to do. It was Friday night, and we didn't have to go anywhere in the morning. Lina was due to come and clean, but that wasn't until later.

"There are definitely more letters stashed around, like the ones we found in the living room," I informed Coal.

"How do you know?" Coal asked, pulling the wall back into place.

"She wrote about it in a diary entry I read. Someone started threatening her. We just need to find out who."

"Have you looked through the attic at all?" Coal asked, the wheels of his brain turning.

I shook my head. "I haven't been there since that day when I was getting the decorations with Lina."

"Why don't you bring the diary with you up to the

attic? You can read, and I can search for clues that might be hidden up there." He seemed to be filled with renewed energy now that we were actually doing something.

"Yes, that sounds great. There's just one thing I want to do first," I said walking out of the library. Coal stood in the hallway watching me descend the stairs.

"Where are you going?" He called after me. "Do you want me to come or wait up here?

"I'll be right back," I called my voice muffled as I was in the sitting room. I returned within the minute holding her picture.

I opened the door to Aunt Ginny's room, my mom's room, with conviction. Coal stayed in the hallway and watched as I returned the beloved photograph to its place in her photo collage.

"There," I said admiring the wall, "everything is as it should be. Now let's find out what the hell is going on."

Following Coal's lead, we climbed the spiral staircase in the library to the third floor. I felt bad this floor of the house was rarely given any attention. That would have to change, I thought as we made our way to the bedroom with the attic access.

Coal pulled the ladder down and I went first up the rickety ladder, clutching the diary to me. He followed swiftly after.

Turning on the overhead lights, the attic glowed. I found a spot that was nicely lit up and sat right on the floor in my green dress.

"Don't sit on the floor," Coal said, dragging over a box for me to sit on. First, he lifted up the flap to be sure there was nothing important inside. We found a bunch of men's sweaters. The box made a good seat.

"I'll read out loud if I come to anything important," I said watching Coal get to work. He looked like he was going to start in the back corner.

"People psychologically hide things at the farthest

darkest corner in an attempt to vanquish it from their mind. It's the logical place to start." He opened his first box to test his theory, while I continued reading.

Monday February 1, 2021

The month of love has officially begun, yet my heart is torn in two. Yesterday I was buying my weekly groceries. While I was picking out kale, I felt a gentle touch on my back. I turned around, and he was there. "God you're beautiful," he said to me. I nearly dropped the kale on the floor. I told him that we couldn't keep "running into" each other like this. Up until a few weeks ago, we managed to both live in Syracuse and never see each other. Now every time I turn around, he's there. Every time I see him, I lose some of my discipline to stay away. I'm sure this is his intent. This is a dangerous game he is playing.

I read aloud the passage to Coal, but he didn't seem to be listening.

"Come over here for a minute, I want to show you something," he insisted.

I walked across the creaky floorboards wondering what he had unearthed in the box. He didn't say more but rather pointed, indicating that I should go in the box. There were hundreds of photos scattered about, photos throughout all the stages of my childhood and adulthood. In all of the photos there was one common theme, they were all of Ginny and me. It's amazing how many photos we posed for, memories captured, suspended in time. I picked up one, clutching it in my hand. Having no memory of this particular moment, as I must have been only barely three months old. I was adorned in a yellow baby sun dress with a matching floppy hat covering my barely there, red locks. Nineteen- year- old Ginny was holding me in her arms beaming at me. I was flashing a gummy smile at her. My heart tugged in my chest. Although I couldn't possibly have a recollection of this moment, I felt her love for me in this picture. She was my life force.

"Thank you for unearthing these." I was crouching on the floor in my green dress. A swelling of happiness ripped through me. I felt the love. "I'm bringing these downstairs, so I can look through them," I said aloud.

"Of course," Coal said, carrying the box and putting it near the entrance. "Can you reread that entry? I was caught up in the pictures."

I reread it.

"We need to both keep going. I feel better that we are getting information rather than just sitting around."

I nodded my affirmation and went back to the journal. A few days later she had to go to London on business. She did lots of shopping and sightseeing while there. I felt a pang of jealousy for all the things she had seen and sorrow for all that she would miss.

Friday February 12, 2021

I'm home from my trip exhausted but happy; I had a wonderful time. I want nothing more than to collapse at home this weekend, read a good book, and get some proper sleep. Around 7 pm, I heard a banging on my front door. The silhouette of a man could be seen through the glass. First, I thought it was my friend, but the way that he was banging gave me pause. I attempted to peer out the window, but it's too dark around my house at night. Note to self, I better do something about that for safety reasons. With my cell phone in hand, the 911 up on my screen, I fretfully open the door. He was standing there, a big box of Valentine chocolate in his arms. A shiny pink ribbon served the dual purpose of securing and decorating the box. "It's almost your birthday," he said, eyes gleaming, filled with mischief as though I had invited him over. I was shocked. I couldn't believe that he remembered. I ushered him quickly inside my house, afraid that someone would see him standing out there. I told him this, and he said that's why he wore a hoodie, with the hood up underneath a nonde-

script black coat. He always comes prepared, he explained to me. He insisted he just wanted to talk, so I put on some nice hot tea and brought him around to the backyard. I didn't care that it was February and freezing, if he wanted to talk, we could do it in the backyard where we wouldn't be seen, and we wouldn't get into any "trouble" He stayed for a half hour, we caught up a little on each other's lives, and we actually had a nice time. He didn't try anything inappropriate. Although, I forgot to ask him how he found out where I live. I was too caught up in the memories, maybe next time. What am I saying? There should be no next time.

"It's amazing how much you don't know about someone's life that you thought you knew so well. Did you find anything?" I shouted across the expanse of the attic.

"I think I did," he said walking towards the box where I was sitting. He was holding a Valentine's card.

Dearest Virginia,

There is no one in the world who can hold a candle to you. I want to wish you the happiest birthday and Valentine's Day. It is only appropriate you came into this world on a day that was meant for love. Regardless if we're together, you are my heart. xoxoxo

"That's quite some declaration," Coal said. "I just wish your birthday was on Valentine's Day because that would make sense for you. Whoever this was had it bad for your mom." After he said it he took a double look to see if he upset me with the use of the word mom, but I was getting used to it. It was ok. In a way, I'm happy I didn't find out when my mom and dad were alive, so I didn't have to feel conflicted and full of guilt about the whole mom thing. Now the only person's feelings I had to consider were my own. I didn't have to betray anyone.

Saturday February 13, 2021

I know I said I was going to stay home this weekend, but I'm partly afraid to stay put because I don't want him showing up here again. We had a nice time, and it was good to catch up but we need to leave it at that. Peter and Amber wanted to take me out to celebrate my birthday. There's a new steakhouse near Armory Square. I mentioned it to him, and he made all the arrangements. It was better to go out today, on a Saturday, than my actual birthday, Valentine's Day. The expensive pre-fix menus and couples everywhere would cramp my birthday spirits. I wore this new deep pink dress I bought that was one piece, but appeared to be two pieces due to the back where it flowed away from me and was mostly bare revealing the expanse of my back. I even went all out and used hot rollers to style my hair. They gave us a lovely table slightly near the bar. Shiny paper hearts spilled across the walls of the restaurant, something I've always enjoyed, ever since I was a little girl in elementary school. I always thought a Valentine's Day birthday was extra special.

We were having a great time laughing and telling stories when across the bar, I felt a pair of eyes trained on me. At first, I thought I was imagining it, but I eventually let my gaze wander in the direction of the stare. The owner of the stare, took my acknowledgment that I felt them looking at me as an invitation to join our table.

Over walked my very handsome, very inappropriate ex. Both Amber and Peter glared when they saw him. I blushed a shade of red which I thought surely clashed with my dress.

"Aren't you a sight for sore eyes?" he asked, undressing me with his eyes. As an afterthought, he briefly glanced over at my friends, "Peter, Amber, a pleasure," before turning his attention back to me. "Out for an early birthday celebration?" he asked, his eyebrow crooked up. After a few more minutes of talking to me, I assume he took our stony silence as a cue that he was crashing our little party. He excused himself, but not before leaning over and whispering in my ear, "You are making me crazy." He said it so no one could hear him tempting me, his hot breath in my ear.

I'm not going to lie, he still did something for me, but approaching me with Amber and Peter was a nonnegotiable situation. I was mortified. They both had the class not to discuss it after he left, cheers to best friends!

Sunday February 14, 2021

Happy birthday to me... I don't dare mention how old I am. Amber reminds me daily that there are twenty-year-olds that are miserable messes, so age is truly just a number. It's what you do with yourself and the years that count. If I count my blessings and experiences, I can think of my age as a blessing, and ...

"Ava." Coal was holding something up. From across the room, I couldn't quite make out what it was. "I think it's more of those letters that we found. Come check it out.

I got up, crossing the creaky boards once more. This envelope was plain, just like the others. I pulled the papers out, unfolding them. All these sets of letters were definitely from the same unstable person. They all came in sets of four, ragged writing adorned the pages. The person who wrote these letters was definitely capable of hurting someone.

I bent down to read the letters. The first sheet was revealed:

We were meant to be.

I peeled that away, placing it face down on the floor. The second read:

You are just an aging ex-beauty queen.

Whoever wrote these letters was trying very hard to convince themself that my mom was unworthy, if they really believed it they wouldn't have bothered to go to such lengths. Someone who we believed wasn't worth anything wouldn't register on our radar. I placed the second on top of the first.

He will see what you really are.

The final sheet read:

I will NOT let you break MY heart.

I took in a sharp breath. I didn't like the reference to her heart. Did this person do something to cause my beautiful mom to have a heart attack? Was it a threat to her? A promise that she'd break her heart before she could do it to her?

Coal, who had been reading the papers over my shoulder, shuddered. "This is the stuff that movies are made from," he stated, holding his hand out to help me up from my crouching position. I grabbed the other papers before allowing him to help hoist me up.

"Maybe it's possible to compare these letters to handwriting samples of people we know?" I thought aloud. "These letters don't make sense with the dolls I've received. In those all the messages were typed neatly. In these, the writing is all by hand and ragged."

"I agree," Coal said, nodding his head. "The person who wrote these letters seems unhinged, however the person who sent the dolls seems very composed. Maybe they have a split personality? He suggested. There was a tapping noise on the leaded glass, Coal and I both jumped before realizing that it was a branch of the enormous maple tree outside the house making the noise.

"Let's put these letters away, with the diary in the library. Even though the letters were written so jaggedly, maybe there's something in the way they are written that will give the person away." I started walking toward the exit of the attic.

"Just want to grab this box of pictures for you," Coal said, remembering the pictures of my mom and me. I began thinking how I would decorate the house with these photographs. I wanted to put up pictures of my parents as well. They were all my family.

I led the way down the stairs, clutching the next series of crazy letters, and I took the box as Coal lowered it down to me. Then he descended the stairs. Upon entering the library, we left the box of pictures on the writing desk. These didn't have to stay hidden anymore. It was out in the open now that Virginia was in fact my mom. It was no longer a secret. It made me who I was. We put the letters and diary in their secret compartment and locked them up.

After getting into bed, Coal and I lay there in the dark. The room looked so beautiful in the moonlight. The shadows cast did not seem menacing; they seemed to illuminate everything beautiful. This business of unwanted letters and boxes needed to be cleared up. I needed answers, but my heart felt so complete.

"You, ok?" Coal asked, stroking my cheek.

"Actually, I am."

CHAPTER FORTY-THREE

Saturday arrived without me waking at dawn. Instead, I woke up entwined in Coal's arms, the sunshine greeting me. Coal was still sleeping, so I tried my best to disentangle myself from him and get out of bed. He smiled but didn't open his eyes. I grabbed my cell phone from the floor and crept down the stairs. While making the trip to the kitchen I was surprised to have a slew of text messages.

First things first, I thought, putting on the percolator before delving into them. Next was Lina asking if it was good to still come at 12 pm today. I wasn't sure what my plans were, but since she has her own key now it was a non-issue. I wrote her back to confirm.

Then there was a text from a number that I didn't have saved in my contacts, but the number was definitely familiar to me. It was nagging at me, but after looking at it a few times I realized it was Michael. A sick feeling washed over me. He must have stolen my phone number from Fiona's contacts.

I can't believe you're back with that loser.

How pathetic, that text definitely did not warrant a response, and I pressed contacts for the phone number and blocked him from calling or texting me. He could call to his heart's content, but I wanted to be none the wiser. I no longer saw him as a threat in this whole thing, rather just a nuisance that wouldn't go away.

Pleasantly surprised, the next text was from Tabitha.

Want to see if we are still on to hang out tomorrow night with the men? She followed her message with a muscle emoji, and I laughed out loud.

"Good morning beautiful," Coal stumbled into the kitchen. He was still groggy despite the fact it was already 9:30 am. "I love your smile," he said, kissing me softly on the lips.

"Do you still want to go out tomorrow with Tabitha and Enzo?" I asked, "She just texted me to find out."

"That sounds awesome," Coal said. "I don't know if you really spoke with Enzo yet, but he is actually hilarious." Coal grabbed himself a mug out of the cabinet and poured the steaming espresso into his mug.

I did the same and settled down at the kitchen table with Coal. I opted to sit next to him rather than across, so we could occasionally hold hands and gaze out the French doors together.

Texting Tabitha back, I told her to think about what they would like to do.

"So, dinner tonight," Coal said, raising his eyebrows at me. "What would my beautiful girl like? I'm really excited to have you over. I want to give you a tour of the whole house, but that is going to require me going home for a while. I want to make sure everything is perfect."

"Surprise me," I said with a giggle. "Whatever you choose will be perfect," I assured him. "Don't make too much fuss. I love you just the way you are, with the exception of your wake-up time," I said laughing again and kissing him on the cheek.

We spent a luxurious morning lazing around drinking our coffee. I fixed us some oatmeal with blueberries.

"I still want to meet your parents," I said as I handed him the steaming bowl.

"You will, I promise. In fact, I texted my mom and

updated her about what happened. Mom said she couldn't be happier, but that she knew we would work things out. She was thinking maybe we could make it to them next weekend?"

We have Tabitha and Enzo's wedding next Saturday," I reminded him. "That is if you're going?" I teased him.

Before he could respond, something occurred to me. "Did Tabitha invite *everyone*?" I asked, worried that Fiona would show up with Michael. I didn't want that man ruining future events for me forever.

Coal nodded his head no. His hair had grown a lot longer since I met him, making his waves more apparent. He looked like a prince from the Renaissance Period. "I don't think so," he said, interrupting my thoughts. "She hangs out with everyone at school, but she doesn't include many people in her private life. That means she really likes you," he said with a smile.

Returning the smile, I said, "I'm glad. I really just want to have a wonderful, calm, drama free evening. Maybe practice our new dance moves?" I finished with a laugh.

After breakfast Coal went home to prepare for tonight. I decided to do a walk-through of the house to be sure that it was ready for Lina. I didn't want to leave any of the letters laying around. I still wanted to keep it under wraps until we figured out what was going on for sure.

The development of finding the photograph of my mom in Amber's linen closet left me feeling uneasy. It should be easy enough to find a sample of Amber's writing to compare to the letters. I really wanted to rule her out as a suspect. The doorbell rang alerting me that Lina had arrived.

Standing on my front porch smiling, she had on her usual uniform of light-colored jeans and a blue sweatshirt, the only item that was different was her white parka complete with fur hood that marked our transition into cooler weather.

"Good afternoon." Lina and I both turned startled to

hear a man's voice. Peter was striding across the lawn towards us.

"Go ahead right in Lina," I said, placing one hand casually on her shoulder. "There's some coffee in the kitchen if you'd like it. I'll be right in."

Lina nodded and made her way inside. I closed the door and stood on the porch waiting for Peter to reach me.

"You doing ok Ava?" he asked, examining my face for a clue to alert him to how I was really feeling.

"I am, thank you Peter, and I just wanted to say thank you for encouraging Amber to tell me about Virginia. I really am grateful." His eyes changed, looking a bit less stressed.

"Thank God, that's been weighing on me since you've moved in. I thought about it every time I saw you, but it wasn't my place. I hope you understand that."

I nodded. "There is something I have to tell you though," I paused. I had a gut feeling I could trust him. I just prayed I wasn't wrong.

"Go on," Peter said, noticing my hesitation. "You have my word that it will stay between us."

"Coal found the missing picture of my mom in Amber's linen closet. He found it when he was waiting for me to get out of the bathroom."

Peter audibly gasped. "Oh no." He covered his mouth for a moment. "I was worried about something like this. I'm so sorry Ava." He grabbed my hand and squeezed it.

"Do you have a sample of Amber's writing? Maybe a card, or a list? Anything that could give me an accurate depiction of her writing."

Peter thought for a minute, scratching his perfectly coiffed black hair. "Yes, I will definitely find that for you. Why? If you don't mind me asking."

Thinking for just a minute before deciding to tell him. "I found some threatening letters that were sent to my mom. I want to see if she could have been the sender."

He inhaled deeply, but nodded his head in understanding. "Maybe I'll drop it off for you later," he said.

"I'm going to Coal's for dinner, but that won't be until around at least five," I said. "Thank you. I know this is not easy for you either. Hopefully Amber had nothing to do with any of this, and we can prove that."

"Agreed," Peter said, giving me a wave as he walked back toward his yard.

Coal called a little while later, after I consulted with Lina about what I'd like done in the house. He said he wouldn't be ready for me until around sixish. That was fine with me, I would go for a run and take the time to make myself beautiful for my date tonight.

Going upstairs, I hunted around in my dresser to find a nice warm running outfit. The sun had disappeared, I noticed while I was still on the porch speaking with Peter. It turned the day gray. The clouds covered the sky in a depressing blanket, immediately changing the atmosphere of the day. It made you want to curl up in a ball and do nothing, which is precisely why I got up. Finding coffee brown running pants, I put on a pair of tights underneath to assure warmness. I found a cozy sweatshirt that stated Coffee Weather in a perfect shade of brown that paired with my leggings. I wore a purple thermal shirt underneath for added warmness. When I got back, I would take a bubble bath and prepare for the night to come.

I originally thought about going on the path that wound through the city, but I settled on running the path that was just around the block. I would save myself a half hour, with just driving back and forth to the path and parking. I finished my look with a brown beanie that covered my ears and my violet running shoes.

"I'll be back in about a half hour," I yelled to Lina from the front door. "In case I'm not back when you're leaving, I left you money on the table in the kitchen. I'm setting the alarm," I added.

"Bye Ava, see you soon," she called, her voice far away working upstairs.

I dashed down the block and turned the corner, onto Adelaide's street. The air was extra chilly now, a strong breeze had picked up lowering the temperature a good ten degrees. It was a good thing I wore a hat that covered my ears.

Entering the running path, it looked particularly dark. The path was abandoned, no one wanting to venture out into this dismal day. I started with a slow jog, enjoying the serenity of the woods, the quietness.

I couldn't believe how once again my life had flip flopped. There was no denying that things with Coal were on the right path. The knowledge that Aunt Ginny was actually my mother brought some understanding. It explained why the two of us had such a big connection. It also explained why we looked so much alike. I still loved my parents the same as I did, so it really wasn't a negative for me. My breathing was even. The cold air felt good. I could breathe freely.

I hastened the pace of my jog when I felt my left shoe laces coming loose. I didn't want to trip on the dark path, so I bent down to fix it. I moved to the side of the path, just in case anyone came by. I was nearly in the neighboring backyard, as I didn't want to block the path.

With no prior warning, I felt an arm hook around my torso from behind. Someone was covering my mouth and nose. They were so silent that I didn't know what was happening. I fought, struggling to free myself from their grip. I tried to see who was grabbing me, but the angle they had me at, all I could see were tree tops and darkness. Whoever it was had the benefit of surprise. They grabbed me when I was down by the ground and unaware. I began to panic. I felt myself slipping. Fight! I screamed in my head, but everything began to get dark. The path. Arms around me, squeezing me tight. The cloth was covering my nose and mouth. Scream! I said inside my head, but no words would come out, like being paralyzed in a dream. The last thing I remembered was thinking I should have listened to Coal. I shouldn't have gone off running alone in the dark.

When I came to, I was somewhere pitch black and damp. The smell was dank. The floor felt cold and wet beneath me. I opened my eyes, but the lack of light didn't give me much of an idea where I was. My right shoulder felt super tight. My mind was racing with questions. Why did my shoulder ache so much? How did I get here? I was supposed to be on a date with Coal at his house. He would be looking for me. How would he know where to find me? How would anyone know where to find me? My phone was gone. I have no pockets. Where was it? The answers were not there, and my mind was so groggy.

"Hello?" I called into the dark. I listened. I could have sworn I heard the sounds of cars swishing by, maybe the honk of a horn in the distance. "Hello?" I said again. I wanted to yell but my voice was scratchy. Water, it was all I could think about. I was so thirsty. I wanted to preserve my energy. I needed to get my bearings, so I could come up with a plan. Questions and random thoughts were swirling around in my head.

My ears tuned-in hyper vigilant, probably due to the fact that I couldn't see anything. I heard that when one of your senses isn't working, your other senses go into hyper drive to compensate. I wondered if this was true. I thought I heard something scurrying across the damp floor, probably a rodent of some kind. The thought made my heart race. I breathed in a deep breath like my mom taught me. Don't let your emotions take over. Come up with a plan. My watch! Was my watch still on?

I realized why my shoulder hurt so badly. My arms were pinned behind my back. I felt with my fingers. It wasn't rope that I felt. No, it was something smooth and plastic. Zip ties? I used my fingers to feel. I had no hope of freeing myself from zip ties without outside assistance.

My watch, yes, my watch was on my wrist. I felt the cool flat surface of the face beneath my sweater. I couldn't believe that whoever did this to me didn't think to take it. Wasn't there a feature where I could call for help from my watch? I remembered I opted for the cellular plan for my watch, just in case I didn't want to carry my cell when I ran. Something in my brain remembered downloading emergency contacts to be notified. My brain was like cotton. It was pounding and I couldn't think clearly. Who were my emergency contacts? I didn't have anybody to call in an emergency before Coal. Who did I put? Ironically, I thought I put Amber. She was the only person who came to mind. Was she the one who did this to me? I couldn't be sure.

Press the button on the side below the crown and hold it down. Yes, that's what I was supposed to do. Was it enabled to work? I didn't know, but I had to try. Survival. That's all I could think of as I used my fingers on my right hand to hold down the button on my left. My shoulder hurt even worse when I tried to utilize my right hand. I needed to get out of here. My life was just beginning again. Who did this to me?

"Hello?" I called again into the darkness. "Is anyone here?" Absolute silence followed. Why would someone take me and just leave me here? Were they ever planning to come back for me, or were they just planning on leaving me here to die? Was I supposed to have emergency services on my watch talking to me? I didn't hear anything. Was the volume turned down?

"Hello," I called again, just in case someone was listening, "I'm being held somewhere, there are zip ties on my hands." I tried to kick, but my ankles were bound. "And my feet. I don't know where I am." I was about to cry, but I forced myself to breathe. Slow and steady, like I needed to steady my heart rate for a long run. Pretend you are running a half marathon. You've done it before, I urged myself. You are a warrior. You are a survivor. I tried to scoot forward on my bottom. The floor was smooth at least. I was afraid it would be rough. Was I in a basement? The first floor of a building?

Beep! I heard it clearly that time. There was someone's horn being beeped obnoxiously. There was life outside these walls. I just had to get to it. I scooted some more, but every time I moved, my shoulders throbbed. Ignore the pain, I told myself. Think of your long-term goal, mom taught me this when my parents died, and I was left all alone. Whenever you feel you can't bear the moment, think of the future. Everything we go through is a means to get us to where we need to be.

Tuning my ears in, I listened. I was definitely closer to the walls. I saw a little sliver of light, probably the size that you might be able to slip a piece of paper through. It seemed that this was potentially where the windows once were, and they were probably boarded up. Whoever did this, brought me to some sort of abandoned building. If only I had paper, a pen, and my hands unbound, I could slip a note through the crack and hope someone found it and actually read it. Was my watch dead? How much time had gone by? It could have been ten minutes or ten hours. I really couldn't tell; I'd lost all sense of time.

Maybe if I yelled, someone walking by would hear me. It was worth a shot! "HELP," I screamed at the top of my lungs. "I'm inside this building. HELP!!!!" If anyone was walking by surely, they would have heard me. I'd cultivated my teacher's voice over the years and could yell over a cafeteria of screaming children.

It was fruitless, nobody responded.

"HELP!!!!" I screamed again.

When I stopped, I heard footsteps coming toward me. "Shut up you stupid bitch!" The voice was hard, cold and calculating and was familiar to me. My heart broke into a million pieces. How could it be? That menacing voice belonged to Fiona, only it didn't sound like her. It was as if a crazy person had taken over possession of her body. I couldn't see her, but I could feel her standing over me.

"HELP!!!!" I screamed again. I felt a blow in the center of my body. Fiona kicked me with all her might, temporarily knocking the wind out of me, leaving me silent.

She flicked on the flashlight on her phone, temporarily illuminating the area. It looked like I was in an old school. She turned it off just as quickly as it came on.

"Why are you doing this Fiona?" I whispered this time. If I could get her to talk, maybe I could calm her down, or at the very least buy myself some time.

"Why am *I* doing this? Aren't you going to take some responsibility? Hmm?" She asked.

"I want to take responsibility," I said thinking quickly. "I'm just not sure what exactly it is that you're upset about. Tell me. Make me understand."

"It's always about you!" Now she was the one screaming manically. "You need to understand. You deserve a good life. Poor Ava, her family taken away from her. You're so pathetic," she spat the words out at me.

I knew better than to argue with someone who was thinking irrationally, so I remained quiet letting her do the talking.

"Michael was using me to get back with you. I bet you're not even surprised. Why would he want me after all? You're the one who walks around like EVERYONE should look at you. He was so angry when I told him you were back with Coal." Fiona's voice stopped and I heard her starting to cry.

"I don't want anything to do with Michael," I assured her, my voice barely a whisper now. Between the yelling and being drugged, my throat was sore and ragged.

"THAT'S the part that makes me the angriest," she hissed. "You don't even WANT him, and you're ALL that he can think about. Maybe if I get rid of you, I won't be invisible anymore."

That's when I heard it. The faint sound of footsteps. My hearing has always been super-sonic. I didn't think Fiona heard it yet, she didn't react, so I needed her to keep talking.

"You're not invisible," I whispered.

"My mom thinks you're so great. She thinks you've got it all together, just like your precious *mother.*" She said the word with such malice that I couldn't stay quiet.

"Don't talk about my mother," I said, suddenly feeling protective, I found the strength to raise my voice above a whisper.

"SHUT UP!" she screamed, her voice echoing through the empty room.

All of the sudden lights were trained on us from several directions. "Police!"

"Back away from Ava," a voice said. It was a voice I had heard before, but where? My eyes were wild, my shoulders and hips ached. My stomach was sore from where Amber had kicked me, and I had to go to the bathroom so bad, I was afraid I was going to have an accident.

The man whose voice I recognized came toward me, but the way that the lights were shining, I couldn't tell who it was. He scooped me off the floor. I was saved. Thank God. I don't know how, I don't know why, but my life was spared.

With the faint glow of the flashlight, I witnessed a female officer, about 5 feet tall with short wavy brown hair and bangs, come and put Fiona's hands behind her back.

Fiona began screaming at the top of her lungs. "NOOOOOOO." The officer cuffed her and walked her out of the dark room while I was carried out by this stranger.

Once outside the building, the first person I spotted was Coal standing on the curb biting his nails. He was surrounded by Peter, Amber, and Lina. Standing away from the group was of all people, Michael. A crowd of people had now gathered to see what was going on. Amber's face was filled with horror as Fiona was put into the back of the squad car. She was still screaming, wild with rage, and with each breath, it seemed a piece of Amber was chipped away.

"Does anyone have a knife or scissors?" the man holding me in his arms asked the people standing close by.

"I do," Coal said, pulling his pocket knife out of his pocket.

The officer who put Fiona in the back of the car was now by my side. She used Coal's knife to cut the zip ties first off of my wrists and then my ankles.

I looked at the name tag of the female officer who assisted me, V. Blonsky.

The man put me down on the ground now. I turned to thank him and to get a better look. To my surprise, it was Mayor Whitherton.

"What are you all doing here?" I asked spinning around first to my group of people, and then to the mayor. "How did you find me?" I was clearly in shock. Was I hallucinating? Fiona took me? I still didn't understand. "I need to use the bathroom." I was near tears.

Officer Blonsky put her hand gently on my shoulder, I winced in pain. "We want to take you over to the hospital to be evaluated. Then we can explain everything to you. You're okay now."

I ended up in St. Joseph's Hospital Health Center. It turned out Fiona had brought me to an abandoned school building near the water company. After being looked over by the doctors, I laid in a hospital bed in one of those flimsy hospital gowns shivering. All I wanted to do was go home. I had a dislocated shoulder, abrasions on my wrists and ankles, and some scrapes along my legs from being dragged. My ribs had some bruising from being kicked, but I was alive and no longer trapped.

At the door of the room, I heard the doctor tell the police officer that they could speak with me now. Officer Blonky approached my bed.

"Feeling a bit better?" the petite officer asked with the semblance of a smile on her face.

I nodded and attempted to not grimace.

"Good, so I know you're tired. I'm going to make this

quick, but it's important I get your statement while everything is still fresh in your mind, for accuracy purposes."

This time I nodded my head in understanding. I realized that she was just trying to do her job. I leaned up and took a sip of water through the clear plastic straw. It seemed I couldn't get enough water since getting to the hospital. I still had a splitting headache and it ached to think.

"So what is your relationship with Fiona Simms?" she asked, pen poised on her notepad to take notes.

"We work together at West Syracuse Elementary. My..." I paused thinking of the correct words to say. "My mother was best friends with her mother."

"Was...?" she questioned.

I take another sip of water. "My mother passed away during the summer, cardiac arrest."

Officer Blonsky's face changed for a moment, a look of sympathy crossed it. "I'm sorry for your loss." She wrote something down on her notepad.

"How is your relationship with Ms. Simms? Fiona," she clarified.

"We've been close since I moved here in the beginning of October. She's been showing me around. I only recently discovered that she is dating my ex-husband," I said, realizing we sounded like a bad daytime television talk show.

"I see," she said, clearing her throat loudly. "Did that put a strain on your relationship?"

"I tried to be okay with it. I just recently started dating someone, and it's going very well."

"Coal Blake?" she questioned. "He also works at the elementary school?"

"Yes," I wondered why she was asking me all of these questions if she already had the answers. Couldn't she see that I've just been through a horrific situation and needed to rest?

"So run me through the events of the day," she said, focusing her chocolate brown eyes on me.

"I went for a run around 4 pm. I went on the path in the woods around the block from my house. "I gave her the street name and point of access I used to enter the woods. "It was just an ordinary run. My shoe became untied, so I bent over to tie it. I moved off of the path, closer to a bordering backyard. All of the sudden…" I had to stop for a minute. My adrenaline started racing. The terror of what just happened to me hitting my consciousness. Officer Blonsky continued to stare at me, "I felt a hand go around my shoulders, covering my mouth and nose with a cloth with some sort of substance on it. I couldn't see who it was. I was panicking and struggling to get away. The next thing I remember was being on the floor in the dark, with my hands and feet bound."

"I see," she said again. "So, you didn't see who drugged you and brought you to the abandoned school?"

"No, they ambushed me and knocked me out before I knew what was happening," I said, ashamed that someone caught me off guard. I prided myself of being aware, especially when I was out running by myself. "When I woke up in the darkness, I was yelling for help and trying to get my smart watch to work to call emergency services. Fiona appeared out of nowhere and told me to shut up. I still can't believe it was her," I shook my head sadly. How could *Fiona* be the one responsible?

"Very well, that should be all for now. I realize that you've been through quite an ordeal today," she said, closing her notepad. "I will be needing to speak with you again but not tonight. I believe you will be discharged soon. Do you have someone you can stay with tonight? In case you have any problems."

I nodded my head thinking of my plan to sleep at Coal's tonight. He worked so hard to make me dinner, and now it was all ruined.

"Just for your edification, Ms. Simms is being held in the psychiatric unit for observation. She will be there for several days."

"Thank you for letting me know," I said, now tears were brimming in my eyes.

"Okay, we'll be in touch. Take care of yourself," she said as she walked to the door.

Coal must have stationed himself outside the door because he burst in immediately after Officer Blonsky left. With tears in his own eyes, he rushed over to me. "I'm taking you home."

CHAPTER FORTY-FOUR

After what seemed like a lifetime, I was discharged from the hospital, given some pain meds, and told to stay with someone for a few days. Waiting to leave the hospital is up there with buying a car and getting a new cell phone. What should take a half hour turns into a night.

Coal informed me that Lina, Amber, and Peter initially came to the hospital. When they were taking hours before I would be allowed visitors, Coal told them to go home and assured them that he'd let them know what was going on.

By eleven o'clock, I was settled into Coal's bed, pillows propped up behind me, the fluffiest feather comforter in the world wrapped around me. I was clad in a pair of Coal's charcoal colored running pants and an oversized navy-blue thermal shirt of his. We didn't talk much on the way home. I was still shell shocked, as was Coal. It was surreal. I was knocked out and dragged to an abandoned building by my best friend. It wasn't until we shut out the lights and lay in his bed that we actually discussed what happened.

"I was so scared," Coal admitted, his words slipping into the darkness like cries for help. "I just got you back," his voice became choked up, "and then you were gone again. Those hours when you were lost, so was I."

"When did you find out that I was missing?" my voice was quiet. I lay on his chest. The feel of Coal's arms around me gave me the strength to talk.

"I called you several times, and it kept going directly to

voicemail. I know you never shut your phone off, so I went by your house and Lina and Peter were there. Apparently, Peter came by to bring you something and Lina was beside herself because she knew you went running and you didn't come back."

"How did you find out that I was at the building? And what was the mayor doing there?" I sat up now, too keyed up to lay still.

"Well Peter called Amber, to see if Fiona went running with you. Amber broke down on the phone with Peter and told him that Fiona completely lost it after we all left last night. She confided in Amber that Michael got involved with her with the sole purpose of trying to get you back, to be honest I wasn't at all surprised about that," Coal said, his face contorting into an angry glare. He now sat up in bed too. "I can't believe you were married to that man."

I shot him a look but said nothing about his comment. "Wow, but I still don't understand how that drove her to do what she did. Something is missing."

Coal glanced at me cautiously, "Well, there's more. Evidently, Fiona demanded that Amber tell her who her father is."

I interrupted, "Yeah, she was upset about that one day when she came by my house. She told me she was going to ask her. Amber never talked about him at all. What does any of that have to do with me?"

"It seems Amber also knew the identity of your dad."

"What?" my heart nearly stopped, momentarily side-tracked from Fiona It never even occurred to me to think about who my dad was. The fact that Aunt Ginny was actually my mom was shocking, but I figured the identity of my dad died with her.

"Your mom knew your dad in high school. They were actually high school sweethearts. She got pregnant after graduation and never told your dad. She broke up with him, and he went away to college, so he wasn't aware that she was ever pregnant. None the wiser, he moved to Washington D.C., attended college at George Washington University."

My mind flashed to the sweatshirt in the hall closet. That sweatshirt belonged to my dad? My heart fluttered at the thought that something that belonged to my dad was currently in my house. Did that mean my dad was still around? Chills went through my body at the prospect. "Who is he? Did Amber tell you?"

Coal grabbed both of my hands. "Mayor Whitherton is your dad."

"You're joking," I said, waiting to see Coal break into a smile. No smile came.

Coal shook his head, "No, I am not."

"My dad! *That's why* he freaked when he saw me and heard my last name. I knew I hadn't imagined it. Coal, do you know what this means?"

He waited, not sure which direction I was going in.

"I'm not an orphan. I actually have a parent that is alive," I paused, remembering something he previously said, "but wait, you said he didn't know about her pregnancy?"

"He didn't at the time. He found out much later, when you were already grown."

I remained quiet for a moment letting this information sink in.

"So how did he end up there, at the building I mean, tonight?" I was so happy to finally get some answers.

Coal smiled, "Amber really came through Ava. When she got word that you were missing, she contacted him. When we found out where you were, he came straight away."

"This is so much," I said my feelings ping ponging all over the place. "How did you know to go to that building to find me? How did you find out that that was where Fiona took me?"

Now Coal had an indeterminable look on his face between being annoyed and grateful. "Honestly, it turns out that Michael's stalking tendencies paid off. Chalk one up to

Team Michael," he shook his head. I imagined he was beating himself up about not knowing where I was. "He followed Fiona because he was afraid that she might do something to you. He witnessed her rage and was scared. Then he contacted Amber. She let all of us know."

I breathed a deep sigh. It was about time he did something to pay back for all the trouble he caused. Deep down I knew he cared about me, but his way of loving was broken and not something that I would subject myself to ever again.

"There's just one thing I don't understand," I said, settling back down, laying on Coal's chest. "Why did Fiona care who my father was? Why would that upset her so much?"

Coal stroked my hair tenderly, "She's known who your father was for a while, since Amber's known." I felt like I was punched in the stomach a second time, this fact upset me because I told her about how the mayor had acted strangely, and she told me it was probably because he and Ginny had known each other. The fact that we looked alike. She purposely kept it from me.

Coal continued interrupting my thoughts, "Amber let her know that the mayor is her father as well."

"Wait, what?!?! Fiona and I are half-sisters?" Now I bolted upright, standing on the side of the bed. "Fiona is my sister?! So, I have a sister, and she tried to kill me?"

Coal was quiet for a minute. When he finally spoke, he continued cautiously. "Not to defend her, because what she did to you was absolutely messed up, but I don't think she was trying to kill you. I think she has some emotional issues. She was angry and feeling slighted."

"Don't sisters just pull your hair or make fun of you?" I asked. "I've never had a sister before, but surely they don't chloroform you and deposit you in an abandoned school."

"I'm sorry Ava. Life is not simple. I'm only telling you this because I want you to think about it from her perspective and not write her off. She's a good person who needs help, a lot of help."

I sat back on the bed. "I know what you're saying Coal. I just need some time. This doesn't answer the questions about the letters and the dolls. Do you think Fiona sent either of them? That part doesn't make sense to me."

"I know. I've been going over and over it in my mind while you were in the hospital. It being Fiona doesn't make sense. Do you think it's Amber? Could they both be behind all of this trouble?"

"Honestly, I don't know. I don't think we ever know other people, not really. Everyone has a part of themselves that they keep hidden. Fiona's part is darker than most, or maybe she just never found a way to manage it." I was quiet for a minute and looked up at Coal looking so beautiful in the moonlight. "I never want to find a hidden part of you that will shatter everything I know to be good about you." I looked at him pleadingly. "That scares me more than anything."

"I can promise you one thing Ava," Coal answered, "We all have darkness, but I've tamed my demons a long time ago. What you see is what you get. Sometimes I get jealous, like the fact that Michael got to have such a huge part of you, but then I remember that I'm the one who gets to share your life now. He gets to skulk around watching from the sidelines."

Pain in my shoulder woke me up early the next morning. I tended to sleep on my right side, and this was the side that ached so terribly. A dull headache was throbbing in my brain. It hurt even more when my eyes were closed, so I was happy to get up and have some of that pain alleviated. Unlike normally, when I opened my eyes, Coal was not sleeping but already up and staring at me.

"How did you sleep?" he asked me, his own eyes red rimmed, looking like he barely closed his eyes all night.

"Alright I guess considering the circumstances." I heard my phone ping and looked for it on the floor. Locating it, I had to physically get out of bed and get it. With my shoulder, there was no way I could reach down to get it.

There was a text message from Amber.

There are no words to appropriately describe to you how sorry I am. I just want you to know that I love you, and I know that Fiona does too. Is it ok if I give your dad your phone number? He really wants to get in touch with you, but I didn't want to give it without your permission. Please let me know, and if there is ANYTHING you need. I am here for you. xx Amber.

I read the text out loud to Coal. "I want to talk to him. Do you think that's alright, to let him call me?" I asked him, nervous about what he would say, excited at the prospect of talking to a dad I didn't know I had.

"Why wouldn't it be?" Coal asked, sitting up in bed.

I thought for a moment, "I don't know. It's just all so weird and new, but I guess he's all I have. I might as well talk to him."

"I definitely think you should then," Coal said standing up and stretching from a long night of tossing and turning, "but just so you know, he's not all you have. You have me."

I smiled and wrote Amber back. A few minutes later I received a text.

Good morning, Ava, I am so grateful to be in touch with you. There are no words to describe how relieved I am that you are ok. I would love to meet up to talk. There are some important things I need to tell you. You are welcome to bring that nice boyfriend of yours, if it would make you more comfortable. Please let me know if this afternoon would work for you and where you'd like to meet. I look forward to hearing from you.

"OMG," I nearly squealed, then an ache in my stomach brought me back to reality. I still needed to take it slow after last night. "He wants to meet this afternoon. He says he has important things he needs to tell me."

"I'm coming," Coal informed me. "That is non-negotiable. You are *not* going alone." He looked at me as if daring me to argue.

"For your information, he told me to bring you," I said.

"Sounds like a nice guy," Coal remarked, softening his tone. "Maybe he'll get my vote in the next election."

Good morning, Coal and I would love to meet you. Would you be able to come to my house around 1 pm? Let me know, and I look forward to speaking.

After I hit send, my pulse pounded wildly. I felt like I had just made plans for a first date. "A second mother *and* a second father," I said aloud, not believing it. Then I turned to Coal who was watching me. "I wish you could have met my parents. It would have meant a lot to me." I felt a rush of sadness, a longing to connect with the people who raised me and loved me my entire childhood.

Coal came up to me and wrapped his strong arms around me. "I know love, you are the strongest woman I know; I am so proud of you."

Then I cried for a good five minutes. The two of us stood in Coal's beautiful bedroom which was decorated in shades of green, the most calming room in the world. I was tangled in his embrace and he let me cry. I cried for all I had lost and all I had found. Tears of sadness and joy became one. When I was good and finished, I finally let go, looked Coal in the eye and said, "Let's do this. It's time to introduce you to my dad."

Feeling in desperate need of a shower, Coal and I headed straight back to my house. I took a long hot shower, there was no chance I could blow dry my hair straight with my shoulder, so I wore it loose and wavy. Putting on a pair of blue jeans, I paired it with a soft yellow sweater. I applied makeup like I was going into battle instead of talking to my dad. When all my preparation was done, I paced the house, not able to sit still.

Coal put on a pot of coffee and set the table in the kitchen for the three of us to talk. It's a good thing he was there because my head was spinning in equal parts anticipation and pain from the night before. When the bell rang at five minutes to one, Coal and I stood quiet for a minute looking at each other. He waited for me to say what I wanted.

"I'll get it," I finally said.

Coal nodded with a knowing glance.

I walked through the sitting room, heart pounding. Coal lingered back closer to the kitchen giving me space, but where he could still keep an eye on what was going on.

Taking a deep breath, I unlocked the door and there he stood, the Mayor of Syracuse, on my front steps. His blue eyes were filled with an odd mixture of pride and sadness.

"I see you are right on time," I said, breaking the ice.

He gave me a sad smile and didn't move.

"Come in," I insisted, ushering him into the foyer.

Finally, he spoke, "I don't want to be presumptuous, but would it be ok to hug you?"

"As long as you're careful about my shoulder," I said with a laugh. "It really hurts from yesterday."

This charismatic man, who all the women were swooning over, was a bundle of nerves. I imagined him as he must have been when he was a teenager and my mom was so in love. I imagined how things might have been different if she had told him that she was pregnant. Then he hugged me, a big bear embrace. Unbeknownst to me, a single tear slid down my face.

When we let go, I wiped the tear away and said, "Come say hi to Coal." I ushered him into the kitchen. He followed eagerly. Coal was waiting by the kitchen island and reached his hand out to him. "Mayor Whitherton, a pleasure to see you again."

My dad smiled at him, not his politician's smile, the

smile of a proud father. "The pleasure is mine," he returned. "How's your dancing coming along?"

"Not bad," Coal said smiling. "I'm looking forward to the fundraiser."

With all the politeness out of the way, we settled in at the kitchen table. Coal played the perfect host and went to serve the coffee. He wanted to be there to support me but still give us some semblance of privacy.

"Where to begin?" my dad said gazing out the window, his finger traced over the silver placemat.

I watched him intently, such a strange feeling being here with a dad I never knew I had.

"The beginning," I suggested, watching him intently.

"Ah yes," he said, taking a small sip of the scalding hot coffee. I watched his face, transfixed, trying to find some resemblance in his face. There was no doubt that I looked like my mom, but I wanted to see if any of my dad's image lingered in me. It wasn't so much in my physical traits, but the look in his eye was familiar to me. The way he tilted his head to the side when he smiled. It was there. "I guess you do have a lot of history that you need to be caught up on. Your mom and I went to the same high school. She was beautiful and vivacious, a breath of fresh air whenever she entered the room. She... was the love of my life," his eyes twinkled as he spoke about her. "I worshiped the ground she walked on."

I felt a tugging at my heart. Knowing that I came from a place of love made me happy.

"When we were graduating, I was going away to school in Washington D.C., and Ginny broke up with me and broke my heart. "He looked down now and then back up at me, "Little did I know that you were on the way. Ginny told me it was because she didn't want me not to go to college, not to pursue my dreams. I didn't know about your existence until this year."

"How did mom tell you?" I asked curiously, suddenly desperate to know everything. Coal settled down at the end of the table with us. He stirred his coffee and looked out the window, not wanting to be intrusive.

"Actually, she didn't," he grimaced a little. A look akin to horror flashed across his face. "Someone else told me."

My thoughts immediately went to Amber.

"Does your wife know?" I asked, remembering the very blonde, very lithe woman I had met at the coffee place.

"This is kind of complicated. I've been married for about twenty years now, only 5 of those years were an actual marriage. We drifted apart several years after being married."

"So why are you still married?" I asked, trying my best not to sound disapproving. Keeping an open mind was hard, but I really wanted to try to see it from his perspective.

"It suited both of us to stay together. She enjoyed the lifestyle of being married to a politician. She's very active in the social scene. She does a lot of charity work. Being married to me allows her the ability to keep this lifestyle."

"What do you get out of it?" I asked, sad because I had the idea of a marriage being something very different. I felt sorrow seep into my green eyes.

He must have picked up on my emotion because something shifted in him. Shame filled his face. "After Ginny broke up with me, I never really fell in love again. I never really got over her, and to be honest, I never wanted to go through that type of heartache again. My wife is a companion to me, she is a suitable wife for a politician, but we are not the loves of each other's lives. To answer your question, yes, she knows about you."

I nodded my head slowly. It was his life to live, and we all needed to navigate our lives in the best way we could.

"I've had casual relationships along the way, as has she. Elise isn't capable of becoming pregnant, something that helped cause our rift. So, when I found out about you, it was like being given the most precious and rare gift that you can ever receive. Not only did I have a daughter, but Ginny's daughter. A piece of her remains with me, in you."

My eyes welled with tears, but I wasn't capable of talking yet, too choked up.

"That brings me to the first thing I have to talk to you about," he grabbed my hand, then looked at my face to see if he overstepped his boundaries. I squeezed his hand to let him know it was ok. "One of the women I was dating found out that your mom and I were talking again. She did not take kindly to this. She knew that Virginia was my one true love."

I sucked in a deep breath. I knew I was on the edge of obtaining some information that I'd been reaching for, for a long time now. I was on the brink of finally getting answers. Nodding my head, I said, "Yeah, I found some pretty threatening letters that my mom had hidden throughout the house. I imagine they must have been from her. The anger in the letters was pretty evident. Do you think she did something to hurt my mom?" I looked at him pleadingly.

My dad shook his head, "No, she didn't hurt her, but she did terrorize her, and I believe you know her," he said looking pointedly at me. This got Coal's attention and he raised his eyebrow at me.

"Who is it?" I asked, anxious for him to release the information.

"I believe you know her from the gym, Marcia," he said. "She found out about your mom because she saw the two of us in your backyard one day. She lives diagonally to you, behind your house."

Both Coal and I sat in my kitchen, mouths hanging open. So many things were making more sense. "Does she know that I'm your daughter?"

He shook his head no. "She probably sees you as competition because you look so much like Ginny. I stopped seeing her a long time ago, but she is having a hard time letting the relationship go."

"How do you know that she didn't do anything to my mom?" I asked, suddenly enraged. "Do you know that the night of my party, the night she was here, someone slipped something in my drink? I woke up with no recollection of the last two hours that people were at my house."

A flash of anger crossed my dad's face, a protectiveness that I was sure was as new to him as it was me. "I wouldn't doubt that she would do that. She's proven herself unstable, but she didn't hurt your mom."

"How do you know for sure?" I said, getting angry at him now for siding with her. How could he be sure that she didn't?

"I know because I just yesterday found out what really happened." He now looked like it physically hurt him to speak. He put his head in his hands, his face seemed to age before my eyes. I was paralyzed in my seat, shocked by his statement. Someone did something to her. Someone hurt my mom. I wasn't crazy; it wasn't some paranoid notion. Someone stole my mom from me. We could have still had a lifetime together, and it was stolen from me.

"Well?" I asked, yelling at him now. He was lucky and had missed my teenage years, but I was giving him a healthy dose of them now.

"This is very hard for me, Ava. What I'm going to tell you now, it rocked my world." His ice blue eyes were trained on me. I just met you officially, but I want you aware of the fact that I love you with all my heart. I want to be part of your life. Your existence has made my life mean something. I have been successful in my professional life, but I have bombed miserably in my personal life. You are the game changer."

I couldn't help myself. Interrupting him before he could drop his next bombshell, "Do you know about Fiona?"

My dad looked down again, like a little boy that was caught doing something naughty. He nodded his head yes, so slightly that I might have missed it if I wasn't really watching. "I am *not* proud of that relationship. When I came back home Thanksgiving break, I was so destroyed over losing your mom. I met Amber out with friends. We had a one-night stand, which resulted in the birth of Fiona. I didn't know about that pregnancy either. Amber and I barely knew each other. I didn't find out about her until down the road either. The fact that she tried to hurt you…" he shook his head vigorously, not finishing his thought.

Coal silently got up from the table and poured three waters, silently depositing them in the spots before us. I sent up a silent prayer to God for giving me the strength to leave my toxic marriage with Michael in favor of being loved by Coal.

"What I'm going to tell you now is very hard. Please try your best to listen to my whole story before making any judgment. I do realize that this is a lot to ask."

What more could anyone tell me than had already been said? I felt that I was beyond being surprised by anything. I was wrong.

"After speaking with Amber, and finding you in that building, I went to speak with my mother. I hadn't spoken to her in quite some time; we had a big argument over my marriage to Elise. She knew about you. She knew about you before I did because she befriended your mom, and Ginny confessed to her. I actually found out about your existence because of her. My mom is Adelaide, and she poisoned your mother."

"No, that's not right," I protested, shaking my head violently. "Adelaide is the lonely woman who lives behind me. She bakes shortbread cookies and loves cats." I couldn't stop moving my head back and forth.

"I'm so sorry Ava, but it is. Your grandmother killed your mother. She poisoned her tea with Nerium. She grows it. It is nearly untraceable, and Ginny told her about her heart condition." I thought about that typed note I found that first day, the one that was with the brownies. I never thought about it before, but it was typed up in the same way that the notes from the dolls were. "My mom's mental health has been on a decline for a while now. I didn't want to admit it at first. I choked it up to just being forgetful, being old fashioned, stuck in the past. It's my fault really; I didn't see what was happening right before my eyes." Tears were streaming down his face now, hitting the table and dampening his sweater. "She told me getting divorced was a sin, but she was so frustrated because she wanted to be a grandmother. When she found out about you, she was afraid I would leave Elise. She couldn't let a divorce blacken the family name, but she desperately wanted to be a part of your life. She told me all about the dolls she sent you. I'm so ashamed."

I stood up, knocking into the table. Both Coal and my dad stood as well but didn't move. They watched me run out of the room. A second later I returned with the three dolls and placed them on the table.

"My grandma made these?" I asked wild eyed.

My dad sat down again and nodded. He crumbled into tears.

I got up from my spot and went and sat in his lap, wrapping my arms around him. "It's not your fault daddy. We are not responsible for the actions of the people we love. We can only control ourselves," I told him reassuringly.

EPILOGUE

The room was charged with excitement and packed with wall- to-wall people. Men in black and white tuxedos, and women competing for the best evening gowns. Everyone went all out. The tables were decorated with white roses in crystal vases. The elite of Syracuse were gathered for the big event. There was a murmur of excitement that filled the entire room. The Dancing with the Stars Event to benefit the After School Arts Program was the talk of the town. Elise Whitherton had worked hard to hype up the event and reach all the privileged people in Syracuse. Now if only the dancing went well, it would be a smashing success. I had butterflies in my stomach as I waited in the staging area with my fellow teachers and the professional dancers.

"Did you see how many people are out there?" I asked Tabitha and Chloe, peering into the crowded room. "I don't know if I can do this." I was adorned in my floor length red Swarovski crystal sequined gown. A high slit going up the front of the dress, so I can perform all of my kicks and flicks.

"You have to be kidding me," Marion said, walking up to me. "You look hot, and you were born to perform. You are going to put everyone else to shame. Well maybe not me," she said laughing.

Thank God for Marion. Everyone served a role in our lives, sometimes it just takes a while to appreciate that.

Coal walked over to where I was standing with the ladies. He had on a pair of tight black dance pants and a white Latin shirt that was cut halfway down his chest. He never looked better, although I could tell he was slightly embarrassed.

"I wish Fiona could have been here," I admitted to Coal as he slipped his arm around me.

"I know," Coal said. "I feel bad about it too, but she needs to put in the time now, so she can get better. She can't rush the process."

I nodded. I knew he was right. Fiona was diagnosed with a psychotic break brought on by stress. The doctor noted that she also suffered from poor self-image. I never pressed charges against her, so she just needed to finish up treatment and she would be free to move on with her life. I was hoping that one day, we would be able to be sisters. I knew that it would take a lot of time and a lot of work, but I was hopeful.

Dad had my grandmother, Adelaide put in a nursing home with around the clock care. She was pretty deep into her Alzheimer's diagnosis, and she couldn't really be held responsible for her actions. She was an old lady who was good at hiding that she had a problem. As long as she was under round the clock supervision, she wouldn't be a danger to anybody else. Despite all that had happened, I felt sad that she was missing this event. I knew how much she was looking forward to it. I both hated her for the role she played in my mom's death and mourned the fact that my grandmother was locked away. I hoped one day I would be able to visit her and try to forgive her. My dad made sure that all of the cats went to loving homes. My little treasure, Restore, came home to live with me early. I called her story for short to remind me that we all have a story to tell, secrets to hide.

"It's time," Samantha said, coming up to all of us. "I'm on first, and Ava you are right after me." Of course I was.

My dad introduced Samantha and her partner, and they went on to do their dance. I waited in the wings backstage. I was on the left side of the stage and Demetrius was on the right. I watched him from the other side to be sure that I got the signal right.

As the music cut and the lights dimmed, I took my position on stage. My dad came back on the microphone, "And now I'd like to introduce my daughter, Ava Zajaczkowski and her partner Demitrus Nowak performing the Argentine tango."

ABOUT THE AUTHOR

J. C. Perkins

J.C. Perkins is an educator, avid reader, dancer, health enthusiast, and cat lover. Although this is her first published novel, the sounds of the typewriter keys could often be detected emanating from her childhood room. She is a born storyteller.

Printed in Great Britain
by Amazon